Mirklin Wood

Mirklin Wood

Book 2 of
Daermad Cycle

Lela Markham

Breakwater Harbor Books, Inc.
Scott J. Toney and Cara Goldthorpe, Co-Founders
www.breakwaterharborbooks.com

ISBN #978-0-9909358-4-1 E-Book edition
ISBN #978-09909358-5-8 Print edition

Laurel Sliney
Lela Markham Publications
P.O. Box 70731
Fairbanks, Alaska 99707
lelamarkham@gmail.com

My Thanks!

To my Lord and Savior Jesus Christ. 1 Peter 5:5-11

To my husband and children who allowed Mirklin Wood to continue the story started in The Willow Branch. The mock sword battles in the back yard that really had the neighbors wondering about us were incredibly fun, but let's face it – writers are messy people who spend a lot of time staring into space trying to envision what comes next. Thanks for putting up with me.

Thanks (again) to Black Dog, canine pirate, for making me believe that animals can think for themselves without being cartoon characters. Joy and Sabre owe their existence to you, you ungrateful beast.

Immense thanks to the writers of the Booktrap for teaching me indie marketing and to those writers who acted as alpha readers and critics. Being in indie author has an exciting liberty to it, but I treasured the support in an area I don't excel at. Special thanks to Scott Butcher (author of the Stillwart Chronicles), Amber Creasy and Scott Toney (Breakwater Harbor Books) for acting as beta readers and editors for this series and going above and beyond the call of duty.

Table of Contents

Map of Celdrya

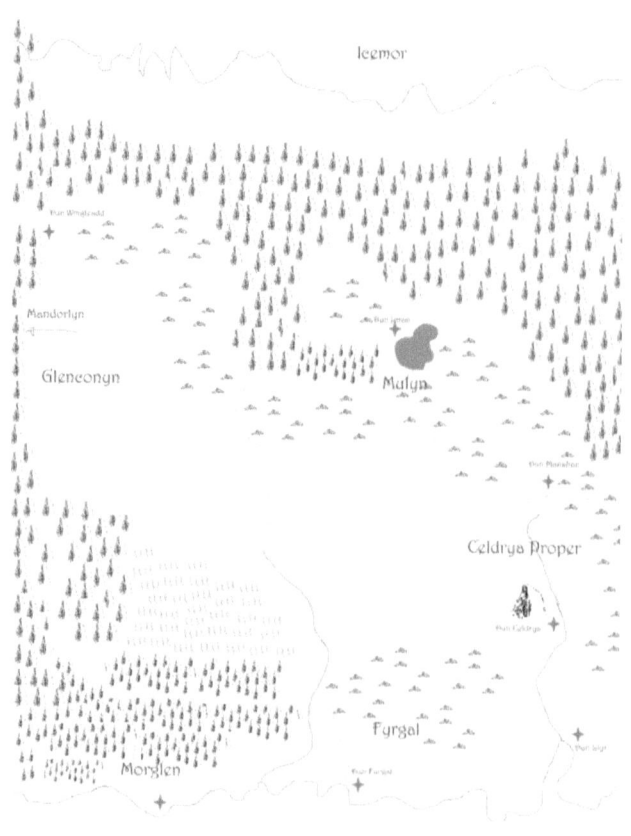

Daemons

&

Dragons

Thus says the One Whose Name We Are Not to Know, hear Me, Kindred, and know that I am One God.

The raptors fight over the aviary, but only one can rule and no bird of a feather will mount the throne. The dragon stirs and the One's Beacon will arise. Go you then to find him and win him free of those who would exploit him. Who shall go? One who knows both worlds and can heal both the body and the rifts of men, one whose brothers rule, yet who would walk barefoot himself, one whose Companion shines like the sun.

And how shall you know the One's Beacon? He will be obscure -- near the rule, but not of it. He will be of the Kin, but not know the Kin. He will pass through tribulation. He will be plain of speech, heroic and thoughtful. The dragon will claim him.
The raptors fight over the aviary, but all will bow before the dragon.
Know this and hear the One speak.

**Navaransen, Sentinel,
Kin Cycle 17602 Old Calendar**

Past

Founding Year 931 – A century ago
Galconyn/Denygal Mountains

*D*aemons of all sizes and shapes choked the paths. Their terrible faces contorted in rage, they pressed toward Donyl and Pedyr, swinging their bronze weapons to meet their iron. Preternaturally calm and rational in this irrational situation, Donyl dealt death as no novice at arms had a right, slicing and parrying, arms burning with fatigue. He understood that they were going to die – that had been a given when the hordes rushed onto the paths -- but the man at his back deserved better. Here was a Believer, a follower of the One, who trusted his god to save his soul, but did not expect him to save his life. Oath-sworn to see Donyl to his destination or die in the attempt, Pedyr fought a last futile battle for naught but honor.

The citadel is within sight!

Could not the Denygal god find it to save this most deserving man? Donyl's rational mind thought this as his exhausted arms continued swinging his sword upon daemon after daemon, with no stop in sight.

I don't know this god and yet, please save Pedyr.

An air-rending roar filled the gorge and the daemon host ducked as if expecting attack from on high. A terrified keening rolled along the paths, echoing off the cliffs, as a dark winged shape glided out of the moon light and swept low. Donyl screamed as the enormous claws reached down and plucked him free of the ledge.

A momentary lift, a silence and then whomp … whomp … whomp. The mighty wings of the serpent pounded downward in deafening strokes to gain altitude and wind tore at Donyl's clothes and eyes. Through streaming tears Donyl saw many hundreds of daemons fall into the black chasm below. Then they were away, careening through the gorge, climbing ever higher. Terror seized the sole-remaining heir of Celdrya as he saw the ground rushing beneath, trees and boulders barely discernible in the moonlight. He flailed, almost dropped his sword, tried to wrap an arm round anything, but there was naught save the smooth curve of the talon that held him firmly and gently across his midsection. His feet dangled beneath him, whipped behind him by the wind. The wings beating slowed and the pounding on his ears eased, but the ground seemed to pass more quickly and the wind tore at him like a ravening beast. There was naught to do. This was worse than the daemon horde … at least he'd been able to fight them. Now there was just the waiting for death either from being dropped to the distant earth or being carried to a nest of hungry … hungry what? What was this thing that had him?

Donyl's reason saved him from utter panic. As he had done all throughout the terror-filled journey into the mountains, he deliberately set aside fear to observe the world round him. He expected at any moment to be sheared in half by the mighty talon that held him, but the pressure was only firm, not painful, as if the beast planned to keep him alive. Maybe it liked to play with its food. His heart hammered in his chest.

Nay, do not think such!

His eyes stung with the wind, blurring the spinning world beneath his feet. He counted himself lucky that he couldn't clearly see the stomach-churning view as onward they sped.

What manner of beast bore him into the high mountains?

What of Pedyr? Poor man! Left against the horde with no one at his back. Best dead by now.

Donyl's terror abated with grief and a sob tore from his wind-burned lips. His fingers, grown numb with the cold, throbbed; he willed himself to keep hold of the sword, glad of the wrist loop. He had but one chance when they reached the beast's nest and only the sword might give it to him.

His heart hammered and his breath grew short. His head felt light and empty, as if he were climbing the mountains once more rather than hanging from the talons of a great wyrm.

Nay, not possible!

It did remind him somewhat of the statues he'd seen of dragons, but that was a bard's fancy and those did not fly to your rescue that often. Or did they? In some of the stories …. *Stories!* He was not being rescued. He was likely about to be eaten. Mayhap he could avoid that, if he was clever. He craned his neck to look above him. The beast's sinuous neck undulated some distance above his head. Iridescent green and black scales caught the moonlight in shimmering waves. The wings hardly beat now. The beast must have set its course and found its altitude. Donyl's lungs fought for icy cold air. His eyes had mostly adjusted to the chill and now he saw the world round him. The moonlight was inexplicably fading, but the snow-capped mountain peaks shone with a white light of their own. Tier upon tier of mountains stretched before them.

The Roof of the World?

No sooner had Donyl recognized what a truly large world existed than the beast dipped a wing and sent them spiraling down into a canyon, giant leather wings barely clearing slate grey walls on either side. Golden light lit the darkness ahead as a stone wall of immense proportions rose into sight. Donyl screamed and pulled his legs up as the beast dropped low to clear it. The talons relaxed and Donyl knew death had come for him. He fainted in terror.

Present

Founding Year 1028
Dun Cenconyn

*T*he closeness of her single tent finally drove a sleepless Sarala into the night. She squatted in linen trews and a sleeveless bodice, staring up at the fell moon, mesmerized until it passed behind a cloud. ll normal calculations, it was dark of the moon, yet the moon shone bright and full out of time. Hearing voices near the council fire, she walked barefoot through the scattered tents until she came upon an animated conversation between Cai, the caravan squire, and his sister Ryanna. Sarala knew it was rude to eavesdrop, but she couldn't help herself. Ryanna had been her mother's bosom friend at Ama'na and Sarala admired her for her strong will.

"Are you certain?" Cai said. "I'm loath to sound like Madi, but as your elder brother I must remind you of your obligations."

"I've settled those, Cai. I've done all a Kin should be required. If Gil lives, he wishes not to be found. He abandoned me and I have been faithful. All that remains is severing our legal ties and I ask you to do that now."

"Because of a fell moon?" Sarala's breath caught in her chest. I knew there was more to it than just a moon.

"Because of a prophecy I can't obey with my braid intact."

Ryanna might easily be the most beautiful Kin alive after Sarala's own mother. Tall and athletic, she scarcely needed to tilt her chin to look into her brother's eyes. She looked wholly human, though you could see her elven blood in her high cheekbones and large eyes. Cai's peaked ears hid among his curly brown hair. Only a single ribband bound his clan braid which had grown almost to his waist, evidence of his high standards in romance. Wrist-thick, Ryanna's waist-length braid was laced with two colors of ribbands interlinked by beads, marking her as a married woman.

"Cai, you have always understood the difficulties of my marriage. I pray now that you remember history and act accordingly."

"Do not use that against me. This is less about Gil and more about Padraig."

"Padraig is the other side of the kingdom and the prophecy sends me to Lindermaden. And how can you deny this?"

She indicated a staff of honor wood at their feet that was nearly as long as Ryanna was tall. Cai frowned, rubbing his rough shaven chin. Like most Kin, he normally walked about clean-shaven, but here at the Cenconyn horse faire, he allowed his beard to grow to increase the comfort of the Celdryans.

"I don't much like you traveling alone into the basketlands."

"I shan't be alone," Ryanna said with a snort. "You can come out now, Sarala. Did you think I wouldn't Sense you?"

There was no use pretending otherwise. Ryanna's talent was more legendary than her beauty. Sarala stepped out into the firelight. Cai looked stunned.

Do you care?

"It's been noised about that you intend to travel into the basketlands alone," Ryanna said. "You'd be safer with a friend, but you should know that I tend to attract adventure."

"I'm seeking what I might learn of the basketlands. I planned to travel alone because no one volunteered, but I would not object to traveling with you. I hear there are advantages to your guidance and, uh, skills."

Cai growled, pivoted on his heel and strode away to his tent. Ryanna's black dog shifted sideways to allow him passage.

"Traveling with me will require certain considerations," Ryanna told her. The turquoise of her eyes shone like a deep pool. "I mean not to get killed defending your honor among the humans. You will submit to the same glamour I cast upon myself and you will need to remove your braid."

Without hesitation, Sarala knelt before Ryanna. The older woman hesitated a moment, then tugged the upper binding down a bit before slipping her dagger beneath Sarala's thick braid.

"Are you certain, lass? It has meaning."

"It grows back and I was going to remove it myself today."

Ryanna's sharp dagger sliced the braid off before Sarala could call back her bravery. She opened her eyes to see Cai standing in front of her looking like a thunderhead. He held two rawhide strips in his hand. He took a deep breath and looked at Ryanna.

"You might as well kneel and get this over with, then."

She looped Sarala's braid into a neat coil of rope.

"You have no family in the caravan. You will need to decide who should convey this to your mother."

My mother? Why her?

"Or to your intended or the Wise," Ryanna added. "I can certainly understand your feelings toward your mother."

She settled the braid in Sarala's hand before taking a rawhide strip from Cai to tie off the top of her own braid as was custom. She knelt and Cai drew his dagger. He didn't ask her to reconsider. He knew his sister's mind well. In a moment, her hair curled up round her ears while Sarala fought tears over her own.

"See that Luc gets that," Ryanna instructed, showing the benefit of years to weigh her decision, while Sarala wiped tears from her cheeks. "I convey my herd into your hands. See that he gets a mare and a gelding should he decide to leave goitan."

"You are not required …." Cai objected.

"No, but Luc is not responsible for Gil and I want him to know this. I'm not divorcing him. I'm divorcing his son. Luc will always have a place by my fire and should I bear children, the first will be kinsman to Luc." Ryanna bent to put a hand on Sarala's shoulder.

10

"We all weep the first time, lass," Ryanna assured Sarala, speaking Celdryan for the first time. "The moon passes and the sunrise is not long. Have you gleaned your gear for the basketlands?"

"Your father helped me do so before I traveled here," Sarala replied in Elvish.

Stop crying!

"Is there no young lass he will not encourage to have an adventure?" Cai asked. That he also spoke in Celdryan seemed significant.

"He ... also ... taught me ... Celdryan," she reported, still feeling her way round that language's clumsy sounds.

"Good. You'll need it," Ryanna said. She turned her gaze toward the walled town. "Reyn is joining us," she announced. "Sarala, I was not planning to travel farther west, so there is much I must settle before our departure. Cai, show her my gear to glean and repack while I deal with other matters."

Ryanna bent to retrieve the honor staff and then shivered, her back arching.

"He is fallen," she murmured in the eerie voice of a prophetess. "The raven has scored a blow. The world awaits the dragon. No bird of a feather shall rule the aviary and darkness has fallen upon the hawk."

She shuddered, then relaxed. The sky above the eastern mountains turned grey as she straightened, wiping her face.

"What is that about?" Cai inquired.

Ryanna shook her head.

"I do not understand what I know." It was not often given to the prophet to interpret what they spoke on the One's behalf. Sarala and Cai exchanged glances, but neither had been given the interpretation.

The couple who crossed the bridge from the faire ground dressed simply, though the man's breecs declared him a noble. The woman's uncovered hair fell in a single braid to her hips. The guards noted them, but let them pass to the squire's fire without confrontation. A merchant's caravan did not seek to antagonize the locals.

"Lord Reyn," Cai greeted. Sarala had seen the rig of Cenconyn the day before as he'd come to visit the squire. He looked a right Celdryan lord, though folk rumored his mam was from Denygal and related in some way to Cai's father.

"My wife Lillirigga informs me that there are dark magicks about this night."

A beautiful woman with dark hair and striking eyes, Lillirigga's delicate features and a slight build belied a well of power only slightly less than Ryanna's, Sarala had no doubt.

"This fell moon whispers evils," Ryanna admitted. They all instinctively glanced at the full moon a fortnight out of time. Its brightness was fading.

"Aye, but the prophecy I received about you was of much more interest," Lady Lilligrigga said. "I saw a hawk grapple with a raven and the hawk fell from the sky to the back of a golden horse. Then afar off I saw a green dragon enter a cave of dreams. There was a black dog in the draon's grip."

"Does that mean aught to you?" Cai demanded of Ryanna.

"Golden horse – Padraig. I think, though it could be Joy, since she is a golden horse. Somewhat's happened to the west. I think Padraig is fine, but there is foreboding. Hawks and ravens – I know naught. Dragons, though ... they've been speaking to me and I rode one in a vision just days ago."

Sabre the black dog nuzzled Ryanna's hand. She scrubbed his head.

"You'd not appreciate a ride by a dragon, I suppose," she said, then turned her gaze to the rig of Cenconyn. "Fortunately, I think I'm the black dog and the green dragon is the king to be. I've been spirit-called south and west to Lindermaden – er, Dunmaden. I wasn't planning such a journey. Might you be willing to aid me in it?"

"Clothes, food, coin ...?" Reyn asked.

"Clothes and food, aye. We've got horses and coin. If you set a task of messenger upon me, would that not speed our travel?"

"It would," Lillirigga said. "Does the lass need clothes as well?"

"I planned this journey," Sarala replied. "I don't require that sort of help."

"I do hope you have a glamour you can cast upon her," Reyn said. "She's not the sort of woman who can ride free in the basketlands."

Sarala then remembered she wore far fewer clothes than either of the other two women. Ryanna had apparently changed into a siarc and breecs when she awoke and Lillirigga wore a pair of plain, dark blue dresses of a Celdryan style. Sarala resisted the compulsion to cover her chest with her arms. She was dressed modestly enough for the holt.

Celdryans are prudes!

"I can make her as plain as a carry sack, though not to folk with your vision," Ryanna assured. "Sarala, repack the baggage. I'll be walking up to the dun."

"Lilli, you escort her while I go ahead and put matters in motion," Reyn suggested, moving toward the bridge. Lillirigga nodded.

"Shouldn't you scry to the holt?" Cai asked.

"I will, but the decision has already been made. It's merely a formality."

Cai growled. Sarala hesitated.

Are we doing it all wrong?

The council had granted her permission to walk about, but Ryanna's plan was much more ambitious.

"You are uncertain," Lillirigga noted. Cai stared at her a moment before nodding. "May I view your aura?" she asked Ryanna.

Ryanna snorted. Although nothing changed as far as Sarala could see, Lillirigga apparently had the Sight.

"That's interesting," Lillirigga said after a moment. "She marches at the orders of the One."

"In the direction of a man she should avoid right now," Cai complained.

"The one with the golden horse? He's far away and preoccupied and she has been an effective widow for many cycles. Even if she weren't – divorce is allowed when a non-believer leaves a Believer."

Ryanna looked startled.

"What do you know of my husband?"

"I met him once in Denygal. And we heard somewhat about him. Those are not the actions of a Believer. You are free to marry under the law of Heaven. But, that is not what she's about, squire. She is truly following prophesy."

"Even the Wise are on your side, sister," Cai complained, but his eyes twinkled. The sun blushed the mountains. "We have things to do if we are to speed you on your way."

"Are you ready for me to follow?" Ryanna asked. Lillirigga nodded. They wandered toward the bridge, Lillirigga assuring Ryanna that she could call her "Lilli". Sarala stood barefoot still, contemplating her future.

"Keep safe out there," Cai said, eyes on the sunrise.

"I will."

An awkward silence ensued between them. Sabre licked his male parts as if what passed between the two Kin mattered not at all. Perhaps it did not.

"So … you might want to know … I'd have taken your braid if you had asked me."

"Why didn't you say?"

"Because I'm too old for you now. I could vote at council the year you were born. It's not appropriate for us to hand-fast yet. You want some weathering. And, I'm glad you didn't ask because if you'd pledged to me, you would feel obligated and that's not what you should take with you on a walk. Find your way and come back or not. This is your time to decide for yourself what your name will be. I would not wish to stand in your way."

Sarala took a quavering breath.

"I would have been pleased to give you my braid in promise, but you are wise. Give it to Gly. There are no others I would have hold it."

He took the thick rope of hair from her, held it like a riding rope in the same hand as Ryanna's braid.

"She'll be back soon enough. You should be about the work or she'll be cross. Guard her back and she'll guard yours. She's bossy, but I can't think of a Kin you'd be safer with than her."

"I'm glad she's going west. You can't see the other side of the hill standing still, but I'd admit I was scared to be going there alone."

"We're never alone, Sarala. The One walks beside us. Much as I fear for you, I know this is somewhat we must do."

Sarala smiled.

"What?"

"It just occurs that we've been speaking Celdryan this whole time and I hardly realized it."

"Their language is not the only challenge they present. Stay with Ryanna and stay safe."

He kissed her on the forehead, then turned on his heel and strode away, leaving Sarala to wonder if she wasn't completely wool-headed for doing what she was about to do.

Wmgleadd

*D*un Wmgleadd sat under a dinner plate full moon, the streets bright as noontide. A caravan had arrived earlier in the day, so the night sang with the great merriment accompanying hardworking men with coin in their purses after a long job is accomplished. Every inn of any reputation spilled over with light, laughter and frivolity, harlots plied their trade and ale flowed like water in a stream.

At the Blue Goose just off the market square, the gaiety was shattered by a scream and the dull thud of a body hitting a grassy yard.

Far from the celebrating throng, Padraig slept soundly, luxuriating in a morrow with no commitments.

He'd been on the move constantly since leaving Clarcom more than two moons hence and a single night without concern for the morrow was a rare luxury that he meant to savor until dawn. When the dream of the eastern mountains began, he though mayhap it was a melting of the blockage he'd labored with for more than a moon, for this had the flavor of vision more than of dream.

The majestic sunlit peaks soared behind Gly as he shouted at Padraig from a great distance. The elven master's words shredded on an unfelt wind so that Padraig recognized only the word "sword". *Sword? What sword?* Gly gestured, directing Padraig to look behind him. He flinched back as lightning rent a storm-black sky. An unnatural raven unfolded enormous wings to launch itself into the storm, somewhat clenched in its talons. Just as it threatened to disappear into the clouds, the raven dropped what it carried and Padraig stared as a sword flashed past his perch to fall broadside upon the grassy yard he suddenly stood upon.

A large fat goose with blue feathers honked at him and waddled off into the darkness. A falcon lifted its beak free of the shelter of its wing in a tree in Mulyn and launched itself into the sky, pushing southward. Ryanna picked up a walking stick of beautiful willow. A Kin woman he knew from the holt told her elfling husband she was with child. Lydia watched Danyl as he slept. A dark and forbidden forest stretched toward unknown mountains. Gly's voice echoed through his head.

~*The broken sword has value. Arise, sleeper, and protect it.*

The dream vision dissolved as loud whispering called his name.

"Padraig of Denygal? Where are you? Padraig?"

Men began to curse the voice that awakened them and Padraig crawled out of the tent in only his small clothes to keep Braeden from being killed … or more like having to kill someone to keep from being killed. Braeden's reputation was no doubt deserved.

"Braeden, over here," he whispered loudly, which brought complaints from the tents round his. Braeden's tall form came toward him in the darkness, backlit by the glow from a fire across the camping ground. "What brings you here, man? Are you ill?"

"Tamys needs you," the captain of Wmgleadd's largest caravan began.All thought was washed away by the deluge of ice that washed over Padraig's body.

No! Oh, God, what have I done?

The Tongue

*O*n a narrow, swampy spit of land thrust into the Stormor like a fist, a collection of buildings lay silent and dark as a black vortex roiled from the ground to the heavens. Amid the swirling maelstrom, lightning flashed and daemons played. Far above the ground, where the air grew thin, the vortex threw off darkling offspring that piled up like thunderheads, spilling across the kingdom of Celdrya, seeking whom they might devour.

A circle of 13 had met in the etheric and built a spell to find the True King. Black mages had attempted this spell twice before in the century since King Perryn had been killed. They had yet to find the True King, but they'd discovered lots of ways to kill black mages.

On this third attempt, the spell had been more finely tuned and the unauthorized choice of a powerful apprentice had provided balance, so that the spell did not pulse out over the kingdom to collapse immediately thereafter, returning a null response. This one continued to grow, to span the kingdom, to reach tendrils into towns and villages, to caress interesting folk, and move on to find others. The True King lived, and the black mages meant to have him ... if they survived the attempt.

Blue Iris Holt

*G*ly tried to remain nonplussed while several council members yelled at him. The Wise of Blue Iris Holt were gathered in the council chamber to discuss Ryanna's choice to travel into the basketlands.

"How could you tell her she could ride onward? You knew the decision of this body?" Melor demanded. As the head of the Council for this five-cycle, he held the authority to question Gly's report and decision, but he sometimes was too eager to remind Gly that he was the former speaker, not the present.

"She reported a prophesy," Gly repeated. "I can't argue with the One. I wouldn't try."

Several of the Wise frowned, for they wished to argue with Gly, even if it might seem to be arguing with the One. Being a long-time member of the Wise Council and past leader did not mean his word was sacrosanct. They had authority and a duty to question him.

"You know this isn't the One. This is my headstrong daughter taking the bit on her own," Marnmara insisted.

Sion smirked in response to her scowl. What angered Marnmara about their daughter Ryanna amused him. It had been the same when this conversation had started more than two 10-cycles ago. Gly wondered that they never seemed to argue about their sons.

"The One can come to the headstrong as well as to the pure," Banara reasoned. Gly's wife was always the voice of reason, even in a crowd as unreasonable as this. "I must admit that I feel more comfortable knowing that Sarala will be traveling with her. Ryanna has knowledge in the basketlands and the ways of the Celtmen."

"How do we know there was a prophesy?" Tavoran asked.

I should not allow you to be here, even if you are my son. The others take it as a given. Why is that? What should I do about you?

"We have to trust Ryanna," Banara insisted, giving their son a sharp look.

The water caught the wheel right there. Most of the people in the room did not trust Ryanna. Sion stood, stretching.

"I do," he assured the gathering.

"And for those of you who still doubt, I can verify the prophesy," Shanara said. Gly had not seen her enter the room. The silver-haired woman could walk through a crowd of those seeking her without drawing notice. It was a rare gift and nnoying at times. "I was at my weaving when it came – dragons and maps. She's to go to Lindermaden and her journey will bring her in contact with the One's Beacon."

"You're sure of this?" Marnmara asked.

If ever there is a reason for Ryanna to be headstrong, it is that attitude. She made a mistake and has suffered for 20 years, but her own mother will not let her move on.

Of course he couldn't say that publicly, so instead, Gly held up a hand for attention.

"Dragons have been speaking to her for months. We must recognize that she is called and accept that the One has a greater voice than we do. This is no youthful lark and time is of the essence. Do you have any knowledge on that front, Shanara?"

"I don't, but I will endeavor to seek it. I must point out to those who struggle with this calling – Ryanna is going to the south near the coast. Padraig is to the northwest. They could not be farther apart. If this is a youthful rush to love, she's going about it all wrong."

An uncomfortable silence fell over the dissenters in the crowd. It was impossible to argue with the One, even about a woman whose past was marked by poor decisions.

"I will keep this body informed of Ryanna's whereabouts and activities," Gly assured. Then he and Banara left the chamber, both feeling as if they needed to protect Ryanna from her detractors, but uncertain if their efforts would be enough. Gly had other matters to be concerned of too. Padraig was well, but his companion had fallen into darkness. Gly did not know how to support him, except through prayer, but the world felt on edge, holding its breath. This was no time to be inattentive.

Maelstrom

The dragon will rise from the mountain and he will fall to the ground. The dragon will die, but be reborn. When the dragon flies he will not be alone. There is one on the other side, preparing. Go west, and hither and to. Keep the sword close even as it is broken, for swords can be mended and reforged stronger than before in the fires of refinement. Wait upon the Lord for the king will rise on dragon's wings.

Andyr of Denygal, Dun Celdrya FY1023

Past

Viking Year 742 – Four years past Hansorfjord

*E*rik didn't like how the jals stroked their beards and held their piss while he talked. He couldn't invade the southern continent without their viks and their silence made him feel like he'd stepped on an ant hill. When his speech ran to a close, he waited for comment, questions, or arguments. He had prepared for those. Samling was all about debate. Silence shivered his bones.

Erik was not yet kong to make sweeping decisions and even his father Magnus could not simply order the jals to follow his leader. The leaders of the islands each had their own vote in Samling and those votes must be coaxed from them by reasoned argument and inspiring ideas.

"Speak," Magnus commanded after several breaths of hearing the wind drive the rain under the eaves.

"It's much bigger than an island," Einar noted. The jal of Jukka clan off Surturey, he commanded the largest navy.

"It's much richer than one too," Jarl said. He was the jal for Hansor clan and hammer to Magnus and by extenstion, Erik, but he did not speak for any of the other jals.

"You've seen these portals?" Sven asked. The Fiskarey folk were white-blond. Their jal had eyes that were unusually dark blue against his almost silver hair.

"Jah," Jarl said strongly.

The peat fire back-drafted as a rain of hail clattered across the shutters. Erik rubbed his nose to keep from sneezing. He'd seen the portals too, had even said Jarl was there with him, but Jarl's word counted more with these men than did that of an untried kong in waiting.

"What if your emissary don't return?" Ivar inquired. Ivar was jal from Steney, an island with plentiful trees.

His question gave Erik opportunity to speak.

"He's gone to raise support for us with the Orental Empire. When the winter storms have abated, he'll return."

"Will he?" Uri asked. He commanded the navy of Spydey.

"If he doesn't, our plan will be revised. If I understand him correctly, anyone with alvi blood can trigger the portal."

Erik's new bride hailed from a family reported to have alvi blood.

"What if the Orental see us as distracted and bite our flank?" Einar asked. His clan had reason for concern, being the closest to the Orental empire. This gave Erik opportunity to show his solidarity with the other islands.

"Then my test will be repelling them rather than taking the southern continent. Either way, it will be a great accomplishment. Imagine if we could take the southlands. Farms, cities, mountains of gold and salt …."

"We're a seagoing people," Uri said plainly. Spydey were more warlike than most. They'd been true Vikings in the Beforetime.

"Not all of us in the old world were seagoers," Magnus countered. "Orma's clan were merchants."

"Bah! Sellers of cloth and trinkets. Do you seek to tame us?"

"It will be a good many generations before that," Magnus replied calmly. Some men would take Uri's comment as an insult to Orma, but Magnus knew that Uri just thought merchants were weak … a condition that could be cured in a generation of working the ships. "Sweeping the seacoast means we can exact payment for use of the harbors. The Celts will work for us like they did in the dawn world."

They liked that, Erik thought, but they weren't won over yet.

"These aren't the same Celts," Ivor announced. "Celts back in the Dawn World lived on islands and they had smidgen armies. These Celts have more resources and they's armies is bigger."

"And they think we're on the other side of their northern mountains. They don't expect us to sail up from their southern sea," Erik said.

That actually won a grin from Einar, quickly hidden by a tug on his red mustaches.

"How many ships?" Thar asked. Jal to the Joppman clan, he might have been slightly annoyed by the comments about merchants. He and Orma were cousins of sorts, from the same island. He was Jarl's elder brother and the easiest of the jals to convince, but also the quietest jal in Samling.

"We could make some feints with 400, but we need far more if we're to overwhelm them and capture the coast before they can mobilize armies," Erik suggested, resisting the urge to glance at Magnus. If he could just show them his strategy, they could be won over.

"How many more?" Thar asked.

"We need a thousand."

"And viks to crew them?" Einar quipped. "That's 10,000. Ambitious, ain't ya?"

"It's been 15 years since the wars and raiding along the Orenthal coast is been near nothing for 10. I've a lot of young pups who want to robe themselves in blood and glory," Thar explained. He deliberately did not look at Jarl, who had left Joppmaney to come to Hansorfjord for just that reason. "I could crew 300 ships myself. What about you, Jarl? Hansorfjord has 400 ships and crew, but you have many more who can't get a ship until the old men die, jah?"

"True enough," Jarl said. He'd been holding his testimony, not wanting to drag jals where they did not want to go.

It's a strategy they play even in council, Erik realized.

"How many ships can Hansorfjord crew?" Uri asked.

"We can crew 600," Magnus replied. "We're building the extra ships now."

"And when do you plan this?" Sven asked.

"I think four years," Erik said. "We need to build the ships and train the young ones, but more we need to work together as a coordinated naval force. We haven't done that in this generation."

"Haven't needed to," Sven remarked.

"True, but the population of the isles is increasing. We need to find more land before there's a bad winter and we starve."

"Why not just take the north coast," Ragnar asked. Erik's new brother-in-law, he was jal to the Fossgrimen clan far to the west and very close to the mainland. He was the youngest of the jals and an unknown in Samling.

"Have you seen the north coast?" Jarl asked. "There's nothing there. We've not enough farmers to make use of it and there's no raiding to be had."

"There's cities. There used to be cities."

"Before our time," Magnus explained. "They've hid their secrets all this time and now we know why the *alva* built cities so far from their main range."

"These *alva* highways ... they really work?" Sven asked.

"I've used them. I sat in the harbor of their main city on their southern coast," Erik assured.

They all looked at each other as if communicating silently, then Sven tugged on his beard.

"Show us the plan and we'll see what we think," he said.

Present

Founding Year 1028
Galornyn

*R*ain fell in sheets from a sullen sky, filling the streets of Galornyn with fetid streams of mud that oozed toward the harbor in thick brown ropes like excrement loosed from a cesspit. The unnatural downpour had kept the city enthralled for three days now. Folk spoke of Hanaloran witchcraft while the merchants of the Southern Isles stood off the jetty awaiting a favorable wind for home.

In the markets, there was news that three academics from the collegiate had died as if strangled by unseen hands the night before the storm broke. The streets and taverns hummed with fear as every man, woman and child saw plague and sorcery round every corner.

Gregyn stood in the shadows of the dim interior of the temple of Bel, watching Naryna's parents mourn their daughter, the whole of his saved wages arranged about her in guilty lavishness. He'd been unable to persuade the priests to provide this time of mercy for Naryn's parents, but the priests of Bel in Galornyn liked coin as much as other men, though they pretended not to.

The failure of persuasion gnawed at him. A symptom of Talidd's murderous spell, no doubt. Gregyn had not eaten for three days and his hands shook when he didn't will them not to. His head ached and every muscle of his body throbbed as if he'd labored for days in a mine.

His gift proved as exhausted as his body. It would be some time before he could work magic again, though he could still feel its power on the edge of his awareness. He'd been fortunate. Others had not been. Naryna had died in his stead as other familiars had died in the place of their journeymen. The magic they'd unleased had poisoned the heavens with its potency.

Naryna's mam held her daughter's cold dead hand as the priest spoke the words that would commend her to the Otherworld. Gregyn knew it should be him departing this world's realm. If he'd only known, he'd ....

What would he have done? Volunteered to die? Used his acolyte as a familiar? The alternatives were limited and unpleasant. Black mages could not afford the luxury of love or caring? Everyone was a playing piece in a massive game of hounds and hares and black mages meant always to be the hound. He'd not meant to kill Naryna, but he'd learned a valuable lesson from her death.

Don't ever link to someone you care about.

The priest placed the wreath of flowers Gregyn had provided across the chest of the dead lass. Gregyn sighed and turned, striding out into the liquid darkness that held no redemption. He'd gone three steps from the door before he saw the Wild Folk standing in the street, oblivious to the poisonous rain. They stared at him with sad eyes, shaking their warty heads, their mouths drawn in silent anguish at his decision.

Intent upon the spectacle that only he could see, Gregyn ran up against a tall, thin man dressed in a sopping grey cloak. Instinctively, Gregyn reached for his shields, but the mental prowess that normally set him apart from other apprentices was lacking in his exhaustion, so that the man's eyes touched his soul as they came face to face.

~It's a dark path you trod, lad, the man thought to him. If I may suggest, there are better treks to choose.

He disappeared into the crowd of huddled cloaks, leaving Gregyn gasping and quaking, staring at the wild folk who nodded their heads solemnly as if they too had heard the unheard advice and thought quite highly of it.

Shuddering, Gregyn hurled the contents of his stomach into the gutter. The crowd bent round him. In this time of plague, none offered to help. Gregyn hunched with water running down his neck, soaking the inside of his cloak as much as the outside. When the worst passed, leaving him cold, wet and aching, he set his face toward the dun and his black future.

Trevellyn

*B*ryan ap Riordan of Clarcom enjoyed his cousins' company immensely. Duncyn always had a jest or a story to lighten the mood. Lord Geran liked to dice and laugh, which left Bryan plenty of time to fraternize with Kefyn, whose mood was less light, but whose heart was so pure, Bryan couldn't resent him for it.

Dun Trevellyn's great hall was empty except for Lord Geran and Duncyn of Moryn, who were playing at field strategy – a more robust version of hounds and hares that Bryan was pretty sure had been created here at Dun Trevellyn. Every time he played, he remembered that the clan Trevellyan were the original royal family. Geran didn't act the sort, though.

Bryan and Kefyn sat at the servitor's table where Bryan could keep his eye on the honor table. Geran would pour his own wine if Bryan wasn't available, but Bryan rather liked what he learned by hanging round the rig and his visitors. Duncyn had traveled the whole of Dublyn and had many interesting tales to tell.

"Denygal nobles live for war," Bryan reminded Kefyn, who fixed him with a hard look. Bryan had spent the afternoon trying to cheer him out of his melancholy over an inevitable life-taking. "All I'm saying is that it's only the Denygal who can afford to grieve their first kill."

"Mayhap that's not a bad thing," Kefyn sighed. "Do you remember each death as if it happened yesterday?"

"Nay. I've lost track since the first. You always remember the first, I'm told, but it must be a half-dozen for me by now. And Trevellyn's quiet compared to other parts of the kingdom. I wager Geran sends me on this skirmishes just to wreath me in glory."

"I wish never to know glory."

"How Denygal of you! Lord Darryl is much impressed with my glory."

"How does Gwendolyn feel about it?"

"I've yet to meet her and it's impolite for a groom to discuss such with his betrothed. It might upset her delicate nature."

"Does the daughter of a lord as renowned as her father have a delicate nature?"

"There is that." His betroth's father had ruthlessly oppressed an area of Dunmaden during a border war some years ago. "The fact is my father is no different and Shyla is far from delicate, despite what men may think when they see her."

"The Denygal rose looks fragile, but it has claws enough for its protection."

Bryan sighed. He'd not wanted to broach the subject, but he knew someone needed to.

"She's betrothed, you know. She's no longer the rough-and-tumble child who you played with in Denygal. She's become a young woman … or near enough to."

"I am aware. You needn't worry that I will despoil her."

"I'm more afraid for you if my father thinks you're fishing a pond you've no right to."

"I've never met your father."

"Duncyn can tell you he's not a safe man to anger or irritate."

"You and your sister deserve better."

"Mayhap, but that's not how it works this far south of the Dragon Wall. None of us has a choice."

"Why not?" Kefyn asked. "Why must marriage choices be made when children aren't yet chewing meat?"

"It secures alliances."

"And enslaves future adults."

It's not like I don't agree, but I can't afford to think that way.

"This is not a debate that occurs here, Kefyn. Your time at the collegiate has turned you into a radical."

"Mayhap, but I'm right and you know it."

He was and Bryan did, but what was he supposed to do with that knowledge?

"If I went to my father with that speech, he'd like as not have me beaten to change my mind and it wouldn't do a bit of good, because I would still be married off to Gwendolyn of the Crossing. Shyla would find herself held in the donjon until her wedding day. Aye, there may be a few noble families who would listen to their children, but most would think we're jesting or insane. I am trying to keep you from pain, cousin. Shyla is not free with her affections. You must realize that and guard your heart."

Kefyn looked even more melancholy, but Geran had just finished off the pitcher of wine, so Gregyn had to replenish it. Duncyn grinned at him from over the game board.

"I do hope my brother is behaving himself."

Bryan glanced at the board and saw that Duncyn was winning with an unusual strategy of holding a small area with a single narrow point of entry. Geran could wear himself down attacking the small area, while Duncyn stockpiled pieces for an eventual surge that would inexorably overwhelm Geran's forces spread-out forces.

"He does not understand our ways and I am attempting to educate him. What are your plans for him? You'll barely have time enough to return to Cenconyn, much less Denygal."

"As always, I travel at the behest of your lady mother, which suits me well and will provide an education for Kefyn."

"A winter in Clarcom might not suit him, you realize."

The bluff Denygalman frowned. Geran had been waiting for him to roll his turn and now looked up. The blond lord's reddish beard was close-clipped like Duncyn's. Bryan wondered if his would ever grow.

"A winter at Clarcom will make a Dengyalman see the world anew," he noted. "It did for you, my friend."

"Ah, aye, I was just about the same age," Duncyn remembered fondly. Bryan sighed. Clearly no one in this group understood what he was after and he doubted he'd be able to spend the winter in Clarcom to prevent a looming tragedy. Young hearts were foolish hearts and Kefyn loved Shyla in the way of young hearts.

Bryan would have to send a missive to his sister with the next post, just to assure that everyone knew the edge of the precipice they trod so casually.

"Lad, I'll talk to him," Duncyn said as Bryan turned away. "We do things differently in Denygal, but he does know he can't poach another man's preserve."

Bryan nodded and returned to the table where Kefyn stared into space. He still planned to send that missive. Shyla needed to know that she had to act honorably as well.

"You're keeping a secret," Kefyn said when Bryan sat back down.

"Am I? Do you know what it is?" he asked.

"No, but I'm certain to figure it with some effort. You've stopped showing your aura, for example."

"You said when you trained me that there was no need to leave it hanging out like a cloak for everyone with gifts to read."

"No need, aye, but in Denygal most folk let their friends and family see it."

"This is not Denygal, lad. Have you not been listening?"

"I have, but I still think you're keeping a secret."

Only that my father forced my mother to whelp another man's offspring so that he might not seem impotent, which means I am not the heir to Clarcom and I am struggling with the lack of honor in all of it.

"Mayhap it is not my secret to share," he explained. "Tell me of Denygal. There are people there that I miss."

In this way, without Kefyn's knowledge, Bryan was able to work the conversation round to Donyvan and Lisbet, former groom and nurse at Clarcom. Donyvan was now equerry at Dun Moryn, where Kefyn's brother was squire. By pretending to have fond memories of Lisbet from his nursery years, he was able to learn that they had two children of their own and that Donyvan was a master horse breeder.

If Shyla's parentage were known, she could marry you.

If Bryan's parentage were known, he would not be heir of Clarcom and Cunyr would purge Denygal for the embarrassment to his manhood. Much as he wished for someone to talk with about this dilemma, he knew that he couldn't share it with Kefyn, who saw the world in Denygal terms and, more importantly, he might seek to act on his beliefs in free will and love. He could not be trusted with the secret.

And, truth to tell, I would be a better vyngretrix than Cullyn or my father. I at least have the One to guide my choices. It's just my honor that must be laid aside for this future to become.

Geran howled with laughter as Duncyn captured the castle once more and Bryan joined them with another pitcher of wine. This time, Geran insisted Bryan play Duncyn.

"Show us what you're made of, lad. Can you capture the kingdom and secure the prize?"

Bryan chuckled for he was widely regarded among the pages as a master at this game. Kefyn came to watch as he and Duncyn squared off across the table, dice at the ready. A shiver ran down Bryan's back as he let the dice go.

It's only a game, but there is a kingdom out there that needs a king and when he is found, he'll need good men to back him. I mean to be one of them.

Clarcom

*T*he sea of grass undulated in green waves from the lakeshore to the horizon. Shyla nee Riordon coaxed her palfry up to the top of a ridge. Macla laughed as she caught up.

"You always beat me. Is it because you ride astride?"

"Mayhap," Shyla said, dropping off the horse into a meadow of delicate blue flowers. She shook out her split skirts before kneeling to pick blooms. Macla took her time dropping out of the side saddle and arranging her fuller skirts, no doubt hoping to gain attention from the lads. Cullyn and Glynn jested with the two riders who had accompanied them.

"My mam says it ruins a woman to ride astride."

"My mam begs to differ," Shyla replied, continuing an old argument. "She has had six children, so it doesn't seem to have harmed her at all."

"You know what I mean. There was no show for the court on her wedding night."

"I've not bled yet," Shyla announced. "Not from riding astride or from the moon."

"It should happen soon," Macla said, smiling, gaze upon Shyla's chest where her dresses were starting to bulge. "It's a bit late, even."

"Mam says she was late also. Naught to worry. Are you going to pick flowers or talk? Can't you do both?"

Macla picked two flowers and then smiled dreamily.

"What do you think Teddryn will look like?"

"I don't know," Shyla admitted. "I'd like him to be tall with dark hair like Bryan, but he's from down on the coast and I hear they're often blonde."

"I read that Dun Galornyn overlooks the sea." Macla clearly thought that was somewhat to dream about. So far, Shyla had picked a half-dozen flowers to Macla's three.

"It would be a sight to see. Cullyn says it's awe-inspiring, slate grey in the winter and green and white in the summer."

"I can't wait to see it … that is, if you choose me for your entourage."

Accompanying a lady to a great dun was a proven way for a landless noble lass with a small dowry to find a suitable husband. Macla might prefer for one of Shyla's brothers to be betrothed to her, but that was highly unlikely. Shyla could not imagine going to Galornyn, let alone selecting her entourage.

"Mam says to wait until I've come closer to the time."

Macla managed a smile, though Shyla could see she was wondering if their friendship was true. It was, which was why Shyla hesitated.

"I understand," Macla said.

No, she doesn't. I feel like I'm being sold off like a prize mare, assuaged by being able to take some brood mares with her. I'm tired of everyone hanging on me as if I might provide them somewhat better than what they currently possess. I'm a slave and naught more. Clinging to me is only going to buy you captivity.

Of course, one didn't say that in their circles. Instead, they smiled and made non-promises while they picked blue flowers for the Lughnasda altars. Far off on the southern horizon, Shyla saw a flash of lightning. Glynn, standing at the crest of the next hill, saw it too. Although they were too far to see each other's faces clearly, she could practically hear him thinking, calculating how long it would take for the storm to reach them.

They had time to fill their baskets before Cullyn announced they needed to head back. A brisk wind bent the grass sea toward the north. When they reached the road, they met the farmers who had brought first fruits to market trundling their wagons back toward their farms, frowning at the storm that rapidly built enormous thunderheads on the horizon.

"We should hurry. That wet will simply ruin my dresses," Macla said.

"Cullyn, can't you take her on ahead and let Glynn escort me? I don't mind storms."

"As you wish, sister," Cullyn said coolly. "Matryc, stay with them."

"Aye, sir," the older of the riders assured. Glynn brought his horse up beside hers as Matryc dropped his pace behind. They rode quietly while Cullyn, Macla and the other rider trotted out of sight. The wind caught Shyla's hair and whipped it out straight, so that it almost touched Glynn.

"We're going to get soaked," he said with a laugh. With the wind guarding their conversation from others, he leaned closer. "What do you want to discuss?"

"Have you told Mam yet?"

"Nay. She's so busy and Cullyn's always about. I don't trust him knowing."

"Nor do I. I will ask her to join me in my chambers this evening. You can meet us there and tell her. She'll be so happy."

"I see that," Glynn assured her. "I am seeing so much different this last eightnight. Colors are brighter, people are different. I want to tell the world and yet … they hang Believers."

"They do. It's our secret in the world, but it's also how I know that it's true. If the world loved what I am, I'd know I am unlovely."

Glynn nodded as soberly as any 12-year-old might. The walls of the city loomed up over them. Thunder rolled from the south.

"After the evening meal then," Glynn told her and then he picked up the pace. "We should move smartly in the right direction. That storm will spook the horses."

Before they entered under the walls of Clarcom, Shyla looked toward the storm and a cold shiver ran through her body.

"There's somewhat about that storm that feels …."

"Aye," Glynn agreed. "Let's be about getting clear of it then."

Inside the town, folk rushed about to secure anything that might be ruined or killed by the storm. Glynn led their clattering way up the broad curving avenue as wind carried a storm of dust over the wall and straight into Shyla's face. Her horse shied sideways, blowing, as she struggled to get her hair out of her mouth and the dirt out of her eyes. When the tears blinked free, she cast about in mild anxiety, for she didn't see Glynn or Matryc. The dust formed a whirlwind at the end of an alley. Her gut tightened. This felt …*deliberate*. Every fiber of her being warned that way lay danger. She stood in her stirrups and spied the towers of the dun in the opposite direction. She'd somehow turned down a side street in the brief time she'd been unable to see. She turned the horse's head and started upward.

A crack of lightning rent the sky and sent a loud rolling boom through the town streets. Her palfry bolted forward, careening round corners, hooves clattering on the cobblestones. It was dangerous to run a horse like this through crowded streets, but she doubted much that she could settle it, much less control it at the next thunderclap.

She met Matryc and Glynn soon enough as they'd turned round to locate her. Her horse, being among other equine it knew, slowed and trotted with them. Glynn looked grim as he reached across to grab her bridle.

"How did you disappear like that? If you'd been lost … I'd care because I'm your brother, but you know how long I'd live after I got back to the dun, don't you?"

She squeezed his wrist and nodded just as buckets of rain began to pour from a black sky. The dun's gates were just ahead. They cantered in and turned their nervous mounts over to the grooms. Before retreating to the dun, Shyla looked up into the swirling mass of clouds over the dun and saw black-winged beings peel off from the vortex, to glide down to the curtain walls and round the broch towers.

"Come inside," Glynn ordered. "What are you staring at?"

"Do you naught see it?" she asked.

"See what?"

A hand settled on her shoulder. She looked back to see her mother standing there wrapped in a cloak and holding another out to her.

"I do," she whispered, fright playing in her blue eyes. "Come inside. There's somewhat nasty about this storm and I wish you all to shelter within walls until it's gone."

Shyla shuddered and followed Lydya. At the door to the stairs that led up to the women's hall, she looked back to see Cullyn standing near Glynn, smiling at the storm.

Can he see it too? And what does that mean? And why is he the only one who seems happy about it?

Bedsports

&

Brooches

Black magery existed in both worlds before the Arrival. The Celtic druids were not all evil, but certainly there were a few who delved into darkness. The Kin admit that there were those who worshipped the elementals as well as the One and wandered further into darkness when they rejected the good news of Jesu. Is it any wonder that the two together destroyed the kingdom?

Blethry of Denygal FY 956

Past

Founding Year 931 – A century ago
High Celdrya

I *have to find Donyl as quickly as possible! As soon as I finish*
with this.

Councilor Dumyr set yet another parchment before
Gerriant, detailing his excellent management of affairs in
the moon and a half since King Perryn had been brutally
killed by his bosom friend. Dumyr could run the
kingdom, if the vingretroi board would allow it. Alas,
that was not to be. They had selected Gerriant as regent,
like it or not.

Gerriant slid the report on the prisoner to the
bottom of the stack before him. There were plenty of
other matters to settle before he dealt with that. The
weavers' guild was disputing with the dyers guild over
their access to the river bank in East Town and the
stonecutters wanted permission to redirect the river to
finish the portcullis they were constructing. Mulyn
ironboats were already complaining of being stopped in
their route through the city by that same portcullis.

Galornyn requested licensure as the port of entry for a merchant fleet from the Summer Isles. Of course, Llyr objected that the Hanolan ships should be hosted in Llyr. Tales of odd phenomena filtered in throughout the kingdom – fell moons, wolf packs, and even dragons. The dun itself wanted repairs to the roof of one of the towers and the spring below the creamery mayhap was running dry.

In many ways, regent at Dun Celdrya was not far different from councilor of Fyrgal, a post Gerriant had held under his elder brother for more than 20 years. Vanyn had always told him that the work of the kingdom was just the work of a rigdon writ large.

Writ annoying! Gerriant thought grumpily.

The afternoon was well-worn by the time Gerriant had naught to address but the prisoner in the gaol. He stood, towering over the shorter High Councilor. Gerriant had once trained for the warband – a long time ago when he'd been a fourth son of a large dun – but he'd broken a leg riding a rogue horse and that ended soldiering for him just as his brother had needed a councilor. His thoughts still flowed best when he had a sword in his hands, though he walked with a significant limp and could not sit a horse comfortably. He ran a wondering hand along the iron haft of King Melchoir's war hammer where it hung above the cold hearth of the council chambers, giving himself time before addressing a stinging nettle. Dumyr asked if he wanted wine.

"Nay. It will not ease this burn," Gerriant replied. Slowly, he turned, walked to the high seat and sat down. "Has he explained himself at all?"

They spoke of Deryk of Trevellyn, accused of murdering King Perryn and suspected of the deaths of both Prince Maryn and King Vanyn.

"He says he doesn't know why he killed Perryn. He seemed genuinely grief-stricken."

"Seemed?"

"The last I spoke with him a fortnight ago, he did not speak in response. I think he's well broken."

The gaol cells would break any man, no less a nobleman who never thought he would be prisoned there.

"Have others given it a try?"

"Aye. You might find the statement of Blethry the priest of interest. He's brother to the bride and at first wanted vengeance as you might expect. Now he has some interesting theories as to what passed that night."

Gerriant sifted through the report to find the statement. Blethry alluded to daemons and ensorcelment.

"Gods, the man cannot be serious!"

"I think he is," Dumyr replied. "The circumstances have unhinged half the kingdom. I counsel a swift end to this. Deryk was found with his hand upon the dagger that killed King Perryn. Although he sounded the warning when King Vanyn was poisoned, he stood right beside him and had access to his goblet. He was with Maryn when he died."

Gerriant nodded, but the hair on the back of his neck tingled. It didn't feel right to execute a noble man without a thorough trial.

"I'd like to talk to some of the witnesses before I make a final decision."

"Maryn's witnesses are scattered to the four winds. Perryn sent several with Donyl. The Mulyn lords saw Deryk touch Vanyn's goblet that day. Many guards saw Deryk with the dagger the night Perryn was killed."

"Aye, the reports say so, but still, this is a noble man. His father and brothers would want us to afford him the full protection of the king's law. I will speak with the witnesses that are available."

Dumyr did not sigh audibly. He'd been a councilor for a long time and was very politic. Gerriant sensed he had somewhat to say, so he waited.

"As the regent, your time is precious. You may trust my judgment and …."

Gerriant had been selected regent in part because he was a nobleman who had labored as a councilor long enough to understand the craft. He'd served twice as regent in smallish duns on his brother's orders. Dumyr had not served as regent nor as councilor to a regent in all his long career. Regents faced realities that lords and kings could best avoid.

"I am not mistrusting your judgment, Dumyr. I am simply verifying the findings. For example, many of these witnesses were interviewed by Lord Deryk himself. How might I trust those reports? Nay, but I will verify." Dumyr's gaze shifted.

I've offended him.

"Dumyr, please do understand. I am not the king to make sweeping judgments. I am only regent. I must be seen as fair beyond measure so that my judgments will not be called into question. When Donyl returns, he will have considerably more latitude than I have now."

Dumyr's mouth tightened, then relaxed and he nodded.

"Well and good then. I'll see to these witnesses being brought to you. Who do you want to speak with first?"

"This one."

Dumyr leaned in to read the name on the parchment that Gerriant pointed to.

"Talidd? I'm afraid I don't know that name."

"Truly? Whose handwriting is this?"

Dumyr took the parchment and held it up to the light, brow furrowed.

"Lord Deryk wrote it, I believe," he replied, handing it back to Gerriant.

"All roads return to him, it would seem. I've a mind to speak with him myself."

"He's been three fortnights in the gaol, my lord, mayhap that would not be the best choice."

Gerriant fingered his moustaches contemplatively.

I am not a king to make sweeping judgments. I must weigh the evidence before I hang a noble man.

"Find Talidd. I'm going to the gaol."

The gaol rested considerable distance from the high council chamber and, shed of Dumyr, Gerriant found plenty of obstructions of a human sort along the way. As he crossed the ward, Burcan of Mulyn watched him from the shadows, but Blethry of Galornyn fell in beside him as he walked.

"Will you see Lord Deryk?" the young priest asked. His shaved head was growing out. Gerriant, being a good deal taller, could see the tonsure on top of his head.

"I will," he replied. "Mayhap you can explain to me your change of heart?"

Blethry stopped walking. Gerriant paused. A servant girl passed with a yoke of buckets. Gerriant smelled milk in the humid air of the ward.

"I cannot, because I don't truly understand it myself. I should want his head upon a pike above the gates, but …. He seemed so shocked at what he'd done and …. I can't explain it."

"If I allow you to accompany me, will you stay back and only listen?"

"I would," Blethry assured him. His simple brown robe with its simple leather belt over simple brown breecs showed no place for a weapon beyond his table dagger. Gerriant continued his course.

The donjon tower of Dun Celdrya was built of plain undressed stone and sealed with thick oaken doors and heavy iron portcullis. As a child brought here by his mother when she'd married King Marcys, who had been Vanyn's father, Gerriant had been terrified of this structure, mayhap because Marcys had thought it humorous to suggest naughty little lads might spend a night within if they were not better behaved than they were at the moment. The gaol always seemed to be full, though the donjon was empty at the moment. Gerriant's leg complained as he made his way down the winding stairs to the first of the gaol levels.

Deryk was held here, in a cell that had a high outside window – meant to be a mercy for the fresh air and light. Gerriant thought it might be a torture to be teased by too little of either. The chains on Deryk's wrists clanged as he shielded his eyes from their lantern light. His beard and hair were grown out shaggy and matted with filth, the unavoidable results of living in a cesspool. His cheeks looked hollow. A bowl of food sat within his reach, flies crawling on the untouched contents.

By prearrangement, Blethry remained outside the lantern light as Gerriant walked forward.

"Do you know who I am?" he asked Lord Deryk ap Trevellyn, younger son of the ancestral dun of House Trevellyn, distant cousin to the royal family.

"If the gods be kind, my death," Deryk whispered hoarsely, letting his head fall back against the stones.

"I might be at that, some dawn soon. I'm Gerriant ap Fyrgal, named regent of Dun Celdrya."

"Is Donyl dead then too?"

"Donyl? What do you know of Donyl?"

"Naught but that he traveled to Dublyn in the company of Maryn's personal guard. What is it that you want from me? Am I to tell the story of killing the king once more?"

"We may get to that. Tell me the tale of Maryn's death."

"I killed Perryn and for that I am willing to face the headsman, but I do not want it said that I killed Maryn. He was my bosom friend. I wouldn't. I couldn't. I didn't."

"Lad, I'm not accusing you. I am simply trying to get the stories straight. You were at all three …."

"So I must have done it, aye? I didn't. Why do you torture me? I killed Perryn. What does the rest of it matter ... except that it does because I loved Maryn like a brother and I did not kill him. You must find Talidd. The servant knows more than he's saying."

Gerriant stared in Deryk's desperate eyes, noted the sweat on his forehead, the sunken cheeks, the sallow skin and turned toward the door.

"I may be back to speak with you later," he explained, taking the lantern with him. Blethry slid up the stairs ahead of him and waited outside the entry door. The gaoler closed and locked it before Gerriant spoke.

"Lord Deryk is to be taken to the top of the donjon, allowed to bathe and dress in clean clothes. He is to have a bed and decent food. I'll send the chirgeon to look in on him by sundown. Blethry, what do you know of Lord Deryk?"

"He likes wine and wenches. I know he can read. Perryn thought highly of his honor, which is ironic, truly, since he --."

"Do you know of a particular lover?"

"Aye. The king's mistress Malona."

"Vanyn had a mistress? I suppose there's a reason no one has shared that information with me."

"I don't know, sir. I haven't actually seen her since the night of the murders."

Gerriant sighed. They left the gaol. He signaled that Blethry could walk with him.

"Mayhap this is all coincidence, but I find it confounding."

"I believe there is some queer magicks at work. Deryk found a raven feather at Maryn's death that was as long as your forearm and near as wide. Have they told you about the fell moon?"

"I've been told some tall tales about a moon bright as day in the dark phase."

"Deryk ap Trevellyn is a soldier, not a poet or a peasant. He didn't have fantasies before killing Perryn, but Donyl claimed Deryk did indeed see a fell moon and the raven feather."

"Hmm. Who is this Talidd that he speaks of?"

"Apparently a servant who was present at Vanyn's death … that naught but Deryk remembers."

"Could he be mad?"

They had reached the back stairs into the council chamber. Blethry closed the door before he spoke.

"Nay, I think not because … truth to tell, I dreamt that night that I was walking with Deryk. I saw him kill Perryn and Lilli and then … there was naught I could do. I woke up outside the chamber in time to prevent his escape."

Face white in the uncertain light of a lantern, Blethry breathed out heavily.

"I know he killed Perryn and my sister, but I don't believe he acted willfully. He appeared … ensorcelled, if ever I've seen a condition to warrant that word."

"Ensorcelled?"

Scoffing came to mind, but Gerriant's heart skipped a beat and he didn't mock.

"Hmph! Queer magicks indeed!"

Present

Founding Year 1028
Wmgleadd

A sullen rain soaked the caravanserai as Padraig stirred a pot of medicinals.

There's evil afoot, he thought.

The gray rain poured from a black sky, turning parts of the camping ground into a shallow lake that crept higher by the watch. If the storm didn't break by morning, he'd take Duglys up on his offer to shelter in his compound. He tasted a drop of the liquid, judged it potent enough for his purposes and moved toward the tarp-roofed tent.

Tamys hadn't moved in the two days since he'd fallen. The cut on the back of his head no longer seeped blood. Truly, that was the only true injury Padraig could find, which in and of itself made no sense. Padraig sensed a growing darkness at the back of his head, which accounted for his failure to waken, but a fall from that height should have killed him or at least left him with devastating injuries. Not that the head injury was not severe enough. If Tamys did not waken at least a bit in the next day, he'd like die of dehydration and there was naught Padraig could do about it. Still, one should expect more than bruises from a three-story fall.

The prophecy that had sent him west had come before healer training in this area. He knew there were techniques elven healers used to support patients through critical times but he didn't know them. As a Celdryan journeyman in herbcraft, Padraig knew how to make Tamys comfortable, but absent God's Healing, he couldn't keep the lad alive as a Kin healer might.

Padraig rolled the lad onto his back, relieved and wondering that there was no sign of posturing. Tamys' long limbs remained straight and flexible. Padraig peeled back one eye lid and then the other. Pupils were equal and reacted to light – a marker for health. His breathing was slow and shallow, his forehead warm, but not deadly hot. Last night, Padraig had feared he would lose him to the fever. Padraig used his finger to dribble the medicinal fluid on Tamys' lips. The lad made no move to lick or swallow, showed no reaction whatsoever. Padraig knew this wasn't enough to sustain life. He'd tried to scry to Gly or Ryanna or anyone who might give him guidance, but so far he'd seen only flames in the fire.

Joy, his sorrel mare, whinnied quietly.

~*Aye?* Padraig sent to her. As a Companion, she only looked an ordinary horse.

~*Someone comes. The dull one.*

Padraig crawled out of the tent to watch Aethyn, a young freesword from Dugly's guard troop, riding his dun through the puddle, leading Tamys' bay gelding warhorse.

~*Do you mean the lad or Tam's horse?*

If horses could chortle ....

Padraig dropped the side of the tent to protect Tamys from prying eyes and walked to his fire to throw on a few more sticks.

"Herbman," Aethyn greeted, swinging from the saddle. "I've come to return Tamys' horse and kit." He looped the reins of the saddled horse round the branch of a nearby tree and proffered a purse of coin. "There's a bit more in there than was Tamys'. The lads took up a collection for his care."

Surprising! Not necessary, but ….

"Thanks to you," Padraig said, dropped the well-stuffed purse into his siarc.

"How does he fare?" Aethyn asked. It might have been the rain and chill that pinched his young features, but the lads had been friends. Water dripped from the hood of his cloak.

"Come stand under the tarp," Padraig offered. He'd built the fire on the edge of the roofed area so that he might have a somewhat dry camp. His own cloak hung near enough to the fire to be warm, but under the roof to remain dry.

"I'll unsaddle his horse first," Aethyn said.

A horseman always cares for the mounts first.

After he'd unloaded the bay and tied it beside Joy and Earnest, Padraig's silver pack pony, Aethyn began to methodically lay out Tamys' gear so Padraig could see that he'd brought it all. He reverently laid Tamys' sword across Padraig's hands. "That was hard to give up," he admitted. "He's noble-born, ain't he?"

"He's in a common enough coma," Padraig countered, his irritation with Aethyn returning full-on.

Aethyn nodded.

"I wager he was drunker than he seemed," he began. "A man would have to be truly drunk to fall backward out a window."

Mayhap he's not an utter dolt, Joy sent.

"How do you know he fell backward?" Padraig asked.

"The way he landed. If he'd fallen forwards, he'd like have landed on his face. You can't turn in midair unless you push yourself in that direction before you leave the ground."

Padraig's memory of arms training tickled.

"He might have flipped o'er end."

"Then his head would have been where his feet were. Nay, he left the window backward. I don't know why the harlot pushed him and then left the purse."

"Harlot?"

"Braedyn didn't tell you?"

"Braedyn only knew what he knew. He arrived at the inn to see Tamys hit the ground. He didn't mention a harlot. Tell me of her."

"Twas simple enough. She wasn't that plum, but Tamys acted as if he'd naught seen such a lovely in his life. They went upstairs and then we heard the scream."

"What did she look like?"

"A ginger." That description and Aethyn's accent told Padraig all he needed to know. The lad was from the east, familiar with Celdryan attitudes toward elves and what they supposed were the traits of elflings.

"Red hair and green eyes is not a curse, lad," Padraig told him.

"She pushed him out of a window. Whatever she was, it wasn't good." Aethyn rubbed a hand through his wet dark hair, spraying droplets. "Mayhap I can tell you this and you won't think me mad. I had a cursed weird dream after you hauled Tamys away."

Why would I … or should I … care about your dreams, lad?

Padraig didn't say that. Aethyn had not meant to put Tamys in danger, though he made an easy target for blame.

"Dream?"

"It wasn't truly a dream. I was awake … or thought I was. After … after … we'd paid for the chamber, so I thought I'd sleep in a bed. I went upstairs and I was thinking about Tam. When I ran outside, I was the first to get to him. I thought he was dead. I looked up to judge the fall and thought I'd see the lass, but she never came to the window. I was thinking on that when I got to the chamber. I was sitting on the bed and the window shutter came open – I'd closed it, you see – and then I saw this woman – she had black hair, shiny as them silk dresses noble women wear, but she wasn't wearing one – just her hair. She turned to look at me and her eyes were golden. Then she flew out the window."

"I hadn't heard that a woman committed suicide that night."

"She didn't. I'd swear she turned into a raven – a cursed big raven. I ran to the window expecting to see her laying in Tam's blood, but I heard wings on the wind and then …." He looked truly uncomfortable before bending to take something from Tamys' s saddle bag. "I

60

couldn't sleep after that, so I went downstairs. I found this in the bushes below the window."

He handed Padraig a raven feather that was as long as his forearm. As Padraig examined it, he said "You can keep it. It's evil, I'm sure."

Joy nickered as a choking sound came from the tent. Padraig turned immediately to see to his patient. Tamys flailed, arms and legs drumming the bedding rhythmically for what seemed like a watch, but was only a double-handful of breaths. God had previously denied Padraig's requests for healing, but when Tamys's breath slowed further, Padraig felt Healing trickle through him into his still twitching patient. Padraig rolled Tamys onto his side after he grew still. Drool ran from his slack mouth.

Aethyn stood staring at his friend.

"I didn't mean for this to happen," he said miserably.

"Nay, I don't suppose you did." Padraig moistened Tamys's lips with the medicinal, knowing it was not enough. "If I can't get water into him soon, he's going to die," he admitted.

"Might that not be best?"

"Mayhap, but I must try."

"Aye. I will think long and hard on this."

A little too little and too late, Padraig thought, but he held silence.

"I'm taking another caravan with Duglys," Aethyn said. "We won't leave until the storm breaks. May I come again?"

"Aye."

Aethyn lifted his hood into place again as it occurred to Padraig that Aethyn had been planning to travel eastward with some of the other freeswords.

How much of the coin in this purse was his?

"Spent all your wages already, lad?"

Aethyn's eyes flashed in the gray daylight.

"Somewhat like that," he said, gaze straying toward Tamys. "He's dreaming," he reported. Surely, his eyes were moving slowly behind his lids which they hadn't done since he'd hit the inn yard lawn.

Padraig turned back to see Aethyn mounting his horse to ride away. Padraig sat down near the fire with his back to his saddle and stared into the flames while contemplating the raven of his dream. In a deep well of coals a window opened and he saw an elven healer dripping medicinals onto a wick of rag tucked into the corner of a patient's mouth.

There was naught a soul to celebrate with, but Padraig thanked the One as he rose to go save his friend's life.

Galornyn

*T*he dark rain soaked everything. Gregyn arrived at the dun shivering from wet and exhaustion, only to be intercepted by Werglidd at the gate.

"Come with me immediately," the court sorcerer ordered. Barely able to stand by this time, Gregyn had not the strength or energy to protest or defend himself as Werglidd compelled him to his tower apartment and barred the door.

"I know it was you, lad," the middle-aged sorcerer fair sparkled with excitement as Gregyn stumbled to the divan before his legs gave out completely. "I knew Talidd was about to work a high-level ritual. Sawyl has been here purchasing supplies. And, of course, for a ritual of that magnitude, Talidd needed his strongest people. Even an apprentice would do when possessed of your power."

Gregyn let his head fall back on the divan, allowing Werglidd's words to wash over him as the chamber spun round him.

"Who were you linked with?" Werglidd asked. Time had passed. Gregyn sensed he'd slept. He felt worse than before. Although normally much stronger than Werglidd and therefore immune to his magicks, Gregyn felt scoured out and beyond the flows of power that had been at his fingertips for most of his life. Werglidd had ensnared him at his weakest. "Who were you linked with, lad? Lying will only cause you pain. I know you were linked, else you'd be dead. How'd you learn that trick? You're only a Level 2, so you've not been taught it. Who were you linked with?"

"Naryna," Gregyn whispered, lips moving of their own volition.

"A lass?! That shouldn't have worked. You're the interesting one, now aren't you? Well and good then. I'll keep your secret and you'll keep mine, if I tell you any. Do you understand what you did?"

"Sexual effluent," Gregyn said. "I stretched my gifts using her lust." He was slurring; his need for sleep paramount.

"Aye. Lasses have lust, but not like men. The lads are so much more powerful, you see. You should not have been able to use her as your familiar."

Werglidd wanted more from Gregyn, but Gregyn's physical weakness dragged him down toward darkness and further questioning only resulted in a seizure … his first not triggered by an awen. Gregyn woke sometime in the night, covered with a blanket, still on the divan. His clothes stank of vomit and his body felt like he'd been stomped by a horse. Werglidd snored in the bed chamber. The man had not pulled off his boots or removed his sword belt. It would be so easy … except that he had all the strength of a wrung-out washrag and doubted he could raise his sword and bring it down with sufficient power to cleave Werglidd's chest. He knew certainly that he could not ensorcel the guards so that they wouldn't remember he'd been here.

He left the sycophant sleeping peacefully to stumble out of the tower toward the barracks. He supposed he'd be squelching rumors about why he'd been visiting Werglidd's chambers, but he couldn't worry about that now. The rain still pounded. His legs weighed stones. He wanted simply to sit down and sleep wherever he was. He crossed near the privies and nearly fell down when one of the doors swung open, revealing Taryn fresh from dumping this night's wine from his system.

"Are you ill, lad?" Taryn asked, grabbing his arm, which kept him from sitting down in the mud.

"Aye," Gregyn whispered and passed out clean then and there.

Clarcom

*E*lora Dyer wept in the silence of the chapel of Bel, huddled in the darkness with her back to a stone wall, hidden from prying eyes and utterly bereft of hope. The cold of the chapel made the bruises on her arms ache more acutely, but she could not yet stop crying and dared not let anyone see her in this state.

Save for the pounding rain outside, the dun lay quiet, so that her snivels filled the chamber like huge shouts. A part of her hoped that Cunyr would come to apologize while a more sensible voice suggested she were safest if he did not.

Two years eight months.

Her dower contract would be fulfilled and she would be free to go – still bespoiled, but with a dowry to smooth over what Cunyr's greed had done to her. And only 18 – still plenty of time to start a family and a life. Two years eight months hadn't seemed so much earlier in the evening, but now ….

A tear flowed down her cheek to catch on her lip.

Gods, what am I to do?

The sound of footsteps cut off her prayer. She tried to squeeze herself more tightly into the alcove where she huddled. Light wobbled across the opposite wall.

Who would be about at this watch of the night?

"Lass, I know you're here," a female voice said. "While it is best to hide from my husband at these times, you do yourself no service by hiding from me."

Lady Lydya?

Elora held her breath, but it took only a moment for Lydya to find her. Lydya of Clarcom, wife to Cunyr, hitched up her skirts and sat down on the floor beside her, setting the candle lantern she carried on the stone. She fumbled in her loose dress until she found a pot that she held out to Elora.

"Lard and pepper dust. Smear it on your bruises and they will fade more quickly."

Elora hesitated.

"The sooner done the sooner healed," the lady advised.

Elora had fled the chamber wearing only a dressing gown. She shed one sleeve to rub the burning salve into her upper arm, then the other. Lydya's gaze stayed on the base of a statue of Bel until Elora was completely clothed.

"It's been about a year and a half, has it not?" Lydya said, handing her a handkerchief to wipe her hands. "That's about when it started for all of them."

I knew I was not the first. Don't cry!

"It's about when it started for me as well."

Her?!

"When he realizes that you can't change who he is, he begins to resent you. The cruel words started some time ago and now he strikes you. Are you ready to go home yet, lass?"

"His lust ruined my prospects. I want that dower."

Lydya nodded.

"It's the power he holds over us. We want somewhat from him, if only to get back what he's taken from us, so we remain in the abuse, which we feel means he owes us somewhat, so we remain in the abuse. At least there's an end to it for you."

"Have the … did the others …?"

"Some."

"But you whelped six times."

"He mentioned that, did he? He wants to prove his manhood with you? Do you want a child with him?"

"I do everything in my power not to get pregnant," Elora announced.

"Good, because a child would bind you to him forever and that's a fate I would not wish even on my rival."

"You are not treating me like a rival."

She'd been as cold as one expected a wife to be toward a mistress.

"Nay. I would prefer if we were allies. There's some land in Denygal and a small sum of coin if you choose to leave. It's not as rich as the dower he can offer, but you won't have to withstand two more years of beatings."

Lydya stood up, graceful. Her simple braid without a hair covering made her seem far younger than she had to be.

Bryan's my age.

"If you allow me to advertise, there are landless younger sons who would wed a former mistress with land."

"I … I'll consider it."

"Well and good then. I've seen some of your embroidery. You have a fine hand. Please do join my court in the ladies' hall during the days. I'm moving your quarters into the women's hall. Should you need to flee him in the future, go to your quarters. I assure you it will be safe."

"Thank you, m'lady."

"I recognize that a lass of 14 winters does not seek the attention of an old man, no matter how powerful he might be. I've spoken to your mam. They would take you back if ever you choose."

"It would ruin them."

"Nay. That's what he tells you, but since I inherited Denygal, he has to treat with me."

"W-why?"

"Because I choose it," Lydya explained. "Tomorrow, he'll be remorseful, apologetic, declare his undying love, bring you gifts. Remember, brooches have value. The more injured you seem ... the more angry ... the more gifts he'll shower on you. Wear them, enjoy them, and be prepared to sell them when you leave. Don't believe his lies. He's not going to change. That is how you survive."

"Is it like this for all mistresses ... all ladies?"

"Nay. I'm sure there are nobles who treat their wives with honor and, if they take mistresses, they recognize the gift she gives them. Cunyr just happens not to be one of those men." Lydya picked up the candle lantern. "I'll leave you to your prayers and see you in my entourage in a day or so."

The lantern sent eerie shadows across the walls and ceiling as she made her retreat, leaving Elora to contemplate the twin gifts of bed sports and brooches.

Remembering

The raven is ever the trickster, familiar to darkness. Black wings against the blue sky. Sitting in trees about the battle field. Sinister, humorous, cunning and entertaining. Is the raven a mere pet or master in disguise.

Grufydd of Fyrgal, FY 783, bard of Dun Mulyn

Past

Founding Year 931 – A century ago
Denygal

Gravity dictates the fate of a dragon dancer. Miss a handhold and gravity wins.

After spending all of yestermorrow climbing the ropes on a sheer cliff face, it would be ironic if a sliding bit of shale on a scree slope sent her tumbling to her death.

Janara jerked her downslope foot off the treacherous slab, dropping to her upslope knee with a teeth-jarring thump and slapping her hands hard on the solid rock. The slab clattered off down the slope, launched into the void with an avalanche of similar stones headed to the river far below.

Janara pretended she'd meant to do that. Settling the pack straps more comfortably on her shoulders, she reached for the water bottle at her side. The late summer sun sent trickles of sweat meandering down her back under her sleeveless linen shirt.

Haste will kill you, girl! A dancer works with the mountain. Forget that at your peril!

The hard blue sky arched above her, wide open to the south all the way to the green valley of Fairhaven and disappearing over the crest of the slate mountain in front of her. Not far now, truly. She'd reach the ridge by noontide. She splashed a little water in a slender, long fingered hand and wiped it across her face and the front of her braided hair. She longed to dump a bit down her back and wet her shirt, but this was not a situation for extravagance. Securing her water bottle in the pouch on the pack, she rose from her knees and began laboring upward once more.

Put one foot in front of the other. Step, breathe in, release, step, breathe in, release, ...

What was that?

She scrambled up the last few steps of inclination to kneel panting upon the warm stone. A dark shape flew along the crest of the next highest ridge. A large bird, perhaps?

A dragon?

She'd seen a dragon flying once, a long way off. It had been a rare sighting, deemed auspicious by her parents, reason enough to train in the Dragon Corpse. She'd dreamt of dragons since, but she doubted to have the privilege of true sighting again, even as she hoped to be granted it. The Denygal rarely found Companions these days and none had Touched a dragon in half a millennia. Why would the One deny such a blessing to one who loved Him utterly?

Why would He grant it, either?

It was an eagle, she decided, riding the thermals at the edge of the ridge. There'd been an eagle in her dream, the one that had prompted her parents to send her northward at daybreak two days past. Lowering her pack to the stone, she knelt to pull out a cloth-wrapped bundle of sharp cheese and thick bread. She took her lunch sitting tailor-fashion on the ground, looking west.

Mam had encouraged her to trek here when she'd awakened from the dream. It did no good to ignore a Prompting. Da had wanted her to wait for her brothers, but none of them were dancers. They'd only have taken her to the base of the ropes. She'd still be alone here, contemplating the vast wilderness beyond the Milk. Janara washed down fruit leather with tepid water and considered the deep valley before her.

The Dragon's Tears scoured down the side of the Dragon's Head mountain, an enormous waterfall fed by a glacier. It stopped halfway down in a churning lake, then spilled on downward, finally becoming a mighty river, the Milk, that carved a canyon through the Roof of the World into Denygal to the south. Few could cross the Milk this far north because there were no bridges up river of Fairhaven, but dancers like Janara had a way … if she chose to use it. She had to be sure of the Prompting because following her heart meant a long dangerous walk back. Stowing her tuck bag, she stood on the verge, looking far down at the gray-brown streak of the Milk and waited for the One's Spirit to speak to her.

A warm breeze brushed her face and dried her lips as she scanned the dark-green forest on the other side of the river. Something pulled at her heart, but she waited for confirmation.

Never trust your heart. Wait for the One to lead.

She prepared to step back from the verge when a rustle of feathers shuffled past her ear. The eagle paused for a moment before her astonished eyes, hovering in space as if frozen in time, and then dropped into the void. For two heartbeats it streaked downward, then opening its wings, it kited off toward the north, swooping low over the evergreen forest.

Janara's breath caught in her throat as she followed the eagle's flight. Perhaps a day's walk from the river, on a ridgeline likely formed by on of the active glaciers that came down from the roof of the world, she saw a plume of smoke.

The One speaks!

Decided, she wasted no time in pulling the faery suit from the pack and donning it. Wide bands of cloth stretched from her wrists, along her arms and sides and down her legs, then between her legs to form a kite that gave the dancers their gravity defying abilities.

The suit does not define your courage.

Securing everything within the pack, which she tied tightly to her body beneath the suit, she stepped once more to the verge and waited, arms half-stretched-out, feeling for the updraft. It started as a gentle feeling of being nudged, followed by a growing sense of being pushed back toward the rock. She leaned into it, stretching her arms further, feeling the fabric between her legs catching and flagging. She wanted to step back, to avoid the danger inherent in dancing. She looked toward the ridge line once more and saw the long slithery shape leave the ground, wings flapping.

Dragon?

The updraft caught the suit full, her feet left the shale, and she became the eagle, headed west toward the fire on the ridge.

Present

Founding Year 1028
Wmgleadd

*T*amys floated above the tent and watched as Padraig bought apples from the passing wagon bound for the town. Using his daggar the herbman quartered an apple and fed the three horses. He then sat down by the cold fire pit to munch a quarter for himself. Padraig had left the side of the tent up so that Tamys would not become overwarm and in the languid warmth of a summer day following a drenching rain, Tamys dreamt....

He stood upon a mountaintop overlooking a wide valley that he recognized, but could not name. The impossible blue sky called him to join it and he took flight, soaring over forests and rivers as if on wings....

His head hurt. His throat scratched. He felt the solidity of the bedding beneath him....

The wind ruffled his hair as he followed a river. He circled a dun of pink stone, dipping lower and lower until he could see men upon the walls and horses in the ward. He thought to land ....

Raven black hair and golden eyes. She tasted of the best mead. His hands fumbled with her clothes as she removed his. His sword belt clanked to the floor. Then he felt the windowsill behind his knees and her hands upon his chest. He grabbed to save himself, but his hands closed on air. There was a moment of weightlessness and ....

He came fully into his battered body, his throat bone dry, paining roaring through his limbs. He thought he opened his eyes, but mayhap he was not fully awake. He groaned. There was a sound to his left and then a hand upon his forehead. Not his step-mother. This hand had calluses.

"Tam?"

His lips felt like they hadn't moved in years. He peeled them apart, but his tongue was too heavy to lick them.

"W-w-water," he croaked.

A bottle of cold water was placed to his lips, but taken away too soon.

"Just sips for now, until you get used to it," the man said. He knew the voice, but he couldn't grasp a name. Not his da, for Corbryn did not believe in visiting the sick. And sick he was. His head pounded with every thought.

"P-padraig?"

"Aye, lad. It's good to see your eyes open again."

"W-where?"

"Wmgleadd."

"Did …." His throat tightened and he coughed. The water came back, a sip more precious than air. "Did I fall?"

"Aye."

"When?"

"An eightnight."

Tamys struggled to clear his throat. It earned him another sip of water. He still couldn't see Padraig. There was light, but it was all a thick gray, like a heavy mist with naught moving in it. He fumbled for and found Padraig's face.

"What time is it?"

"Middday. You needn't worry about that right now. You need rest."

As if by magic, Tamys felt sleep dragging him back into the blankets. He remembered falling and his hand tightened on Padraig's arm, then he floated free of the ground and let the dark take him.

The next time he awoke, Padraig was slower to respond and he was more aware of the pain. Bruised and stiff his body was and his head pounded with every pulse. The water felt glorious, but his empty stomach clenched and he retched before sleeping.…

In his dream, he floated far above the earth as if on wings, seeing small birds in trees far below. Sometimes he heard voices he knew. Aethyn, Braedyn and Duglas the caravan master visited at different times. Padraig let him sip milk once and then another time it was bread soaked in milk. The pain subsided slightly and he became able to think for short periods.

He woke from a dream in which he flew far above a dun he recognized from Mulyn. The misty gray beyond his eyes greeted him. He lay listening to Padraig talking with Duglas. The caravan was leaving for Mandorlyn and Duglas had brought Padraig somewhat. It had been a fortnight from some event that Tamys must have slept through. Padraig was saying somewhat of needing to travel south.

"This will make taking him with much easier."

"I could provide a wagon," Duglas said.

"Nay. This will do much better. Thanks to you for all of your assistance."

"I wish there were more I could give. Do you think he'll ever be well again?"

"It's early days yet and he heals uncannily well."

"I wondered about that. He's not from the east, but I saw the signs."

"His grandmam, I think."

Tamys put out a hand to pull the tent flap aside, thinking he'd protest being spoken of as if he were a piece of kit, but his hand encountered only air.

"Ah, lad, awake, I see," Padraig said. "Let me get some water for you."

When the bottle was pressed to his lips, Tamys swallowed once and then stayed Padraig's hand. His energy was limited and he needed to know.

"What watch is it?"

"Midday," Padraig said. Tamys could hear the catch in his voice.

He knows.

"Am I inside a tent or in the open?"

"Under a tarp, but mostly open. It's been hot today."

Tamys put his own hand in front of his face and saw the gray change a little, but he did not recognize his hand.

"I'm tired," he whispered, trying to avoid the truth.

"You're mending, lad. What is it you want to ask me?"

His heart pounding in his chest also began to flutter in his ears. It felt like the ground was spinning slowly to the left.

"I can't see," Tamys admitted.

"I thought that was the case."

Tamys opened his mouth to say somewhat in reply, but there was naught to say, so he closed his lips and swallowed hard. The dizziness spun him lazily into the black and then he floated far above the ferry on the Avermulyn on a warm summer day. He let the dream take him to a place where he didn't need to think about what blindness meant for his survival.

Galornyn

A tingle ran up Taryn's back as Berdda rubbed one of Teddryn's legs. Was she why his brother could still move when so many others were palsied or dead? The thought brought a stab of grief to his heart once more. This illness had taken Lord Daryn's life and though Taryn wasn't a child to shed tears after the funeral, he couldn't shake the sadness.

"That hurts," Teddryn complained in a weak voice.

"You say that every day," Berdda chided. "Taryn, help sit him up."

This was the part they all hated because Teddryn had never been a coward about pain, now sitting up made him weep. When he'd first become ill, he'd been able to push himself up, but his back and neck were tightening despite Berdda's best efforts and magicks. Tears rolled down Teddryn's cheeks as Berdda massaged his shoulders, back and neck. Taryn could feel her power coursing past him and for a little bit, Teddryn would have relief, but those times were getting shorter.

After that, Taryn was free to go and he fair fled. He found a wash barrel and a scrap of soap and washed his arms, neck and face and felt cleaner, if no more safe. In a dun rife with plague, you did the best you could to stay well, but if its victims were your family, you couldn't avoid contact.

Egoran held court in the great hall, settling a matter between two farmers. Taryn dipped himself a tankard of dark, but as he lifted it to his mouth, Maddw's huge hand closed on it.

"Bit early for that, brother."

A man fully grown who could make two of Taryn, Maddw's black hair and ruddy complexion favored their grandfather, Berdda's husband Lord Marcyl.

"How is Teddryn?" Maddw asked, pouring the tankard's contents back into the barrel.

"Still fevered and still in pain. Grandmam' s best efforts only hold it at bay."

Maddw nodded. Truth be told, he was Taryn's favorite brother, but there often seemed to be a great deal unspoken in their family.

What are you thinking, brother? Is it better for Teddryn to die than be palsied? Do you care that he's in pain? Why do I have to visit him every day when you do not?

"Egoran wants you to go collect a page from Clarcom in Teddryan's stead."

That would be that weasel Cullyn. Can I lose him along the way? Clarcom?!

"Me? Am I to carry a message to his betrothed?"

"You are to collect the dowry. She's not of age yet. You'll leave when the storm breaks."

"After five days, I begin to doubt that it ever will. Why are they sending me and not Rogan?"

"Egoran makes decisions that differ from Da. It should be an adventure. You can pick a band of 15 and get a taste of command."

Taryn's tongue itched for the taste of ale more than he itched to command men.

"You mean you'll pick these men."

"Nay, but it is somewhat you will do with guidance."

The farmers were leaving, one of them frowning and the other smiling. Egoran strolled over to them and dipped himself a tankard of dark. When he saw Taryn's eyes upon him, his mouth formed a cool smile that did not reach his eyes.

"You can at least wait until sundown to drop into your cups," he said. "Has Maddw told you?"

"Aye. I look forward to it. I'll get started on selecting my escort this very afternoon."

Taryn donned his cloak and headed for the barracks. Owing to the rain, many gathered indoors, trying to escape the chill as much as the damp, though the coastal humidity made it too close above the stables to warrant a fire in the hearth. Gregyn's bunk sat empty as it had been for days.

"Where's Gregyn?" he asked.

The healers said he'd left. Where else would he go?

"Cleaning tack," one of the riders, Ethynan, reported.

Gregyn mayhap had healed from his illness quickly, but his boots tucked under the bunk made Taryn suspicious. When he'd taken him to the infirmary, the healers had assured he'd be taken care of, so Taryn had not been surprised when he'd been gone the yestermorrow morn, but he'd yet to catch up with him and was beginning to wonder why.

"When you see him, tell him that I'm wanting to speak with him." Taryn scanned round the room, noting who seemed healthy, who he'd seen sit a horse well, who was sharpening their swords while the rain dripped from the eaves. He didn't need to make this decision today. The storm would hold for days more, he somehow knew. He headed for the tack room to find Gregyn.

The tack master thought he might be working in the armory. The armorer thought he might be working in the infirmary. The herbalist who had examined Gregyn night

before last claimed not to have seen him for an
eightnight. Taryn knew that to be untrue since he'd
fetched the man to see to Gregyn himself after the lad
had fainted at his feet.

Having left messages with many who thought the
rider somewhere else, Taryn meant to try the barrel of
dark again, but met with Werglidd, a councilor of sorts,
at the door of the great hall.

"I hear you're seeking the rider Gregyn."

"I am," he reported. "I want him to be part of an
escort to Clarcom."

"Gregyn would be glad to accompany you, sir,"
Werglidd said. Taryn felt a tingle in the hair of his arms.

"How do you even know this rider?"

"You do not recall that I cared for him just the
other night?"

"Nay. It was not you."

Werglidd's normally cloying attitude became evasive.

"Odd," he said as if to someone else. "I believe your
mother wishes to speak with you."

Peddryna had never spent any attention on Taryn,
so he found it highly unlikely she was seeking audience
with him now. The young lord leaned in to the servitor
and whispered.

"I know what you're trying to do. You needn't
bother. It doesn't work on me."

He smiled and headed to find Berdda. As he
approached the greeting chamber she shared with
Marcyl, Taryn felt a buzzing like bees down his back and
then he could hear Maddw speaking to her on the other
side of the door.

"You can't ride both horses, Gran. He's growing beyond your hiding. Either we allow him to dull his senses with drink or you must tell him what he needs to know so he can protect himself from her."

"Mayhap you sensed it wrongly."

"Mam's gift is very small, but she is shrewd. And he grows in strength. Sooner rather than later, she will come to realize that he is what she seeks."

"Is that why you're sending him to Clarcom instead of going yourself or having Eg send Rogan?"

"It will give you time to decide how best to approach this battle."

"What, truly, can I do except train him to slough off her predations. Were that I knew what cracked my hiding."

"I don't know. Mayhap it's maturation. I grew into my gifts."

"You were stimulated by interacting with that page from Cenconyn."

"Padraig. Aye, though he himself lacked strong gifts, the very fact that he wasn't frightened by them made me bold."

"I never blocked your abilities. Your strength of character was always so great – and she didn't have sorcerers about then."

"I could see that taken care ... do you feel that?"

Before Taryn could reverse directions, the door was flung open and Maddw dragged him into the greeting chamber.

"Ah, lad, we did so much want to talk to you," he said as Taryn gawked at the blue globe floating in the center of the room and casting an eerie light upon the walls.

"That tears it. There's naught for it but to tell him," Berdda decided right then and there.

"Do you wish to tell me that you're a sorceress, Grandmam, or that Maddw is?" Taryn demanded. "I've known that for a good while now."

Berdda raised an eyebrow. Anyone looking at her silver-streaked blond hair and trim figure would think her twenty years younger than she actually was.

"I've never tried to hide my abilities from you, lad," she chided gently. "How long have you known about Maddw?"

"In the winter. So it is true that I have also inherited some small portion of your gifts?"

Maddw and Berdda exchanged a significant glance.

"Of my offspring, you may well be the strongest ... although Rhodda remains to be judged."

Taryn tried to recollect his experience with this "gift" and shook his head, gaze straying to the glowing orb near the center of the ceiling.

"I don't feel strong," he admitted.

"Do you want to be?"

"I want to know why it's important that my abilities remain hidden. I want to know why Werglidd tried to ensorcel me just now. I want to understand."

There was that significant glance again.

"If that is all you desire then you might be ready for the gifts I sealed you from."

The Tongue

*M*aster Talidd lay as if dead. As Jaryn mixed herbs and minerals into a pedestal, he wondered if mayhap he should not be doing this. Outside, the storm pulsed with dark lights and daemons, invited into this world's realm by the Master of the Black. Did he sustain the spell? Would it collapse without his vigilance?

What happens if he dies?

This was a new thought for the maimed man who mixed medicinals with one hand because the other was coiled against his side in useless spasm.

Nay, not new. Reborn!

Still he mixed the medicinals and did not include poison. He wasn't ready to make that decision just yet.

An acolyte sat crouched at Talidd's bedside, awaiting his orders. Many had died this time, but not all. There was somewhat different about this spell from the one that had included Jaryn all those years ago.

"Ches … spreh … foha …." Jaryn told the lad. He'd been about long enough to make sense of Jaryn's speech, especially if Jaryn included gestures. The lad scrambled to do what was ordered. Jaryn leaned on his stick to lurch to the window and stare out at the black jungle.

Did we find the king this time?

There was somewhat he'd forgotten. What, of course, he did not know. If he knew, he'd have not forgotten it. Somewhat from before the last spell.

The secrets in the scrolls.

For a long time he'd been unable to read them. For so long, Talidd had assumed the condition was permanent. He'd been wrong. Jaryn's reading had improved. He'd slipped scrolls out from time to time to find that which he'd forgotten. Now, when he wasn't treating Talidd, he had all the time he needed to read the scrolls.

"Sssay mmme iffff channnnge."

The lad nodded. Jaryn lurched into the workroom and unrolled another scroll. It wasn't easy, scrolls, when you just had one hand. He had to use cups to hold it open and hold his head in such a way that he could bring the words into focus. This scroll held arcane knowledge. He needed to know what he had forgotten, but he remembered this … spells of various sorts. That had gotten better too over the years and without Talidd's notice.

Jaryn let the scroll close, tucked it into the fold of his useless arm and lurched toward the cabinet where the scrolls were housed. He'd taken them all out when he'd realized Talidd's condition. As he went through them, he put them back, one by one. The ones he hadn't read were stacked on a side table. His leg spasmed as he made his way there, so that he stumbled sideways into the scrying table, causing the bowl of black ink to dance.

In the reflective surface, Jaryn saw the powerful apprentice whose name he could not say tossing upon a cot in an infirmary. He'd never seen the lad's aura before and found it curious.

What sort of being has an aura like an oval flame? And who or what is tapping into him? Will he live and be as I am or will he die? Pity to waste such strength of gift.

Now a man dressed in grey robes entered the infirmary, speaking with the herbalist. Jaryn felt the ensorcelment through the link. Men brought a stretcher and lifted the lad onto it. Jaryn remembered the grey mage, though not his name. Names were hard to hang on to since that last spell. Talidd had taken him to him once, when he'd still been unable to walk or talk. Jaryn had not understood what was spoken and he'd slept through most of it, but he'd begun to get better gradually after that visit.

Talidd cares for no man, so why does he care for me? I have forgotten somewhat. I must find it.

The next scroll proved frustrating because it was larger than the others and harder to hold open. He almost gave up trying to read it, but when he did focus his eyes on it, he realized that this was mayhap what he'd been looking for.

Mulyn … Cadda … Joran … Perryn … Donyl … spell … True King ….

As he scanned through it, not actually reading it, but trying to see if it pertained, he saw a name he knew well, over and over, and this meant he had to read the whole scroll carefully. That name … he had not forgotten that even at his worst, though he struggled to say it.

Joryn. Joryn is me and I am Joryn. Why am I in this scroll and is this what I have forgotten?

Blue Iris Holt

*P*alsynedwynchela squeezed water from her hair, looking wistfully at the pool where some of the other females swam. While Chela was glad to be pregnant after so many years of waiting, she hated the changes it imposed on her life. Even simple things like bathing were now complicated by a small swelling in her white belly.

The bathing pools in the lower reaches of the holt were mostly dark except for fungus light and the distant shine of the cooling deck's open door. In the summer, the air lay languid with humidity. Chela rested her head on her knees and wondered if Melim was even thinking about her right now. Males had it so much easier. They didn't have to carry the child. She knew he loved her and he seemed so happy to be a father, but it was hard to be alone with this task while he was out droving.

She turned her head as she heard bare feet on the stone behind her. Shanara gave her a brief smile before stepping under the sluice and pulling the lever to pour warm water over her head. Chela turned her head so she wasn't watching her and closed her eyes, smelling the lavender in the soap Shanara was using. She remembered a day of walking through a lavender field with her mother.

"How are you feeling?" Shanara asked, wrapping a towel around herself before sitting down on the stone.

"Better," Chela replied. "The midwife thinks it's a girl since I wasn't sick for long."

"That's a blessing then. Of course, every child these days is a blessing."

It went unspoken that the Kin birthrate was dwindling. Some couples tried their whole lives with no children to honor the effort. What had once been thought a problem of full Kin mating with Celts now seemed to be a problem with Kin in general. Chela and Melim had tried for nearly a century. The healers had no theory as to why, but it was known that any pregnancy that made it past the birthing sickness was the future of the holts.

"Have you ever been married?" Chela asked.

"No. Most males don't find me attractive." Her wolfen eyes twinkled. "Truthfully, I'm content in my singleness."

"You never wanted a family?"

"Briefly. There was a young man I liked very much, but he never smiled back. And then I found my Calling. If my eyes were not intimidating enough, prophetess sealed that jar. I mothered a child for a bit though."

"You did?"

"Yes. His mother died in childbirth and his father needed someone to help tend him, so I did. He offered to marry me, but I thought that was grief talking."

"Do I know the child?"

"No. That was in Northholt when I was a youngster. I used to drop by now and again on my travels. But it's been a good long while since I've been. Since my father passed, truthfully."

"I remember something you said, about how you look. What does it mean, about your father?"

"That he took his bride from a northern holt?"

"Yes."

"I don't remember my mother, but my father said she looked ordinary enough. He didn't expect me, though he surely loved me. He could have left me with my grandparents when she died, but he didn't."

Chela stared at Shanara's winter pale hair. It wasn't the silver of age. It was simply palest blond, with hardly a hint of yellow in it.

"And, yes, I do sometimes wonder if he was fibbing, because clearly I have Winter People blood in me."

Chela touched her belly where the barest bulge now grew.

"I sometimes wondered which she'll look like – more Kin than Denygal. I suppose I'd be surprised if she came out completely different than I expected."

"My father doted on me. If it surprised him, he got over it quickly."

"That's good to know. I've asked Melim if it would matter to him. He says not, but … I think pregnancy is an insecure time for some of us."

"Melim loves you."

"Is that prophesy?"

"No. Observational skills." Shanara stretched. "I should be about my bath so that I can continue my scrying."

"What are you scrying for?"

Did Shanara seem a little sad just now?

"For knowledge. Rest well, Chela. And … well, do you want to know what I see of your child?"

"I do. Really? You've had a Sighting?"

"Yes. She has a grand future. I'm not sure the details, but many people will follow her. And she's not the only child you will have."

"How do you …?"

"I don't know. I just do. Goodbye for now."

Shanara executed a shallow dive into the pool and stroke off into the dimness. Chela lay back and traced the outline of the bulge under the firm muscle of her stomach.

"Hello, my daughter."

In her imagination, she thought she heard a child laugh as red hair streamed away from her as she ran through a lavender field. *Red hair? Oh, my!*

Cousins

The Celt call it the Southern Confluence now, but the Kin — what the Celt call the Fey -- called it Peace River. That's what Ama'na translates as, you see. That were the hope and it started well enough. The community had been growing for a few years when we arrived and they'd settled the worst of the conflicts.

When I say conflicts — you shouldn't confuse the way it turned out with how it started. It were a beautiful place and beautiful people.

We called it Peace River because that were what we were after — peace. I don't think anyone were looking for paradise, but they were hoping for a place where Celt and Kin could be friends and raise some wonderful horses. My mam would have said it were a good place to raise children — a place where young ones could run freely and even strangers wouldn't harm them.

It were a wondrous place to raise horses. Ama'na were on the other side of the lake from Clarcom ... far enough from civilization that there were no uninvited noses to enter our business, but close enough that we could take horses to market when we like. It were right at the end of a Kin trail ... they'd used the meadows between the two streams for generations. Some of the early Celt settlers called it the confluence because the two streams — small rivers really — came together just off the mountains and then spilled toward the lake as one. The grass grew lush and green and the lake was filled with eating fish. It had everything a drover were looking for to raise horses and a nice community besides.

Duglas of Fyrgal, apprentice merchant, fireside tale, FY 1012

Past

Kin Cycle 24574 (Four years ago)
Orental Eternal City

*F*arenlucgilyn gazed over the Eternal City, trying to make sense of what he saw. The buildings seemed chaotic – square with peaked tile roofs that turned up at the eaves. The bright hues of the roof tiles were only matched by the facades of the buildings. In narrow alleys and broad avenues, every building seemed to strive to outdo the others for attention, every surface lacquered like one of the trunks Ryanna favored.

In the street below his window, a dozen lively conversations could be heard. Although the Goddess had given him the gift of Orental translation just as she had when he negotiated with the Svard, he had not grown used to the sharp sounds of this language. There was a music to it that seemed at once tonal and discordant. He could not, therefore, tease out a thread of conversation from a babble.

A soft voice called sleepily from his bed and he turned to see Mei Ling resting against the red silk sheets, her black hair fanned out across her peacock blue robe. As a bed warmer, she was well-versed in the arts of pleasure and easy on the eyes for an Orental. As an agent of the court, she could not be trusted.

"You ordered the morning meal, I see," she remarked, rising to help herself to the tray of fruit and *baozi* Gil drained his cup of *jook* and moved to get more.

"Today, I am to take you to see Zhu Chian Gak."

Gil took his time chewing a dried fig to hide his annoyance. Five moons since he'd come to the city. He had been passed from one functionary to another. Within the first moon, he had acquired Mei Ling as an agent of the court. She had pleased him in bed, but she had always had an excuse why he could not see the emperor. He had expected some warning so that he might have opportunity to confer with the Goddess before the audience.

"How long has that been arranged?" he asked.

"Why does that matter? A quarter-moon or one day – it is immaterial so long as you see the Emperor, no? Eat your breakfast. There is much to do before you gain audience and it is often a long day of waiting."

She swung her feet up to rest on his thigh. He pushed them off. Her brown eyes watched him from behind hooded lids.

"Is it the custom in your land to treat an honored guest like a common *jinu*?"

"My apologies," he replied. "I find it frustrating that I have waited so long and then to be given no notice."

"You are a foreigner. You have no standing."

This bitch has no idea of my standing. She will see … as will her employer.

Gil pulled a cord by the door and waited while a steward came. The slight man with the dark face and long braid bowed slightly.

"Please have hot water brought for a bath."

"As you say, *lawai*." Everyone here called him that and it was offered respectfully enough, though he knew it meant "foreigner" They called the other guests *keren* and he would have preferred *zhu* meaning master, but he knew his situation here depended on his acceptance of their customs … for now.

With the departure of the steward, Gil turned back to Mei Ling and the tray of food.

"Please instruct me in which clothing I should wear."

Mei Ling smiled in that mysterious way she had, looking away, then inclined her head in acquiescence.

She chose black linen trews and a black silk tunic. They argued about what shoes he should wear. He would not wear slippers, no matter how respectful it might seem. They limited a man's agility. He wore his soft elven riding boots because they were black. The Orental did not wear cloaks except in the winter, so she pinned his golden horse brooch to one appellate and pronounced him acceptable. They hailed a paladin and rode to the court.

Gil didn't know the source of the coins that paid his room and food. They appeared in his purse as he needed them, just as the junque had appeared when he needed a boat to ferry him to Svardland or Orental or clothing appeared as he needed it.

Mei Ling herself appeared to be quite wealthy. Certainly her clothing was opulent even among the opulence of the Glorious Court, her black braids dripping with pearls and gold coins. Gil had been to the outer courtyard on several occasions and had struggled not to be awed by the majestic silks and brocades even the servants seemed to wear.

The Court itself outshone the city around it in its lacquered woods and tile roofs. The plaza to the main building was paved in blue stones further across than Gil was tall. The Imperial Palace was built to impress – large with wide white marble stairs and ornate columns across the front. The doors were taller than most duns and the building was the tallest Gil had ever seen.

They entered the cool interior of the building. Servants offered them bowls for washing their faces and hands. They were then ushered into an ante room where a cushioned chair awaited Mei Ling and a stiff wooden one awaited Gil. The walls were painted with fantastical scenes of peasants harvesting rice as a stylized dragon flew overhead. Dragons were everywhere – huge statues out front of the building, at the ends of the arms on Me Ling's chair, on the urns in the corners.

"How long is this --?"

"Do not speak," Mei Ling said softly, but firmly. "Meditate on the privilege of meeting the Holy One."

How, Goddess, do you expect me to treat with a man who thinks himself a god?

In the year since he'd accepted the Goddess' mission to enslave the Kin and Celt alike, he'd traveled far and risked much and he'd only seen her three times. The first time, they engaged in bed sports while the Kin camp around them burned. The others he had seen her at a distance only. He might have despaired at knowing her will but for the coin and clothes and other tokens of her guidance.

Time passed slowly. Gil thanked the Goddess for arranging the meeting with Zhu Chian Gak, but his mind quickly wandered. He knew himself well-shed of his mate Ryanna, but thoughts of her occasionally surfaced when he was bored. She would have laughed at the formality of the Orental city and its self-possessed court. She would have been quick to discern the weaknesses of the system of protocol, which would have given him an advantage in the coming meeting. Leaving her behind had not been a mistake, but it was hard not to compare her to Mei Ling. Ryanna was a stranger to silks, a horse drover and huntress who had come into her powers late. She could easily have run the Orental agent through with her long knife.

Bah! She's Wise now! There's nothing of the woman I mated left. I couldn't even beat it back into her.

What was the meaning of all the dragons about? He would have liked to ask, but Mei Ling remained resolute in her silence.

The day must be well-spent. Mayhap it is even night.

The hair on his arms stood up and a shiver ran down his back.

Somewhat is happening.

The inner door to the ante room swung open and Mei Ling rose, indicating that he should follow. A long corridor of columns stretched ahead to a high red throne where upon a man dressed in blue silks awaited them. Mei Ling had explained the protocol on their way from his lodgings.

They walked bent forward at the waist, perpendicular to the floor for most of the way to the throne. Then they dropped to their knees and crawled the last 20 feet. They put their foreheads to the floor and waited.

How incredibly denigrating! Does this man truly believe himself to be a god? The Goddess will eat his spleen.

"This is the *lawai*?" the man on the throne asked. "His hair is very light. Sit up that I might see these moon-struck eyes."

Gil swallowed his pride and obeyed. Zhu Chian Gak appeared younger than Gil had expected, a slight man made tall on the throne. Like all Orental he was dark, but his large almond eyes were amber rather than dark brown.

"It is reported to me that you are conversant in our language."

"I am," Gil replied.

"You are from the west, beyond the sand sea. How you come here?"

"My mistress sent me." Movement behind the throne resolved itself into a woman wearing red silks. She put a long fingered hand upon Chian Gak's shoulder.

"Your mistress?" Chian Gak asked.

"The land beyond the sand sea rightfully belongs to her. She invites you to join her in recapturing it."

"For what purpose?"

"It is a rich land filled with hard working people who will make excellent slaves."

The woman smiled at him. Gil watched as the Morrigan leaned to whisper into the *zhu*'s ear. Chian Gak nodded, reaching up to touch her arm. The intimate gesture sent jealousy surging through Gil's loins, but she touched a finger to her lips to caution discretion. A furtive glance to his right assured that Mei Ling could not see the Goddess.

"Our interests may be aligned," Chian Gak agreed. "Tell me of your alliance with the Svard."

Present

Founding Year 1028
Llyr

As the unnaturally dense storm eased to a miserable drizzle, Howedd ap Maille stepped from a coach at the door of the Golden Unicorn. The sprawling inn complex looked almost like a dun with its stone towers and high walls. Two servants were cleaning the street in front. When the rain stopped the cobbles would gleam like the ones in the ward at Dun Llyr.

How did I not see the connection for all of these years?

He hadn't known what he was looking at. Or mayhap he'd been prejudiced by the attitudes of others. Harlots were harlots after all, not the great granddaughters of the last legitimate king of Celdrya.

The servants knew him and made no effort to slow him in his progress. Doors were swept open, staircases cleared, his cloak taken. His mother Nanyna waited in her greeting chamber, a handsome wood paneled room that looked over the gardens and, more significantly, commanded a view of the dun. A pleasant fire crackled on the hearth, a cat curled up nearby.

I always assumed my father built this as the price of being her paramour, but this house goes back much further than that – further even than Prince Maryn.

"Wine?" she asked. She wasn't exceptionally tall, but she'd maintained her figure after four pregnancies. Her brown hair had a hint of henna in it these days, set off by the rich green of the silk dress she wore.

"Mulled, please! This infernal damp sinks into the bones."

She served him herself, pouring their wine into ceramic goblets. They exchanged pleasantries. Then he asked the question he'd come for.

"Why the secrecy, Mam?"

"He never told you and it is not our place to tell the boys. The blood is carried in the female line so there is no question of that it is true lineage."

"But they put the boys in the book. They even legitimized one."

"Aye, but the timing was bad on that one. Did you not see the age at which he died and the notation?"

"Poison was suspected. Why? And who?"

"It's a difficult secret to keep. In the early days, there were those who knew. Gilyan was not planning to birth a dynasty. She just wanted a bit of land for her babe, mayhap a small dowry for a girl. She inquired of King Perryn. Although her daughter grew up safe within these walls, her grandson was not so lucky. He would have been a spare heir anyway. It is much better that you are Umaille now."

"Why?"

"Tren and Corbryn continually fight each other to a standstill and Fyrgal's claim is only a regent's claim. The High City hungers for a king. You may have your will with it if you but choose to exercise it."

"Many men thought that and have failed."

"Ah, but they don't have what you have, my love."

"What is that?"

"A noble name and a common heart. You know how to woo the people to you."

"Do I?"

"Ponder it a bit. What do a starving and neglected people want? Not a king to rule over them and suck the life from them."

Howedd sat listening to the pop and sizzle of the fire, watching the firelight glint here and there off reflective surfaces. Flowers in a vase freshened the air.

Corbryn and Tren do offer to let the people of Celdrya fill their coffers and warehouses as befits the kings they wish to be. What if a regent offered protection and reclamation for a reasonable share of future prosperity?

"I think I'll send Randodd on a scouting expedition. Best to know the lay of the land before one claims it."

She smiled at him warmly.

"Shall we toast to your success?"

"Nay, but we will toast to your cleverness."

Aye, indeed, this may be the best of times for such an endeavor.

"May I ask?" She raised an elegant eyebrow over the rim of her goblet. In this world, men did not question women. She was no noblewoman to command. "I always assumed we had different fathers, but …."

"The girls are your father's. Randodd was a spot of fun I chose for myself. Lord Sedd was done with me and there was a young man who looked delicious."

"Which explains my brother's good looks. It also explains why the girls have been given positions. Randodd … what becomes of him in this world?"

"That is for you to decide. He's stayed here far longer than common-born lads normally stay and that only because he is my son and my blood line is a valuable commodity to the House. I gambled that you would take him in when you ascended."

"How did you know I would?"

"I didn't. I hoped."

She's not telling the complete truth. Do I want to know it? Mayhap not.

He couldn't imagine Nanyna dealing death, but recognized Shyralan, the madam of the House, might well have poisoned his father's heir to assure Howedd ascended.

"I will find somewhat for him … a position he can grow into."

Best I get him away from Shyralan. I've never trusted her and I think my instinct was correct.

"What about you, Mam? I can find a place for you at court."

"Gods, no, child. This is my place and I enjoy it."

"How much of the House do you own?"

"Half and land in my own right."

"And you don't wish to have titles? You are, after all, Maryn's great granddaughter."

"We can talk about that when you have the kingdom."

Howedd smiled at her, because he truly loved his mother and admired her political acumen.

"To Gwenydd's line," he toasted.

She smiled.

"To Maryn's seed," she returned. They tapped goblets and drank.

Dublyn

Sunlight slanted through the trees, dancing off dust motes, turning the air golden. Ryanna led their procession of four horses as she had since Cenconyn. Sarala rode steadily behind her, no doubt sulking at the rough treatment Ryanna had served to her at every point of the journey.

She reined in her horse and stared down into a vale. Sarala rode up beside her.

"What do you see?" Ryanna asked.

The girl had learned to hold her tongue and think in the days of travel. She considered the scene before them.

"There is a structure there," she said in Celdryan, pointing. "Could be a smallish dun, but as we've only just passed one this morning, it's likely a temple of Bel or the Moon."

Ryanna nodded her approval.

"You're learning. What do you think I will do now?"

"The sun is three-quarters across the sky. These temples have caravansaries. You wish to stop for the night."

"Why is that?"

"Because Celdyrans do not have our eyesight. We need time to set up camp before the sun sets."

"Good. Except for the certain clumsiness with the language, you are doing well."

"What did I say wrong?"

"Naught," Ryanna replied and started forward with her horses.

Truth told, Sarala's Celdryan would not betray her as an elfling. She would learn the music of the language in time. It was just the word misplaced here or there that would likely not be noticed by any who did not know to listen.

"Secure the caravanserai for us," Ryanna ordered when they reached the closed gate with the carved moon. She stayed nearby as Sarala pulled the rope that rang the bell and waited until a sister came to the gate and spoke to her through a small door just large enough for a head.

"May I help you, lad?" the Daughter of the Moon asked.

~I do not like this place, Sabre informed Ryanna as he sat upon his haunches staring at the walls, tongue lolling like an ordinary dog. *They make the poison juice here.*

Ryanna had tried to explain wine to the dog before, but he insisted upon calling it "poison".

~I'm listening. Silence!

Ignoring the vision he sent of pissing on her favorite boots, Ryanna turned her attention to the exchange at the gate. Sarala introduced themselves as Saryl and Ryan, travelers from Cenconyn, and asked after the camping ground for a single night. They settled on five coppers to include fresh bread and a couple of apples.

The hair on the back of Ryanna's neck prickled. She resisted the temptation to look round, for she knew she would see no one and only betray her own skill. Someone with power observed them. Ryanna felt tendrils test round the edges of her shields. Sarala shifted, and then turned to stare at Ryanna.

"Someone …."

"Aye. The temples have druins … sorcerers. Mostlike they test everyone. Did she breach?"

"Nay. I was better trained than that."

"Gly was always an exacting tutor."

The daughter of the goddess returned with a bag of food and instructions to the caravanserai. It was easy enough to find and deserted but for them. After unloading the horses and putting a kettle on the fire, they practiced at swords while the two squirrels they'd taken earlier in the day turned on spits.

Ryanna was determined to make a passable swordsman of Sarala before they got much farther into the kingdom. She needed to know how to protect herself. Like many elven women, she was proficient with bow and had been trained in shield work, but her sword handling was clumsy, made worse by being short enough to be forced to the long knife. Ryanna had reach and weight on her.

"Do herbwomen need such training in the kingdom?" Sarala asked, panting, as they passed the water bottle between them.

"Not usually, but if an herbman travel with me, there's need." The fool girl still did not understand that human men were wolves. "I'll gather more wood. You should tend to the fire and make sure the meat does not scorch."

"Aye, brother," Sarala said, for they were careful with their appellations. The afternoon grew muggy even as they considered the night.

The caravanserai had several stores of wood, but it was elven custom to refill these. Ryanna walked off to the west where a road from the east bordered the caravansie, filling her sling with wood while taking stock of their situation.

~What do you think, Sabre? Is she ready to go among folks?

~She follows her alpha, Sabre replied. *Can the pack leader ask for more?*

Ryanna turned as a sound came to her ear … a baby wailing and the sound of struggle. A woman cried out. Ryanna dropped the sling and ran in the direction of the commotion, drawing her sword and long knife as she ran.

Through the brush, she could see the wagon on the road – two men struggled with a woman each as an infant wailed at the rough handling by a third man. A fourth stood upon the wagon, tossing its contents.

Ryanna sent to Sabre – ~*Get the one on the wagon* -- as she rushed the one who had the baby. She sheathed her long knife, then used the pommel of her sword to batter him into unconsciousness, while catching hold of the child with her free hand. She set the little fellow down as gently as the circumstances allowed while scoring a touch on the leg of the brigand who held the baby's mother. He howled and let the woman go to protect himself from Ryanna. The mother rushed for her baby while the brigand made the fatal mistake of taking a swipe at Ryanna with his dagger.

Should have gone for his sword, she thought as she ran him through.

The third man tossed the younger woman aside and drew his sword. Taller than Ryanna by half a head and outweighing her by several stone, he also wore a much-patched mail siarc while she wore only a leather jerkin. As she blocked his first cut on her blade, she knew she was in a fight for her life.

Against his weight and strength, she had speed and a long knife. They circled, feeling out each other's weaknesses. He feinted. She brushed it aside. He cut. She sidestepped.

Heavier tires quicker. Keep him dancing.

She parried another cut, feeling his power through her arm up to her shoulder. In a mob, she'd never have selected such an opponent, but here she was … alone and responsible for these women.

His breath came harder, but she felt his blows more heavily. She feinted with the sword. He parried and she cut up into his left side with the long knife. Blood blossomed under the mail. His eyes widened as he saw his death in her face. She drove her sword into his gut up to the hilt and lowered him to the ground upon the blade, killing him with the withdrawal.

Behind her, she heard the sound of steel leaving leather and knew she'd made a fatal mistake. She'd spent herself too early. She turned as she heard the footsteps advancing, raised her long knife to block the sword, saw the shield coming round, then watched as the fourth brigand stumbled to his knees at her feet, a Kin hunting arrow sprouting from his upper back. He gasped, spit blood and spilled over onto his side. Cleaved through the spine, he'd live for a short while before he bled out, but he couldn't move or speak. Sarala had already nocked another arrow, but the only brigand moving was Sabre's quarry who was backed up against a tree trying to hold the dog off with a fallen branch.

"Briganding will get you killed, lad," Ryanna remarked. The younger of the two women had armed herself with the wagon whip, but Sabre controlled the brigand without assistance. Horses nickered in the trees across from the caravanserai. Ryanna found a coil of rope tied to a saddle and used it to tie the lad to the tree he leaned against.

"Who are those men to you?" she demanded, noting how scared his eyes seemed in a face too thin.

"One was my brother."

"They earned their deaths, lad, as you will earn yours if you continue this life. Those horses belong to you or are they stolen?"

"We're not horse thieves. We just wanted food."

"Aye and that warranted threatening a baby."

"I didn't do that," he said. Truth be told, like most Celts he wore his aura like a cloak and she could see that he wasn't a bad sort – yet.

"Nay, you just let them do it," she said. "Best keep silent while I consider what to do with you."

~Sabre, watch him.

The black dog bared his teeth and growled. Ryanna joined the women at the wagon.

"Thank the gods you lads came when you did," the elder of the woman said. She was trying to sooth the baby with a breast, but the wee lad was most upset. Sarala examined the other woman's arm, which had been bruised in the scuffle.

"Going to market, I see," Ryanna noted. "You've no men with you?"

"There are so many travelers on the roads that it didn't seem needed," the younger lass said. "My husband Sion had a late calf to deliver and Rudda's got other children at home, so her husband needed to remain. I'm Marya by the way."

"Ryan and Saryl." Ryanna glanced up at the sky. "Sunset's upon us. You're welcome to our fire before you push on to the town."

The two women exchanged uncomfortable glances. Sarala asked with her eyes and Ryanna gave her leave with a simple nod. She leaned into Marya's ear and spoke in whispers. They left the young brigand to stew while Sarala took the two women to their camp and Ryanna buried the dead. She sited the burial mound far enough from the young brigand that he couldn't see that she did not use the shovel she carried with her. She doubted he was bright enough to wonder at what short time the burial took.

"What will you do to me?" he asked when she approached in the darkness. She unstoppered a water bottle and gave him a sip. "I'd rather you killed me clean than you took me to the dun to have my hand cut off."

"I plan to do neither. If you get yourself killed, it's none of my affair. Briganding is a short life, but some 20 years ago, near this spot, a brigand saved my life, so I will return the favor by saving yours." She slit the rope at his wrists. "If I were you, I would take those horses, sell the three you don't need and buy yourself a prentice to a better employment than this."

Ryanna left him the water bottle and walked away to let him win free of the rest of the ropes himself.

~Don't let him come to the caravanserai, she told Sabre.

He suggested he should hamstring the horses, a request she denied. She knew the dog would make sure the lad was clear away before returning to camp.

Approaching the camp, Ryanna watched Sarala joking with the women and wondered if she had told them the full story or just that she was female. In that instance, she slipped into Marya's memory of a tall, handsome man with a golden horse. Padraig had passed her way and given Marya medicinals to help improve mating. They had worked, though Marya seemed unaware and may not have needed them. The brief touch told Ryanna the lass was at least quarter elven and there was somewhat familiar about her.

Ryanna removed her sword belt and laid it inside her tent. The farm women had added food to their supper of squirrel, including a small bag of ale that Marya and Sarala both cut with water. Ryanna enjoyed a good swallow of it full strength first.

"I'd never have thought you were a lass," Rudda remarked. "You're so tall and you fight like a lad."

"But I can see where it would be wise to travel as lads," Marya said. "You are less like to be set upon by brigands."

"And less likely to have anyone question why I wear a sword," Ryanna agreed. "Where are you from, lass? I feel as if we've met."

Marya stared at her for a moment, a thoughtful expression on her face. Without her headscarf, her blond hair gleamed in the firelight. An image formed in Ryanna's mind. At Peace River, there'd been a lass named Laryssa, a half-elf who had gained nearly as much attention as Maryanara. Looking from Marya to Sarala, Ryanna saw a resemblance that couldn't be denied. Ryanna scoured her memory as she prepared to roll into her blankets, but she couldn't remember ever seeing Laryssa after Peace River. She fell asleep contemplating it.

When Sabre lay down at her back, she awoke to see Marya sitting up on her blankets staring at Sarala curled within her own blankets.

~My mam said my sire was a wolf with an unseeming attraction to Kin women, Marya thought to her psychically. After a moment of stunned confusion, Ryanna replied the same.

~You must be only a quarter. That's a strong gift nonetheless.

~So my mam says. I did not expect to find a sister bringing cheeses to market.

Satisfying her curiosity meant asking uncomfortable questions. Ryanna chose to be bold.

~Did your mam give you any details?

An image washed through Ryanna's mind – shadows and light – the council fire, a boy dragging a terrified girl into a shed, a hand over her mouth, the pain. Some elves could share their memories with others and this had the flavor of that. Ryanna sensed the fear and images, but she didn't feel it as intensely as she might have. The scent of lemons confirmed what she had suspected for a long time.

~I knew it wasn't Dylan when he claimed it was a hand fasting. He was just trying to protect Marianara, Sarala's mam.

~But you knew it was a rape? Marya's thoughts were immensely sad.

~Later and she didn't deliberately tell me. Her distress broadcast to those of us who could hear it.

Marya wiped tears from her cheeks, gazing at Sarala's sleeping form.

~Should I tell her?

~I cannot guide you with that decision. I am often too bold.

Marya sighed and lie down on her blankets. Ryanna felt the need for guidance slip away. She slept, and dreamt of riding up to Marya's cottage with Sarala.

Trevellyn

*T*here was no reason to rush about trying to find folk when you knew where they would be. Well, he knew where they intended to be and where they were when he looked in on them. The actual future was locked to him, as it was to most men. But he knew where they'd be in their intentions weren't thwarted.

Thus, Kefyn waited.

Duncyn had left him yesterday to travel more quickly to Clarcom, trusting that Kefyn could take care of himself in fairly settled land. Kefyn had camped nearby last night, and now sat leaning on a bollard of the bridge. The stream grew broad just below. A shimmer of ripples caused him to look up as a doe entered the water. Her dusty red coat shone in the sunlight as she dipped her muzzle into the water. She raised her head to stare at him, water dropping silver from her nose. Kefyn sent restful images her way and she bent to drink again.

Comforting to know that my gifts work just as well below the Dragon Wall, Kefyn thought.

He spied movement in the brush. A moment's intense gaze brought the weircat into focus. Kefyn put out a hand and "called" his bow and quiver to him. They floated to hand with simple thoughts. Few could work magicks such as this or even knew that there were those who could. Kefyn drew an arrow, stood up on the railing and nocked. The deer sensed his concern as the weircat closed the gap and launched across the water. The deer startled into deeper water as Kefyn's arrow sliced through the cat. He nocked and drew, tracking movement in the brush. A second weircat burst from cover, only to tumble to the ground dead. Other traces of movement reversed direction.

Kefyn nocked a third arrow and waited until he heard the jingle of tack from the road. He threw out a Sensing to assure that the weircats were routed, then turned to look at the two women and their four horses. The dog ran into the woods, growling.

"Go see what he's about, lad," the warrior of the two said, turning to draw her own bow and scanning the woods.

"They've gone," Kefyn told the lass who rode up to him. He allowed his shields to relax so she would know he wasn't a threat.

"What are they?" she asked. "Ryan sensed them, but I only saw the bushes moving."

"You needn't bother with me, lass," he said in Elvish. "I see two Kin women dressed as Celt lads." The dog was coming back toward the road. "I'm calling them weircats. They showed up in Denygal last summer. My father set me to seek them this year. This band is coming out of the mountains."

"We saw the same such near Blue Iris Holt," Ryan said as she joined them. "Weircat is a fanciful term, but right enough." She cocked her head to one side, her blue eyes slightly unfocused. "That's an interesting aura – quarter elf with magicks from both sides. Rare."

"Not as rare as thought," he said in Celdryan since they were both speaking that. "Kefyn Donyl of Clan Shyr."

"You do know that's folly?" Ryan asked. "You'll only reveal yourself as an elf and they kill elves in this part of the world."

"I only see two Denygal and none to hear us, but I will style myself as Kefyn of Donylshyr from now on. May I know your names … or the names you are using."

"Ryan of Moryn and that is Saryl of Ama'na."

"Where's Ama'na?"

"It translates Peace River," Saryl said. Both women were beautiful in the elven way, but she was by far the lovelier. Her cap of black curls gave her a flirty aspect, like a young boy, only prettier. Those without Sight must see a handsome young lad.

"Peace River? I have heard of that, but I don't know where."

"The Celts call it the Southern Confluence," Ryan explained. Saryl's mouth tightened. "So how do we come upon a Denygal this far south?"

"Tracking the weircats to the best of my ability. We heard from Lillirigga that you would be passing this way. They suggested three young men traveling in company would attract less attention and I was eventually going to visit Clarcom anyway. My brother Duncyn's already gone on ahead."

Ryan's chin lifted in resistance and then she relaxed.

"Let's go collect your arrows, see if we can see anything Sabre's nose missed."

"How closely are we related?" she asked as they pushed through the undergrowth.

"If your father be Sion, then he is first cousin to my father."

"The Donyl's children have survived then?"

"Aye. Culyna traveled to Mulyn many years ago. We hear from her occasionally. Her husband fades but she has children and grandchildren. My father remains hale and his sister Barantha was mother to Lady Lydya of Clarcom, rig of Denygal."

They came upon the first cat, floating in the shallows. Ryan dragged it from the water and turned it to show the unusually long teeth, while Kefyn worked his arrow loose from its spine. They moved toward the second cat, which had fallen in the bushes.

"When I can, I'll send to Sion so that he might know. If you mean to travel with us, you should know that as long as you are in company, I am the leader. If you want to travel elsewhere, that's fine, but if you travel with me, you accept my leadership."

"Aye. Fair enough. I've naught traveled so far south and that place you were talking about – it was near Clarcom, aye?"

"Close enough. Have you ever seen cats hunt in packs before?" Kefyn bent the shaft working this arrow lose, but the fletching and arrowhead were still good.

"I've read that lions in the desert country do, but nay, not this side of the Back."

Ryan frowned, then straightened.

"We should be moving on. We lost a half-day nurse-maiding some women beset by bandits and I don't want to lose more. Where are your horses?"

"I'll gather them. What do we do about the weircats?"

"There's not much to be done. Somewhat is amiss in the spiritual. I've seen lions, but not these cats. I've a mission to be about. If you want to stay hunting weircats, I've no argument, but I'll be about what was set before me."

Kefyn turned toward his horses. The younger of the women had taken their four horses down to the stream to water them. Saryl indeed! He wondered if they truly thought they could hide that one even with an elven glamour.

The dog trotted up to sniff at Kefyn's mounts. His horses twitched tails and his saddle mount stomped a hind foot. The dog showed him some teeth and sauntered off toward Ryan. There was somewhat about him … Kefyn couldn't quite place what he felt … not as yet, anyway.

Dark Wings

I should put a pillow over his face, but I cannot. The Black have no children and we're taught not to love our apprentices too much, but I raised him. I cannot go forward whole and well if he must die in my stead. The Grey have healers. It is ill-advised and foolish. I will no doubt owe those schemers somewhat. But I must do somewhat or I will have failed my love for Joryn. I should not have risked so much talent, not even to find the True King. I shall not do it again with another.

Talidd, Master of the Black, FY 994

Past

Founding Year 931 – a century ago
Denygal Mountains

*D*onyl's teeth chattered in the cooling breeze as he tried to start a fire with flint and steel. He'd spent the majority of his life in a dun where servants had tended and mended the fires and cooked the food. He ought to have paid better attention, but none had ever said he should. A dozen sparks had failed to ignite the wood and he knew naught a remedy for it. He shoved his hands into his underarms and tried to warm his fingers for another round of attempts.

A shadow passed over his campsite and he ducked. Whatever it was cast a large shadow. The air vibrated with a down thrust of its wings before it passed out of sight. When the great beast waddled into view, it held a deer in its massive jaws. It dropped the deer beside the fire pit and stared sideways at him with one eye. A melodious voice boomed out syllables that he could not comprehend.

It has to be a dragon, he thought looking at its beautiful green and silver scales. *But why is a dragon helping me and not just eating me in a single gulp. There is some fell magic here that I am not privy to.*

The pain eased in his fingers, so he caught up flint and steel again to try to light the fire. There was naught for it. Spark after spark died on the log. *Must I eat the deer raw?*

He'd read somewhere that dragons could breathe fire, but this one apparently lacked combustion. As big as a dun, the creature was long and sleek with a slitherin neck and a tail as long as its body. While it could walk for short distances on its hind legs, leaving its clever looking front talons free, it was clearly a four-ped in practice. Its scales had felt thick and hard and they glittered slightly in the late evening sun. When it opened its mouth, razor sharp teeth winked white. It nosed the deer and stared at him with its catslit eyes of purple.

His intense scrutiny of the dragon allowed the lass to slip up to him unnoticed. When she stepped into his peripheral vision, he flinched so hard a muscle in his neck spasmed. That slowed him pulling his dagger as he tried to scramble to his feet. Then his bad leg folded under him and he ended up on his back staring at this utterly alien woman.

She stared at him with green catslit eyes set in a face that was all angles and planes. Music flowed from her full lips. He managed to get his dagger up.

"Keep back," he said. *I sound afraid, and rightly so!*

She tilted her head and seemed to smile.

"Celtic?" Her gaze ran along his body. "You've had a rough trek." She looked at the dragon who sang at her. "A Celt with a dragon. Tis an odd relationship."

She seemed to listen to the dragon as it sang a series of musical notes. She laughed and returned a song to the dragon. Then she drew her dagger and carved out a large roast from the hind quarter of the deer. The dragon caught up the remaining portion and waddled off a distance to dismember and consume its kill.

"You can put away the dagger since you didn't carve out a meal so she could go about her own life. I mean to save you, not hurt you. I'm Janara."

"You speak my language," he squeaked.

"Obviously. Learned it from my pa, who lived for a while below the Wall. I'm your first elf, aye?"

"Elf?! The Fey are a myth."

She ran a hand down her side.

"Nah, I feel real enough." She stared at him again. "Is your leg injured?"

"Nay. It's an old injury."

She nodded.

"It's really rude to hold a dagger as if you think I'm going to hurt you. I'll get this fire started and spit the roast. We'll need more wood for the night. It'll be dusk soon."

She walked a distance away and returned with an armload of dried grass and leaves. Shifting the logs off the fire pit, she built a small pile of grass, leaves and finger sticks. She paused, seemed to take a deep breath and then flame licked the kindling. She added sticks, building the fire. Donyl rolled from his back to his knees to climb to his feet. A freshening breeze blasted over the ridge, sending a shiver through his body.

"You were actually trying to start a fire without kindling?"

"I don't know about such things." *How did she start it without flint and steel?* He feared to ask.

She sat back on her haunches. Dressed in a leather jerkin that left her arms bare, she looked comfortable, though gooseflesh raised on her tanned arms. She wore leather trews and a pair of leather boots. She removed the coil of rope from her torso and swung the haversack off her back. He'd never seen such that looped over both shoulders. She pulled a light siarc that opened in the front out of the pack and donned it over her tunic. All the while, her gaze was on the majestic mountains round them.

"How did you get here?" she asked.

"The beast brought me."

"That beast is a dragon," she announced. "They avoid the world of mortals, so you're somehow important to the One. What brought it to you?"

Donyl shuddered to think of the two nights before. The fell moon, the pathways filled with daemons, the desperate battle with Pedyr at his back, and the dragon coming out of nowhere to pluck him free of the ledge.

"You won't believe me," he explained.

She traced one of her furled ears with a long finger smiling mischievously.

"I think you might find I believe a lot that is alien to you."

He stared at her. *Don't trust her!* She turned back to mending the fire. Soon the roast was speared with a stick, which she braced on rocks across the fire.

"The beast brought you here – you flew?"

He nodded. Grief over Pedyr had formed a cold knot in his chest. How could he feel this way about a common born rider he had not known but a couple of months. The dragon let off its feeding to speak again. Janara listened respectfully, responding in the same language from time to time.

"My, you have had an awful time of it!"

"The season's turning. Mayhap you can explain how I've lost so much time," he asked. "I remember two nights, but it's been many more."

"The dragon explained that you slept in her cave for more than a moon. She doesn't know why. Then yestermorrow, she received guidance to bring you here. That would have been about the time I started my climb, so the One was arranging all."

He understood the words she spoke, but she described madness. He didn't remember sleeping in the dragon's cave. He doubted very much that dragons built plazas before their lairs. Mayhap that had been a dream?

What of Pedyr?

"So you know, you are in Denygal. We've a lengthy walk to get anywhere, but we can deal with that tomorrow." Her pronunciation of Celdryan words was perfect, but her cadence rendered it into musical notes. She rummaged through her pack. "How are your water supplies?"

Donyl hadn't thought of that. He limped over to where he'd dropped his pack. One bottle was half full, the other empty.

"There are no streams up on this ridge. It'll be night soon. I'll collect dew."

She pulled somewhat out of the pack, a cloth suit, and wandered off on an errand of her own. Shamed by her skill, Donyl gathered wood where he could. There were not many trees this high up, but he found fallen wood here and there. When the dragon left, he fell down in startlement.

"Where's it going?" he asked.

"Where is *she* going, you mean? She didn't say, only that we don't need her. You've yet to tell me your name."

Surely there was no harm in that. She seemed gentle enough.

"Donyl. And yours is – J-janara? It's very unusual."

"Not in Denygal. Donyl's not a common name hereabout. Do you have anything useful in that pack?"

"I know naught."

She cocked her head to stare at him again. Was her eye sight better in the horizon plane? She strode over to his pack and began to pull out the contents, inspecting his filthy small clothes and other garments before setting them aside.

"What happened to your traveling companion?"

"How are you knowing I had one?"

"Because *this* is half a kit. You couldn't have survived in the wilderness with this alone."

Donyl's throat hurt as he swallowed.

"I don't know. Pedyr and I were fighting the – the daemon hordes off when the dragon came. I've no idea – mayhap he fell after I was gone."

She bit her full lower lip and then stood.

"She didn't tell me of that," she admitted. "The daemons – well, close enough, I suppose. Some form of elemental bent to evil purpose. She recognized them. The archaic word she used translates somewhat close to daemon. Throw some wood on the fire so we can eat the roast tonight. That rock overhang will make a good shelter. I'll get busy with that. If the fire gets too high, dampen it with dirt. Don't waste the water. We'll be tight on that until we reach the Chet'na."

She finished the night preparation just as the roast began to smell delectable. Donyl watched her cut it up into chunks and dole them out in bowls from his kit. She threw another stick on the fire and sat down near it. Her long chestnut braid coiled across the ground by her hips.

The meat flooded his mouth with juices and he had consumed one whole chunk before he could think of aught else but feeding his hunger. She ate more slowly, cutting the chunks into strips, chewing delicately. Now that he wasn't starving anymore, he stared into the fire.

"Janara, why are you here by yourself?"

"I'm a dragon dancer and the One sent me to bring you in to Farhaven."

"I don't understand."

"Nay, it is not your world." A shiver ran through her body.

"Are you cold?" He was warm this close to the fire.

"Nay. My spirit resonates, is all. This is not your world, but it will be."

Donyl opened his mouth to protest that he didn't much want to live on a mountain wrapped in cold winds,

but a shudder ran down his own back then and he didn't
speak.

Present

Founding Year 1028
Galornyn

*N*aranddal had sedated him, Gregyn supposed. In this
dark windowless place, he couldn't track the passage of
time, but he sensed it had been days rather than watches
or eightnights. The gray mage brought bowls of
medicinals that left him thick-tongued and confused,
while also allowing him to hold down broth for the first
time since Talidd's ill spell.

Between bouts of madness when Naranddal spoke
to a column of glowing light, Gregyn had heard a bit.
Naranddal was a gray mage and some sort of herbalist.
He was no friend of Talidd, judging by his muttered
comments. There seemed to be people coming and
going. Sometimes he thought he heard a woman's voice.

Gregyn swam up from darkness into the light and
felt the bed for the first time. He cast about the chamber,
noting the paintings that graced the walls here as they did
in the cellar at Dun Galornyn. These were old painting
of the Fey times. A blue ball of aethyr light hung above a
small table where Naranddal sat reading from a codex.

Gregyn felt surprisingly well given all that had befallen him. His movement caused Naranddal to glance his way.

"Awake, lad?"

"We met on the street," Gregyn remembered.

"Aye."

"How did I get here? Or did I dream going back to the dun?"

"Nay, you went back to the dun and took thoroughly sick. When they took you to the infirmary, one of our brothers assured that you came here instead. It was touch and go for the first day, but the last two have mostly been you sleeping."

"Sleeping? I didn't dream."

"Nay. The medicinals prevent it, in case Talidd is snooping about in the Gatelands. It wouldn't do for him to think I'm poaching his strongest apprentice."

Gregyn remembered now and reached for the Source, but it was as if his arm were too short. A wave a nausea washed over him and pain stabbed through his head.

"Lad, you're still on the mend. Don't waste my hard work by mucking about."

"I can't ... but I've always ...." Gregyn moved to sit up, but Naranddal laid a hand on his shoulder and suddenly Gregyn couldn't move a muscle below his collarbones.

"It's not permanent. You will heal. For now, though, you mustn't. You'll only do yourself harm."

"Talidd's spell?"

"Aye. Do you have any idea what you were doing?"

"A finding spell."

Naranddal's long face grew longer.

"Is that what they tell the apprentices to get them to sacrifice themselves? I suppose it could be used to find someone with a certain etheretic signature, but its most often resulted in death for whomever they were reaching out to and for many of those doing the reaching. It's a nasty spell at that because it uses a net of familiars to draw strength from. The familiars often die or they're left broken. In most instances, they're low-level hangers-on, but occasionally they are apprentices. I am actually curious as to why Talidd would risk you."

Gregyn refused to say, turning his gaze away so Naranddal could not ensorcel him. The gray mage rubbed his shaven jaw as he considered his next question.

"I don't want to force information out of you, lad. I actually know more about Talidd than he believes I do. I don't need to get it from you."

Gregyn managed to turn his head enough to stare at the flagon on the desk. Naranddal poured water into a cup and lifted his head so he could sip.

"Physically, you're fine. Mayhap easily tired for a fortnight, but not dying. You will not be able to use your gifts for a moon or more. I've shielded you. I can Sense your terror, but you must understand why I've done this. Mages weave energies through our brains. Some of us can wield a great deal of energy. Others cannot weave so much. But we can also weave more than is healthy for us individually, which is what has happened to you. Talidd had a soft spot for his damaged apprentices in the past.

Jaryn was quite a promising apprentice who drew more than he should."

Gregyn swallowed tightly, remembering the old man with the paralyzed body and only a handful of words.

"That might have been you if you hadn't formed the sexual bond with the serving girl."

"If I'd formed it with a male, what would have happened?"

"You'd undoubtedly both be dead. This is the dirty secret the black does not tell you. Women in a circle can overcome all sorts of difficulties. They balance the energies in ways that men cannot. As near as I can determine, far fewer people died from this spell than is usual. Some of that is because you were in the circle, but some of it is also that a woman was involved."

"Because I was – you mean because of the sexual bond?"

Gregyn's chest tightened with anxiety as a wave of exhaustion crept down his limbs.

"Nay, lad. Surely you know that you mayhap be the strongest of the black in well-over a century?"

Gregyn shook his head in denial, but Naranddal only laughed.

"Lad, Talidd and his journeymen want you ignorant of what you are until much further along in your apprenticeship. They may even desire to keep you in the dark until well into your journeyman phase. It gives them control of you. Because of the way the Black trains and harnesses power, you are a risk to them if you realize how much stronger you are than even Talidd. I want you to know that when you heal … if you allow yourself to heal … there is not a mage alive today who has your capabilities."

"W-why d-do you w-want mmmme ttto know thhhhis?" Gregyn's teeth chattered. Naranddal allowed him to sip of some sweet medicinal while he explained.

"The Grey has followed the Black for generations and watched as they grew stronger through nefarious means. We watched them destroy the royal family. The True King walks and lives and you will find him. I have seen this. If you find him for the Black, the nation is destroyed. You must know this, so you can decide what you will do."

Gregyn tried to speak, to ask more questions, but his tongue was thick and the bed was spinning. He let it spin lazily into darkness and healing rest, knowing he was safe enough here for the time being and mayhap for the first time in his life.

High Celdrya

A great city fallen was High Celdrya. The gaps in the walls were many, the merchants and trademen were already leaving, mayhap fleeing the bowels and infant palsy, or the next siege. It had been Tren last time. Mayhap it would be Corbren this summer. Or Fyrgal. Or his brother.

Randodd had spent three days in this flea-ridden, piss-stinking city and hadn't found any compelling reason to invade it. He understood the symbolism of the high city, but Llyr could bankrupt itself rebuilding it to withstand the next siege. It would take years to attract new tradespeople and there was a risk to the armies of contracting the plagues.

Still, Randodd had promised to thoroughly inspect the city before giving his report, so he walked up yet another hill. It appeared a better quarter than some he'd seen. The houses were in good repair and the shop signs hung straight and had paint on them. He rounded a building fronted by a stone fence sheltering a small vegetable garden and entered an alley. A shop at the end showed the traditional mortis and pedestal of an apothecary. The door stood open and a lovely aroma wafted out, spurring Randodd's curiosity so that he entered.

A group of people were gathered round the board, eating pastries that were scenting the air with a warm, spicy aroma. Randodd swallowed saliva.

"May I help you?" one of the three men asked, standing.

"I know it's rude, but mayhap you could tell me – what is that delicious smell?"

They laughed and one of the two women placed a pastry on a pewter plate and offered it to Randodd.

"I didn't mean to interrupt," he said, embarrassed.

"Nay, you're more than welcome. It's called cinnamon. It's imported from Hanalan, but it also grows in swampy areas along the southern coast."

Randodd savored the morsel. He'd eaten sugary pastries before, but this was heavenly.

"Do you sell this spice?"

"I do," the tall man, who appeared to be the proprietor said. "I'm Andyr. This is my shop."

"I will take some now," Randodd offered, pulling out his purse. "This area of the city appears better than the rest."

The women's mouths twitched with suppressed smiles at the compliment. The men exchanged uncomfortable glances.

"We try to keep it up," Andyr said. "Closer to the walls, it's harder to keep hope. They've been burned out year after year. You're not from Dun Celdrya, are you?"

"I'm Randodd of Llyr, sent by a merchant to scout the markets."

"There's still activity in the city," one of the other men said. "It's less than it used to be, but there are some of us committed to remaining."

"Why? I don't want to be rude about your home, but it's looking dismal."

"It is home," the woman who had given him the pastry said. "My family has been here for as far back as any of us know."

"The True King is coming," the third man said. "I feel it."

"The city starts to heal when he does," the other man said.

Andyr explained it was a copper a curled stick of cinnamon, which seemed reasonable for something so mysteriously delicious. Randodd took 10 sticks. He would use this intoxicating spice as an example of what the city had to offer.

"Have you been to the upper market?" he asked.

"Nay. I found the market faire near the gates, but it looks like it's been abandoned."

"There's another near the western gate that still has a good deal of commerce. The upper market is only two days an eightnight now, but it's the largest in the city. It's in the plaza before the old Bel temple."

"The priests allow that?"

"The temple burned during one of the sieges and was never rebuilt. The market's been there for decades now. It was here when I came to the city more than 20 years ago."

Andyr hardly looked old enough to have been here 20 years, but Randodd assumed he had come here as a child. This was the sort of information he'd been seeking during his time in the city and these are the sorts of people who made a city worthwhile to their lords. They were hard workers who didn't intend to leave next season. If they survived the plague, they could rebuild the city.

Mayhap that was the answer he sought. Mayhap it was not strength in arms that Howedd needed, but strength of character.

Galornyn

*B*ranwyn nee Manahan of Mulyn plied a fine hand at embroidery. While the other attendants laughed and gossiped, Berdda had been watching the lass carefully count the line of stitching for the dolphin device and begin the next line of blue thread. Most seamstresses of her age would simply have followed the pattern given her, working the yoke of dolphins in light blue and silver, but Branwyn had highlighted her work with two shades of somewhat darker blue that truly made the dolphins seem to be cutting through waves. It was appropriate to spend this much time on a wedding siarc. Farm wives spent the time before their wedding in such intricate detail, though usually an arranged marriage like Branwyn's would have Egoran's mother do the needlework. Daryn's death had given Branwyn time to finish a wedding siarc for her husband.

Lady Berdda glided up behind her chair and watched while she worked.

"You have a fine hand, Branwyn," she remarked. "Very fine indeed."

"Thank you, m'lady. I confess to still being surprised at the light blue as opposed to the dark, but I'm sure that will ease with time."

"I still miss my own family's colors," Berdda admitted. "I am pleased that you are willing to join us while you wait."

"What else would I be doing?" Branwyn reasoned. "I expected to be in the marriage by now, but during this period of mourning, it seems appropriate to spend the time in productive work."

"Aye, especially with this pestilent rain," Lucynda, the equerry's daughter, remarked. "I do so weary of this seaward clime." Her marriage had been arranged to Dunmaden, so sun or rain, she found fault with Dun Galornyn. Berdda wondered if Branwyn had felt the same about her northern home.

"Well, there's not been a rain like this in the 30 years we've been in Galornyn," Berdda assured the entourage.

She returned to her seat and picked up the banner she was working on.

"It's better than snow," Branwyn added. "We've four to five months in Mulyn and wouldn't object much to rain."

Ah, aye, the long winters of the north. My mam used to talk about them.

"This rain feels different," Camilla commented. The middle-aged spinster had come from Dunmaden with Berdda and knew enough to recognize magicks when she saw them. "It feels malevolent." She shuddered for effect.

"It's only because it is so dark," Derdydda said. Rogan's wife was newly from the birthing bed. She'd brought her little lass to pass about as if to remind Branwyn that she was expected to produce an heir just as quickly as possible.

That's unkind. She can't help it that Egoran's first wife died at childbed and that Branwyn's father delayed in paying the dowry to pay for wars instead. It's neither of their faults that Daryn died just as Branwyn was arriving. The poor lass must feel the pressure. What would she think if she knew this was the rest of her life?

A knock on the door was answered by a serving lass who brought a message tube to Branwyn. Outside, a crack of thunder shuddered the walls. The baby started crying when several of the women gave startled shrieks. Branwyn paused in her needle work, took a deep breath and resumed. In and out, in and out. She waited to the end of the line before pausing to read her message.

She will use her time to good purpose. Wise lass.

"You look pale, lass," Rhyla, Perdydda's only attendant, come to spy for her mistress, said. Branwyn read through the message twice and tears came to her blue eyes.

"Somewhat?" Berdda asked. Derdydda settled in with the babe at her breast and the gossip resumed.

"Naught that I can do anything about, although you might wish to know about it." She held out the scroll.

You owe me naught, lass, and yet ….

Galryen, heir apparent to east Mulyn, who did not style himself as High King, wrote to his sister:

> *Gwen*
> *The Lughan accused Tamys*
> *of conspiring with Lord Tren and*
> *Father in his infinite wisdom has*
> *chosen to dishonor and disown*
> *his spare heir. Tamys was*
> *traveling east when last I heard,*
> *but should he happen to turn up*
> *at your door, please ask your*
> *husband to spare his head. I*
> *don't believe a word of what he's*
> *accused of and I hope you won't*
> *either. He was in an odd state*
> *after Trevyr's death and he made*
> *a bad decision, is all. If Father*
> *does not recall him, I will when I*
> *ascend. He knows this and has*
> *promised to contact you when he*

*can. Please light incense for him
at the temple. I'm sure the gods,
if they listen at all, hear your
prayers better than mine.*
  Gal

"It must have happened not long after I left Dun Joran."

"This is your youngest brother, aye."

"Aye. My stepmother has only had lasses. I don't know why Da would do that given the circumstances."

"Nor I, though I will see if I can find out for you. I should see about the evening meal. Will you get on well here on your own?"

"I thank you for your consideration. I'll be fine. When I finish the siarc, mayhap you'll allow me to work on the banners with you."

"Indeed. Anyone with such a fine hand ought to be set to such careful work. I'll be off then."

Berdda left the women's hall to go to the greeting chamber she shared with her husband, a boon their son-in-law had provided them as they were willing to come and fulfill Perddryna's duties when she had proven unsuitable.

Berdda poured water into a bowl, lit a candle lantern and set it beside the bowl, then swirled the water to create a scrying portal. After a bit, a misty image formed in the reflections in the bowl. It was always that way when one didn't personally know the person you scried to. Culyna probably saw her just as out of focus.

"What is it, dear?" Culyna asked. Scrying was done mind to mind and usually silently, but when one didn't know the other personally, it was somewhat strengthened by speaking the words aloud.

"Branwyn received a message from Galryen today. Do you know aught of Tamys' disownment?"

"We received word after he'd departed for the east, else we would have offered him lodging in some hidden corner of our demesne until his father calmed down."

"What happened?"

"Some nonsense with one of Tren's riders. Tamys was captured by Tren's forces a couple of years ago when he was an extra heir. He was scheduled for execution and one of Tren's riders let him go. That rider was captured in the winter and Tamys returned the favor."

"Why didn't Corbryn simply flog him as an example?"

"The Lughan claimed dark sorcery drove Tamys to it. They know, Berdda – if not about me, then about my daughter."

"Has Tamys ever shown signs …?"

"No, though we tried to keep him here as page so I could watch and train him if needed. He never showed any signs. It's Corbryn's father though. Before he died last year, he was very vocal about the witches of the Arrival. He had the age madness, but mayhap someone thought there was somewhat about it."

"There was, Culyna. You know this."

"Yes, but that was before my time and had naught to do with the Dun at the Pass. It was all at Dun Joran."

Berdda felt the hair on her arms stand up.

"Did the old man mention aught about ravens?"

"Yes, babbled about them all the time. Why?"

Berdda rubbed her arms, cold despite the muggy heat from the storm.

"What do you know of the Morrigan?"

Llyr – Golden Unicorn

Clinging to the thick rope tied to the rafters, Barbaryan bellowed in agony, sweat trickling down her body. Nanyna counted heartbeats. A good strong contraction. Shyralan wetted a rag and washed down the lass' shoulders. The water felt good as it also washed down Nanyna's breasts. The midwife prodded with practiced fingers.

"It's coming along nicely, lass. A few more good pushes and you'll be seeing your babe."

"I'm so tired," Barbaryan admitted, leaning back at Nanyna. "And it hurts so much!"

"'Tis a first babe and those are always slow at coming," Shyralan assured. Nanyna wanted to say somewhat, but it was her job to count and you couldn't do that and talk at the same time.

"Oh, I think another one's coming," the lass announced. A moment later, she sucked air and then let it out in a long, deep, growling groan, half climbing the rope with pain. "Oh, gods!" she shrieked.

"You're crowning! Another good push," the midwife instructed. She'd scarcely said that than the lass pushed again. The back of the baby's head became visible. Three more pushes and the child slid free into the midwife's hands. Shyralan helped Nanyna lean back so that the lass leaned back. The midwife laid the babe on her stomach and concentrated on delivering the afterbirth.

"Oh, what a fine lovely lad," Nanyna said. Truth-to-tell, that child would be Barbaryan's heartbreak, but you didn't say that to a lass who'd just given birth. The boy began to cry. Shyralan brought a towel that had been warming by the fire to wrap the wee one.

A watch later, the young harlot was asleep in bed, having nursed her baby for the first time, while Nanyna and Shyralan were fresh from the bath. Lantern light sparkled off the copper vases in Shyralan's room while Nanyna slowly worked a bone comb through the harlot's long, beautiful hair. Even wet it felt like silk thread in her hands, heavy and glossy. Sometimes when they pleasured each other this way, Nanyna considered the cold truth that Shyralan never seemed to age. From her earliest memories, Shyralan had always been the same and now Nanyna was the elder. Birthings were more tiring with each year.

"Do you think he'll do it?" Shyralan asked.

"I think he's tempted. We didn't raise him to be foolish though. He'll weigh the options and think before he leaps."

"It's taken the House nearly a century to make this happen. It's worrisome to think it rests on the decision of a noble male."

"Oh, close your mouth! Howedd is no nobleborn sop. He's my son and a product of this House. He'll make the wise choice. We did not raise him to be hasty."

"Women can do the best we can and it still rests on the odd sense of honor that men think they possess. Just braid it and be done with it. I'll do yours then."

Nanyna set the comb aside and gathered the thick hair to plait it.

"Do you ever wish you could have kept your boys?" she asked.

Shyralan laughed.

"Nay, I never did. I was glad to give them to their fathers knowing that they would have good lives."

"Not all," Nanyna reminded.

"I don't wish to talk about that. Are you done yet?"

Nanyna bound off the end of the braid with yarn and turned so Shyralan could work on her hair.

"I wept when it was time to send Howedd to his father. I was so glad that Randodd came later, when my time was past."

"We all do what we must, Nan. Someday, the House will not need to send our children away."

"Mayhap soon," Nan said with a smile. She could hope that for Barbaryan. She heard the comb slide slowly along the length of her hair. Shyralan had such a practiced hand. "Do I need more henna yet?"

"Nay. Another eightnight."

"I used to want another baby when I sat in on the births, but now I'm glad they're not mine. I couldn't do the late nights any longer. Are you still having your monthlies?"

"They aren't so regular," Shyralan said.

"That's what Ederra used to say."

The subject shifted to a harlot they'd known when Nanyna had been young. She'd been old enough to be their mother, but she'd held her looks for a long time.

"The beauty of your middle years is that your monthlies aren't so regular."

She'd been a favorite of several of their older customers.

"We need to order some more Fyrgal wine," Shyralan said. "And, there's a Hanolan ship in port. I should go see if they have any fortified."

"Tyna is developing a new recipe. I tasted it this morning. Citrus chicken."

"That sounds intriguing. Does she need somewhat?"

"Nay. She's not quite ready to serve it. Another few rounds. Elyana is about to whelp."

"That land near Galornyn will be a lovely dowry for the House. Imagine the rents. Oh, messages from Pryna arrived just before we were called to the birthing. The note's on the desk. She's enjoying herself as mistress to Lord Dralas of Fyrgal. His wife is apparently very supportive of her."

Pryna was Nanyna's daughter with Lord Sedd. Her fingers itched to feel the paper her daughter had handled, but there were protocols here, the patterns of years. She would wait because the House was more important than the children, had always been more important than any one harlot's life.

She relaxed under Shyralan's practiced hands, thinking of all the years since she'd lived in the complex that was the Golden Unicorn. Unlike a common whore, her mother had been of Gwenydd's line and her father had been younger brother to Galornyn. She had been groomed as mistress to the Umhall from a young age. Sedd had known her purpose and favored her highly. She'd had three children by him because he had preferred her bed over that of his wife. When she had tired of him, the House had sent a mistress to live in the dun. Her skill with politics and ability to balance a ledger sheet had brought her to the highest office in the Golden Unicorn, Shyralan's second.

It should have been enough. It wasn't, truly. She wanted to be the mistress of the brothel. Shyralan did not age. Her skin showed not a wrinkle. Her breasts did not sag. There were no stretch marks on her taut stomach, though Nanyna had held her hand as she birthed a lad and Ederra had told her that Shyralan had had a lass, though Nanyna had never learned the girl's name.

"Will Howedd want a favorite?" Shyralan asked.

"Hmmm, he has not mentioned. Truth-to-tell, he's never really needed our services. The noble lasses like him well enough."

"I suppose he needn't worry about getting one pregnant, being the vyngretrix now. Will Randodd stay with us or is he moving to the dun?"

Randodd had not been sent away as was customary. The lad made himself useful running errands and could easily go between the brothel and the dun without stumbling. It had been Shyralan's concession for the coin Nanyna brought to the House, to allow her to keep her common born son. Lord Sedd had never complained about her seeking pleasure with some other man after she'd given him a stable of bastards to suit his needs. He'd not loved her enough for jealousy.

"There you go, all tied back for the night. I am quite tired myself." Shyralan stretched, moving toward her bed. "In the morning, you and I need to go to that Hanolan ship."

"Right after we break fast. I'm for my bed."

Shyralan paused, her robe half open.

"You know, you and I have been friends a long time. Don't let's make a muck of it by you asking inconvenient questions about my age. I shan't tell you and I daresay it's dangerous to you to ask. As your friend, I ask you not to."

Nanyna's breath caught hard in her throat. Shyralan gave her a small smile and then turned toward the bed once more, dropping the robe to the carpet as she went. Nanyna swallowed, turned and let herself out the door.

Nay, I won't ask again, nor wonder. She's got a secret and I don't think I want to know it.

Dwarven Roads

Many feared the Fey, but I find them beautiful. The one lass we captured was lovely, tall and fierce. Her intelligence was clear as she learned Gaulish in a fortnight. She lacked understanding of proper government, spoke much of freedom. She also would not raise her hand to fight us. My da said they were creatures of the One same as us. I talked to her about what we believe, that we are also outsiders among the Celts. She explained that they also worshipped a singular god who had no name, but they had sinned against the land and were being punished. I tried to explain the love of Jesu and the forgiveness given. I can only hope I was successful.

King Gwin didn't view the Fey as Da did. He said they meant to harm us and that we must act to protect ourselves. The lass was soon slated to be killed like all the others, so I cut her bonds and told her to flee. If that be a sin against my own, I'll gladly take the penalty.

Ryla, Druidess of the Krystan Celts, Year 39

Past

Founding Year 931 – a century ago
Mulyn – Dun Joran

*T*ariq heard the servant moving in the chamber beyond his view, but apparently whatever the man was about had naught to do with him. The room required cleaning quite apart from his direct needs. The shutters were still closed on the window, but his stomach rumbled in anticipation of the fresh baked bread made nearby.

Hungry.

He took that as a good sign as he'd been unable to eat in the days since he'd dragged himself to the dun from the ritual cave. Balastyr's nasty spell had left him only slightly better than all the others. He assumed they were dead since he'd not heard from them. If Balastyr lived, he'd assert his control soon enough. For now, Tariq had all he could manage with his own concerns.

Would apprentices strive to become journeymen if they knew the price of drawing too much power?

To even roll out of bed right now required he reach for the Source – a painful experience given his psychic injuries. He pretended to sleep until the servant left lest his attempt to alleviate his agony result in more pain than he could control. Alone, he channeled a trickle, breathing through the coursing fire that radiated from his head into his limbs. When the shaking eased, he rolled onto his side and eased his spasming legs from under the blankets. He meticulously gathered his strength of will and body and sat up, using his cooperative arm to catch the bedpost, so he wouldn't spill face first onto the carpet. Nausea washed over him in waves. When the worst of it passed, he let go of the bedpost to rub his clenched left hand until it relaxed enough to use the arm. His feet touched the carpet and his left leg shot out straight, foot twisting. Everything took time. He channeled a trickle of the Source and his leg relaxed. He clung to the bedpost as he took weight on his feet.

The door to the bed chamber opened to admit Ryla, Lady Cadda's lady in waiting. A stout woman with a deep voice, she approached him with a rustle of silk after setting down a tray.

"You shouldn't be out of bed," she informed him.

"I need the chamber pot and breakfast," he fussed, resisting her attempts to make him sit down. Had he had his full strength, he might have dried up her ovaries for touching him.

"I've been sent to assist you, Councillor Talidd" she explained. "You may lean on me."

Tariq resented that he needed to rely on this saeffic, but truth to tell, he was nearly falling down. Her use of his assumed name reminded him that he had urgent matters to attend to, so that he must regain his strength as quickly as possible. *Rest is healing.* He allowed her to help him to the chamber pot and was grudgingly grateful that she turned her back to allow him an illusion of privacy. While he waited there, he wondered why she did not have an aura. Was he unable, in his weakened condition, to view it or was there somewhat afoot?

How many of Lady Cadda's attendants are part of her inner circle?

Ryla helped him back to bed and brought the breakfast tray to him.

"Has Cadda whelped yet?' he asked her.

"The night of the fell moon," she reported. "A fine healthy squaller. They'll name him Jaryn."

Born during Balastyr's spell? Twice-blessed it would seem, though that wicked moon seemed ill-omened.

His left arm and leg started shaking, forcing him to settle back against the pillows.

"We hear that the men who work moon magic suffer apoplexies," Ryla announced. "Our moon blood protects us."

Fool saeffic! I could end your moon blood and stop your heart if I were at full strength.

Yet, he had to admit to himself that she might be right as to what had happened to him and the others. It was an ill-concealed secret among the journeymen that this was a risk they took on to achieve mastery of their craft.

"I'm well enough for now. Thank you for your assistance. I will sleep now."

"I'll return at sundown to assist you upon Lady Cadda's instructions. If you need somewhat in the meantime …."

"I won't, I assure you."

After she left, he stared at the bed draperies for a while, considering what had happened over the last eightnight and the 25 years previous since being sold as a slave to a black mage at age 6. He'd wept bitterly when his mother closed the wheel house door and shut him out. He'd hoped the mage was his biological father, but of course, wishing never made fiction into truth. He'd passed from one mage to another until Balyster had acquired him several months later. He'd learned the Celdryan language by then and stopped missing his mother and siblings. He'd realized that he was only half Morikan and that the other half must be Celdryan. When Balyster had introduced him to the rituals, he'd felt his first taste of power and there'd been no turning back. He'd been the acknowledged master of journeymen by strength for a half decade.

Mayhap, he was the only journeymen left from Balyster's spell circle. If so, what did that mean for his rank among the Black? He would need to ponder and assess that. If none lived from the circle, he may well have become the Master of Journeymen as Sherwyn had been part of that circle.

Rubbing his twitching left arm, he withheld his celebration until he was better healed, but began making plans immediately.

Present

Founding Year 1028
Glenconyn

*P*adraig waited for Tamys to fall asleep before he headed off to the town on errands. Three eightnights had passed since Tamys' fall and Padraig felt the passage of time acutely. The lad mended well, but he'd suffered a grievous injury that left him in pain, dizzy and exhausted. He generally took a long nap in the heat of the afternoon, which had allowed Padraig time to gather supplies for the upcoming journey.

Kath, a short, barrel-chested man, looked up from a map he was working on when Padraig entered the door of his shop. Kath smiled and stood to cross to him.

"Padraig, welcome back to my shop. Please, take a seat. Take a seat."

Though he came only to Padraig's chin, Kath was powerfully built with arms that could have served a smith – which indeed his father might have been. Dark with a thick beard and eyes of jet black, he might have some desert-dweller or Hanalan in him, but Padraig had recognized dwarven blood immediately. It was a testament to how foolish Celdryans could be that Wmgleadd had been built to repel the dwarves and yet a half-dwarf had owned a cartography shop within the city for decades. Padraig would have loved to know Kath's life story, but though Kath acknowledged recognizing elvish blood in his customer, he did not divulge personal information, beyond the fact that he had traveled widely and was himself a Believer.

"I suppose you're in a rush again," Kath said.

"Somewhat, but not as badly as before." As Tamys recovered strength, he became less afraid of being abandoned. He slept more solidly and could be soothed by the camp girl Padraig had left to watch him.

"Good, good. Come take a look at what I've found. Sit, sit. I'll bring it to you."

Kath hurried off to a back room while Padraig sat down on one of the two stools. After a wait that seemed to stretch into the next day, Kath returned with a scroll about as long as Padraig's forearm. He unrolled it onto his long work table and Padraig gasped, for the map was drawn on elven paper sewn to papyrus, a technique unknown among the Celdryans and rarely used by modern elves, though he'd seen it in the Kin libraries. He glanced up to see Kath noting his reaction.

"I suppose you want to know where I got it from?"

"I am curious."

"Found it in a street bazaar in Dun Llyr on a trip several years ago. I've no idea who made it, but it's old. The edges are starting to crumble."

"Old, aye, but it can't be original. This sort of paper can't survive a thousand years without a controlled environment. In fact, the library in Denygal has naught that old."

"Nay, it may very well be a more recent copy of an older map. The gravings are in Celdryan, but the map shows none of the human settlements. I don't know. It's been a mystery for the 20 years I've owned it. Come take a look."

They leaned over the map.

"This be Wmgleadd," Kath said. "You can see the Portal marked on the map, but no town. I suppose the elves were not so afraid of the dwarves as the Celdryans are."

The beautifully-drawn map was very reminiscent of the elven style of maps. The paints had faded with time, but each line remained clear. Human mapmakers stylized mountains, rivers and lakes, but here the mountains were finely drawn, rivers looked like rivers and showed waterfalls as pictures and forests were drawn with trees myriad and diverse. The Portal was shown as mountains bracing a road.

"Now you follow down this way." He traced the road as it went south from the Portal to a drawn city of rectangles and squares. "Do you know this city?"

"Aye. The elves called it Traelagaleana - the Farwesting City of the Plain. At least, I think that's what it was. There should be a river there, but there's naught. It's in the right place, I think."

"Aye, well, it's not there now. But, a dwarven trade road's not as delicate as an elven city. I've seen paving stones here and there to the south. You see that the map shows the road running far straight into the forest to the south and across the mountains to Morglen. Morglen seems to have had little but fishing villages back then."

"Elves mostly lived in what is now the central kingdom, Mulyn to Dun Llyr. They spread along the coast a bit, but not like the humans have. If there was once a dwarven trade road, then the mountains must be passable."

"Aye. Even after a thousand years, there'd be a bit of our road left, I'm sure of that. Do you want the map?"

"I don't need it," Padraig assured him. "You'd make more money selling it to an antiquities dealer. I am curious, but I can't make full use of it."

"Do you know what these glyphs mean?"

Kath pointed to a series of symbols scattered across the map.

"The symbol means highway," Padraig said. "They're oddly placed. I don't know of any dwarven highways in these areas of the east, and I've traveled there extensively."

"And the highways are not marked on the map. There's just the symbols, almost like waypoints."

Padraig stared at the map a good many heartbeats before saying what he thought.

"The elder Kin who remember the time before the Threshing are mostly dying off now and they were children at the Arrival, but I've heard them tell tales of being able to travel the length of the basketlands in a matter of hours."

"How is that possible?"

"I don't know and more importantly, they don't either. They were very young and mayhap remember it wrong."

"I'll tramp round here to see if I can find somewhat. On your journey, you'll pass near two of them, you see."

"I'll keep it in mind. I'm grateful for the help." He laid a handful of copper coins on the table. "Can you tell me what's south, as far as you know?"

"There's a Celt road through farms – an area called Traelyn, coincidentally of course - then a lot of ramshackle ruins. Farms, I supposed, abandoned for some reason. The children went off to war, or mayhap there was plague. I never thought to ask."

"And farther south?"

"The Mirklin forest. No one goes there. The Celdryans say it's haunted. You hear tales of haunts, true enough. Some say it's the ghosts of vengeful elves."

"Virgin forest, then?"

"Most like. I can't imagine any Celdryan entering it."

"I must have asked for an adventure," Padraig said with a smile. "I'm certainly having one."

"There's a proverb, 'may you live in interesting times.' You live in such, my friend."

Kath and Padraig parted with clasped hands and warm speech. Padraig returned to the campground a couple of watches later to find Tamys sitting on his blankets talking to the lass who'd been paid to keep him company.

His eyesight had not returned as Padraig had hoped it might, but yesterday he'd admitted to an awareness of light. Melancholy about the future, he had asked more than a couple of times what was to become of him.

Padraig rode under the command of a Great Lord who ordered to travel south to Morglen. Already the time was short for reaching that temperate coastal plain in time to plant herbs. The only roads to Morglen required returning to Fyrgal to travel south and then along the coast, a long journey of nearly a month, longer with Tamys in his present weakened condition. It would be an exhausting journey for the lad and one that he might not survive. Nay, Padraig thought the lad mended well. Likely the journey would not cause his death, but it would tax him sorely. On the other hand, staying in Wmgleadd made little sense. The laws hereabouts didn't allow an itinerant herbman to ply his trade within 10 miles of the town walls and there weren't many people living outside that radius. It wasn't for Padraig to stay the winter here. And, he simply would not abandon the lad. Nay, the lad needed him and compassion was somewhat Believers rated highly. He'd counseled Tamys to bide time for healing, but that didn't mean they couldn't make some progress while they waited.

The sunny little lass with the dirty face and the wild curls smiled when she saw Padraig and leapt to her feet.

"He's fine and I'll take my coin now," she said.

Padraig laughed as much because she couldn't have been older than his nephew Danyl, but also to hide his dismay. He'd certainly never met such a mercenary child in Denygal or the kinholt. Padraig paid over the coppers he'd promised, plus a bit more since it seemed the lass had cheered Tamys a bit.

"Did you know Morglen was founded within our lifetime by the younger sons of some of the great houses?"

"Truly? I knew it was but 15 or 20 years old. I didn't know that bit about the extra heirs. You'd think with the wars they'd have plenty to keep them home. Was Jaryna spinning tales?"

"I don't think so. She's been there and she likes to talk. She tells me Morglen is too far to reach it by winter."

"What do you know about Morglen, lad?"

"It's where you were headed when I was hurt. I've learned a bit from her the last few times you left her with me. You can't practice your trade here and summer's turning. Do herbmen traveling with invalids make better time than minstrel troops?"

"You've stopped being worried that I'll abandon you?"

"Nay, I'm still worried about that, but you keep insisting it isn't true, so I'm trying to believe it."

"Well, first, we are leaving soon. And, second, we don't need to stop to entertain folks as Jaryna's family does. Third, we'll not take the roads her family would."

"There's other roads?"

"There are."

"Either way, how are you planning to take me? I can barely crawl from the tent without getting dizzy. I can't sit a horse. And, I sleep half the day away plus the full night."

"You'll not be riding at first. Duglas had his carpenter make a travois so you can sleep while we travel."

Tamys nodded, but then put a hand over his eyes.

"What, lad?"

"Just dizzy," Tamys said, his voice trembling. He swallowed spasmodically. "How long before we go?"

"A day or two. I have all the supplies gathered. I just need to pack them --."

Tamys fumbled round to the side, located dirt by touch and vomited explosively and repeatedly. When his stomach was empty, he dry heaved several times. Padraig ran to the well to draw a bucket of water. They'd been through this before. Padraig wetted a cloth and placed it on Tamys' neck as the young soldier curled into a shuddering ball. Between renewing the cold cloth, Padraig cleaned up the vomit and prepared some willow bark tea. The willow bark tea wouldn't dull this pain because Tamys wouldn't hold it down when the headache was full on, but when it began to ease, the tea would shorten it.

Padraig couldn't do much more for him. His elven teachers had cautioned against the use of pain-dulling medicinals like opium, alcohol, and valerian when a patient was recovering from a head injury. Padraig had asked God for permission to take the pain away, but he'd been overwhelmed by the feeling that the pain wouldn't be stopped. He did what he could, stayed near, put cold compresses on Tamys' neck and forehead, tried to find ways to ease Tamys' pain without venturing into forbidden territory.

"Padraig," Tamys whispered.

"Aye," Padraig replied.

"Did I survive because you did somewhat?"

"I have no control over death, Tamys. Only God does and there was no need to ask for permission for such, even if He would grant it. You lived because you lived."

"Blind," Tamys grunted.

"I can't explain that. I can tell you what happened inside your head, but I can't explain why it affected your sight."

Tamys covered his eyes with one hand, groaning. Padraig wet another rag and replaced the other.

"I keep seeing flashes," Tamys murmured.

"Flashes? Of what? Light, color?"

"Both. They seem to make my head hurt more."

"Does keeping your eyes closed help?"

"I – I don't know."

Padraig rummaged in his workbag for a strip of linen and tied it round Tamys' head so it covered his eyes.

"Let's give this a try, see if your headache eases with it."

Tamys had no energy to argue. They remained quiet for a good long while, Tamys occasionally groaning in pain. In time he slept and Padraig lay down near him to rest. He awoke when Tamys awoke.

"How do you fare, lad?"

"My head hurts, but not so much," Tamys whispered. "Why does it hurt? It didn't at first."

"Your skull is made up of bone and they're mending." Padraig thought it the probable answer, though he was not entirely certain. The Sight revealed the darkness at the back of his skull was shrinking. Padraig thought that might have somewhat to do with the flashes of light and color that Tamys was "seeing". He hoped it meant returning sight. Still, the darkness was at the back of the head and the eyes were at the fore.

It made no sense that one would be connected with the other. Except ... a vague memory floated to the surface of Padraig's mind now and again. Somewhat to do with head injuries. He couldn't quite find the meaning though. If only he could scry to Gly, but his best efforts had resulted in naught and he knew not why.

The headaches really set Tamys back, leaving him weak and melancholy.

"I should have died," he lamented. "I'm in the lowest hell and your god cares naught. You healed that child on the Mandorlyn road, but you've done naught for me. Your god won't give you permission, will he?"

"Nay," Padraig admitted. "God's ways are mysterious to man, Tam. I don't know why, but the answer isn't really nay, but wait. I can't heal without His permission."

Tamys' face contorted with rage.

"Damn your god!"

"Lad, I know that it seems like your life is over, but when the pain abates and your strength returns –."

"I'll still be blind."

"You haven't given it time enough to know that. You might heal. He might give me permission to do that which I desire greatly. There's no way of knowing yet."

"Wait?! And do what? I don't have any family I can go back to, Padraig. I can't see and my only skill requires sight. I can't even find the road so I may beg beside it. What do I have to live for?"

"Hope," Padraig replied. "I never considered your father as an alternative for you. He's a man who hates weakness, I'm sure. I know you're not well enough to make this decision now, but you need to know what I'm proposing. My Lord's bade me travel south to Morglen for the winter. We'll need to leave soon to miss the snows in the mountains. I propose you stay the winter with me, wait for your healing to complete. I'll train you in herbcraft. It's a useful trade, sighted or no. I propose you give yourself the winter to heal."

Tamys lay still, not speaking. Padraig waited.

"I'm tired," Tamys announced in a thin voice.

"Rest then. I'll give you time to think on what I've proposed."

Padraig sat by a fire that night. It was warm enough not to need one, but he felt the need of the comfort of the cheery light. Tamys awoke, calling softly for him. Padraig went to him immediately. After sipping some water, Tamys slept again. In the dark of the night, after Padraig had fallen asleep, Tamys awoke again.

"Is it night?" he asked.

"Aye," Padraig replied, drowsily.

"Are there stars, the moon?"

"It's the waxing quarter moon," Padraig reported. "The stars are large, summer stars."

A tear rolled out from under the cloth that covered Tamys' eyes.

"I'll never see them again." He drew a deep shuddering breath. "Mayhap."

"Mayhap," Padraig agreed. There was no use lying to the lad. He'd have to face the truth sooner or later.

"I don't feel like doing aught but lying here and dying," Tamys admitted.

"I know that."

"You won't let me, though, will you?"

"Nay, I'll fight you to your dying breath."

Tamys grew so quiet that Padraig thought he'd fallen back asleep, but the lad stirred finally.

"I'll try to have hope."

Padraig smiled, but he curtailed any show of enthusiasm since Tamys was so melancholy. This was not a journey of joy they were undertaking, but it might be a journey to hope.

Galornyn

*T*aryn winced at the sunlight as the warband rode through the city. Gregyn rode beside him as his sergeant. That lad intrigued Maddw. His luck was uncommonly good – finding well-hidden brigands by chance, surviving a plague that had killed his lover. He was a taciturn young man, given to quiet smiles, with an observing nature. Taryn had taken a liking to him, but no one else seemed to know aught about him. Even his fellow riders gave various tales. He was from Dunmaden, some said, while others noted the Llyr accent. Maddw didn't rightly trust him, but he could find no real objection to his position. The lad had saved Teddryn's life earlier in the spring, during the raid on the brigand camp. Gregyn had proved to be a man you wanted in a mob, but Maddw was not altogether certain that he would trust him alone in an alley.

When they reached the city gates, the warband dismounted to give their horses water and to do one last check of the gear. Taryn rinsed his face in the trough like a common rider, then leaned his forehead on his saddle, looking like he might vomit. He'd not taken the news of his gifts as well as Maddw would have liked. He'd been drinking almost constantly since. It didn't help that Teddryn had taken a turn for the worse yesterday. Maddw reminded himself that the lad was young … and he had a plan for the trip that might help.

Gregyn checked the catches on the wagon gate, nodding peaceably to Maddw.

"Sir," he said. What little Maddw had dealt with him, he'd found him private, but today he seemed ill-at-ease, like a soldier whose come out without his sword belt.

"Gregyn. This is your first command, aye?"

"I got a taste of it a bit guarding caravans," he said. "It's an honor to serve Dun Galornyn."

"I'm sure it is," Maddw said with a wry twist of his mouth. "For this journey, however, I'd prefer if you served my brother."

Gregyn glanced to where Taryn leaned.

"Taryn detailed that two kegs of mead be secured in this wagon. I had them replaced with two kegs of ale. He'll be cross and I tell you because you have my permission to blame me."

"Aye, sir. It seems like a … an appropriate measure."

"Taryn's ways are not mysterious to you?"

"We're of an age," Gregyn said simply. "May I suggest …There's an old king's road south of the Black Forest. We could shave three or four days off our journey. It has few duns or villages where we might resupply."

"Taryn will rely on your guidance as he has not traveled eastward before. You understand the way of it. Good journey."

Maddw left the young sergeant to his preparations and walked over to Taryn.

"You fell a bit too deeply into your cups last night," he remarked.

"Are you here to lecture me?"

"Nay, only to provide some last bits of journey wisdom and somewhat else. I can't completely release you from Grandmam's binding, but you'll have a bit of use of your gifts on this journey. It might last a month."

"I don't feel any different."

"Nay, at the dark of the moon, it will present itself. That's an eightnight hence. Mostly, it will be child's play, what you'll be able to do, but this taste may help you to decide if you truly want to be unbound."

Taryn let out a long breath very slowly, swallowed convulsively and stood up.

"I still wished I knew what Egoran hoped to accomplish by sending me instead of you on this journey."

"I cannot say," Maddw said. *I wish I knew to tell you, brother.* Maddw and Taryn looked toward Gregyn at the same time. "Pay attention to your sergeant. He's young, but he seems to have seen a bit of the world."

"I will. Thanks to you for allowing me to pick my own men."

"You surprised me."

"How so?"

"You picked Janyr and Baryk … sober men of middle years not given to much drink."

"I've never seen Gregyn drink more than a tankard," Taryn noted. "I asked myself what you would do. I don't want to embarrass the family on my first journey."

"Good. You've made a good start … hangover notwithstanding." Maddw handed over a silver message tube and a purse of coin. "Lady Lydya is the sister of a very dear friend of mine. Give the tube to her and bring it back to me and none others."

"Aye. Is there somewhat I should say about … Teddryn is growing weaker."

"Nay. Egoran wishes to hold that to his chest for now. Truth to tell, we need the coin."

"What happens if …?" Taryn looked stricken.

"Egoran hasn't made me privy to his thinking on that, but you are to say naught. If anyone asks after Teddryn, he is hale. Do you understand that?"

"I do." Taryn uncorked a water bottle and drank deeply. Maddw poured heat into the bottle. *By noontide it ought to be vinegar.*

"Good journey to you, brother." They embraced and then Maddw walked toward his horse, passing Gregyn, who met his gaze briefly, nodded and walked to where Taryn waited.

Taryn had done well to select the band that he had. Maddw shouldn't be nervous of it at all. Mayhap it was just that his brother was taking his first band outside of

Galornyn. He watched the band mount and set out and felt a cold fist clench his stomach tight.

The Tongue

*T*he spell vortex collapsed at dawn. Jaryn awoke to feel Talidd's mind hammering desperately against the prison of his useless body. Jaryn debated whether to work magicks on him, but one of the apprentices had a gift for sensing that had not yet been bent to dark purposes.

"There's bleeding," he told Jaryn. Talidd's eyes had been open the day before, but now they were closed and his breathing grew more shallow as the day passed.

Jaryn remembered that Talidd's had been the first face he'd seen when he'd woke up those many years ago. He thought it only fitting that his be the last face Talidd saw before he passed. He sat down and patted the master's hand. Talidd's eyelids fluttered and eventually opened a slit.

Pictures flickered through Jaryn's mind – the farm they'd lived on when he was a young child, a woman with blond hair who he didn't know, but resembled the face he used to see in the mirror, the early training in magic, his initiation into the power of effluent. Many of these memories had been lost to him. These were Talidd's memories passed to him.

Black wings flickered across his inner eye and Talidd's raven alit in his mind. It turned its black eyes to stare at him. Jaryn sensed a question. He'd not seen the raven since Talidd had unleashed the spell and he was uncertain that he was seeing it truly now. Mayhap this was Talidd's own soul, asking to continue in the way as a part of Jaryn.

All these years, Talidd had thought Jaryn was held by name-magic, but he had not known that Jaryn had lost his true name in the seizures that had nearly killed him decades ago. Jaryn had stayed and obeyed because he'd felt unable to function on his own. Now he knew this was not true. If he had magic to heal Talidd, he had magic enough to heal himself somewhat. He could go and do and be.

Or he could let Talidd in.

One of the scrolls had touched on it. Talidd would largely cease to exist, but his essence – his power – would pass to Jaryn, who would retain control. This was only being offered to Jaryn because he was the only black mage about. He should pass it to one of the faces that flickered through his mind – Sawyl, the grey-eyed apprentice whose name he could never remember, about a half-dozen others. The scroll said Jaryn had a choice.

He held out his hand to the raven and it leapt up onto his right wrist. Outside, the rain stopped and birds began to sing raucously. He opened his eyes to see Talidd had stopped breathing and the raven perched on his right wrist, which for the first time in decades was not twisted with palsy, but straight and supple and fully useful.

The raven bowed its head and quorked. Jaryn bowed his head in imitation.

"H-hello," he said. He paused, surprised at how clear the sounds came and with so little effort. "I am your new master."

The raven shifted its weight on his wrist and then pecked his forearm hard enough to draw blood. A rush of images filled Jaryn's mind, too fast to process. Faces and places and words … it left him dizzy just to experience them. In the end, there was one overwhelming thought.

Talidd might be gone, but the raven remained and Jaryn was not to mistake himself in any way as a master. This raven was no mere bird and he must never forget that.

Liquid Rock

We hiked for a fortnight north of the Dragon's Head and found rivers of ice that supplied the Milk and its tributaries. These frozen rivers came out of the north mountains grinding rocks up and pushing mud ahead of them. At the foot, there was a large lake of frigid water that would slowly trickle away to make a torrential river that scoured out huge canyons through the mountains.

The vastness of the One's creation takes my breath away.

Ryladd, apprentice researcher at Collegiate Moryn, FY 965

Past

Founding Year 931 – a century ago
Denygal

*H*e followed Janara along a mountain trail several hundred feet above the Milk, a wide, powerful river that boiled with life as it cut down through granite mountains to some distant sea. To his right, a granite cliff rose grey against a crisp blue sky. To his left, tangled daermon's club guarded the slope to the river. An occasionally breeze tossed the odd knot of branches that composed the tree tops and kept the insects at bay.

I wonder what created this trail. It's not natural, I'm sure.

With strong, lithe legs that brought her slightly taller than him, Janara had a tendency to range ahead of him like some sort of deer hound. The upward slopes no longer winded him, but his leg dragged a bit from exhaustion born of spending half the day sliding down a loose scree slope and then struggling through a wood of choking daemon's club where black flies bit mercilessly.

She stopped at the crest of the trail, waiting for him to catch up.

Is she a female?

He doubted it. He'd thought Janara was female because her voice was light and her hair was long, but she dressed more like a male and she had no breasts under that jerkin … he thought.

"When will we camp?" he asked when he reached her.

"Soon. We need water. We have to keep moving until we get to it."

"Can't we climb down to the river?"

She blinked and cocked her head again.

"The Milk isn't good to drink," she explained. "When we get to the Chit'na, you can see why."

She said somewhat like that to almost every suggestion he made and he'd become quite tired of it. Aye, this was her world, but she never explained her edicts. Why was the Milk not good to drink? It was a river after all.

This is why they don't put women in charge.

Was she a woman? He thought of her as female, even as he wondered if he was right. What did he really know of her people … if they could be considered people? He could believe the stories that they cropped their babies' ears, but that didn't explain the vertical pupil of her eyes or the unnatural green shade of their irises.

They toiled up another hill and rounded a corner. She paused for a moment and then her pace picked up on a downward slope. He followed her, his leg burning with the effort. Although the cliff remained to their right, the land dropped away to their left to open into a creek valley. The creek at the bottom moved with a breathtaking speed, though it seemed small for the valley it tumbled in. Looking downstream, he could see where it entered the Milk in a churn of mixing waters, silver and brown.

Janara leapt from boulder to boulder along the edge of the creek until she reached the confluence. He followed more slowly in the gravel. The tumultuous Milk boiled against the rock she stood on.

"It's like liquid mud," he remarked, shaking dirty water from his near-frozen hand.

"It's glacial silt from the north mountains," Janara explained, raising her voice over the babble of water and wind. When he frowned his lack of understanding, she added. "Rivers of ice scour out rocks and deposit the ground material in the water. The early Denygal called it the Dragon's Milk, but it has naught to do with dragons."

"It does look a bit like milk. Have you seen these ice rivers?"

"I haven't, but I've a brother who has trekked north for studying them."

"Who would study such?"

"The collegiate in Moryn does."

"I was bound there," he told her.

"Were you now?" She seemed distrustful of his story, since he'd told her he was Prince and possibly King Regent. Not that they'd talked much during the day's journey. Mostly she had led and he followed and he'd needed all the breath he could spare to keep moving.

"We'll get water and build our camp over in those trees," she announced, following the creek back by the same method of leaping from boulder to boulder. He knew his leg would prevent him from doing it, so he followed her through the gravel again.

The sun had touched the mountain on their right where the creek slashed down from the heights, splashing over rocks in a fall. Janara dropped her pack, and filled her water bladders. Donyl imitated her, fingers growing numb in the fast-moving icy-cold water. She strode into a copse of wind-battered trees, located a sandy floor and dropped her pack. Once the wood had been gathered and a fire laid, but not lit, she doffed her tunic and trews on top of her boots and walked in her small clothes to the stream, where she jumped in, shrieking from the cold. Donyl had never met a woman so comfortable with the out of doors or near-nudity. Her bare arms had bothered him before, but now there was no question but that she was a female, for an odd sling covered two small breasts above a well-muscled stomach.

Donyl found a rag and wet it to wash down his neck and arms. She came out of the water, streaming rivulets from her hair.

"That felt good," she enthused. "You should try it while I catch our dinner."

She pulled a net from her pack, lashed it to a stick and waded into the stream to fulfill the promise of food. He gathered more wood and worked to light the fire. The flint and steel cooperated this time and he managed to light the kindling and then build a fire of the larger sticks.

Janara stuffed the single large fish with forest fruits she'd been gathering as they walked. The aroma of roasting fish caused saliva to squirt into his mouth so that Donyl felt he could have eaten forbidden meat. The sun set behind the mountains, casting all in grey, while they set up a tarp and spread blankets.

"May I ask – you don't have much in the way of gear," he noted. "What are you doing so far from settlement?"

"I'm a dancer," she said. "This is what I do."

"Hike through the forest with lost princes?"

She laughed. Her bare skin looked warmed by the sun.

"Do you see that big mountain there?"

She pointed to the mountain that never seemed to go away. Every time the landscape opened up a bit, the dominate mountain thrust up on their southern horizon. Though they were in shadow, the mountain remained kissed golden by sun.

"That's the Dragon's Head, highest point in all the Dragon's Back. Women of Denygal – some men, but mostly women – train to fly into remote valleys to help stranded travelers or deliver urgent messages."

"Fly? Do you mean like the dragon?"

"Somewhat, I suppose, like the dragon, though that was the first one I'd seen. We use a glider suit." When he stopped tying knots and stared at her, she shrugged.

"I'll show you tonight after we've eaten."

The fish had meaty orange flesh with easily removable bones. Janara ate in her small clothes with her loose siarc covering her, clinging suggestively on her curves. After she'd sucked the juice from her fingers, she took her pack into the bushes and returned to hang her small clothes by the fire, wearing an odd suit with fabric like wings from her wrists to her ankles.

"The wind catches these flaps and allows us to glide for miles under the right conditions," she explained, holding her arms out at shoulder height.

"What if the wind fails?" he asked.

Her delicate forehead wrinkled and then she shrugged. Her full lips embraced humor.

"I suppose I would regret being a dancer for the heartbeats remaining to me."

Where before he'd found her features alien, now he saw a beauty in them. Her eyes remained hard to meet.

"When the – the dragon lifted me free of that ledge – I felt only terror," he admitted. "In time, though, I saw the world round me – round us and there was a terrible beauty in it. Is that why you risk your life in this way?"

"We risk our lives every day. Dozens of things might have killed us since we woke this morn until this moment. You wear a sword. Does that not invite the risk of violence? We cannot avoid risk. Dancers are needed and I was called. We may not always die of old age in bed, but neither do men who wear swords."

She gestured round their camp.

"The One protects us so that we may do His work."

"The One?" he asked.

She tilted her head and then sat down on the blankets they'd spread beneath the tarp. She wrapped her arms and therefore the flaps around her knees in a way that made him think of bats.

"I forget that Celdryans believe in multiple gods," she said. "We believe in the One."

"A single god?" *Disconcerting. Intriguing.* "When I was planning to study at Moryn, I heard that your folk had some odd philosophies, but I was assured that educated folk believed rightly."

"We do," she assured him with her characteristic confidence. His expression must have betrayed his astonishment at her impertinence. "The problem with being trapped in a forest many days hard hike from any other thinking being is that you are rather trapped with me and what I believe. I do not ask that you believe it; only that you give me the respect due your rescuer in accepting my right to believe it."

"Your right to believe it?" He sat down on the other blanket, offered his top blanket for a wrap. She shook her head, indicating that the gliding suit was warm. "I know of this concept of rights. It comes from the old world – the idea that the Celts had a right born of being thinking beings to choose their own kings rather than submit to the Rawmayns. When we came here, however, it became obvious that we needed to have strong leadership."

She tossed a stick on the fire, sending shadows dancing against the cliff behind them.

"The elves of old also believed in rights – the right to choose their leaders, the right to speak their minds, the right to believe as was right. It was this adherence to rights that has caused us to continually move away from the Celts who do not respect those rights."

"How does your rig feel about these rights?"

She frowned.

"My what? I do not know this word 'rig'. What does it mean?"

"Originally, it meant king, but here it means lord."

"We do not have such in Denygal. We have squires – those who serve as elected leaders for a period of time prescribed by the electors."

"Who are these electors?"

"All the adults of the land."

How could I not have known of this? Did Father know?

"Does Denygal consider itself part of the kingdom?"

"No," she said in her odd Denygal term of negation. "We are independent, neither part of Celdrya or the elven holts."

"Holts?"

"Holt – it's – a village. Although my family are Kin, we have chosen to cast our lot with the Denygal. My mam is an academic and so wants to remain at the collegiate."

"They have female tutors?"

"Yes, of course they do. Why wouldn't they?"

"Women are ill-fitted to the scholarly arts."

Janara breathed in deeply and let her breath go slowly.

"I think that I am tired and it would be a good time to rest," she announced and lay down and closed her eyes. Donyl waited to see if her abrupt need for sleep was a jest, but she didn't move.

"I said somewhat wrong?" he asked, but got no reply. Lasses are difficult, he thought. Surely this is a known. Why would it anger her if I speak the truth? I do not believe her mother is an academic. Mayhap she works in the collegiate, but not as a scholar. We've encountered a language barrier. It is naught more than that.

Rain splattered on the tarp. Janara rolled onto her right side, facing the fire, away from him. He lay down and listened to the rain and wondered about what had become of Pedyr. He fell asleep imagining his friend overwhelmed by daemons and carried over a cliff.

Present

Founding Year 1028
Clarcom

*L*ydya of Clarcom, wife to the vyngretrix of Dublyn and herself rig of Denygal, understood that mating was at the heart of all kingdoms. A rigdon rose and fell on the quality of its heirs. That could make an unhappy life for a noble wife of good character whose spouse blamed her for his inability to plant his seed. Her marriage to Cunyr ap Rhiordan had revolved round that fact and it had fallen to her mother Barantha to find what happiness could be made of a pig's slop. A noblewoman took what she got and made the best of it. Bryan would be a wonderful heir – a fine replacement for Cunyr when the time came – a great improvement. Cullyn would be … Cullyn. She couldn't decide what to make of him.

Arrogant, willful, very much his father's child – mayhap Cunyr's only child, the others having been conceived by a kinsman-redeemer .. all except Danyl. Danyl was more worrying these days than Cullyn for the wild blood had shown itself in full.

Lydya thought all of this betwixt the time it took Danyl to leave one balcony and alight on a nearby roof. She took in Cullyn's grin and her retainers' gasps, felt horror at her son's risky behavior and then relief that he landed safely.

This is not good. If Cunyr becomes aware of it, he'll start to ask questions and others may as well. This straw house is easily blown over. This sort of thing cannot be.

But it was and she must do aught about it.

"Did you encourage him in that?" she demanded of Cullyn.

"Mam, he didn't need any encouragement. He's wild as a new-broken colt. But if you mean, did I enjoy seeing him do it … aye, it's very entertaining."

"Go to your chamber and stay there until I come to speak to you."

His jaw hardened. *Aye, you're Cunyr's. You've got the jaw.* Then he turned on his heel and strode away. Far below, there was a clatter in the ward. She looked over the parapet to see young Kefyn from Denygal in the company of two Dengyal women dressed as men. *Nay,*

*there's a glamour. They seem as men to others. Best to remember
that when I speak to them.*

"I really must find Danyl. Millyna, dear, would you
be so kind as to locate the lad and take him to the
nursery?"

"Aye, m'lady." The girl dropped a curtsy before
rushing off in search of the wayward boy. Lydya hurried
down the circular stairs to meet Kefyn whilst still in the
ward.

"Duncyn was thinking he needed to go fetch you,"
she chided.

"The people I was meeting took a bit longer than I
thought they would. I must introduce you to a messenger
from Reyn – this is Ryan and Saryl."

Unlike common-born riders acting as messengers,
Denygal did not take a knee. The taller of the two
Dengyal looked the male part better than the smaller, but
she was quite one of the loveliest women Lydya had ever
seen for all that she wore a sword and no doubt a jerkin
under her siarc to cover her femininity. There was
somewhat about her that reminded of her grandmother
Janara. For all that Janara's eyes had been cat-slit, there
was somewhat ….

"Are you Sion's d – offspring?" she asked.

Sion, the son of Barantha's brother, had departed
into the eastern mountains when Lydya was just a child.
She'd never heard confirmation of the rumor that he had
mated with an elf before now. Ryan's shields were
formidable, but the power she could wield practically
overwhelmed them.

"Aye. I suppose that makes us second-cousins or some such," the Kin said.

"As close as me, as I said," Kefyn said. "Where's Shyla? I've much to tell her."

"She's at her lessons. You should go clean up from your journey. And this young l—lad?"

"Saryl is from my home," Ryan said. Kefyn took his opportunity to take his horses toward the stables. The Dengyal were uncomfortable with turning their mounts over to the grooms. You could judge it a bigoted stance or that they simply loved their mounts.

"Not related?"

"Mayhap more distantly. Are we related in any way, Saryl?"

"Not that I ever heard. We've messages for you, Lady Lydya."

"Reyn and I only just exchanged messages. Is it urgent?"

"He thought it might be so," Ryan said.

"Then let's go to my greeting chamber so that we can continue this conversation in private."

Lydya turned toward the dun and saw a small body fly across the open gap between roofs once more.

Ryan paused in her stride and stared at the roof. Saryl's mouth dropped open like a village lass seeing the town market for the first time.

"I'm sure you'll explain that when we're in private," Ryan said with a twinkle.

Lydya ordered a flagon of water on the way and led the two Denygal up to the third floor of the central dun, where she had carved out a generous slice of the floor for her private abode. She had benches with cushions, Morikan rugs, and real glass in the windows. When she threw up her privacy weave, she bumped against one already in place.

"My apologies," Ryan said. "I assumed you couldn't …."

"You'll find that quarter elves here are much stronger than they are in Denygal or the mountains. My theory is that it is the closeness to the basketlands, but I have no proof of that."

Ryan seemed to look inward for a moment.

"Mayhap you're onto somewhat," she agreed while Lydya worked the knot on the message tube.

> *These young women are bound on a mission. Do what you can to help them. There are prophesies that suggest the One's True King may be rising and there is an army amassing in the northern sea that we believe will one day turn its attention to Celdrya. Anything you can do to warn the vyngretrio, the better.*
>
> *While she will likely not admit it to you, Ryanna is betrothed to your brother, Padraig. Also, Ryen and I have a difficulty. Servitors are starting to*

> *ask about our fertility. How do*
> *you overcome such issues?*
> *Lillirigga*

How would I who have six children know that? Lydya wondered. *Marry a man with less Kin blood than my brother? Find a Kin herbalist to prepare the right tea? I suppose I'll have to suggest somewhat. Later.*

Lydya turned to the Kin women who hadn't sat down. When Lydya offered the upholstered benches, they looked ill-at-ease. Finally, Ryan said "We've not bathed, cousin."

"Of course, I forget the manners of Kin. Why do I keep seeing images of my brother Padraig?"

"He's a friend," Ryan said. Saryl snorted. Ryan looked annoyed. "We smiled at one another."

"I see. He mentioned you, though not by name. He's far off to the west now."

"I've not been called to follow him." Ryan's voice was dark enough that she could pass for a male. Some Celdryan men were shorter and she looked comfortable with her thumbs hooked in her sword belt. Saryl looked much more feminine.

"And you, why are you on this journey?"

"Walkabout. My father was Celdryan. I want to know about his people."

"But not about him?"

"He's dead," Ryan said. "I knew the man who killed him."

That was a lie of sorts, what one keeps not to hurt someone they care about. The lass does not look distressed. Surely there is some mystery in this, but they seem unwilling to share and it's really not my concern.

"What is your mission?" Lydya asked.

"Travel to Dunmaden. That's all of it that I know right now."

"There's brigands upon the roads twixt here and there and an occasional pirate foray. Best to travel in caravan."

"Are there any headed out?" Ryan asked.

"I'm the wife of the rig, not the merchant's guild master. I do know that an escort is coming from Galornyn to take my son back to page and other commerce. They're mayhap a day out of Galornyn, so it will be some days before they reach us."

Ryan sighed before speaking with Saryl.

"It will give us time to canoe across the lake to Ama'na. You can see the settlement and decide your next course."

Saryl nodded. Lydya went to the door to receive the flagon of water and detailed the serving lass who brought it to see to a private bath for her guests in a shared chamber in an auxiliary broch.

"Will you continue to comport as men or be women while you are here?" she asked.

The Kin looked at each other and Lydya felt the illusionary weave dissolve. She still saw two Kin women dressed as males, but others would now see their true faces. Ryan might still be able to pass as a male without the glamour.

"What is your part in this mission?" Lydya asked Saryl.

"I'm just traveling with Ryanna," Saryl explained. "I'm still waiting for God's guidance."

"You are much too trusting," Ryan snapped. "She is a Believer, but she might not be."

"I took you're dropping the glamour to mean …."

"Never take aught for granted this side of the Dragon's Back. You stand to get us both killed."

"But all is well as I am both a Believer and a Denygal, though truly Ryanna is right to be wary. Saryl – is that the name you wish to go by?"

"We'll be maintaining the glamour outside of these rooms," Ryanna said. "At least for as long as you ride with me. Getting killed defending your honor will not be fulfilling God's mission. This isn't a lark for me."

"I accept that," Saryl said."

Another tap at the door brought a platter of meats, cheeses and fresh berries. The Kin women accepted stools and asked after conditions farther to the west.

"Lord Cunyr has strengthened patrols to the Blyan crossing, but Blyan lacks the coin to patrol as often and Dunmaden suffers from its separation from Galornyn. We heard they managed to rout a lot in the spring, but others may have taken their place."

"Has it occurred to anyone that the nobles are causing the brigands?" Ryan demanded.

"It's occurred to me, lass … lad, but I have naught to say about it outside of Dengyal, which last had a brigand problem in – never. A king … the right king …

might help the matter, but there's no one been found for that task and who would want it anyway?"

"The True King lives," Ryan intoned and Lydya felt the truth of her statement vibrate to her core.

Outside she heard a whoop and a terrified lass's scream, followed by the sound of feet clattering on roof tiles. She ran to the window and saw Danyl disappearing over a parapet.

"Yours, I assume," Ryan said.

"My youngest. Wild as a spring hare."

"It's the bane of parents of elflings," Ryan noted. "He's a powerful personality. I could feel it from here."

"I just want him to stop this foolishness before he falls and breaks his neck."

Ryan stared after Danyl with unfocused eyes. Lydya felt the power behind her shields.

"Somewhat is … I know naught." She shook herself like a dog coming out of water. "I'll try to catch him up and see what can be done by someone with Wisdom."

"I thought that might be what you are."

"Reluctantly, but you're right about the lad … he's risking his neck."

"I climbed the rock face from the horse meadow to the baths when I was scarcely any older," Saryl reported. "I survived, but they also found other tasks to divert my attention after that."

"I'm sure I was doing somewhat similar," Ryan admitted with a laugh. "But we'll see what we can do."

A tap came on the door. It was a serving lass to take them to their chamber where their baths awaited.

After they left, Lydya leaned in the window for a while, staring where Danyl had disappeared, shaking with cold dread. Then she remembered that she had sent Cullyn to his chambers.

The lad had obeyed and was sitting at the table with a book open in front of him, mayhap actually studying the Annals of the Celtic Migrations. He stood up as soon as she came into the room.

"You encouraged him, didn't you?"

"Nay, he overheard Glynn and I talking about how we'd done a similar leap a few years ago."

"I believe that, but you're lying about not encouraging him further than that. Do you really want me to ask Glynn for details?"

Cullyn's jaw hardened.

"It doesn't take much to encourage him, Mam. He's wild. If you won't acknowledge it, that's your fault, none of mine."

Lydya restrained herself from smacking him across the face.

"You will stay here in your chamber without food until I come to you on the marrow. Do not stir past this door or I will have you flogged."

She turned and left the room, shaking with rage.

I mayhap made an error in bearing Danyl, but I know for certain that I erred in bringing Cunyr's spawn into the world.

Galornyn Road

Gregyn felt ill-armed without his powers. He couldn't so much as light a fire by magic or sense brigands a mile away. He went to bed the first night carrying the secret of having turned to the southern road, quite exhausted from living like a wholly natural man. Being the sergeant, he shared Taryn's tent and enjoyed the luxury of his table, the cook acting as serving man. When the mead in his saddle bottle turned to vinegar, Taryn grew testy. When the exchange of the two casks became known, he became petulant. Still, he hadn't kicked Gregyn out of the tent, though truth-told, he wasn't the most restful of tent mates. He tossed and turned most of the night and left the tent early in the morn to go for a walk, leaving Gregyn to detail the men and make preparations for travel.

It wasn't until the morn of the third day that Taryn remarked that the road between duns seemed very long. Taryn had awakened late rather than early, so they were hardly upon the road by midday.

"Maddw suggested we take this route because of the brigand activity in the north."

"You seem to know the road."

"I've traveled it a time or two." The southern route took Gregyn to the Tongue more directly than the northern, but he preferred to keep that sort of knowledge to himself.

Where are the other mages? I can't sense Talidd, I've had no contact with any of them. Yet I feel Naranddal. Has he ensorcelled me? Of course, he has. How else might he block me from my gifts.

Taryn gazed about at the forest to their left and the long stretch of seaward prairie interspersed with second-growth trees to their right. His eyes lingered on a remnant of stone wall.

"What used to be here?" he asked.

"This was a king's road," Gregyn supplied, gesturing to the paving stones that could be seen under decades of debris.

"Aye and most of the king's roads have settlements along them still. Why is this one neglect?"

The question had never occurred to Gregyn before. It was simply a faster way to the Tongue and, by happenstance, to Clarcom.

"I don't know," he admitted. "Do you expect somewhat dangerous?"

"Nay. Maddw is a skilled and experienced war leader. He would not suggest this route without knowing what it would lead us to."

Truth-told, I suggested the route, but I've encountered no danger on this way.

Gregyn weighed whether to tell that truth and chose not to.

"How far to the next dun?"

"The Averblyan is six days by the route I know well."

Taryn turned toward him with a weighing gaze.

"You aren't describing the duns."

"I'm a common-born rider. What would I know of duns?"

"You'd know if you'd seen any, I think."

"We've got enough food."

"Was part of his plan that there'd be no mead or wine and no resupply?"

"I'm not privy to his plan."

"But you agree with it?"

"I'm a common born rider and not fit to judge your noble brother's plan."

"My brother isn't here and you clearly were aware of the condition of this road."

There it is. The crack of noble authority, driven by annoyance.

"Who is in command of this trip – me or Maddw?"

Gregyn's instinct was to bite his tongue, but in all honesty, if Talidd was dead, he'd have to make his own way in this world. That meant proving to noblemen that he fit in their world. Taryn was a child playing at adulthood, but he was one place to start.

"Respectfully, these mornings it has looked as if I was in command."

"This doesn't sound respectful."

"I believe your brother teaches that a captain must listen to his sergeant. I mean my advice in respect. If you sleep til noontide and complain at having to drink as the men do, you make yourself look like a child rather than a commander. There is more to command than riding at the front of the column and getting special food and drink."

Taryn opened his mouth to protest, then snapped his lips shut, cheeks darkening. Gregyn waited for an explosion that did not come. An odd feeling washed over him like the touch of another mage's power, but in his incapacity he could only experience it, not analyze it.

"You may drop back now," Taryn finally said and Gregyn obeyed, still ruminating on the sensation he'd experienced.

Could Talidd be reaching out to me? Sawyl? Or did Naraddal set someone to follow me?

Instinctively, he reached for the Source, but it remained stubbornly out of his grasp. And then a sprite materialized on his saddle peak.

She grinned at him, her blue face actually lovely for all that her teeth were pointed and her eyes were catslit.

He'd not seen the Wildfolk since the day in the rain and he hadn't really felt their absence until now, but her appearance was fortuitous – if he could speak to her without power. He formed a picture in his mind of rising up over the forest and the prairie and looking about. She blew him a kiss and popped out of existence. He didn't know if that meant she'd understood or if she'd simply gone off on an adventure of her own.

I should slow to check on the men.

She materialized on the saddle peak once more. She spread her long fingered hands all round her, pointed to her eyes and shrugged, then shook her head. Then she winked at him and disappeared once more.

I hope that means she didn't see anything. Wildfolk are so unreliable!

The day proved beautiful for traveling, the sky hard blue and the air hot, but humid enough to keep down the dust. A gentle breeze from the coast washed the road. The horses had a jaunt to their step and the king's road was a good surface for the supply wagon. If the sprite told truthfully, they hadn't a care in the world before stopping to camp for the night.

Without my power, I have naught to do but ride in the column and wait upon my commander. Gods help me that it is a child and a sot.

When the afternoon shadows came, Taryn showed no sign of stopping, so Gregyn took command once more as they passed a copse of trees on the far side of the road from the forest. Taryn was a quiet presence who chose to sit away from the men. Gregyn turned aside to check the horse pickets, thinking that it would be another uncomfortable night in the tent, when he heard gravel crunch under a boot. Taryn stopped well-back.

"You don't think much of me, do you?"

"I think nobles don't see much of life before they leave page. Did you even serve page?"

"I spent a year at my uncle's dun. I didn't understand why it wasn't more, but Maddw included me in arms training. I kept waiting for my father to offer me to the temple, but he didn't. It always seemed as if they were waiting for somewhat, but they've taken their sweet time in telling me what it is."

"Have they?"

"Aye. You wouldn't understand. It's not an ordinary sort of occurrence. Now I have to decide what I will become."

You would have been a truly remarkable apprentice. Who is currying you now?

"Mayhap you are meant to help me. I've been very lazy," Taryn admitted. "It was easier to play than to take life seriously. I am near a man and I've not learned what I should. Mayhap you will guide me."

"Me, sir? I'm but a common rider."

"Aye, but you are a man and one who has lived life and led men."

"A bit."

"That's a bit more than I have done. I think that Egoran sent me on this mission to make a man of me or break me. I wish to return home a man. Will you help me with that?"

"Aye, if you're willing … starting in the morn."

"Good then. Now I'm going to go have a tankard of ale – just one – and not complain about it."

Gregyn grinned at him, but did not follow. He needed time to think and to plan. Mayhap he could not take Taryn to apprentice, but he could use him as a means to an end nonetheless. Mayhap.

Clarcom

Shyla nee Riordan waited in the darkness of the garden, surrounded by the fragrance of blooming trees and roses. The sound of merriment drifted through the warm evening from the open door of the great hall. A lithe male figure emerged from the shadows, smiling at her.

"I've been trying to catch up with you since I arrived this afternoon," he said. Kefyn ap Shyr had grown several inches and his voice was magnificently deeper since the last time she'd met him in Denygal two years before.

"My goodness, look how tall you are now!"

"You've blossomed."

Shyla felt her cheeks redden. Her long hair still flowed down her back unrestrained, but she more and more felt uncomfortable with the sound of a male voice or the gaze of lads only slightly older than herself. She'd known Kefyn her whole life and had never before felt this odd feeling in her lower belly when in his presence.

"My Mam says I must stay in public places with lads now."

"Your mam sounds sensible. I saw Bryan on my way here."

"He visited in the spring. We met his bride's father."

"He's putting a brave face on that one."

"Her mother's pretty enough. Mayhap not that bright, but the daughter's young, Mam says."

"And not a Believer."

"We who live here in the south cannot guarantee who our spouses will be."

"Being a Celdryan noblewoman is akin to slavery, my Mam says. Do you think your mam will allow us to go riding?"

"We can ask. My hair is still unbound, so mayhap."

"Nobility is so messy."

"It is. You brought the two Kin lasses, didn't you?"

"Shh, they're under glamour."

"I know, but they're fascinating. The taller of the two is going to compete in the tourney."

"There's a tourney?"

"When Cullyn rides away, we'll have a day. Will you compete?"

"Mayhap in archery. I'm trained at arms, but I hope never to test my mettle in a real scrap."

Shyla turned and frowned as a wave of somewhat unpleasant washed over her.

"What has happened to you?"

"Nay ... naught. Some time, men must do what they wish not for the good of folk, but it makes us sad no less."

When they touched hands, Shyla felt the bow in her hands and saw the sheep thief at a distance. She broke the vision before he could complete the memory.

"I am sad for you," she said, brushing away a tear.

"I've not shared that pain with anyone else."

"I am honored that you would share it with me."

Her stomach felt funny – cramping, like she'd eaten too much meat. They walked together to the stairs that led up to her chamber. Kefyn pushed a tendril back from her cheek. Heat washed through her.

"I shouldn't go further," he decided. "Ask your mam about the riding. If naught else we can wander the public grounds together."

He gently handed her into the stairwell, closed the door and left her. The candle lanterns hung on hooks lit the stairs as she climbed. By the time she'd reached her chamber, she felt the wetness in her small clothes. She'd looked forward to this day for years and yet ... what did that mean for riding with Kefyn?

Veil Parted

It's a curious custom of the Kin that the Denygal also use. The elvish word is goi'tan. It means "silent man". Men and woman alike serve a time of silence, their heads shaved, working as servants, when they break the rules of the Fey religion. They are not slaves. It is voluntary. Some of these people seem to have really benefitted from their time and speak highly of the practice.

**Nolyn, Priest of Bel,
Dun Moryn (FY 978)**

Past

Founding Year 931 – A century ago
High Celdrya

*B*urcan ap Manahan of Mulyn sat on the wide sill of his chamber window, watching the dun's goings-on. He had tarried here since Perryn's death, awaiting the vyngretroi decision and then had remained in hopes of seeing Deryk hanged before returning to his bride and newborn son. He'd grown restless, but with the arrival of his twin brother Joran today some of his pent-up energy had dissipated.

"The messengers must be headed northward by now," Joran said from the table where he was viewing a map of the kingdom. "You'd think they'd have caught Donyl on the road by now."

"Donyl mayhap is already dead," Burcan said. Joran blinked at him. They bore striking resemblance to one another, except that Burcan bore a scar on his cheek from a youthful duel.

"Why do you believe that?"

"I'm not certain, but no one actually saw him leave. Mayhap Deryk did away with him and just left us all to believe he rode off to Denygal."

"Truly? You believe that to be the case?"

"I believe a regicide would have no problem killing a prince."

"I actually like Donyl, you know? Maryn was altogether too confident in his place and Perryn would have been an annoying king, but Donyl is smart and well read."

Joran's admiration for the intellect always left Burcan with little to say. This was a world that needed men of action, not intellectuals. Donyl had not been fit to be king.

"What does it mean if he is dead?" Joran asked.

"It can pass in the female line. Cadda should have been named regent with you named her protector."

"They hesitate over the matter of Donyl's fate. Cadda would stand as regent for … Jaryn?"

"Aye. Your son might be the future king."

"That feels odd as your boy is the elder of the two."

"True enough. It's also true that there's some question if Loryna or Cadda is the older. Twins are so hard to tell apart." They grinned at one another because a similar situation existed between them.

"But Cadda is recorded first." After finishing the joke, Joran sobered. "I am grateful for what you have allowed me to do as a younger brother. I do not seek to put my son upon the throne."

"Neither of us sought it, Joran. It's what fate has brought to us. You will raise a fine king and I think my son will enjoy the benefits of their close relationship."

"Of course … if Donyl is dead. He may turn up."

Which is why you should raise a king and not me, because I find myself hoping he doesn't.

A bell tolled the 5th watch and Burcan straightened from the window sill.

"I've a meeting with Gerriant."

"My bath should be ready by now. Shall we meet after to discuss it?"

Had they been in Mulyn, Burcan would have joked "the bath?" but he took Joran's meaning with due solemnity.

"We should. Gerriant is merely a caretaker until Donyl's fate has been determined."

Gerriant's council room door was open when Burcan arrived. The windows had often been covered in Vanyn's day, but today sunlight washed across the floor and the sitting area where Gerriant waited.

"Close the door so we can have some privacy," the elder lord requested. He sounded as jovial as his reputation but Burcan's father had taught him never to trust other lords beyond his brother. He obeyed and took the seat offered.

"Would you care for tea? I find it a bit early in the day for ale or mead."

Burcan thought tea sounded like drinking dishwater, but he accepted the hospitality. Gerriant was younger than Vanyn by several years, though the step-brothers had reportedly been good friends as adults. In addition to the tea, there were tea cakes and a platter of fresh fruit. Gerriant poured and offered a plate.

"I hear you're a father now," he began.

"I am, as is my brother."

Gerriant leaned back in his padded chair and sipped tea.

"Both babes healthy, then?"

"Aye, both healthy boys. What of the search for Donyl?"

If the news of Mulyn's fertility concerned him, Gerriant's expression did not let on. *How politic a man is he!*

"Ongoing. I'm hoping that Deryk can give us better information about his journey plans once his fever has broken."

"Why heal him for the noose?"

"Because he is a nobleman and the killing for both Prince Maryn and King Perryn smacks of fell magicks."

"Not to mention King Vanyn."

"Far as I can ascertain, Vanyn was poisoned. That suggested the Assassins' Guild, but three murderes in short order does rather make one think."

"You don't think I got them all in Clengaryn?"

Gerriant selected a grape, savored it, took a sip of tea and poured himself fresh before answering.

"I rather think you burned a village of innocents and there were no assassins at all in that inn."

Stunned, Burcan forgot to breathe for several heartbeats as he remembered women and children being pushed back into the flames.

"Why would you think that?" he demanded gruffly.

Gerriant drank another sip of tea.

"To gauge your reaction. You clearly thought the assassins were in the village. Why?"

Why indeed!

"Malona's eyes and ears found them."

"Malona? Vanyn's mistress?"

"Aye. She was a shadow hunter before Lady Rhodda's death."

"Curious occupation for a woman," Gerraint noted. "I honestly do not remember much about her. I saw her at the last council meeting. Did Vanyn task her with finding Maryn's killer?"

"He tasked us all with that, did he not? She came to me the day after Vanyn's death and said one of her eyes and ears had learned a possible source of the wolfsbane, a witch woman who lived near Clengaryn. I rode there immediately, but this woman was merely an apothecary who was known to sell abortifacients on the sly. She told me of the assassins in the inn."

"Did you verify her claim?"

"Of course. I sent two of my riders in and they spent two days assuring that the men she'd marked were assassins."

"How did they accomplish that?"

"Listening to conversations, chivvying the serving girls. They are men I trust. They found a nest of five."

"How did you come to fire the entire village instead of simply arresting the assassins?"

"While my men were at the inn, I had others getting acquainted with the village. The assassins had been socializing with the mayor and other prominent citizens, including the innkeeper. I couldn't be sure who had been compromised and I never got an accurate count of the number of assassins."

"Children and women, Burcan?"

A young mother with her babe clasped to her chest ran out of a cottage, her hair on fire.

"I followed Dumyr's orders."

"Dumyr? I can't imagine that he would make such a bold gesture with his lord dead and the succession in question. When did you speak to him?"

"I didn't." A silver tube knotted with scarlet, sealed with golden wax and the stallion rampant of House Trevellyn. "A messenger brought my orders. It was signed by Dumyr."

"And it said …?"

"To fire the village and let none escape."

Cold dread crept into Burcan's gut and coiled itself round his heart.

Why does this feel like a lie?

"Deryk had aught to do with this?"

"Nay. He stayed behind to be questioned over both incidents."

"Who led the questioning?"

"I assume Councillor Dumyr, Chamberlain Rhys, Equerry Joffryn, and Steward Llorthyn. I was not privy. Truth be told, Deryk was in his cups from Maryn's death to the funeral and little help in finding Vanyn's killers."

Gerriant ate a slice of apple.

Why am I telling him more than I had planned? Is it his silence that compels me?

"Was your brother Joran part of this campaign?"

"Nay. He was in Mulyn at the time of Maryn's death and arrived the day after we moved on the village."

What are you about, old man? Seeking a way to deny Cadda her right?

"I'm trying to sort out all the evidence. Do you have any idea where Malona might have got off to?"

"I knew naught of her missing before you mentioned it. I simply thought she was staying out of sight before connecting herself to another man of power."

Gerriant set his tea mug aside.

"She was Vanyn's mistress for some time. Had she moved on to any others?"

"Lord Deryk."

"Deryk and Malona? Was that a pre-existing relationship?"

"I'm not a member of the court to know such things. I was here for the wedding and I saw her slipping into his chamber of an evening."

"Were there others?"

"Mayhap. I've no knowledge."

Should I tell him of the rumors of Perryn in her bed? Nay, it will be better if some other tells him. Mayhap she knew what Deryk did with Donyl's body.

Gerriant stared into his tankard as he poured the last of the tea.

"I'll be questioning others. Is there more you have to add?"

"Nay, my lord." *Now is not the time to broach the subject of Donyl or the succession. Soon enough, they'll know the obvious.* "Thank you for the audience. May I go now?"

"Aye. Stay in Celdrya until I release you." Burcan nodded and turned to leave. "And ... ask your brother to join me at the next watch."

"Aye, my lord," Burcan said with wooden lips, inclining his head slightly before withdrawing.

The man is more cunning than I imagined. Might he challenge us for the regency.

Present

Founding Year 1028
Glenconyn Prairie

*T*he dreams became clearer. He skimmed over the earth, a shadow sweeping across the passing landscape. At first he'd enjoyed seeing, but with every day that passed, he became more aware of other senses. He was flying, feeling the wind all around him, hearing a city's life as he passed overhead. Even as he puzzled over these sensations, he rejected the obvious implications. It was a dream, mayhap a consequence of his injuries. Then whatever body he seemed to inhabit stooped on a rabbit and he tasted blood and fur in his mouth.

He jolted awake, a throb of pain stabbing through his head. Laying quiet, trying to control the pain, he realized that the travois had stopped moving. He listened to the world round him, trying to sort out where they were and what time it might be.

He didn't think they were near a town. He couldn't hear the ordinary sounds of the caravanserai – the well windless, horse tack, folk calling back and forth, children chasing dogs. He didn't think it was night – it was too warm and the insects weren't biting yet.

He pushed the blankets off and sat up, feeling out of step with his environment. He gripped the side of the travois, swung his legs over the edge and found that the travois was off the ground by an arm's length.

"Do you need help, lad?" Padraig asked.

"I need to piss and I need you not to hold the jar."

"Of course." Padraig had moved closer and now he touched Tamys's arm. "I'll take you there and leave you to it. It's all grass here, not many trees, so walking barefoot is probably fine."

Tamys allowed Padraig to guide him over to a tree. He left him with his hand on the trunk. Everything took extra time. Moving quickly hurt and made his head spin. He thought he'd never get his breecs back up and laced. When he called, Padraig came and guided him to a blanket by the fire. Tamys could smell game bird cooking on the spit.

"Where are we?" he asked.

"Out on the prairie south of the villages. I think we've left actual civilization. According to some folks, there's some elvish ruins farther south."

"I thought your folk were on the Eastern mountains."

"When the Celdryans pushed through the northern passes, they moved along the Aver Celt. The elves hung on in some parts of the east for several years. The ones to the west may have stayed for longer since the Celts were slower to move to the west."

Padraig portioned out the food and they ate in companionable quiet. Tamys couldn't eat much, but he thought his appetite might be returning.

"How are you feeling?" Padraig asked, giving him a wet rag to wipe his fingers on.

"I'm mending, I think."

"There's a pond here and you, my friend, could really use a bath."

"Do I smell?"

"Aye."

Tamys agreed, though he panicked when he first stepped into the water. The water was warm from the sun, but the sensation on his legs felt too harsh. He flailed and grabbed at Padraig's arm.

"Easy, lad. The water stays shallow. There's naught to worry about."

"It feels like it's biting my feet."

"That's your senses trying to sort out the world without sight, I think. There's a rock here that stands above the water. Do you want to sit on it while you get used to the water?"

Padraig guided him to the rock, helped him remove his small clothes and the cloth over his eyes, then left him to rest. Tamys sat listening to the lap of the water and a light breeze through the trees. The stone was warm under his bare bottom. He felt the roughness of the stone with his fingers while he listened to Padraig scrubbing his clothes some distance away. There were flowers blooming nearby, but not the ones he knew from Mulyn, so he couldn't identify them. Behind him, one of the horses had defecated. His legs stopped crawling with imaginary ants and when he rinsed water up his legs, they didn't react negatively. He risked opening his eyes.

The multi-tone gray that had greeted him for a month had been replaced with multi-tonal colors – scarlet, gold and blue.

"Is there a sunset?" he asked, pointing forward.

"Aye. You can see it?"

"I can see colors. I can't make sense of them." He held his hand before his face, but couldn't see it. He turned it, flexed his fingers, but all he could see were the field of colors.

"I can't see," he muttered, easing himself into the water. "Why did you camp so early?" he asked.

"You're fulfilling my plan," Padraig said. "When I saw the pond just after midday, I thought we'd bide here until I got you into the water."

"The smell must truly have been offensive." A dark image appeared in the colors, causing him to flinch. He reached for it, but his hand met air.

"Nay, though you needed a bath. I'm hoping you'll start to feel better after this. I can see you're healing, but your melancholy is slowing your recovery." Tamys heard Padraig wading about. "There's a bowl with soap and a rag here now. I'll help you shave when you're ready."

Wiping his hand over his face surprised him with a soft beard. He'd always hated facial hair. *How could I not have known? Is this what the bards mean by stone of melancholy?*

"I've never had another shave me," he admitted.

"Then you'll be committed to learning to do it yourself. Clean up. I've clothes to rinse and hang."

Tamys fumbled about until he found the soap and rag on the rock. For some reason, sinking down in the water filled his chest with anxiety, so he used the bowl to pour water over his head. When he opened his eyes after, someone was standing in front of him and he slammed his back into the rock before he realized there was no one there.

"Somewhat, lad?" Padraig asked from a distance.

"I don't – there's – I can't explain it. What I can see makes no sense to me."

"Best not to try, then. I'm taking these to the fire. You'll get on fine here. I'm within earshot."

"Aye." Tamys wondered if "these" were his clothes.

Padraig returned to shave him. The field of colors had faded to multi-tonal purple.

"Is the sun going down?"

"There's mountains to the west – a good deal away. The sun is hopping along the tops, but the sky is darkening and the sunset fading."

"Is there a moon?"

"There won't be. Maybe a thumbnail. It's dark of the moon."

It's been a month. That's why he thinks I should be adjusting. How do you adjust to having no eyes?

"There. Managed without nicking you. You getting weary?"

"Aye."

Padraig helped him up onto the rock and into small clothes.

"Your clothes are drying, so let's just wrap this round you." The blanket of northern wool felt soft and warm round his shoulders. He let Padraig lead him cross the camp to the travois.

"How is it elevated?"

"A fallen tree on one end and a log I rolled over on the other. Before you sit down …" Padraig put his hand on a tree trunk then directed it upward to a rope. "That leads to our squatting area, should you wake in the night and need to." Padraig directed Tamys' other hand downward to the travois.

"Thanks to you," Tamys said, sinking onto the waiting blankets.

"If you need somewhat, I won't be far. Just over at the fire."

Tamys located it by the smell of burning wood. After a few breaths, the rosy glow filled his sight.

"What do you know of blindness?" he asked. "I'd always heard that it was darkness, but I can see light and color – sort of."

"Your pupils still react to light as well. I left before that part of the training. I don't know why you are blind, but not quite. I can tell you what's going on inside your head. My gifts allow that much. Why it affects your eyes …." He sighed.

"Mayhap it isn't permanent. It appears to be getting better … a little."

"Aye, that's the spirit. You should sleep. Tomorrow night, I hope to get you on your horse."

"A blind man riding a war horse?"

"War horses are used to clumsy handling, trained to take wounded men off the field. And there's not a thing for miles that you might run into. We'll see how you feel on the morrow. Lay down. Get some rest."

Tamys yawned as if in agreement. He lay down. The world spun round the travois, gently depositing him into darkness.

The Tongue

*M*agic flowed through him as it had not done in decades. It straightened his limbs and cleared his mind. He knew what he must do and he set about to do it. What journeymen remained to him must be found and called to heel. There had been an indwelling. This was no time to scatter to the four winds.

Outside the lodge, the jungle came alive with a riot of bird song and the grunts of bull crocs. The acolytes prepared Talidd's body with reverence. They apparently did not know what Talidd had been – did not understand the true black heart of evil.

There were few high-level journeymen left. Traegyr in Clarcom, Werglidd in Galornyn, Melchyr in Mulyn responded quickly through the scrying length. Jaryn could sense Sawyl, but the mendicant seemed somehow shielded. There were mayhap a dozen lesser journeymen plying their trade as poisoners. Most of the apprentices responded quickly. Jaryn did not know what to make of the grey-eyed apprentice who went by the name Gregyn. Jaryn wondered how Talidd could have gone so long and not realized that the lad's true name was not Gregyn. Did the lad himself know his own true name? At any rate, Jaryn couldn't try name magic on him because whenever he reached out, it was if the lad were covered in a glass dome. He still lived, bit he was shielded in someway Jaryn and what remained of Talidd had never seen before.

Nay, he had felt this before. It felt somewhat like a grey mage shield. How those dabblers erected them was unknown among the black. Was Gregyn therefore captured?

Unable to sort it out, Jaryn left the mystery of Gregyn aside for the time being to deal with the disposal of Talidd's body. The acolytes had acted without direction except for the oldest, who had no doubt participated in burials before. Their preparations would not do.

Talidd did not deserve a celebration. Even at the risk of angering the raven-god, Jaryn would not have Talidd honored.

"Sssstop," he ordered. The acolytes all turned toward him. The eldest might have been 14. Jaryn limped into the clearing between the buildings and tapped the platform with his walking stick. "Nnnah. Wwwe ddddid nnnnnot lllllllllllove hhhhim. Hhhhhhe wwwwwas cccccrrrrruel annnnnd hhhhhurt us innnn eeeeevvvvvilllll wwwways."

He paused. He had not said this many words since the last time Talidd had conducted a spell of this magnitude. He was drooling and his jaws hurt. He wanted to be understood. A few deep breaths relaxed his mouth. In the silence, the eldest asked the inevitable question.

"What should we do with his body then?"

All knew that you couldn't bury bodies in the swamp. They floated to the surface eventually, spreading disease.

Jaryn nodded, pleased that one so young was wise.

"Wwwwhat wwwwould yyyyyou dddddddo wwwwith ttttthisssss eeeeevvvvvvilllll mmmman?"

The acolyte, whose name was Daryl, considered a moment. Jaryn could hear his heart beating faster.

"Leave him for the swamp beasts," he decided.

Jaryn smiled and saluted him. Some of the younger ones began to cry, but the older acolytes laughed to be about this business. They used a sledge to drag Talidd's body out to the edge of one of the green lagoons, then rolled him into the mud. They all found places to sit in the mangroves and waited. After the sun had moved a thumb's worth to the west, a bull croc stumped up out of the water. Grabbing Talidd's leg, it pulled the body into the green water. Blood left a dark trail as it bore the master of evil into the bayou and then, Talidd was no more.

Best forgotten, Jaryn thought … except for his twisted body, halting speech and the raven, of course.

Southern Galornyn

*T*aryn twisted beneath his blankets, awakening for the fourth time that night. He lay drenched in sweat upon his cot, know that he was done with sleep. Tossing the blankets aside, he stared up at the canvas ceiling. Somewhat pulled at his mind's eye. Else he was missing mead more than he should. Or ale. He'd been drinking watered for the last two days, trying to disprove to himself what he knew to be true.

I am too fond of drink.

On the other side of the tent, Gregyn's cot lay empty. Taryn couldn't really blame the rider for seeking another sleeping arrangement.

How many times did I wake him tonight before he left?

Gregyn made a habit of passing unnoticed, so that Taryn never heard him leave.

His tongue stuck to the roof of his mouth, Taryn sat up and rummaged in a saddle bag for tepid water. It helped a bit. The sweat began to dry on his chest. The band had camped along a lake this night. Taryn wrapped his cloak over his small clothes and carried a towel barefoot to the water's edge. A fire lit the circle of tents. There were three on guard, but the rest of the men were sleeping. It must not be near to dawn as the cook wasn't mending up the fire.

The water was still sun-warmed as he launched into the deeper shallows. He saw one of the guards turn to mark him, but there was enough light from the crescent moon to be seen. Rolling onto his back, he lazily stroked out into the deeper water and then just floated, looking up at the stars. The sky reminded him of the black cloth his mother wore as she pretended to mourn his father. That got his mind chewing over thoughts of Teddryn. Then he turned to Gregyn and his lover.

He assumed Naryna had been Gregyn's lover. Clearly, he'd cared for her. She'd been taken right fast by the plague. Taryn could have sworn he'd seen her hail that day, Gregyn whispering in her ear. Gregyn's disappearance during his own illness still nettled. Taryn liked the rider well enough, but his curiosity piqued to know more of the lad's history.

Why do such odd things seem to happen round him?

It seemed that everyday he felt new sensations and thought new ideas.

Unchain these gifts and then send me on a journey. Aye, Maddw, that was a sensible choice. What could possibly go wrong?

A guard shouted, muffled by the water in his ears. Taryn's eyes flew open to see a flight of large birds cross the sky above them. With his head out of the water, he heard the flight as birds of prey. He returned to the shore and walked out of the water as the last of the birds headed west. The night was warm, but goose flesh covered his arms. Wrapped in his cloak, he met Gregyn at the fire.

"That creeped my flesh," he reported.

"Then this will creep it even more," the rider said, holding up a feather longer than his forearm.

"What is it?"

"Raven, but cursed big – the biggest I've seen in my life."

Tamys put out his finger to touch the feather, but a feeling of filth crept up his arm before he made contact, so that he withdrew his hand.

"Do you feel that?" he asked.

"Power?"

"Power, aye, but more … evil," Taryn identified, shuddering violently.

Gregyn frowned.

Does he not feel it? Taryn watched as Gregyn set the feather down on a rock by the fire and wiped his hand on his breecs. *Does he not feel it or is he simply not surprised by it?*

They walked to the tent.

"Should I dress for the day?"

"It's barely past midnight," Gregyn assured him.

Who are you? I know you're not just a rider. The signs have been there all along and I was too distracted to question them. But now …. And, yet, you don't admit to feeling somewhat from the feather. Are you a liar or ….

Gregyn had been different since his illness. There was a tentativeness that was wholly unlike what Taryn was familiar with. What had happened to him and was it somewhat Taryn should be concerned with?

Gregyn had set the feather down on the table. Taryn stopped to stare at it. Black, as long as his forearm, as wide as his hand. What manner of bird might shed such? Gregyn said a raven.

I can't trust him to tell me the truth, even if he knows it.

Taryn touched the feather with a finger. A shudder ran down his back. He picked it up and stalked out to the campfire to throw it in the flames. A guard gazed at him from near by, but nobody asked what he was after. When he returned to the tent, Gregyn was sitting on his own bunk. Whatever he was thinking, he kept it to himself, but there a sheen of sweat glistened on his face.

Blue Iris Holt

*T*he stone beneath her bottom had begun to push its way up through the pad. It was time to admit her limits. She was no closer to the information the holt needed than she'd been when she'd started this meditation.

Sometimes it was like this. She couldn't turn her Calling on and off. It came when it came or it did not and she could only wait and hope.

Shanara rolled up off the floor, working out a cramp in her left leg. Her cupboard contained some dried venison and some hearth bread. She made a meal of that along with some soft cheese. Beyond her isinglass windows, the summer day tempted her. She had been at this all morning.

She tugged on boots and walked out into the box canyon where she lived. She could hear the sounds of the holt at the far end of the canyon, but folk rarely disturbed her because she was known to value her privacy. In the summers, she set up a sitting area and bath just outside her door, the bath enclosed by a wood screen. She walked almost to the opening of the canyon where it narrowed down from three men's arms span to little more than a single man's arms span. She turned sharply on her heel to walk back to her outdoor living room. She dipped water from the bucket to drink, but the reflections caught her eye. She looked through them with her spiritual eyes and saw ….

A vast flat land stretched for miles, covered with low brush and myriad crooked streams. As her view wheeled along the rock-dotted shoreline of a great grey sea, she focused in on a broken city. As she grew nearer, she recognized the stone as lumina, though unmaintained for many centuries. As she rounded the ancient buildings, hovering like a seagull, she saw the hundreds of long, narrow ships and the men with light hair and reddish beards dressed in boiled leather interspersed with iron.

They laughed and talked among themselves, shifting gear and supplies from some ships to others and then a young man stood up in the bow of one of the ships and began to talk. Shanara did not understand what he said, but the men seemed inspired by his words.

And then she saw the tall figure dressed in dark grey standing in the back and her shock caused the vision to dissolve.

The dipper sank into the water as Shanara ran down the canyon toward the holt. Kin tended to be spontaneous in their activities, so no one thought it amiss that she was running. She wove her way through a crowd of drovers fresh back from their assigned duty and turned into the Hall of the Wise. *Goi'tan* blinked at her as she cut down a small corridor to bang on Gly's workshop door. The Wise leader gave her a curious look when he answered.

"Bad news?" he asked.

"Not yet, but it is coming."

Gly blocked the door open only a crack and set up a Hiding.

"You saw something?"

Shanara explained what she had seen.

"Those sound like what the Celts called Vikings. Fierce warriors, very good sailors. I've never heard of them going inland by more than a few miles."

"Gil would not be involved with them unless they were moving to attack the holts."

"I would agree with that. And you're sure it was a future vision?"

"Yes. It was spring, not mid-summer. It had to be at least a year from now."

"The city is Malektropher" Gly stared at the ceiling for a long time. *Why are visual memories stored in the top of your brain?* "There's somewhat ... I need to do some research. That city was so far from the basketlands. Why?"

"Did it fall to the Celts when they got here?"

"I don't remember, which is why I must research. Please keep searching as only you can. Did you attempt to reach anyone?"

"Padraig's young friend is awake and Padraig is now beyond distant once more. Ryanna told me the council could sit in silence or prepare for what's coming. She is riding at the command of a greater Commander."

"That answer does not surprise me in the least. I really do need to finish my herbal duties for the day, so that I can spend the rest of it researching not just Malektropher but also the other cities. I don't know what it is that ... feels ... odd. It's like when you can't quite remember a word, but it's just on the tip of your tongue." He shrugged. "I must research."

Shanara thanked him for his time and walked out into the holt once more. In the common grounds, she paused to look around at the high walls. On the other side were steep mountain slopes. There were a few old dwarven highways that connected them to the rest of the world, but Blue Iris Holt was relatively protected. Before Ryanna's husband had succumbed completely to his evil nature, he had taught the holt how to defend itself. The guards still walked the gangways above the entrances and they could close the canyons with a few well-placed hammer blows. Blue Iris had tried to spread its knowledge to the other holts, but most had rejected the proposals.

The threat was real. She needed to let other prophets know of her vision, so they could prepare … if they would.

The summer sun beat down on her head and back as she walked back toward her home, thinking of the long hours of scrying ahead of her and praying that it would be enough.

Peace River

The Kin call them ali'ko'tan. It means "those who are confused by the spirits of drink." They don't see many in their society because there is not much fermentation about, but the Denygal see them more often. Both Kin and Denygal value sobriety highly and find ali'ko-tan annoying, but they are also people of great compassion. They feel the ali'ko'tan are suffering and need support. There is a controversy whether serving time as goi'tan helps. I suppose I will be here long enough to find out.

**Nolyn, Priest of Bel,
Dun Moryn (FY 979)**

Past

Founding Year 931
High Celdrya

*L*ady Wymffa, wife of Dumyr, High Councillor of Dun Celdrya, knew her place in the world, but she also occasionally listened to the still small voice that whispered to a compassionate heart. It was that guidance that sent her up the donjon on a sunny late summer day. The climb to the highest floor gave her time to think about what she was going to say, and not just to the prisoner. Her husband would be quite cross with her for her compassion, for he believed Deryk to be a regicide. Wymffa was not nearly so certain.

The marshal unlocked the door to the chamber.

"I'll wait here unless you wish me to accompany you."

"That's most kind of you to remain here." She continued into the large chamber alone. Gerriant had shown great compassion to a doomed man when he had sent Deryk to the top of the donjon. The views in this quarter chamber were breathtaking, encompassing a wide swath of the city's better houses and a slice of the Dome of Arrival.

Deryk's eyes opened when she neared. He'd lost a good deal of weight since last she'd seen him on the night of Perryn's nuptials – the night of Perryn's death. The chirgeon reported he'd stopped eating in the gaol. He'd eaten a bit when he'd been raving with fever the last few days, but now he was returned to setting his jaw against the spoon.

She set her basket on the floor near the bed and dragged a stool across to sit at bedside. He still stared at her while she made herself comfortable. Nay, he did not stare at her. He took her in, but didn't meet her eye. Deryk ap Trevellyn had always been a forthright young man, for all the 15 years she'd known him. That he could not meet her eye spoke volumes.

"I've brought you a selection of treats that I'm hoping will open your heart to me," she told him, lifting the basket and balancing it on the edge of the bed where he was sure to smell the aromas. After a moment, he swallowed and sat up, keeping the blanket arranged to cover his nudity.

"If Gerraint will not take my head, then I am left to starve myself." His voice was flat, lifeless.

"Gerriant must investigate the whole of it before he can grant you peace."

He stopped breathing and tears flooded his eyes.

"There won't be peace for me, Lady Wymffa. Men who did what I did linger in the Gatelands."

She set the basket on the floor where he could reach it if he chose.

"I know what you did and I suspect you yourself do not know why. What happened before you went to Perryn's chamber?"

He wiped the tears from his shaven cheeks with the back of a callused hand.

"My memory is moth-eaten. I was at the feast. I remember you there."

"We danced," she said with a sad smile. "And after …?"

"And then I went to the privies, but … I don't remember the next. It gets foggy until I woke up with that bloody dagger in my hand."

He stared at his hand as if the dagger were still there. Wymffa's heart twisted for him. She didn't want to force him to remember such horrible events.

"Malona disappeared that night," she announced.

His continued his transfixed stare at his hand for several heartbeats and then raised his gaze to the ceiling.

"I didn't kill her."

"I'm sure you didn't. Unlike my husband and others, I am certain you didn't kill Maryn or Vanyn and that you were but an unwitting tool in Perryn's murder."

Deryk's gaze met her eyes for the first time.

"You believe me? Why?

How to explain the inexplicable?

"Maryn was your bosom friend. I cannot imagine you killing him. Vanyn … what would you gain from that? Perryn … rather against your interests, I think. He gave you an honored position. It makes no sense."

"But I did kill Perryn, though I don't know why," he said to his hands.

"True. You were witnessed. Is a sword guilty of what a man does with it?"

"How could someone force me to do somewhat like that?"

"I don't know ... yet, but I think it has somewhat to do with Malona's disappearance."

"Somewhat?"

"Nobody knows when she left. Her chambers were just empty, her horse and carriage gone from the stables. Did she say to you where she might have gone?"

"Nay, why would she?"

"The court claims you were lovers."

Deryn stared at her in frank astonishment.

"I –" He paused, eyes twittering. "I feel that is right, but I can't remember our ever ..." His pale cheeks flushed with embarrassment.

"It's all right. If what I suspect has happened to you is true, you weren't meant to remember."

"I don't ... understand."

"Wicked magicks are at work, Deryk. If that be the case, then I will work to save your life."

He blinked, then shook his head.

"You needn't," he assured her. "I will stand the consequences for what I did. I just want to know why."

Wymffa felt a momentary flush of relief that he understood the truth of his situation.

"I will do my best to answer that question and I hope ... well, if I can do more, I will."

"Nay. You needn't. If my head rolls and I know the truth, it will be enough."

Heartbreaking!

"Lad, you should know – regicides do not face the headsman. They receive Roman executions." Deryk looked stunned as if she'd struck him between the eyes with a stick. "I would spare your life if I can, but to spare you that …."

Deryk remembered to breathe.

"Men dishonor themselves when hung upon the tree."

"Just so. This is why you must remember all that you can so that I might help you avoid that," she explained.

"Why will you help me?"

"Other than I hate fell magicks?" He nodded. "I am a Believer and we seek that no one shall die without knowing Jesu." He stared at her, slowly swallowing. "You are not asking the obvious questions."

"Nay," Deryk replied. "Dun Trevellyn is in the east. My grandmam hailed from Denygal. I know the tales."

"If you tell me to be silent, I will, and still continue my investigation. If you wish to make peace in case you die, I will try to guide you."

He nodded, haunted eyes gazing at his hands once more.

"I would hear you, for surely without this One god, I will be damned."

She reached down for the basket again.

"You should eat a little, to give you strength, so that you might listen the better."

Present

Founding Year 1028
Southern Glenconyn

*H*e wanted it to be real, but he knew it a dream because he could make out the hand before his eyes. The night round him was silver and white, light reflecting off a pond a stone's throw away. He swung his legs to the ground and stood up, wary.

Padraig slept curled in his blankets on the other side of the fire. The horses drowsed near the pond. A raven tekked and a blanket of snow washed down his back.

She seemed to materialize from thin air, wearing only her luscious black hair. He gawked. He'd been lifting the skirts of serving lasses in his father's dune since shortly after his voice changed, but he thought he'd not seen a lass without dresses. Even the harlots of Celdrya had worn gowns.

"There you are," she said, her gaze settling upon him. "Nice, isn't it?" she said.

"The view? Aye."

"That you can see at all is what I mean. We've only a time. It took great will to be here now, but he's taking you to warded ground on the morrow, so it had to be. Do you want to see again, lad?"

"What a ridiculous question! How do I know you?"

"You were promised to me as a lad."

~*Watch yourself, Tamys.* This second female voice felt real in a way that the naked women did not. ~*That one wants your death if you give your trust to her.*

How did he know her? He'd met her … somewhere … before.

"How are we connected?"

"Your father pledged you because you were hers. And if you renew the pledge, I'll give you your sight."

Tamys shuddered as he felt a window sill at the back of his knees.

~*What do I do?*

~*Now you ask the right question. The swords of men can be used against the Ceeley Court.*

An image formed in his mind of Padraig wrapping Tamys' sword in a blanket and installing it in a pannier. Tamys gazed round the camp until he saw the pack saddle and panniers. She slid up beside him.

"Do you want to lay with me?"

"Aye," he said, catching up a blanket from the travois. Her image shifted and he thought of ravens, cursed tall ravens. "The other side of that bush is good. Let me just get some ale to wet our throats."

He walked toward the panniers. She flowed behind him. He flipped the top of the pannier, felt the familiar sword and pulled it from its sheath as he turned.

She howled and backed away.

"Why are you so cruel?"

"I could ask you the same thing, wench. The last time you offered to bed me, you pushed me out a window. Who are you?"

She smiled, but her eyes were not warm as she calculated the distance to the sword.

"Some call me Macla. You don't need that. I will give you your sight back."

"I have my sight back."

"It is but a vapor, gone with the fell moon. I gifted you this so you would know that I love you, but you must consummate our love or your vision will fade."

Tamys' heart contracted painfully in fear of the darkness while a shudder of warning coursed through his body.

"I can't love someone I do not know. You're asking me to bed you, but that worked out poorly in the past."

"You've known me since you were a babe at the tit. And I know you don't want to be blind for life."

"Did you take my sight? Is that why my blindness is different?"

She frowned. *She doesn't understand.* Then, cutting through his thought was the strong female voice. *You should push away, lad. She's tricking you.*

"Or you are," he said. The dark lass reached for him, but he stepped back, holding the sword between them. "I remember the window and I think I should not trust you."

"What window?" she asked. "Who has clouded your desire for me?"

She doesn't understand. How can that be?

He opened his mouth to ask, but she shattered into a cloud of sparks. He saw Joy, Padraig's sorrel mare, an iron-clad hoof raised, and then everything faded to black.

He sat up with a shout and landed a panicked blow on a surprised Padraig.

"Lad, you were muttering in your sleep."

"Padraig? Where is she?"

"She?"

"The wench that threw me out of the window."

"There's none here except …."

He can hear me, you know.

"Is that the voice you're talking about?" Padraig asked.

"Nay, that's the voice that warned me. Who is it?"

"Joy is a Companion – an animal bounded to an elf. I thought you were beginning to hear her on the trip from Mandorlyn."

"Why? How?" Tamys' head began to buzz with confusion.

"I dunno the answer," Padraig assured him.

Pain sliced through Tamys' head and he feared he would vomit. Padraig responded immediately with willow bark tea eased with honey and a cold rag for his forehead.

"Padraig?" he asked after a long while of waiting for the pain to ease to controllable levels.

"Aye." He was sitting with his back to the log, waiting. Tamys could "see" him in his mind's eye.

"Was there … is there a fell moon?"

"Nay. It was a fingernail moon. Sky's lightening toward dawn now. Why?"

"It was the lass – or whatever it was – who threw me out the window."

"I wondered if you remembered that."

"It's not very clear, but seeing her brought it to mind. It didn't feel like a dream."

"Mayhap it wasn't, Tamo. Certainly someone pushed you out that window – the red haired wench."

"Red-haired. Who told you she had red hair?"

"Aethyn originally, but I asked a few of the other riders and that's what they saw."

"She had black hair and amber eyes. I don't know what they saw, but it's the last sight I have."

"A shape-shifter of some sort, then, and she came at the fell moon, which is a witching time. What did she want?"

"Apparently to push me out a window."

"Nay. Tonight, what did she want tonight?"

"For me to bed her. She offered me my eyesight in return. I could see her, by the way. I could see you sleeping and the pond."

"How'd you hold her off?" Padraig asked.

"My sword, actually. Is it in one of the panniers?"

"It is. Where'd you get that idea?"

~The swords of men sometime have power.

"Who is that?" Tamys demanded.

"Joy. I told you. Not every Kin has a Companion, but when we do, we can speak to them mind to mind and they to us. I've no idea how you can hear her too."

"She knew what to do. She made the daemon flee by pawing her with her hoof."

"It didn't flee from the sword?"

~The sword wasn't real in the dream, but my hooves are real here.

"What does she mean by that?"

"Dwarven steel, I think. And to think I was going to pull those shoes tonight to trim her hooves and chose to wait for the morrow. Dwarven steel is different from Celdryan steel. I'm not sure of the reasons, but there are Denygal stories of dwarven steel chasing off the ceely court."

"What does that have to do with my sword?"

"I don't know and we need to get on the road. You can sleep while we travel and we'll work on this later."

"What if … she comes back?"

"We'll deal with it," Padraig said. "The One is more powerful than the ceely court. He protects those who worship Him."

Tamys wanted to protest, but the words wouldn't come. If Padraig's God protected Padraig, it was all well and good, but would a god protect a man who didn't believe in it?

Galornyn

*B*ranwyn fondled a tapestry, studying the stitches. If she was to help Berdda with banners, she would need to know the house stitches. While every seamstress would add their own touches, the overall design must seem a whole. These were older banners hung in a side broch, but they were illustrative of what she needed to learn to become valuable to the dun. Out of the corner of her eyes, she caught a bit of black and then a hand touched her elbow. She turned to Lady Perdydda.

"My lady," she greeted, curtseying.

"Good morning." Pedryddaas dark to Berdda's blond. Her brown eyes held secrets that Branwyn was certain she did not want to know. "You've traveled such a long way to wait longer to be married," she remarked.

"I understand. There is a fit time for mourning."

"Do you think that's the reason?" Perdrydda pursed full lips as if judging a wine. "I suppose that's what they tell you, truth or not, and you've no position to judge, knowing so little of us. Egoran is quite pleased his father passed, as am I. You've no idea what that man's moralism meant for the raven. He simply could not accept that my mother's ways are not to be. But your father understands. There's more than one way for a child of his body to sit the High Throne. You'll be …."

"Mam, leave the lass alone."

Perdydda's eyes widened as a large shadow fell across her and then she scurried away. Branwyn thought of spiders and shuddered. Lord Maddw, Egoran's brother, sketched a bow.

"My apologies! That woman! If Egoran knew what she was about …."

"Doesn't he?"

"Not to my knowledge."

The family at Dun Galornyn was large. She'd arrived the day before Taryn had departed for the east and so had hardly said hello. Teddryn remained quite ill and in isolation. Maddw was older, the third son, master at arms and jovial. She'd not spoken much to him, but she liked his merry blue eyes that contrasted sharply with his blue-black hair.

He scarce seems the son of that one!

"How are you keeping?" he asked. Tall and broad shouldered, he wore clan breecs and an emaculate siarc.

"Trying to hold patience. Berdda said you were looking into my brother's situation."

"I am. According to the Lughan, he was accused of sorcery, somewhat to do with the raven cult."

"That's an old myth from the time of the Wars of Succession," she supplied. "Your mother referenced it just now. But it was never more than tall tales to explain odd behavior."

"I believe you, lass, but the Lughan found your brother's behavior suspicious of witchcraft. Your father set him upon the roads to prevent his execution. Your brother Gal has let nobles know that when he ascends they will be rewarded for not executing Tamys during his travels."

"Tamys guilty of sorcery – it is ridiculous. I've seen more hints at sorcery here under this roof than I've ever seen in my brother."

"I understand what you mean, lass, but I'd not be saying aught where others can overhear."

This side broch was so rarely frequented that it suddenly became curious-making that Perdrydda had found her at all, let alone that Maddw had interfered.

They stared at each other a moment in awkward silence.

"What was your mother babbling about?"

"She believes, has believed, for a long time, that Egoran is the True King."

"Is that all? I'm sure every noble mother in Celdrya has wondered that at one time or another."

"Aye, but you might have noticed my mother is far from normal. She's rather made a big noise about it over the years, prompting your father to offer your hand in marriage."

"There's more than one way for Clan Manahan to sit upon the throne? Is that it then? I'm a prize brood mare?"

"And Eg has been put out to stud. Aye, somewhat like that."

They smiled at the floor in their mutual joke. What little Branwyn had seen of her betrothed since arriving, she had not thought he had a sense of humor, but mayhap, if his brother did …. Their mother worried her greatly.

"What happens if Tamys rides up to this gate?"

"We're not Lughans. We shan't kill him."

"Of course, Old Faith. I admit I don't rightly understand what you believe. I assumed it was just to hold the Lughan at bay."

"Nay, we have a different way of viewing the gods. You should speak with my grandmam if you truly want to understand it. Egoran is the only Lughan in the family, but he's got to live within the context of Old Faith because so many in Galornyn are."

"I'll ask Berdda. Thank you."

"Certainly. When you see my mother out of the corner of your eye … it's best to choose to have somewhat else to do. You understand?"

"I do."

They had reached a corridor that led into the heart of the main broch. Maddw bowed now and left her, allowing her to find her own way to the Ladies Hall."

Llyr

*B*aku had worked at the Golden Dragon for near five years now. While he missed the warm breezes of the Summer Isles and the lithe sway of the *wahinis* in their *lole*, he loved the smell of Shyralan's hair. It reminded him of the flowers on *Maku'aine* and made his loins ache for her. He knew she'd never return his feelings, but guarding her felt like he had a place in her world, so he volunteered for the honor as often as possible.

Today's guard duty had a bonus because Shyralan thought to secure fire wine from the *Makani'ku*).

Shyralan walked beside him through the press of the crowd, dressed in a fashionable gown, kol lined eyes watching the folks. Baku carried his *hili* and enjoyed the look the *haole* gave him as they walked together. Baku stood taller than most *haole* and broader cross the shoulders. This was good thing for a guard.

The Makani'ku occupied a berth in the side harbor, the better to view its hull. Although Baku had trained as kahu, his father had been *holomaku*. Baku knew ships almost as well as he knew *hili*. Almost. *Makani'ku* was a good ship and her captain treated his mistress with care, not allowing a build up of barnicles.

Shyralan paused at the foot of the gangplank and asked the *kapa'kai'kahu* if she might speak to the *mo'i'moku* about fire wine. Of course, she asked in her own language, though Baku would have translated for her if she asked.

"The *mo'i'kane* is too busy for *wahini*," the *kahu* said to Baku, recognizing his as *kanaka*. "Come back on morrow."

Shyralan blinked at his back as he turned away. Baku would not have been so quick to turn his back on her when she wore a dagger.

"Do you speak the same language as this man?" she asked in a low tone.

"I do."

"Give him this and tell him I would speak with his captain right now."

Shyralan produced a silver piece from her sleeve pouch. Baku smiled at her. She smiled back, but not the way he wished.

The *kahu* turned when Baku approached him.

"The color of silver is most beautiful, my friend, but *haole wahini* is not welcome on ship."

"She wishes to buy fire wine and she will pay fairly."

The *kahu* tested the coin.

"Go rest in the pavilion." He nodded to the bright tent erected nearby. "The *mo'i'kane* will answer yes or no. We'll see."

"Come-come," Baku told Shyralan. "We may have talk. He has sent for captain."

The tent was mostly open on two sides and a handful of canvas stools sat about waiting for customers. One was occupied by a large man wearing bright *lole'wa* and a white *palule*. Shyralan's blue eyes twinkled, for this was clearly the captain. When he saw her, he stood.

"Pretty wahini wants somewhat from Manu?" he asked, eyes only for Shyralan. He knew a *kahu* when he saw one.

"Aye, captain. I would like to purchase fire wine."

""'Tis strong drink for pretty *wahini*. Please do sit. Do you want guava?"

Shyralan glanced at Baku, who was pleased she saw him as more than a guard. He nodded slightly. Soon Manu had seated himself on his stool and poured a cup of guava for Shyralan. The ritual of entering into a merchant relationship gave Baku opportunity to size up the man his mistress was dealing with. Manu had been *holomaku*, not born to the ship. His open *palule* showed off the fighting scars that had gained him entrance to the ships and then had secured him as *mo'i'kai*.

Shyralan had expected guava to be somewhat alcoholic and remarked on its mild flavor.

"Have you tried fire wine?" Manu asked.

"I have. I serve it in my inn."

"It makes *haole* soldiers insane."

"In large quantities, is true enough. May I sample yours?"

"If you must." A dark boy emerged from the fabric at the back of the tent and poured some dark red liquid into a cup. Shyralan took it and sipped. Her eyes crinkled a little at the corners, but she did not cough or even flinch.

"This is a fine vintage," she remarked. "I will offer five silver a cask, 10 casks."

"Ten! You must have very large and expensive inn."

"I do."

"I cannot let such excellent vintage go for less than 10 silver a cask."

"And I cannot pay more than six silver."

They haggled back and forth, finally settling on eight silver. Shyralan advanced 20 silver and promised the 60 upon delivery. She would send a wagon.

Manu took the silver, his broad face somber. He was a man who smiled easily, so that it was curious to see him look into dark pools.

"I will give you this for free, *wahini'hana*. There is a dark wind of red beards coming your way. Watch the seas and prepare."

Shyralan frowned and looked toward Baku.

"The Svard?" Baku asked. Manu nodded. "How do you know?"

"Black rain in Galornyn. Many hana die. Our makani'hana say means dark magic. Last time, they swept the islands. You remember or know stories. This time, they're coming here."

Shyralan was wise enough not to interrupt with questions, though her eyebrow arched when Manu made a statement completely to Baku.

"*Kane*, this one is *nahele'hana*, wrapped in *wahini*. Be careful what you love."

"Thank you for your wisdom, *kupa* I like *nahele*, but I will think on what you say."

They were a distance from the pavilion before Shyralan asked what the last part had been about.

"The ship's wind-witch says the storm in Galornyn was caused by black witches."

Baku watched her face and saw this did not surprise her.

"Who are the red beards?"

"They say Svard, come from the old world. *Kane* found them here when we arrived. They very fierce warriors, sailors. They sweep the Summer Isles when I was small child. Kill, take, move on. We thought they died, but I guess they are returned."

"By dark magic?"

"This is true. There were black storm then too and then they came."

"So what was that what he said about me?"

Baku wished she had not understood that part, but now that she asked … it was good to keep her secrets.

"He say you are wood witch."

"He did? Do you believe this?"

"You bewitch my heart the day I see you, so it may be."

"It may," she said. "I mean you no harm so long as you do your job well."

"I do know this," Baku said, giving her a wide smile, which she returned. "We should return to the Golden Unicorn to arrange that wagon."

"Let us go then."

Ama'na

*T*he ruins of buildings sagged on the lakeshore as Ryanna pulled the canoe onto the pebble shingle. Sarala tossed her boots to her as Sabre jumped free and tore off up what might have been a trail.

"That was the boat house," Ryanna explained, pointing to a ramshackle stone foundation right on the shore. She let Sarala take it in while she finished donning her boots.

"That's where my father died?"

"Dylan did die there, but he weren't the man who planted the seed," Ryanna told her. She donned her sword belt, shouldered a pack and hooked her bow and quiver on its points.

"Are you going to tell me who that was?" Sarala asked. "I know you know."

Ryanna strode away from the water. She'd been clear that this was a day trip. They'd not be staying overnight in this place of ghosts.

"You can see how the fire took it, the stones are cracked."

Sarala joined her at the top of a stone ramp. Timbers had fallen into the foundation then been overgrown by vines and grasses. You could still see that a building had once been here, but the evidence was growing scant.

Ryanna walked the length of the foundation wall, leaping a void here and there, before dropping off near where the real woods began. Sarala dropped to the ground sooner. Her legs were not long enough to leap one of the collapsed sections.

"This used to be a wide avenue," Ryanna reported as they entered the narrow trail Sabre had followed. Second growth trees grew to either side, the log paving had been filled in with dirt and grass. Sarala spied log walls leaning in the woods, trees growing up through what were houses at one time.

"What happened?" Sarala asked. "People talk about it, but most of those who do weren't really here. Why did Peace River die?"

Ryanna had turned aside to enter a house that had the remnants of ovens to the side.

"Your family lived here?" Sarala asked.

"And your mother." This house had a stone floor as well as a foundation and the trees had not grown up in it yet. Stone exterior walls had started to fall, but although the roof had been fired, some of the interior walls of log had survived to help hold the structure together. A door still stood in one opening. When Ryanna pushed on it, it fell with a bang and a huge wave of dust.

"Our bed chamber," Ryanna said, wiping dust off her face.

The beds had become nesting material for small animals. Ryanna pushed a timber aside and pried at a stone near one of the beds, pulling out a rusted metal box. She dropped a necklace of amber beads into her neck pouch followed by two gold Regals.

"If I poke around at the stones near the other bed, will I find somewhat my mother left behind?"

"She had already gone back to the holt by the time this happened," Ryanna said. She walked to the other bed and did her own exploration not of the stone floor, but the timber wall. She brought out a cloth-wrapped bundle and handed it to Sarala.

"What is it?"

"Not sure. It's yours to unwrap."

Sarala hesitated for truly it was not hers to unwrap. Her mother had left it behind, mayhap a symbol of her destroyed childhood.

Sarala unwrapped a necklace of silver links and a bronze arm band set with a green stone.

"Gifts, mayhap?" she asked.

"Dylan gave her the silver necklace, which is quite lovely when not covered in tarnish. The armband, however, I don't know."

Sarala dropped them into her neck pouch as Ryanna stared out what had been the window opening before the fire had taken the roof.

"Dylan was the mayor's son. I never once believed he killed himself. I think if I'd reacted to the moon and the dream as I should have, I might have saved his life. He was new dead when I found him. His father was the mayor and when he and his wife died suddenly right after, it sent some folk into a state. They rode away to report it to Clarcom. They sent Clarcom men back bent on destroying this place, on killing Kin. The town folk fired the village to give us a chance to escape."

"They died here?" Sarala asked. She didn't really need to. She knew.

"Most. Over the years, I've heard that some of the women survived, raised the children they led away. Cunyr would have sold the boys into debt slavery. They'd all be free now. Some of the girls my age might have been sold to brothels."

Sarala hadn't much liked Lydya's mate before, but now ... healers took an oath not to harm except when there was no choice, but she wished someone else would harm him.

Ryanna stepped over the window ledge and continued up into the village. Sarala had to scramble over to follow her. The village square became obvious. The bathhouse was still somewhat intact. It had been made of fitted stones and had not been burned. The chapel had also been constructed to last, but it had been burned. Ryanna stood in the doorway, staring in. At first Sarala hadn't understood what she was looking at and then she realized there were skulls.

"A common pyre," Ryanna reported. "I had heard that, but to see it …."

She turned away, wiping a tear from her cheek. She stood by what might have been the council fire pit for a moment. Sarala put a hand upon her shoulder in sympathy. Ryanna straightened and pointed to a large three story façade. As with many of the buildings, it had been fired, but you could tell it had been somewhat important at a time.

"The inn. Dylan's family ran it."

"If he's not my father, why do you act is if this were my inheritance?"

"Because it should have been. He may not have been your seed father, but he wanted Maryanara and her child. He would have loved you as his daughter."

"He died. Why do you keep my seed-father's identity from me?"

"Marynanara never told you. Why is it my business to do so?"

"Because I am of age and have that right."

Ryanna sighed.

"She didn't lay with him willingly."

"I know that."

"Perhaps I will tell you when I am ready and not before. I am not yet ready."

Why not? What do you care if I know the name of the human wolf who is my father?

Ryanna turned toward the mountain and Sarala followed her. The village had died by fire, but most had not been set by Clarcom men, but by the villagers themselves, trying to slow the riders so that the Kin could get away. In a meadow hip deep in grass, Ryanna pointed up the mountain.

"The pass," she explained. "See those boulders to the left there?"

Sarala shaded her eyes and nodded.

"That's where Gil and I took up position with our bows, to cover the others so they might escape." Ryanna swallowed. "I'd never killed anyone before," she reported. "I didn't much think about it … until later. There are still nights when I wake up hearing the horses screaming as their riders died on their backs."

This has somewhat to do with why you won't tell me the name of my seed-father. I shouldn't push. This is a place of ghosts.

Sarala could see why the Kin and Celt had come together at this place. This meadow in a fold of the Dragon Back was rich and watered by two streams that conjoined to run down to the lake. The mountains loomed to the east, climbing steeply to the stark peaks that inspired its name. It looked like the skeleton of a dragon's spine.

"There's rain coming," Ryanna reported. One did not argue with a Wisdom about such. They knew. "I do not want to spend the night here."

"No. We should head back. I've seen enough." They started back toward the lake. As they crossed in front of the inn, Sarala paused for a moment. She'd gathered flowers in the meadow and wove them into a grass wreath. This she laid on the inn's stone steps. She laid a second one on the steps of the chapel. "Thank you for bringing me here," she said to Ryanna. "I know it was no an easy choice for you."

"The past is dead, Sarala. This is just part of it I had not yet had a funeral for. We're going to get caught in that rain if we tarry much longer."

When they got to the canoe, Sarala glanced round.

"Should we call for Sabre?" she asked.

"No. He's Sent to me that he'll hunt his way back to the city for when it is time to continue west. He doesn't much like cities."

"Was he here in Ama'na when this happened?"

"Yes. He was born here and just a pup when Clarcom came for us. That's a tale to tell some other time. We need to paddle for the city now or get soaked."

They shoved off, caught up their paddles and drove westward.

Stone of Storms

The brain's curious thing. It's reversed from the body. Damage the left side and the right side of the body doesn't function anymore. My investigations have shown that eyesight is located at the back of the head. Why this fascinating physiology would be so is not yet known.

Paringalsynmeldor, Dome Collegiate, Kin Cycle 16430, Old Calendar

Past

Founding Year 931
Llyr

*S*hyralan's hair smelled of jasmine and Caedyn ap Maille inhaled deeply in desire. He traced the curve of her hip with a fingertip. She looked like a maiden, but he had no doubt that she was older than she seemed and wise beyond her years.

"We've business to discuss," she reminded him.

"Has my coin run out? Has my father outbid me?" It was a jest between them.

"Your father has not favored my bed in years," she informed him, rolling to face him, settling her head in the hollow of his shoulder. "The bearing sickness has passed and she's becoming restless."

"Then there's hope she'll whelp?"

"The midwife believes so. The babe has quickened."

"That's a dangerous child, you know? Perryn had reason to want my sister dead, but now a whole kingdom would be shed of her inconvenience."

"Hmm," Sharyalan hummed, her hand trailing the muscle across his ribs.

"What are you thinking?" Caedyn asked. When he'd first came to her bed two years past, he'd been smitten. Now 19, he knew that she was merely conducting a financial transaction with him. Still, he liked the flattery of her touch.

"The rule can pass in the female line if there's no male heir."

"Aye, that is true. Do you mean to stab me?"

"Nay, of course not. You're not worth the blood on the sheets. I'm speaking of the child."

Caedyn pulled back to see her face more clearly.

"I do not follow your train of thought."

"Maryn and Perryn are both dead and there's rumors afoot that Donyl is missing."

"Aye."

"The rule can pass in the female line. What would the succession be? To the elder sister or to the heir's offspring?"

Caedyn sat up to stare at her.

"You're suggesting that this child could be king of Celdrya?"

"Mayhap. Am I right?"

"Mayhap. It would be worth it to ask the Lughan to verify the thought." He rolled off the bed to pour some wine into two goblets. "My father mustn't know, at least not yet."

"That needn't be said. He wants her dead. So unlike him."

"He's not rational on the subject. I've never seen him like this on any other matter. Gilyan has always been his favorite. He was so pleased that she would be Maryn's bride."

"You know he tried to match her soon after the boy was born. There was a bit of an age difference, but he had hopes."

"You weren't his lover then, surely."

"Nay, but my predecessor kept records and notes about such things." She sipped of her wine.

"Why?"

"Why else? Gossip is as useful to us as our physical allures. We have a prince's child residing within our walls now. Of course that is useful. Your father's previous attempts to get a royal alliance through marriage make his current behavior all the more odd and it makes us wonder what's in back of it."

The recognition of her as an educated woman stunned him. She could read and write, do figures and understand politics. All that separated her from being his wife was that she was common-born. *Or is she?*

"You seem to know a great deal about the politics of the kingdom. How is that you are a harlot?"

"Harlots are sometimes born in the houses, Caedon – of noble women who had an inconvenient affair. There are at least three bastards of great clans here at the Golden Unicorn and another five of minor clans. Some even have two noble parents. Your sister is the highest in the roost. We could almost form our own clan and ask for lands and a seat on the vyngretroi board."

"Women are not permitted," Caedan said with a laugh. "But, aye, you could be a rig in the Denygal style.

Galconyn had a female rig a generation ago. If my sister whelps a healthy boy, I will set lands on you."

"You'll set lands on me if it's a girl. This house is protecting the future of the kingdom and the glory of your clan. Our service is worth a smallish demesne that we can gain income from."

She sat straight backed on the bed, her appraising gaze upon him.

"Aye. You drive a bargain. Who were your father and mother?"

"Someday I might tell you. For now, it only matters that your sister's coupling with Maryn is sworn when the babe is born."

He leaned into her until she fell back on the bed and he peppered her left shoulder with kisses. He knew she was just conducting a business transaction, but it was a highly enjoyable enterprise for him and he hoped she was not terribly disappointed in it.

Present

Founding Year 1028
Glenconyn

*R*iding a horse blind terrified for only as long as it took Tamys to realize he'd been sleeping for a moon. Then pain replaced terror, followed by exhaustion. He'd fallen asleep before Padraig could prepare the midday meal.

With the sun still up, Padraig faced an afternoon of boredom. They'd not even reached the modest mileage he'd hoped. Restless, he pulled Tamys' sword out of its sheath and examined it. All who had ever seen it acknowledged it a fine weapon that marked Tamys as noble-born, but truly, it was a rather plain sword unadorned by jewels or heraldic marks. It felt lighter in the hand than it should and was perfectly balanced, testifying to its craftsmanship. When Padraig tested it by swinging at a clump of grass, it sliced the grass rather than bent it. A dwarven blade, sure enough.

Padraig had only ever seen Tamys oil the blade. He couldn't remember seeing him sharpen it. Padraig compared the sword to his long knife and dagger, both dwarven steel and was convinced. Tamys had admitted to the dwarves trading with the dun at the Pass of the Arrival. As Padraig moved to put the weapon back in it sheath, light glanced off the shank and he saw, for only a moment, the elven runes writ along the pommel.

"Dwarven-wrought and elven-blessed."

This was not Kin work. The Kin no longer blessed blades. The elves of old had done that. To Padraig's knowledge there were no elves that still did. The Winter People, mayhap, but one of their blades would likely never have come into a human market.

It could be that old. You know what this reminds you of?

A month ago, Padraig had been more or less convinced that Tamys was the One True King, but the fall and blindness had washed that hope from his heart. The Kin mayhap would accept a blind king if he were wise and devout, but the Celts believed physical infirmity to be a curse by their gods.

Despite the reality, he circled the thought. There were still stories about King Gwin's shattered sword replaced by an elven witch. It had been the royal sword for centuries, seen on ceremonial occasions along with the royal artifacts, said to also have been given (or stolen) from the elves. All had disappeared after King Perryn's death a century ago.

Keep the sword even when it is broken, for broken swords may be mended.

Padraig had not understood the prophesy given to him by Andyr the apothecary, but he remembered the vision of Gly shouting about the sword even as Tamys had been hurled from a window. Could "the sword" have a dual meaning – a physical sword of mythical origins abruptly brought out of obscurity and a man who would protect or advise the One's King?

If so, he was doing what was right. If not, he was still doing what was right, but he was no closer to his mission than he'd been when he started.

Padraig placed the sword next to the fire and went for a walk. This had once been an elven town, he was sure. The grass had grown up to conceal the rectangular blocks and they were not made of lumina stone, but he saw elvish design in the patterns – wide avenues, rectangular houses and trees at most corners. He was no archeologist to read a history in what he saw, but he guessed the town had been abandoned more than a century, but not more than two. This was not the fabled city of the West. As the sun sunk low over the mountains, he thought he saw somewhat out on the plain, but he couldn't be sure. It might just have been sunlight winking off the surface of a lake and not a place of broken spires long abandoned. He climbed a wall for a better view.

The plain swept round the town, dead level with wave upon wave of ripening wild rye. The sun's dying light gilded the grain with rich hues. Padraig blinked against the westering light and considered a distant grouping of rocks, mayhap an outcropping, but unlikely in this land of grass. It was too far for Padraig to make out, but he thought there were enough stones to be the remains of a destroyed city, the stones of which had been turned into these now-abandoned dwellings.

Padraig remained upon the wall until well after the sun slid beneath the horizon. He stayed to watch the stars come out one by one. When the wheel spread overhead, he climbed clear of the wall to hear Tamys mutter somewhat in his sleep. Padraig crept close to settle a blanket over his shoulders. The lad was recovering well, Padraig supposed, though it was a slow turn, mayhap owing more to the melancholy than the head injury. Padraig reasoned that Tamys had sat the horse longer than expected and that promised good for the days ahead.

Traveling with a convalescent meant plenty of time for napping, a state that he was unused to. Naturally, he wasn't tired at night. Denygal eyes needed little more than starlight to make out details among the stones and the encroaching weeds. Padraig poked about in a ruined house, finding the remains of the hearth and of a small bath. Ancient elven homes were reported to have such, but Padraig had always thought it unlikely.

He emerged from the house into the black and white world of night to head toward his blankets near to where Tamys slept. He blinked for a trick of the light sent a spectre of whiteness across his path to hover near Tamys. Padraig halted as his eyes adjusted and he saw the lad standing over his friend. It was the lad from the Mandorlyn road, he that had asked for a ride into the town. Padraig had not thought of him since the gates had opened and was about to call out to him a friendly hallo when an icy hand grabbed his stomach and threatened to spill its contents onto the broken paving stones beneath his boots. In that moment, the night was lit by an impossible full moon.

"God help me," he prayed and instantly courage more than he could have mustered strengthened his spine. "Halt there. Are you friend or foe?"

The lad turned toward him and the icy hand crushed his stomach once again, but this time Padraig didn't hesitate, for he felt the Spirit of God standing at his back. He continued walking forward toward the lad and his sleeping prey.

"How come you be here?" Padraig asked.

"I have business here," the lad spoke, but it was not quite the voice of a child. Padraig could hear the daemon speak beneath the false tones. He felt filthy just at hearing it. This was his first daemon and it disconcerted to see the face of a sweet child, though it still wore the rags of a waif. Its hair was dark in the low light and its skin white. Its eyes seemed deep pools of blackness, bottomless wells.

"With whom?" Padraig asked. The lad smiled an evil smile and looked at the sleeping Tamys. "I don't think God has given you his life," Padraig said.

The lad turned to glare at him with hate-filled eyes.

"Your God has naught to do with me!" the daemon snapped. "He was promised to me a long time ago."

"Was he now? Not by God!"

The lad spat at him, turned and reached for Tamys. As Padraig stepped forward, his foot encountered Tamys's sheathed sword. He caught it up and called out - "Halt in the name of Jysu Cryst."

The daemon faltered as if he'd stabbed it in the back. Padraig, still feeling the Sure Swift Hand at his back and with an elven-blessed dwarven blade in his hand, ran forward and slashed the sword between the daemon and Tamys. The daemon screamed in agony, backing away from the steel.

"Fool! He's mine from birth and you will never get him!"

"That's his choice, neither of ours."

Padraig had stepped between it and his charge, sword held downward, ready to parry any attack. No great swordsman, he would wonder later how he'd known to take such a stance.

"In the name of Jysu Cryst, I command you to speak, daemon! What is your name?"

The daemon spat at him again, but it couldn't resist the power Padraig wielded.

"You know me by many names," it growled in a decidedly feminine voice. Then it wrenched free and fled, leaping onto a wall and disappearing into the night air. The sound of a huge raven echoed back. Padraig's pursuit met with darkness.

After a moment of gagging and gasping, Padraig began praying and as he prayed, he walked the perimeter of the compound, setting God's seals upon the area, praying for protection that only the divine could accomplish.

Dawn found him nodding on his blankets, his back to the wall, Tamys' sword across his knees and his long knife beneath them. There'd been no more disturbance, but he'd been unable to sleep after the experience. Rising, Padraig washed his face and drank some cold water. He knew that with morning her power was diminished. She was a creature of the night, capable of working mischief only in the mind of man during the day.

~Warded ground.

Joy's thoughts in his mind were clear. She thought he ought to move deeper into the elven village.

Padraig yawned, bending to pick up a raven feather as long as his arm, wishing he had a gift of discernment. It didn't feel evil, but he knew its owner was.

~Very tired. What do you mean?

~The she-witch told Tamys that you were taking him to warded ground this day. We're on the edge, but not close enough.

~How do you know that? Padraig asked.

~My shoes tingle. Dwarven steel does know elven wards.

~There's been no elves in these parts for many cycles.

~Somewhat wards the ground. She has no power there and it's just a mile along this road. And … there's somewhat here that recognizes him.

~Him? Padraig was genuinely confused.

~Tamys. I feel it. Joy seemed to mentally shiver.

~Is that good or bad?"

~I'm a horse, not an elf. I think it's good, but I think I could also not understand elves.

~Tamys is not an elf.

~Isn't he? she asked. *He smells like an elf.*

~We smell differently?

~You don't know this? She seemed puzzled by his inability. *Not as different as a horse from a donkey, but near as great.*

Padraig didn't have the mental energy to consider this at the moment, so he hooked up the travois with the sleeping Tamys on it and dragged it to where Joy said her shoes sang. Then he slept, secure in the knowledge that they were safe from the raven goddess.

Dun Llyr

*T*he Golden Unicorn had a wonderful reputation for meeting the needs and tastes of every client. Sawyl had enjoyed the company of a young man of exquisite beauty and skill for the entire evening. When he'd tired of him, the lad had withdrawn with grace. A plate of food was left upon the table by a serving lass who could easily have been one of the harlots, but who brought in his laundered clothes and offered to draw him a bath.

Of course, such care cost coin and Sawyl could only afford a night, but he felt he deserved it in celebration of his appointment as chief chirgeon of Dun Llyr. That had been quite the catch, requiring every bit of skill he possessed. He'd had to have documents forged and reference letters written. He had been shocked by Lord Howedd's layman's knowledge of field care and infant palsy. Apparently, the plague had passed through the Bottom when he was a child and he'd seen its ravishes.

It was interesting to view the Golden Unicorn's grounds and recognize that this was Howedd's childhood home. It really had the look of a dun about it – tall walls, several brochs, formal gardens, a full stable ….

By tonight, he would be in an actual dun, serving as chirgeon to the future king of Celdrya. Oh, Howedd may not realize his destiny just yet, but he was the descendent of Prince Maryn and with the right guidance ….

Standing at the window, Sawyl smiled to himself while idly watching a bird glide across the sky. It dropped to a branch on the huge oak tree in the garden and turned its head to stare at him. Ice formed a hard ball in Sawyl's stomach for this was a raven he was fairly certain he knew well. In the weeks since the spell, Sawyl had heard naught of Talidd. There'd been naught communication coming out of the Tongue and the news about the surviving Black mages was that nobody knew what had occurred. Many had died. In fact, Gregyn appeared to be the only one in the circle to have survived and Werglidd claimed he'd needed to seek help from the Grey to save the lad. And yet, Gregyn was not acting like a supremely powerful young apprentice who had just survived a spell that had granted him his freedom. He had escorted Lord Taryn to Clarcom.

Does he not realize that when your master dies, you must either seek another or become your own master? Is it possible Talidd still lives to hold the power of the name?

The raven staring at him might well be the answer to that question. Sawyl had never been blessed with a familiar, so he didn't understand how it all worked. Could the bird do Talidd's bidding? Was it a spy for Talidd? Did Talidd see through its eyes?

Or is it seeking a new master now that Talidd is no more?

The raven launched into the sky and was soon out of sight beyond one of the rooftops. Sawyl shivered in the warm air. He would have to find the answers to some of these questions soon. For now, he needed to be about becoming the chirgeon of Llyr.

Southern Blyan

*T*aryn stood at the flap of the tent, watching the rain fall. They'd awakened to a driving thunder shower with high winds, far too dangerous to attempt travel. The men huddled under a tarp among the trees, trying to keep a fire going. Gregyn sat on the ground near the back of the tent, sharpening his sword.

"It won't stop raining one moment sooner by you watching it," the sergeant said, sighting down the blade before setting aside his stone to pick up a cloth.

"Am I annoying you?"

Gregyn had become more outspoken as they traveled and Taryn appreciated that he allowed the illusion that he was not the apprentice to Gregyn's master. The men treated Taryn with more respect since he'd begun to act the commander rather than the 15 year old lad. He missed ale. He now allowed himself only watered with meals. Taryn sat down on his camp bed and began to sketch the scene outside the tent. Gregyn stowed his sword stone and stretched. Taryn looked over his shoulder when his back made a popping sound.

"Are you feeling better?" he asked.

"What do you mean?" Gregyn often tried to avoid answering personal questions this way.

"When we first started this trip … you were still not recovered from that illness."

"It's mostly pasesed."

"Were you ever frightened that it might be the plague?"

Gregyn shrugged.

"I feared not to die. There are worse fates than death."

"Aye." The image of Teddryn's emaciated limbs came to mind. "There will be many halt in Galornyn when this is done."

Gregyn pointed to the sketch.

"It's almost magic, what you can do there?"

Taryn shivered. When he'd begun doing this as a child, there'd been a few folk who had suggested it was some sort of sorcery. He turned it so Gregyn could see it better.

"Remarkable from just paper and a bit of charcoal. This … it's a dun."

He indicated an area Taryn had left blank on the paper.

"A dun? We're soaked to the skin when there's a dun nearby?"

"Nay," Gregyn said with a laugh, countering Taryn's rising ire. "It was abandoned a very long time ago. There's no roof left. I just thought you might like to finish it."

Taryn considered the gap in the sketch, thought of a fractured dun he'd seen earlier in the journey, and began filling the image.

"Why are there no standing duns in this area?"

"I never thought to ask. I do know there were pirates in south Dublyn and Blyan for a long time. Mayhap the duns couldn't protect their small folk, so they had to abandon the land."

Gregyn's perspective on the world differed from anything Taryn had been exposed to before. He supposed his brothers had interacted with common born soldiers who had risen to command positions, but Gregyn was so young that it was almost like having a friend. He trusted to have him at his back.

While Taryn sketched, he was vaguely aware that the rain slacked. Gregyn confirmed this from the open flap of the tent.

"I think it is passing. It is past noontide and we couldn't make the next caravanserai by nightfall, so I recommend you decide we remain here til morning."

"Sounds good." Taryn put his sketching material in the box where he kept it. The tent flap's view showed the men venturing out from under the tarp. "Let's go speak with them."

Taryn told the men of their travel plans and suggested they use the time to relax a bit since they were in a safe location. Gregyn's expression said he'd left somewhat out. He added that a guard still needed to be set.

Gregyn suggested they walk to the road. It had been a king's road once with wide paving stones. The rain had washed away the debris that had built up on the surface, so that they could actually see the stone in many places.

"Do you ever wonder what it must have been like to travel the roads here when there was a king to order them repaired?" Taryn asked Gregyn.

He was only a few years older than Taryn, but he'd lived a much different life. Gregyn bent to gather a handful of mud from the road.

"My folk would have been consigned to the common roads," he reminded calmly. "There were tolls on these to pay for the paving."

With the sun come out, fog had begun to rise from the trees. Taryn could see the dun now.

"I'd like to explore that," he said.

If Gregyn thought it a frivolity, he didn't say so. Stone duns lasted a long time without care. The curtain wall remained strong, though the gates were gone. Inside the stable roof had collapsed into the horse stalls, but a three-story broch looked to be in better shape. Water dripped down from the upper levels as they peered into the dim interior.

A chill ran down Taryn's back of the sort that he was beginning to recognize. He knew naught why, but he had to venture within.

He lifted a candle lantern from its hook and found a fat candle still within. His flint and steel did not light the wick on the first two times, but then he remembered what Maddw had said about his abilities – that he'd be able to light fires and play with raindrops. He thought about the wick blazing with flame, struck the steel and flint together and the candle awoke. Gregyn turned from trying to gaze up the stairs. His grey eyes seemed enormous.

Did he somehow sense what I just did?

If Gregyn did, he pretended not to.

"The stairs appear to be intact, but the floors above have been open to the elements for generations, so we'd better keep to the stone."

Taryn nodded, but his real interest was on what he could see of the great hall and the kitchens that occupied the back third of the main floor.

"There's a lot of furniture here, almost as if they had no warning," Taryn said.

"Mayhap they didn't. Pirates move in small bands, fast and silent."

"The postern gate was taken by fire," Taryn said. "Did you see the black above the lintel? An army would have battered the main gate and mayhap have been turned away. The postern gate is not honorable."

He shuddered again, feeling the pull to climb the stairs even as he knew it was folly. Those floors wouldn't hold their weight. He started up the stairs nonetheless.

"Careful," Gregyn warned. "Mind the wet."

He followed behind. Taryn paused on the second floor landing. Here wicker walls had fallen, revealing cobweb-covered furniture.

"Women's hall and council chamber," he indicated. Swinging the light about, he saw tables and chairs and chests.

Climb farther.

He headed up the stairs to the third level.

"That floor will be even more dangerous than this one," Gregyn warned.

"I'm being careful," Taryn argued. He'd already climbed halfway, so there was naught Gregyn could do to stop him.

"You're not. Careful would be staying on the ground floor."

These had been family chambers. With the roof gone, Taryn realized that the afternoon was beyond them. The long strands of sunlight reached across the floor to a chest at the end of what had been a fine bed. Taryn put a foot on the floor. The wood didn't groan. He trusted his entire weight to the slick moldy surface. Good so far.

"What are you doing?" Gregyn demanded from the stair below. "That whole floor might collapse."

"It's good. I just want to see somewhat."

"We've no chirgeon with us. If you break a leg, you'll be crippled for life."

"I'm fine," Taryn assured.

The surface of the floor felt rotten, but the deck held as he light-footed his way to the trunk. Gregyn's head came into view.

"Are you mad?"

"Curious."

"Curiosity drowns the cat."

Taryn lifted the lid to the chest. The leather hinges had rotted away, so that the lid fell with a clatter. Taryn lifted away shredded gowns and a moth eaten pair of slippers to find a small box in one corner. He pulled it out, shuddering again. He glanced at Gregyn who looked stunned.

"What is that?" he whispered.

Taryn opened the box. A lady's jewels. In a smallish dun like this one, jewels were few. A malachite brooch, a string of pearls, a medallion of lapis lazuli bound in bronze wire and hung from a heavy chain. It was this that Taryn felt drawn too. He grazed it with his forefinger and felt ice water rushing a torrent in his veins.

The floor beneath him groaned. Snatching the box to his chest, he stepped quickly to the landing.

"Let's go," he suggested. Gregyn stared at the box. "We can inspect it out in the fresh air.

The ward was overgrown with grass. Taryn set the box on a tumbled garden wall and opened it. Gregyn's lips pursed. This was no doubt more wealth than he'd seen in his lifetime. It was only a small portion of the jewels his mother Peddryna possessed.

"These are just a lady's baubles. There's somewhat about this piece, though." He drew the medallion out of the box. "This feels old." He heard Gregyn swallow. "You feel it too."

"Aye," Gregyn admitted. He reached out without permission to touch the stone and Taryn let go of the chain. "It's marvelous."

The light seemed to bend toward the stone and Gregyn, for the first time since he'd been ill, seemed completely well.

"It is. Far more than just some lady's bauble. It's old, too."

"How old?" Gregyn's whisper spoke of awe.

"The stone is called lapis. It's rare stone … sacred among some circles. The druids of old said the elves favored it highly."

"That's why you think it's old?"

"Nay, the chain, that's called elven gold. My grandmam wears a ring that's wrought of it."

"It's marvelous," Gregyn said, handing Taryn back the medallion. "Some lady will appreciate the pretties."

"If I but had a lady to give them too." Taryn plucked out the malachite brooch. "Here. For going with."

"My purse has never been so fat. I'll take it though. Never know when a man might want to impress a lass."

Gregyn grinned and dropped it into his neck pouch before following Taryn across the overgrown ward and out the gate. Dusk fell as they walked back toward the fires. As they neared the camp, a shadow crossed their path. The wolf looked up with its silver eyes, its cub held gently in its mouth. Taryn and Gregyn both froze, wondering when the whole pack would arrive. The cub opened its blue eyes to stare at them. Then mother and cub disappeared into the dripping woods and the moment passed.

"Its eyes are like moonstone," Gregyn whispered.

"What?" Taryn said, feeling as if he'd missed a part of a conversation.

"The bitch. Her eyes were silver, reminded me of moonstone."

A shudder quaked down Taryn's back.

"Is that your first wolf?"

"Aye. I grew up in a dun in a city," Taryn reminded him. "I've never been hunting. You?"

"It's not my first wolf."

He keeps secrets, but why?

Another shudder ran down Taryn's back as the sky darkened from aubergine to indigo. At a distance, a wolf howled. Taryn glanced at Gregyn, realizing the rider was watching him with a weighing look.

"What are you thinking?"

"You're the one sensing it."

"You too."

"Not like you, but aye. Somewhat just changed. It's as if the wolf was an omen."

Taryn stopped just shy of the ring of light from the fires, shuddering again.

"Not the wolf. The cub."

Gregyn cocked his head and smiled.

"Aye. You'll be seeing him again."

"How do you know?"

Gregyn shook his head and headed into the camp. He liked to keep secrets and that could be annoying, but Taryn rather thought this time the secret was not Gregyn's but his own and that the rider was allowing him to discover it for himself.

Blind Sight

They treat their women like slaves when they marry them. They can't own land or leave a husband that beats them. The only women truly free are, oddly enough, sexual merchants — harlots, women like Rahab, who own their own business and employ others like themselves. While I cannot admire the product they sell, I do wish that spirit of independence would become evident in the rest of the women

**Macla of Llyr nee Moryn,
Lady Umhall
(FY 1002)**

Past

FoundingYear 1024
Hansorfjord – Four cycles ago

*F*arenlucgilyn leapt from the junque to the shingle and started the long climb to Hansorfjord dun. He thought of it as a dun. Unlike his prior visits, he was known and the viks cleared the passage up the stairs. Orma met him at the terrace and directed him into the great hall where the northern summer was considerably cooler than out of doors. There were doors set in the gables to catch what little breeze there was and the stone beneath their feet exuded coolness that kept the heat at bate.

"Magnus and Erik have gone to the outer islands to garner support. I've set aside a chamber for your use. Do you wish to see it now?"

"I'm not tired, thank you. I would like to see the preparations for the invasion."

"We could start with the maps in the ward room. Please do come." Unlike most of the Svard, Orma was dark haired. She commanded the eye, a woman born to power. She faded when the second woman stood. A mere slip of a girl with eyes a penetrating sea-green and hair red-gold, she sucked all the light in the room to herself. Orma paused.

"This is Erik's wife, Sygna. Daughter, this is Farenlucgilyn, Emissary to the Orental."

"The man who can command the wyrding roads? Please to meet you." She held out a slender, strong hand.

Goddess-made, he thought. *Do the Svard turn them Wise or do they let them run free?*

"Sygna comes from Westaberg. They have the best boat wrights."

"My fader has commissioned 400 boats toward this invasion. It will be a glorious fleet."

And you will be a glorious ornament upon my sleeve.

The Goddess had allowed his dalliance with Mei Ling, so he supposed she would permit this one. *Does she see when she is not here?*

Orma drew him along toward the ward room, but leaned into his ear.

"Leave her alone, emissary. My husband and son will feed you to sharks if they even suspect your attraction, and I will be the one to put poison in your food if you do more than admire. Do you understand me?"

He restrained his hand from reaching for his dagger only because Orma's hand was already on hers and he suspected she had skills beyond what he wanted to test in these circumstances.

And how would I explain her death? Patience! You will have all you deserve and desire in time.

He stared at her collar bones while inclining his head. She accepted that as apology and continued to the ward room. It was all he could do not to throw his dagger at her back and take Sygna to bed.

Erik's maps were exquisite. The lad knew strategy that Gil did not. He indicated the prongs of his attack, an invasion that he expected to take more than one season. He'd even indicated which islands should participate in which prong of the attack.

"Provisions seem inadequate."

Orma raised a fine eye brow.

"Viks live off raiding," she explained. "Small crews can go from battle to battle without much baggage. In the Before Land, crews might be gone for years without resupply and return with boats overflowing with *skatten*."

"How did your people come to be here?" he asked.

"That's a many and varied tale. We did not all come through at the same time. We term them the 1st, 2nd, and 3rd Migrations."

"But you all somehow gathered here?"

"We were some of us very suspicious of others until Magnus united all the islands. There is a far westing tribe that settled on the mainland that has not joined us. They've intermarried with the trolls, is what we hear."

"Far westing? How far?"

"Beyond the boundaries of Celdrya, Sygna says."

She would know, wouldn't she? Magnus made a good match for Erik. I almost feel sorry for the boy. Every man of intelligence will want to possess his bride

He'd been careless allowing Orma to see his ardor. No matter. When the time came, the mating would be the girl's idea and none of his. He would be ruler of the world and many women would desire him. He rather liked the desert-dweller notion of a stable of females to fulfill his needs. For now, though, he must carry out the Goddess's plan and that meant he must exercise restraint … if only for as long as it took Sygna to come voluntarily to his bed.

Present

Founding Year 1028
Clarcom Court

Ryanna finished wiping down her pack horse and stood back to take a final look. A small figure swerved round the end of a stall and slammed right into her. Instinctively, she grabbed his siarc and the arm under it.

"My goodness! You're a lass!" Danyl gasped, gawking. She wove Air round them to keep that secret close and to prevent the young whirlwind from escaping her. He stared about and then faced her boldly, his green eyes alive with curiosity.

"How do you do that?"

"How do you see it?" she asked.

"It's a transparent cone of silver."

Ryanna's mouth dropped open. She'd never had it described thusly, though it was true enough. It's how she would describe it if someone asked.

"You're an interesting one. First, I am a lass, but no one must know that about me or the other lass I'm with."

"The pretty one? Everybody already knows she's a lass hiding in lad's clothing."

"You don't think I'm pretty?" Ryanna asked, not actually offended. She wanted to hear how he answered.

"Nay, you're beautiful. There is somewhat different in your beauty over her prettiness. Yours is – deeper and it comes from someplace inside, like the silver cone."

He glanced round the stable. He was tall for his age and thin, reminding her of a bow string vibrating with energy.

"What do they hear?"

"Us talking about the horse. Who are your parents?"

"Lady Lydya is my mam. They say Cunyr is my da, but I doubt it. His offspring have a sour taste."

"Who are his offspring?"

"Cullyn and Elora. She's not his child, but she has his sour taste on her."

Ryanna flashed through her store of faces and names from the last couple of days and recognized the pretty young merchant's daughter who warmed Cunyr's bed. Had he got her with child recently? And, if so, how did Danyl know?

"You have several more siblings," Ryanna said.

"Aye, but Lydya is their mam and someone else must be their da. I don't think mine's the same as theirs."

Truth to tell, however he knew it, Danyl was likely speaking the truth. Ryanna had met Shyla, Ygerna, and Glynn and they all had more elven blood than their mother. Danyl, however, had more elven blood than Ryanna, as much as Sarala, mayhap more. They were truly elves who just happened to look like Celts.

"You know you shouldn't be telling me this? You could get your mother killed."

His was mayhap the prettiest face she'd ever seen on a Celt lad. He smiled and won her heart even before he spoke his thoughts.

"There's a cone of whispers between us and them. I wouldn't say this to just anyone. Do you not know what your aura says?"

"You can read my aura?" Ryanna felt momentarily naked. She purposefully held her aura away from the sight of Wise and mages alike and yet this child could read it without training.

"Of course I can. Can't you read mine?"

Well, aye, she could, but she'd been a good deal older before the gift had manifested itself. His aura had the usual flux of a small child, but it was, she had to admit, the steadiest she ever seen in one so young. It was a golden candle flame, indicative of a great deal of elven blood.

"What does mine tell you?" she asked.

He stared at her.

"You have much power. You have a pure heart. You lack trust. You've killed. Someone hurt you badly. Your baby died. You love another who is a great man. Your future …."

"That's enough. The future should be closed to us."

He frowned.

"I didn't know that," he told her. "Mayhap that is why I cannot see my own future."

"Well, I know somewhat you might not know. Little boys who jump from roof to roof sometimes fall and break their bones. You're scaring your mother, so you should stop."

His face sobered for a moment, then he nodded firmly.

"I see what you mean," he announced.

"I will let you go then, but first – what do we not tell others?"

"That you and the other lass are lasses and that my mother put horns on Cunyr's head … but he puts horns on her head all the time. Am I allowed to say that?"

"Nay, it would be impolitic and impolite."

"May I say that Cullyn is a hound?"

"He appears to be one, so it's probably allowed. Is it wise … now there's another topic."

Ryanna released the speech glamour.

"It is a lovely horse," Danyl said. "I want a Regal, but the equerry says I'm not old enough yet for a horse. I must ride a pony. I'm growing fast though. I must be off. Cook has popovers this afternoon. Will you want one?"

"Nay, that's most kind, but I have other business to attend to. It was nice talking to you, Danyl."

The lad dashed off, leaving Ryanna feeling bereft of activity. She led her pack horse into the stall he was sharing with her saddle horse and headed out of the stables. The ward buzzed like a hive. A farmer had brought a wagon of cheeses for taxes and another had brought oats. A page strode across her path. She could hear the clang of practice swords somewhere off to her right. The chirgeon Traegyr hailed her as she entered the great hall.

"I've been trying to get a moment with your friend Saryl, to discuss Dengyal herbs. Would he have any for congestion of the blood?"

"I would hardly know what any of his herbs do, my lord. You'll have to ask him."

Traegyr made her nervous because he had no aura and because he was shifty. Somewhat about the man simply didn't set right. That historically meant he was a mage, but she had no clear evidence of her suspicion.

Cullyn ap Riordan, likely the rightful heir to Dublyn, stood talking to Cunyr ap Riordan, rig of Dublyn, near the honor hearth. Cunyr lacked the ability to shield his aura and Ryanna could see it wrapped tightly round his soul, a poor sign for any man's future. Did that have somewhat to do with Traegyr's request? And those black stars in Cullyn's aura set her teeth to grind. Rightful heir or not, she hoped he never ascended to the rule. She'd not met Bryan, but she could only hope he was a better man. Kefyn seemed to like him, which might mean he'd make a fine ruler or be eaten alive by the politics of rule before he ever got a chance to prove his worth.

Lydya and Elora were coming down the stairs amid the other ladies. Ryanna watched as Shyla met eyes with Kefyn. Those two were being very unwise, given that she was daughter to the rig, who likely knew she was no child of his flesh. Ryanna just couldn't imagine Lydya cockholding her husband, no matter what a monster he might be. She remembered her father's tales of how the nobility treated their women and she thought Cunyr rather lucky he had not been married to her. He'd be very long gone from this world if he had.

Danyl's reading astounded her. How did a young lad know so much about a stranger?

There was a time when you would have bent your will to obey … to make Gil happy even when he would not be happy. You are no different than Lydya. Mayhap she is the stronger for taking the route that she has. Your rage is not God's path.

Then why select her for such a task?

She could only ride at the One's command and hope He would reveal His plan when the time was ripe.

Why am I languishing here, waiting for an escort I do not need, when I should be about the One's business?

Ryanna had no answer. She felt as if the whole world held its breath, awaiting … somewhat she could not foresee.

Southern Glenconyn

*T*amys surprised himself by posting a trot his second afternoon in the saddle. Of course, Padraig had hold of the halter rope, but it felt good to know he could keep his seat even though he couldn't see. His eyes were covered by the strip of cloth because the sun made his head hurt. Not that what he could see really made any difference in what he could see. It was all an incomprehensible blur.

Tamys flinched when the field of purple burst across his vision.

"I've told you. There are no trees."

"I know. Where are we?"

"Just south of the elven ruins. We'll be circling back soon."

"What do you see?"

Tamys waited through Padraig's momentary pause. Describing things was a newly acquired skill.

"Prairie. Lots of golden green grass, wild wheat."

"Flowers?"

"Aye, just ahead."

"Purple flowers?"

"Aye. Do you know these flowers?"

"This is the farthest south I've been in my life, so likely not. It's the oddest thing. My eyes are covered. You cook bacon and I see pigs. I smell flowers and then I see them. It's like a hallucination, I suppose, but it's not entirely, is it?"

"I've heard of this. Scent drives memory. Smell a flower and it can trigger visual memories associated with the scent."

"I've never before …"

"I can't explain that part. It does explain the pig, however. Turn your horse to the left. Tell me when you think he's lined up with the road."

"I can cheat at that, Padraig." Tamys pulled the horse's head round until it lined up with the road. "War horses are trained to take the path of least resistance, which is the road. There are subtle shifts in his body that tell me when he's aligned. And the scent of the flowers is now behind me."

"I don't care how you do it. We're going to canter back."

"I suppose you'll have me galloping on the morrow."

"I know you think I'm pushing too hard, asking too much of you when you can't see, but …."

"Nay, you need to get through a forest and over the mountains by winter. My choice is to do what you need me to do or die here. Besides, I think I'm feeling better, at least until I begin to feel what I'm doing."

They walked, trotted, cantered all the way back to camp. Although Tamys expected to be exhausted after a half day in the saddle, he found he wanted a wash and dinner before he collapsed into his blankets. He had removed the blindfold and was eating dinner when he hallucinated the hawk. For all the times he'd felt like he inhabited the bird's body, he'd not seen the bird itself until it landed in the misty grey that was his vision. He reached out toward it, expecting it to dissipate like mist in the heat, but his fingers touched feathers.

"Careful, lad. That's a wild raptor you're petting," Padraig whispered. "Don't make any sudden movements."

"I can see it and feel it."

Tamys heard Padraig's breathing cease.

"Have you been dreaming of this bird for some time?"

"Since I woke up from the coma."

The vision of the hawk tore apart as if shredded by an unfelt wind. With a rustle of feathers, the hawk launched itself into the sky. Tamys tried to pull his hand back slowly, but he was grateful the raptor didn't attack.

"Surely you are a puzzle," Padraig proclaimed. "Where'd you get your sword?"

"My grandmam gave it to me." Tamys yawned as a dull throb started in his forehead. Sometimes breathing deeply helped. "I don't have the energy for this mystery. I need to sleep."

"Of course. We'll have lots of time to discuss it and mull the possibilities over while we're riding."

Padraig led him to his blankets, helped him with his boots and then let him settle down into dreamless sleep. Sometime in the night, he dreamt he was the bird, dozing in a tree, the branch beneath him softly swaying in a wind, a fire near at hand to two sleeping humans and three drowsing horses. He settled back into the dreamless sleep, secure, watched over, oddly fulfilled.

Dun Llyr

*H*owedd had expected to need to hire another chirgeon following his father's death, but he'd not been certain of how to go about it. Every last one of the under-chirgeons had declared themselves unqualified for the post. To have a chirgeon just show up at the gate had been disconcerting. Sawyl was beyond qualified, having worked at duns across the kingdom. Having grown up outside of noble circles, Howedd had knowledge of field care and herbal remedies. Sawyl had tolerated his questions calmly. The under-chirgeons reported his knowledge of surgery and bone setting to be greater than their own. The turning of the tide had come when they had discussed the infant palsy. Howedd well remembered when it had swept the Bottom and the Gold Unicorn when he was a child. Sawyl had observed some of the same things Howedd had and that gave Howedd great comfort.

Now if he could just shake the feeling that somewhat was amiss with the man, all would be well. He couldn't place a finger to the reason, but he did not wholly trust Sawyl in matters other than medicine.

Howedd had been watching Sawyl detail gardeners in the medicinal herb garden near the Mendicant's tower, musing about his distrust of the man and wondering what he should do about it when Sawyl had spied him. Leaving the gardeners to dig in the dirt, he strode boldly up to the vyngregtrix.

"This will be a fine garden. Rich soil," he reported. "How is it that you are acquainted with herbs?"

"I didn't grow up here in the dun. The place where I was raised had its own herb garden for food and another with medicinals."

"I had heard that you were legitimized only recently."

"Aye, what do they call me behind my back?"

"The whoreson," Sawyl informed. Shock flashed across his face when Howedd laughed.

"It is what I am," he explained. "Naught is gained by trying to deny it. But I am their rig and they will come to appreciate me in time … well, mayhap not the nobles. To some of them, that's all there will ever be of me."

"You seem remarkably sanguine about the situation."

"I cannot change the circumstances of my birth. I can only conduct myself in as honorable a way as I can, so as to silence the loudest of the whispers. But you can never silence the thoughts that are in men's heads." Howedd looked out across the new straight rows. "It seems there were herbs here before. Why are you planting new so late in the season?"

"We can get another crop this summer. You can see there was once glass in the frame structure. If it were replaced, we could grow herbs all year long."

That's an expensive undertaking.

"Truly? That's a lot of glass. I'll have to consider it."

"Of course, sire."

I really should consider his suggestion, and not just for herbs, but for vegetables. We would feed many more people if we had winter gardens.

He thought that an odd idea considering the expense, but it was also a good idea. The Golden Unicorn had a winter garden and he had cherished certain vegetables in the middle of winter.

"I intended to ask, why you haven't married yet, sire."

"I haven't truly had time. My father tried to marry me off a handful of years ago, but it's harder to find a bride for a bastard spare heir. Then my brother died and things changed, but I wasn't interested in wedding his widow and my father was loath to force me to marry against my will."

"Who decides such things for the vyngretrix?"

"I do. I can do the unheard of and select a bride I like rather than one chosen by others."

"Do you have advisors for it?"

"My mam."

Sawyl looked uncomfortable trying not to look uncomfortable.

"Aye, there are those who would question a harlot's choice in noble brides, but trust me when I say, I trust her in this implicitly."

"They don't marry often, do they?"

"Harlots? Nay. Husbands are a liability. There's a tendency for them to become jealous over their wives' pasts. Some of them do take their wages and buy a farm or business with a husband, but it generally works out badly. They come back to settle in to what they know. It's an easier life than farming, to be sure."

Sawyl nodded.

"I would think sons would be a liability as well."

"The Golden Unicorn has resources. My brothers would have places in the world even without their connection to me. The House would have bought them prentices or dealt with a dun to get them honor position. But, aye, the lesser brothels – lads are turned out as soon as they can care for themselves. It is a world of women ruled by women."

"Fascinating."

Sawyl seemed sincere, but there was still somewhat about the man ….

"I've been meaning to ask … your time at Galornyn … did you get to know Egoran well?"

"Nay, but I was an under-chirgeon. The family were above my station."

"Well, then I'll leave you to your garden."

"Before you go … I understand your brother has traveled to Dun Celdrya. May I inquire about the reason?"

"Not as yet, Sawyl, mayhap another time."

What explains the sudden urge I have to tell him everything?

Whatever it was, Howedd meant to resist it, for he truly did not trust the chirgeon on some level he could not evaluate.

Southern Dublyn

*O*ne of the horses picked up a stone, causing Gregyn to call a stop for the evening. They were still ahead by two days, so camping just off the road before it reached the main road from the Blyan crossing wouldn't interfere with their overall travel plans. Upon seeing what walked in the grass, he considered it a good time to put some fresh meat in their diets.

"What sorts of birds are these again?" Taryn asked, as they watched the heavy-bodied copper-and-gold feathered fowl forage among some dwarf willow.

"Pheasant. Very good eating."

"I've eaten pheasant. What are the brown ones?"

"Female pheasants."

Taryn laughed, causing the pheasants to alert.

"It's the females who paint themselves in our kind. I just find that funny."

Easy. Remember that this is his first hunting trip. I'm tired. I spent half the night dreaming of that medallion.

Gregyn could feel the power of the medallion just out of reach, even as he held it in his hands. It bothered him that he could do naught with it, while at the same time he wished to know what Taryn might do with it.

He can work magicks. For some reason, they've blocked him, but it's blossoming now. Am I the cause of that?

"Aye, well, the males are bigger, which makes them better eating, but we'll take a couple of the females as well."

"*We* will." Taryn gestured with the bow. "I've never used this thing outside the practice yard."

"Where you do very well. This is what you've been asking for – lessons in manhood. Men hunt."

"And if I don't skewer it, what will the men think?"

"They'll think naught because I've sent them to the south to gather wood and turf for the fire. Come now. He's large and bright. Get on with it."

Taryn did know his way round a bow and arrow. He planted his feet and nocked the arrow. He drew in a deep breath, let it out slowly, drew in a second one … and released the arrow. The pheasant struggled briefly, but the arrow had caught it right behind the chest, so its death struggle was brief.

The rest of the flock scattered. Gregyn clipped the arrowhead bindings and slipped the shaft free before dropping the bird in a bag. Taryn looked doubtful.

"Squeamish?"

"It just seems so sudden … life to death."

"It's the nature of hunting. The females are harder to spot, but do you see her there?"

Taryn nocked the arrow, but this time he missed.

"Your nerves are a bit up, no doubt. Take some deep breaths. Let's see if we can find another."

Stalking pheasants in the summer sun was pleasant enough, though Gregyn had to keep his impatience with Taryn to himself. The lad had never had this opportunity.

Not terribly different from you when you got to the Tongue. You'd hunted rats for food.

Taryn skewered seven pheasants in total. Gregyn got the last one. They headed back to camp where they turned the plucking over to the cook.

"These would be better stuffed with mushrooms and acorns," the cook suggested.

There was an oak tree surrounded by smaller oaks and willows to the south, so Gregyn showed Taryn the fruits of the forest. They found gold chanterelles near the roots and wood hens at the base of the tree.

"You have to watch carefully with mushrooms because they can make you sick," Gregyn explained. "Smell."

"It's … peach … or … apricot?"

"That's what you're looking for in the chanterelles, aye. We'll leave the wood hens for someone else."

"They do look rather like chickens. How do you know which acorns are good?"

"If they rattle, toss them."

Did I ever think to see a noble gathering acorns for dinner?

Camryn, the cook, seemed as amused by Taryn's culinary participation as Gregyn was fascinated, because he asked them to crack the acorns. Taryn had no idea about this either, but soon was an old hand at placing an acorn on a flat rock and smashing it with a fist-sized one.

While the pheasants were cooking, Gregyn accompanied Taryn to the tent so the young lord could change his siarc.

"Thank you for the lessons," Taryn said as he fingered water through his sweaty hair.

"You're my employer and you asked me to help you with this."

"Aye, but you don't seem to snicker at me behind my back, I appreciate it."

"I would have no idea how to greet a vyngretrix or what foods are acceptable to offer him. Nor do I know ought about wines. Am I a fool for not knowing or have I never had occasion to learn?"

"The second."

"It's the same for you … except now you do know … somewhat."

Taryn nodded, turning to where his siarc sat on the bed.

"I want you to have this," he said, turning round with the medallion in his hand.

"Indeed? Are you serious?"

"Very much. I think we both know that it is somewhat special. It felt at first like it should be mine, but the more I think on it … you know what I'm trying to say, aye?"

"Somewhat." The medallion felt heavy. The chain spoke of wealth and strength. The stone itself was smooth and cool, a deep blue with darker veining. "Are you absolutely certain? Isn't it worth a lot of coin?"

"I don't think so. That dun wasn't plush. The other jewelry was common enough. I can't explain it, but it isn't for me. It should be yours."

Now that it was in his hand, Gregyn felt uncertain. He could feel its power still, but he couldn't exercise his own. It left him hollow feeling, more hungry than the span since midday could account.

But he's right. You can feel it. It is for you, somehow.

He dropped it into his neck pouch with the malachite brooch.

"Thank you. If you change your mind, you should say so."

"I don't think I will, but it's good of you to offer." He raised his nose like a dog smelling a cooking fire. "I'd say dinner is just about ready." He buckled his belt over his siarc. "Stopping here was a thoroughly inspired idea."

"It wasn't mine. Unless we wanted to cripple a horse, we needed to stop. It just happened to be a wonderful camping ground. Tomorrow, the city walls ought to come into view. We'll be there the next day."

"Good. I'm ready to collect the dowry and the page and to head back home. I can't shake the feeling that there's somewhat back there I should be attending to … which, when you think about it, is a very odd thought for a very spare heir to have."

Gregyn felt a tingle down his back that mimicked the shudder he saw run through Taryn's body.

"It's likely naught," Gregyn assured. "You're homesick."

Taryn nodded. Proceeding him out of the tent, however, Gregyn thought that Taryn might have the right of it. Mayhap this feeling of dream had less to do with his own disability and more to do with whatever was on the horizon.

Dublyn Grasslands

*T*he small rodent squealed and tried to flee, but Sabre pinned it with a large foot, grabbed it with his mouth, slammed it against the roof with his tongue and ate it in one gulp.

The grass bent round him as a wind swept the prairie. There were farms nearby, but nobody had noticed him on his journey from Ama'na. Some had thought they saw him, but the Companion link came with benefits. He couldn't exactly ensorcel other species, but he could make them think they hadn't seen him. Their dogs were more of a challenge. Those he could ensorcel though, make them think he was a friend, a litter mate even.

He sometimes missed his litter mates. He'd been thinking of them a bit as he hunted the prairie. They'd been young, eyes just opened, when the Celt had come to Ama'na.

~Mama, what is that smell? he had asked.

~Death, young cub. The two legs have killed one another.

She had carried them into the cellar of the bathhouse, hoping to keep them safe. The smell of smoke and roasting meat was very close, however.

~The girl is not one.

~What girl, cub? his mother had asked.

~The one I see in my sleep.

His mother had not understood what he meant. It had been the first thought that he was different from his litter mates. After the fires had found no more fuel and the two legs had deserted this place, his mother had mourned for her master and then allowed her pups to explore the village. She had punished some of them for going into the place where the two-leg bones were. Sabre had not been punished because he had not touched the bones. He'd assured to himself that his girl was not there. No, she was off to the northwest with a dark mind. His brothers and sisters had not understood why he cared. His mother wanted another two-leg. It was the way of dogs. They had played the rest of the summer and then fall had come and she had told them it was time to find two-legs. They had followed the lake to the south, toward where the women had taken the children. But Sabre had known he should not go with them. It was time to leave his mother and siblings. He'd nuzzled his mother's nose, turned north and never seen them again.

They'd be long dead now. Companions matched their life length to their Companion. Ryanna would live centuries, so he would too. But he missed close relations with his own kind. *Ah, yes, the scent of female nearby.* Unlike Kin, dogs did not care who their fathers were. Sabre neared the farm and laid down in the grass. It was near sunset and two-legs would go into their den for the night. The female was tied, but she wouldn't object to his visit. She wanted pups. Sabre waited as the night grew dark. He smelled food cooking. He walked close. A cow sounded alarm. He Sent to it that he was its dog. A goat bleated. He soothed it. The female wagged her tail at his approach. She was a lighter color with a short coat that didn't shed water. Her two-legs would be impressed with his pups. She offered him her food. Unlike most males, he did not take it. He could hunt. He would give her pups and then he would go to his girl.

~*Where are your two-legs?*

~*Near. They are travelers.* That was near enough to the truth to not be a lie.

~*My two-legs want me to mate with a dog next farm over, but you're here now. Will you give me pups?*

~*I will and they will be beautiful, good hunters and protective of livestock.*

~*My two-legs will appreciate your seed.*

Their time together was brief, not like the two-legs, but he nuzzled her nose before he trotted off into the night. Far off in the night, he felt Ryanna's mind. She didn't want to know what he did when he was not with her. He Sent warm thought her way and she responded. There was time. He needn't come immediately. There were lots of rodents out here in the grass.

Forgotten Past

There were objects of power given to the Royal family, supposedly by the elven king himself. A sword, a goblet, a medallion, a key, a ring and a message tube. These disappeared when Donyl fled the city. None know where they have gotten to. Mayhap they are in Dengyal, if Donyl did indeed reach that outpost.

**Dumyr, Chief Councilor to Court Trevellyn,
Summer FY 932.**

Past

Founding Year 931 –a century ago
Denygal Wilderness

*W*hat made this highway?" Donyl asked as they trod a more or less flat portion.

"The dwarves." Janara indicated the rough stone of the upland cliff. "It must have been under construction at the Scourging because it was never finished."

"The Scourging?"

"It's what the Kin call your Arrival. Do you know what scourging is?"

"It's a punishment meted out to soldiers. They are whipped many times."

"Do you understand why the Kin might call it the Scourging?"

"It must have seemed like a punishment to them – forced to live in villages instead of wild in the forests."

She stopped and stared at him as if he'd just grown two-heads.

"I've gotten somewhat wrong again, haven't I?"

"There were grand cities in the basketlands – the lands your people took. Cities bigger than Clarcom and smelling more pleasant. There were a dozen collegiates scattered across the basketlands. There's only one left. You very much got history wrong, Celtman."

Donyl saw the stubborn set of her full lips and offered his next comment carefully.

"I grew up in a dun library with tutors who thought themselves very learned. Mayhap they didn't know history so well." She relaxed. "Or mayhap your own people have created a fiction to sooth them." She stiffened. "I don't know which might be true. It was one of the reasons I was coming to Denygal."

She breathed out forcefully, pulled her water bottle free of its pouch and settled her bottom on the ground with her back to the cliff.

"How old are these tutors?" she asked.

"I don't know. My father's age. Mayhap 50-60 years."

She smiled at the sky.

"My mother is more than 300 years old. I've seen 60 winters myself."

"Nay! You're my age!"

"Am I?" she asked. "By the laws of my people, I am nearing my majority. I suppose that makes me the equivalent of your maturity. But elves number our lives in centuries."

"I don't believe you."

"Because your tutors didn't tell you it was true? My father was born in southwest Galconyn before your family purged the region and they fled to Denygal."

Donyl stared at her, not sure to be shocked or stunned.

"That was in the 6th century."

"Aye. That's what I'm trying to tell you. There are Kin who remember the Scourging. There are few old enough who remember Before, but they grew up with the threat of Celts just over the ridge. When you met me, you didn't know what to think, aye? I'm not part of your experience. You knew almost nothing about Denygal or elves. Well, now you know different. You've seen an elf. My ears weren't cropped when I was a bairn and my eyes really are catslit. So, when I tell you there were elven cities in the basketlands and that my parents are old enough to remember when the corner stone was laid for your dun, you shouldn't scoff. Consider that when you make assertions about us running round the forests like woodland creatures, you're believing fairy tales told by men who live entire lives in fewer years than we spend in childhood."

He saw a young lass before him, but the things she'd said began to come clear. Her knowledge of the trails, her sure confidence in the things she did … it was consistent with being much older than she looked.

"Let's say I believe that you're older than my father. Why have I never seen any of these cities?"

"Did you ever venture into the cellars of your dun?"

"Rarely."

"Were there fantastical paintings of people who looked like me?"

He swallowed tautly and nodded. That's where I've seen someone like her before.

"Many of the great cities of Celdrya are said to be built on the ruins of elven cities. What better way to hide them than to put your duns upon them."

"And in hiding them, it would allow them to make up history?"

"Aye, because it serves your leaders more to have people believe that they brought light into darkness and civilization to the wild fairies than that they destroyed a civilization."

Why doesn't she seem angry? She's so calm. Is it the many years of life that teaches them patience?

"I am not king to make edicts, but I may well be regent when I return to Celdrya. What may I do to rectify this?"

"Rectify? As if you can put right two generations — well, from your perspective 30 generations — of occupation, purges, rapes and death? You can't and you shouldn't try." She sighed. "Mayhap you should allow elves to return to the basketlands. Mayhap that would end the cycle of death."

"Cycle of death?"

"Elves lived 1000 years before the Scourging. Now most perish before they're 600."

"Of what?"

"Old age. They wither and fade, like fruit cut from the branch."

She tilted her head to look at the swiftly scudding clouds, then rose gracefully from the ground.

"We need shelter. Storm's coming."

She disappeared over the verge of the downslope, slithering between the bows of wind-torn daemon's club. He followed her downslope as big raindrops began rattling the broadleaves. He landed on his bottom and had to follow like this as she grabbed tree branches and moved far more quickly than he was capable of. When she found a rock overhang, she grabbed his siarc to keep him from continuing down the slope and they sheltered under the low hanging roof. He spread the tarp over them, so that they were relatively dry as rain began pounding all round. Lightning rent the sky and thunder rolled after. For a bit it was too loud to think, let alone talk. Wind tore at the trees and here and there out in the storm they heard boulders falling. The air grew cold as the rain slacked. The sun was going down.

"We'll reach the bridge on the morrow," she told him, fog coming from her mouth. "Might as well sleep here and wait for the rain to stop. You look chilled."

"It's very cold."

"Aye. Northern summer does not last so long as in the basketlands."

"Why do you call it that?" He shifted his weight. His leg didn't like holding still so long and the cold was starting to sink into his bones.

"Basketlands? That's what the folks who remember living there call it. I suppose it's like the idea of the Promised Land flowing with milk and honey."

"The Promised Land. I'm confused. Your folks lived there before. How is it promised?"

"Nah nah nah. From the Scriptos. Ysrael was promised to the Hebrews. But your folk know naught of this."

"Nay. What is Scriptos?"

"It is the writings of the One."

"That's your god, aye. Who wrote these?"

"He guided the hand of the writers."

"How do you know this?"

"How do I know many things that you do not? The Promised Land was in your old world, I think."

"You're saying this Scriptos came here with us."

"With Ryla of Krystan Celts, aye. Her father was pastor of the church at Trevorri. They came through with King Gwin."

"Your folk don't happen to know how they came through, do they?"

"Nay. If we could have stopped it, we would have. Well, I'm not being truthful. If we'd stopped it, the Scriptos would not have come to us and we would be living in ignorance still, so perhaps your folk coming was wrought by the One."

He yawned and then a shudder ran down his body. He needed sleep and dry clothes, but the second was not likely as the rain continued to fall. He leaned his head back against the rock and listened as she talked. He quite enjoyed her soothing tones. The One rules all with a loving hand and He asked only obedience. This came from the old world. Believers had lived among the Celts, but had come to live among the elves when the Celts had persecuted them both. He would question it in the morn when he woke, but for now, it was enough to listen while the drip-drip-drip soothed him into sleep.

Present

Founding Year 1028
Southern Glenconyn

*P*adraig couldn't shake the image that had flashed across his retinas a moment before the creature had disappeared – that of a beautiful woman with long black hair flowing out behind her as she fled. He woke early, disturbed by his thoughts. Tamys was still sound asleep, so Padraig walked about the outskirts of their campsite, muttering prayers to himself before settling down to inspect the raven feather. It felt like he held filth in his hand, just as it had when he'd held the other feather Aethyn had brought to him. Aye, this had been left by the daemon, just as the first had been. Padraig put them both back in the pannier, uncertain what to do with them. He wanted to toss them away, but a part of him knew that someone, somewhere, would know more about this than he and the raven feathers would help with the answer.

Tamys groaned and groped about his blankets. Padraig grabbed a water bottle and approached him.

"You slept hard, lad. You want water?"

"Ale would be better, but I know I'll get naught from you."

Tamys took the water bottle and drank down a long draught. He held his face up to the light.

"It's morning, aye?"

"It truly be. I'll set the breakfast provisions out so that you may eat while I load the stock."

"For a moment, I thought I saw light," Tamys reported. He wriggled his fingers before his eyes. "Has that bird been back?"

"Not that I've seen."

Tamys still had not the energy to regret his inability to help Padraig. He nibbled a spare breakfast and struggled to find both boots to wear. Padraig came back to find him kneeling on the ground beside his rolled blankets. Tears were spilling down his cheeks.

"Somewhat the matter, lad?"

"I can't find the rope," Tamys whispered.

Padraig's heart twisted with compassion. The rope lay within reach, but just out of where Tamys had tried. Life would be fraught with these sort of difficulties for a long time to come and there was naught for it.

"Here you go. You finish up while I eat a bit myself."

Tamys managed to get his bedroll into a fairly compact bundle, then sat back on his buttocks as if straining to see somewhat, his back against the wall. Padraig didn't disturb his thoughts.

He'll be needing time such as this to heal. Mayhap I cannot help with that, but if I might, God, you must show me how.

Tamys hadn't been a particularly chatty companion before his fall, but the melancholy pulled him into even deeper silence. It was half the morning before he spoke.

"What's about?"

"Prairie still. There's an abandoned elven farm village. They kept the livestock enclosed by houses with fences between. Their fruit trees have taken over though."

"How far to the forest?"

"On the morrow, I think. I've seen the hawk once, by the way. It was a distance off, but Denygal have good eyes."

Tamys swallowed, breathed deeply and chose to stay positive.

"What do you think it wants with us?"

"I think it wants naught from me, but somewhat from you.

"Me? What?"

"I dunno. Mayhap it's to do with the daemon."

"You mean the she-witch that threw me out the window?"

"That's no lass," Padraig said. "She manifested into the physical the other night."

"You saw her?"

"I talked to him."

"Him?"

"Remember the lad on the Madorlyn road? He said his brother was a brigand and asked us for a ride into the town?"

"Aye. Somewhat about him creeped my flesh. You're saying he's the daemon?"

"Or the daemon chose his form, but more like it's one of the forms the daemon takes. Fairly effective – taking the form of an innocent-seeming child or a beautiful temptress."

Tamys grinned and blushed.

"Somewhat?" Padraig unstoppered a water bottle and took a long swallow.

"She …" Tamys' voice squeaked. "The other night in the dream … she weren't wearing clothes."

Padraig choked on his water, which made Tamys laugh.

"I'm starting to sort out some of what I hear. You were drinking water, aye?"

"I was," Padraig croaked. "I can see why you did not resist her immediately."

"I didn't remember her at first. That night's not in good focus."

"That's normal considering your injuries. There's the hawk again. He's got somewhat in his talons."

The hawk swept in low and landed on Padraig's saddle peak. It fixed its amber gaze on him for a moment before it fluttered away, leaving a still warm rabbit behind.

"Did it – a rabbit?"

"Did you see that?"

"Sort of. It's not like sight. It's – like a hallucination, but vivid. I can't explain it. Why would a wild hawk deliver a rabbit to us?"

"I've some thoughts, but I must mull them. Will you wait?"

"I've little choice. I fancy rabbit stew for dinner."

"We'll stop early enough for that, I think. You've lost a lot of weight, so eating good food is important for regaining your strength."

Tamys sighed.

"What will I be regaining my strength for?"

"I'm not convinced your blindness is forever, but even if it is, blind people are not inherently weak."

"Just reliant on others."

"For now. I think you may find, with time, that you're not as dependent as you think. You've mastered horse riding. We'll work on other areas as you have energy."

"Your optimism is annoying, you realize, aye?"

"In time, you'll thank me for it."

Southern Dublyn

*G*regyn woke before dawn and eased out of the tent. Taryn often was awake by this time, still getting used to not sedating himself with spirits, but he slept deeply tonight, exhausted by the power he'd channeled in the ruined dun.

Gregyn had felt Maddw's wielding of power at the morning of their leave-taking. He'd been surprised to sense the incredible power because Maddw so rarely used it. Gregyn assumed Maddw had unlocked whatever restraints were on Taryn's abilities. Still, it was only a trickle of what Gregyn knew Taryn was capable of.

Why? What are they afraid of? Your mother? Peddryna's gift is middling at best. Do they fear she will sell you to the mages? What would they think if they knew about me?

From the squatting pit, Gregyn set off into the cane grass that surrounded the marshes. When he thought he was far enough from the camp, he leaned against a tree and pulled out his neck pouch. The medallion seemed to shimmer in the dark. The lapis stone was a thumb's length across and a bit longer, oval in shape. He could feel its essence of incredible power, but he couldn't touch it with his mind. His gift pounded against Naraddal's barrier, unable to push beyond it. He felt round the barrier, trying to find a weakness, any hole where he might channel a trickle of power that could become a larger flow. He'd tried this before and made himself ill, but today, with a talisman of incredible power in his hand, he felt well. But he had no more success than previously.

The sky to the east flushed with the first light of dawn. He smelled the cook mending up the fire. He knew he needed to head back to the camp. The grey light of dawn washed the tree and the amulet grew warm. The dark blue stone drew him in like a deep well. His vision faded into a world he'd not seen before – a band of horses and people coming down a mountain trail. A sense of concern washed over him as he saw the group. He tasted blood in the air and knew that the world was changing in a disastrous way.

The vision faded and the stone no longer was a well. He heard riders jesting as they used the squatting pit. He returned the medallion to the pouch and walked toward the road, gathering an armload of wood as he went.

Why did he give it to me? Surely, he could feel the power of it. He was drawn to it, after all. Why give it to me? What if it is meant for him?

Gregyn did not know the answer to those questions. Taryn was dressed and directing the men to break their fast and break camp. They'd lost a day of travel, but they'd already been two days ahead thanks to Gregyn's choice of route. Still they needed to be on their way now. One of the men offered him a tankard of ale, but Taryn told him to enjoy it himself. He dipped a tankard of water for himself.

You're learning what stands in your way. What am I missing here?

The pouch against his chest felt warm. A vision formed in his mind – Taryn running his hand along a building stone as what could only be a dragon flew overhead. He didn't know the reason, but he felt like he was going to know soon enough.

Dun Clarcom

My brother is a lovely idiot!

Duncyn watched as Kefyn chatted with Shyla in the flower garden. They stood much too close together when in public view.

I am the least likely person to make this stand. If my father could see me now.

He gathered his arguments like stones to hurl at the couple and walked boldly up to them. Kefyn caught him in his peripheral vision and took a step back.

Aye, you know what I'm about to say.

"Are you trying to get yourself killed, lad? And, you, lass. What do you think your father will do if you cost him his investment?"

Kefyn had the grace to look embarrassed, but Shyla's blue eyes flashed with irritation.

"We're not doing anything wrong."

"Wrong is in the eyes of the beholder and your father could be the beholder. This is a man who killed his own brother, who beat his first wife until she was fit only for the Temple of the Moon."

"He won't kill his prize mare."

"Won't he? I doubt that. I'll make this easier for both of you. Kefyn, you will no longer speak with Shyla." Kefyn looked shocked but before he could protest, Duncyn spoke over him. "Our father made me your guardian on this trip. You will do what I say or I'll take you back to Trevellyn and you can wait there for the winter. Is spending time with a woman you can never marry worth the cost of your defiance?"

"I thought you were a nice man," Shyla complained tearfully.

"I am a nice man and I'm trying to save your young and foolish lives."

Kefyn is hearing me. The lass ... she's younger. Scared of somewhat besides me.

"I won't force you to make a decision this moment. Kefyn, arm's length and I'll allow you to set things at rest."

Duncyn left the two and didn't look back. He trusted Kefyn to love Shyla enough to take the wiser choice when it was offered.

He hadn't gone more than a dozen steps and rounded the curve of the broch when he found the taller of the two Denygal women in front of him.

"Ryan," he greeted. "Are you looking for me?"

"Aye. Lydya tells me she's sending you as a messenger to the west."

"And you're headed west, so you're hoping to travel along."

This one knows how to handle herself, which she will need if she brings that lass with us.

"When will you be leaving?"

"When Lydya commands it. She wants me to travel with her son and the dowry to Galornyn."

"Has the embassy arrived yet?"

"Nay and it will be some days after they arrive before they'll return. Patience not your highest virtue?"

She laughed. Denygal often seemed ageless. He suspected this one was a half-elf, so while she looked a lass, she was mostly likely twice his age. It explained the wisdom in her eyes and the self-knowledge.

"I could set off on my own, but my spirit says I shouldn't be defiant just yet."

Duncyn nodded, though he had naught to say about spirits.

"You're welcome to come with us when the time comes. May I ask … why are you traveling west?"

"Your brother didn't tell you?"

"My brother is a faithful young lad who sees the world colored by the One. I think you are more astute than that."

"The One gave me a vision that sent me on this course. I can only assume that the One will grant direction when I reach where I am being sent. Kefyn says you're quite the man with a fighting staff. Mayhap we can spar."

She stood just a hand-breadth shorter than he and he could see by the way she stood that she'd had training with the sword she wore. Staff fighting was often where Dengyal women began.

"Aye. Meeting you in the morning on the sparring grounds would be a fine entertainment. Now it's time for a tankard of ale and a game of hounds and hares. Do you play?"

"Badly. You'll find better competition among the riders. I have things to do. See you at dawn."

As she continued toward the stables, he found himself watching her back in admiration. She only played the part of a male, but she was all female under the breecs and sword belt. He would have to watch himself round her or he would give her ruse away and he suspected she would not deal kindly with him in those circumstances.

Blue Iris Holt

*M*orynsynsioncai finished coiling the last bit of rope while Morynsion folded the last tarp. The storage cave looked neat and tidy. Father and son sat down on a bench to admire their handiwork. Cai sighed with exhaustion, content with having finished another successful caravan.

"How is Madi handling the news of Ryanna's mission?"

"Your mother is very upset," Sion said with a rueful laugh. "She cannot separate God's guidance from Ryanna's romance with Padraig."

"What does one have to do with the other?"

Sion sighed and shrugged. He spoke in Celdryan.

"Marnmara sees things concern Ryanna through a glass darkly, still stuck in the morass of 20 years ago."

"Does she blame you?"

"For Ryanna's decision at Ama'na – for my not spending more time seeking her rather than taking the others to safety – aye. That will always lay between us. But this … nay. She blames this on Ryanna completely."

"She does not acknowledge the One's Long Hand in all of it?"

"She says she does, but she still does not see Ryanna as obedient."

"And you?" Cai asked.

"Adulthood reaches out to all of us eventually. I can only hope Ryanna is responding to that call now."

Cai scratched fingers through his dirty hair. He needed a long bath.

"I think she is obedient. I wouldn't have taken her braid if I hadn't." He pointed to his pack saddle. "I'll give that to you when I've had a bath and some sleep."

"No rush. You know we never got the first one. They burned it when they thought they might be found out among the Celtmen."

"That sounds like Gil."

"And, you, son? Did Sarala give you her braid or does it go to another?"

"She sends it to Gly and Banara."

"Does that sadden you?" Sion asked.

"It does. I would have waited."

"And now?"

Cai sighed.

"I need a bath, sleep and food before I can answer that, Da. And maybe not even then. Mayhap Earmon will make you a grandfather soon."

"Mayhap I am content with your lives as they are. I just want you to be happy."

"The One will lead in that area when the One leads, then. Now I'm for that bath."

"Marnmara most likely wants my presence for the evening meal. Will you join us?"

"Nay, but if you want to leave a bowl in my quarters, I would not object."

"I'll do that then. First, though – Shanara has called the alarm. She believes the Svard amass on our northern border sooner rather than later."

"It's turning winter north of the Roof, Da."

"I know, which gives us time. She's been scrying to the other holts, trying to warn them. There's been no response from some of the north."

"Her home holt?"

Sion nodded. Cai rubbed his jaw where a moon's worth of beard scratched.

"I need a bath, sleep and a meal before I decide to ride messenger to the northern holts. I'll consider this in the morning."

"Of course, son. Mayhap Earmon will want to go with you."

"You sense somewhat?"

"Just a cold breeze coming out of the mountains … or an old man worried for his sons."

Cai felt a shudder run through his body. He needed a long hot bath before thinking about this journey.

Elemental

The royal items hold power for those who know how to use them. The vexation is that none remember. There's not been a king in half a milennia who has been able to make them work. It is said that when that king appears, he will live forever.

Caelen of Dun Celdrya, third son to King Marcel (FY 847)

Past

Founding Year 931
Denygal

*T*he sensation of being watched bore into his spine as it had nagged all day, but the need to move forward couldn't overcome his terror.

"You mean to cross that?" Donyl asked, staring skeptically at the affair of rope and board that she called a bridge. Although he'd followed her instructions to lash his gear tightly to his pack, he saw no way forward.

"I know of no other way to cross the Dragon's Tears."

"It does not look safe."

"It is," Janara said confidently.

The river here was narrow, the canyon walls high. Narrow was relative. The far shore was a long distance and the bridge looked frail, swinging in the wind.

"What if it fails?"

"Death will take you quickly. The Tears is cold beyond imagining and there's a cataract not far downstream."

She grinned at him like a berserker preparing to charge into battle.

"Follow me, but keep a distance so that our combined weight doesn't affect the swing of the bridge."

"The bridge swings?" he croaked, mostly to empty air since she was already starting out on her journey over the chasm of death.

She walked with hands on both rope rails and her feet at hip width. He hesitated, stomach churning, trying not to look down at the boiling river so far below. She didn't look back, so that eventually he knew that he would be left behind if he did not follow. That feeling of being watched from the stones cast ice down his back. He grabbed the cable railings to step out on the deck. The bridge moved slightly in the wind and with Janara's light steps, but it seemed stable enough. The far shore was a long distance and the distant river was a tumult of brown eddies that sucked whole trees down and spit them out as kindling. Janara had not halted her forward movement. He followed to not be left behind.

The farther from the shore anchor he got, the more the bridge moved in the wind. It was disconcerting because the bridge moved in an opposite direction of the river current. An occasional gust of wind swung the bridge harder than average, frightening him into freezing. Janara kept walking. He swallowed nausea and followed her.

Wind tore at his clothes, his ears froze and his nose ran. Though dry, the deck slanted toward the river as the wind lifted the whole bridge upriver. He continued walking, grateful for the ropes that held the deck, because they kept his foot from sliding to the down rail ropes.

Janara reached the far shore and knelt to reorder her pack. Anxiety relaxed its taut grip on his chest and he moved forward with more confidence until a gust of wind caught the bridge and it shuddered. His left hand slid free of the rope rail and his feet skidded across the deck. He caught his stomach on the down rail and wrapped his arms around it, screaming as the bridge bucked like a stallion and his pack straps bit into his shoulders, threatening to drag him free to his death.

When he dared to open his eyes again, Janara stood at the end of the bridge, hands upon the rails. The bridge no longer bucked, the wind barely gusted. It was as if the world were holding its breath. Remembering the daemon paths and the dragon, Donyl released his convulsive grasp on the railing, straightened and started walking toward Janara again. He wanted to run, to be off this uncertain road as soon as possible, but he knew better. One step, then another. Panic never served well. The bridge's arch turned upward now. The wind grew less. He kept walking until he could link hands with Janara and fall to his knees on solid ground.

"I've never seen a wind like that," she reported breathlessly. "Are you well?"

"I'm intact. It felt like someone grabbed the far end of the bridge and shook it."

Her face taut, she glanced toward the far shore, straightened and glared. He slewed round on his rear, but he could not make out details.

"What do you see?" he asked.

"I thought I saw a woman with flowing black hair. We need to go. If it's an elemental force, it can't cross the river, but there may be others."

"What superstition is this talk of elementals? Tis fairy tales!"

"Naught. Donyl, this world is not yours yet. There is much you do not know. I'll explain as we walk. Come."

The path turned away from the river, though the granite remained on both sides.

"Elementals exist all throughout Daermad. They were here before the Arrival. Some have taken on the image of Celtic gods. They are opposed to thinking beings."

"Mayhap you saw wrong. It was a fair distance."

"My eyes are not the same as yours," she reminded him. "I can see farther and in the dark."

He'd suspected that she could. Still, a half mile was a fair distance.

"You said it couldn't cross the river. Why not?"

"Rivers are elemental forces too and elementals are pulled apart by the forces of other elementals. My worry is … daemons were attacking you when the dragon rescued you. You may still be of interest to somewhat."

The days had somewhat gotten away from him. How many days have passed?

"Is it almost dark of the moon again?"

"An eightnight. We'll still be on the road when the time comes."

"Can hurrying change that? Trust me. We don't want to be out here at dark of the moon."

For the first time, he told her the whole story of his journey to their meeting. She took it rather well, did not call him mad, and didn't seem overly frightened. He'd never met a lass like her before.

"You're right. We need to be moving as quickly as possible toward Farhaven. We do not want to be out here at the dark of the moon."

Present

Founding Year 1028
Clarcom

*T*he air was cool and fragranced with the morning's baking. Ryanna set her staff of honor wood on the battered outdoor table used for staging practice weapons while Duncyn warmed up with a routine of stances. Ryanna stretched her legs and arms, slowly craned her back. Duncyn finally faced her.

"Do you have experience?" he asked.

"Some, but not near enough."

"That's a beautiful piece of wood. Marks you as somewhat more than a mere rider."

"Aye," she agreed. "It came to me by magical means."

Duncyn picked it up, tested it.

"It's perfectly balanced. This should be interesting."

He tossed it to her then picked up his own staff. Before she knew what he was doing, he swung it at her head. She stepped back to avoid the blow, twisted and countered the backswing.

"Good. You don't trust me. That's the first lesson." Duncyn scored a touch on her leg. "Second lesson. Don't let me distract you." He swiveled to tap her arm, but she blocked it. "Good. Now you attack me."

Ryanna danced in swinging the staff, but every move she made, he countered. He called a halt after five blocked moves.

"You're aiming where I am, not where I will be. And you're announcing where you will strike with your gaze. Make use of your Denygal vision to see me out of the corner of your eye and fool me by looking where you don't intend to strike."

They danced round one another, Duncyn scoring more taps than Ryanna. She began to sweat. Duncyn circled. Ryanna blocked. She moved in to tap him. He swept her feet out from under her.

Lying on the ground, looking up at the sky, she realized they'd attracted a small crowd of observers, mostly riders who had come out here to practice. Duncyn held a hand out to help her up.

"We'll have to cede the field soon enough, but we can go another round or two. Don't be gentle. I outweigh you. Don't be worried you'll hurt me."

Ryanna wiped sweat from her face with the sleeve of her siarc. Duncyn took a defensive stance, his staff held horizontally at waist height. Ryanna circled him. She looked down at his feet, then quickly at his right shoulder, dipped her left hand and scored a sting on his left knee. He stumbled. Ryanna dropped the right hand slightly, felt rather than saw him try to counter it, and then swept his left foot out from under him. He landed on his side and rolled away from her, but as he tried to regain his feet, she put the end of her staff on his throat apple. A roar from their audience told her she'd just won the match. She set the staff at her feet and offered him a hand up.

"You need more practice, lad, but you've got the basic idea," Duncyn assured. Then he leaned in to whisper in her ear. "Your sweat is going to give you away."

She grabbed up her cloak and tossed it over her shoulder so as to somewhat hide her physical form. Several of the riders complimented her skill, but nobody asked after her physiology. She quickly walked toward the gate out of the practice yard. Sarala met her along the way.

"That was quite somewhat to watch," she remarked.

"Thank you, but I think he let me score that point at the end."

"Mayhap, but you are so very athletic and strong. Sweat aside, you seem to be one of them."

"In this case, I must say thank you for saying so. I'm off to the baths, though. You and I have practice this afternoon."

"Again? I am meeting with Traegyr to provide him with medicinals."

"Watch him. He doesn't have an aura."

"Neither do half the people in this count, but you don't warn me about them."

"Just remember what I said, because you only get one chance if he's as evil as I think he is."

"We're meeting in the great hall. Off with you now. I'm actually joining the riders for sword practice, so you can spend the afternoon doing somewhat else."

Ryanna turned to her to wish her good luck, but she paused, turning toward the west.

"What is it?"

"I don't know. Power. A great deal of it. It comes this way."

Sarala stared off toward the west as well.

"I see only the ramparts and sky. Are you certain?"

Ryanna felt the sensation ebb away. She tried to locate it again, but it was gone, the vestiges of it disconnected, dissipating.

"I am certain, but …. It's gone now." Gooseflesh raised on her arms. "We know there is more to this fight than what we can see. I'm going to the baths now."

In the bath, Ryanna wiped away the suds from the surface of the water and saw Padraig riding through green grass. The image was weak and fuzzy and then it faded to naught.

Southern Glenconyn

A dense thicket grew at the verge of the old-growth forest. After assuring himself that it was impenetrable, Padraig paused to consider his options.

~*I'd turn toward the setting sun myself,* Joy advised.

~*Why would you?* Padraig asked her.

~Dwarven trade roads went from city to city, not across empty land and the city was that way.

~How does a horse know such?

~I'm not just a horse, of that you can be certain. Please, trust me.

Padraig looked west and decided to do just that. Although they had left the remains of the elven city behind on the plains, Joy's instinct proved quite trustworthy. Within a sun's span he'd found a break in the thick brush where the trees grew less close.

"We've entered the forest," Tamys said a moment after they passed under the canopy.

"Aye. How did you know that?"

Tamys frowned, considering it.

"It's cooler here," he observed. "The sun might have passed behind a cloud, but I can smell rotting wood and fresh earthy growth. Just seemed like a forest, somehow."

"Learning to use that which God gave you to overcome what you've lost. 'Tis a good thing."

Tamys seemed unimpressed by this accomplishment, but Padraig thought it a good sign the lad had taken notice of the world round him. Mayhap the melancholy did not grip him as tightly as it once had. Padraig wondered if it had somewhat to do with the daemon. Had she been drawing somewhat from the lad, depressing him more than his injury already had? Had Padraig slashed some connecting spell? He was not a Wisdom to know such things.

The forest was surprisingly open, with much less undergrowth than Padraig had expected. He'd seen very little virgin forest in Celdrya. The elves claimed there'd been quite a lot in their time, but the Celdryans didn't seem to like trees very much. They'd reduced what the old stories said were vast expanses of forest down to only a few pockets throughout the kingdom. Most were hunting preserves of lords and not very large. What Padraig had seen of them brought memories of dank, weed-choked forests of rot or manicured stands of trees lacking any undergrowth at all. Only in a few places were forests more than a day's ride across. He'd grown up within two days' ride of the true primordial forest in Cenconyn, but he'd never been there. He'd been to the verge of the Black Forest in Dunmaden, for his master Lyam had gone to gather herbs there, and he'd heard of the Devil's Tongue along the southern coast. Then there was this – Mirklin Wood, they called it locally. This was indeed his first journey through one of the old forests. Some claimed elves had a special connection with the forest lands. Padraig supposed they'd find out.

Padraig had more common concerns to occupy his thoughts as they forged into the deeper forest. He rarely had to warn Tamys of low-hanging branches for the lad ducked away from the few they encountered without warning. Padraig remembered the Sense Tamys had shown during a brigand raid in Mandorlyn and how he'd felt a lad healed. The origin of his sword, his vigor at healing, and the hawk all pointed to a question Padraig needed to ask.

The Sight didn't appear often among those without elven blood, but it had been known to Celdryans from the earliest times, since before the Arrival. The druids of the Old Faith were holdovers from that time. It was remotely possible that Tamys' Sight, if indeed it existed at all, was a natural gift rarely, but occasionally born among the Celdryans. Or not. Padraig couldn't help to remember the old saw "a noblewoman marries where she's sent." Where had Tamys' mother hailed from?

A question worth asking.

Tamys, you're altogether too quiet back there," Padraig began. "And I rather miss our conversations. You feeling up to a bit of a chat?"

"I guess," Tamys replied, sounding like he wasn't. Padraig forged ahead, taking opportunity where he found it.

"Somewhat's nagging at me. You talk about your father a good bit – not in the most complimentary turns, but you acknowledge him. Where's your mother?"

"Dead," Tamys answered glibly. Padraig glanced back, thinking the reply too flippant. In the silence, Tamys elaborated. "That's not exactly true. That's the story he tells folks and he's had such rotten luck with wives dying on him that they believe it readily enough. Only thing is, she's not got a grave – naught that I ever found – and my grandfather told me once that he – Corbryn – put her aside."

"For what?"

"He didn't say. I asked Trevyr once, but he smacked me cross the cheek and said it was forbidden to speak of it. Gal said somewhat the same, but he gave me this odd look, like he knew somewhat he wanted to tell me, but daren't not."

"You don't remember her?"

Tamys sighed. Padraig waited.

"I remember a face with long brown hair and a voice singing. I'm not truly certain if that mayn't have been a nurse, but I rather think it was my mother."

"Do you know when she left?"

"I'd guess I was about five, since he remarried when I was six. I know that because his current wife likes to remember firsts. The first time she saw me, she says, I was six and I was up a birch tree in the inner courtyard, hiding from the tutor. She's been round my whole memory, but I actually remember her as my first clear memory. She's a kind lass."

"Lass? How old is she?"

"He likes them young. My mother was 14 when they married. Marya was mayhap 15."

"He does like them young. Where did your mam hail from?"

This had been the whole point of the conversation.

"Pass of the Arrival. My grandfather is lord there."

Padraig thanked God that Tamys couldn't see his disappointment, but then a second thought came to him.

"That's marrying rather close to home," he noted.

"It was a third marriage, mind."

"Third? Where did his first two come from?"

"Trevyr and Galryan's mam was from Galornyn, the current lord's niece, I think. My sister Branwyn's mam came from Galconyn. He'd secured his allies in the north and bought a spot on the sea and the way to it. I supposed the Pass was important enough to marry to it."

"Aye, that's most likely true. Does your grandfather have any alliances of interest?"

"You'll have to tell me sometimes why you're so interested in politics," Tamys mused. Then he ducked under a branch before Padraig might mention it. "I don't truly know. My father and grandfather don't get along. I spent a winter there as a page because my father mistrusted anyone else, but they never spoke round me. I know that my grandmother was a second marriage, as well. His first wife died of a fever after giving him two heirs. My mother was first of two children. Her brother died young."

"That's too bad. Well, I suppose there are many family mysteries. Tell me about your brother Galryan. He's heir now, aye?"

"Aye. I can't imagine him actually being king, though he'll do well enough as rig of Manahan. He'll struggle with his conscience as vyngretrix, I think."

"It would be truly hard to be vyngretrix. Would Trevyr had been better?"

"Aye. Da raised him to be and he was born to it. Gal is more – honest, I suppose is the word."

Padraig had gotten little from that exchange beyond the mystery of Tamys' mam, but that was enough.

"Do you know where from your grandmother hails?" Padraig asked.

"My mam's or my da's mother?"

"Either, truly."

"It doesn't matter, truly, for I don't truly recall. My mother's mam hails from somewhere called Farhaven, but I know naught of it."

Padraig felt that name tickle round the back of his mind. He'd been somewhere called Farhaven – or near to, but he couldn't remember where that might be. He warned Tamys of an encroaching branch.

"My head begins to ache again," Tamys announced.

"Do we need to stop now or can it wait a bit?"

"A bit, I think, but I'd like to be quiet for a while."

"Aye, of course. I've my own thoughts to consider. You let me know if you need a rest."

Clarcom Court

*T*hey arrived in Clarcom in the early afternoon, dusty and hot, having crossed a vast treeless sea of grass with hills like rolling waves. The striking blue of the lake made Taryn's head hurt for shade. They rode their horses slowly through the streets. The city was impressively built, with thick high walls and gates staggered as if expecting war. Taryn's fingers itched for a charcoal and paper at several of the sights they saw – towers and gates, shops and stables. The ward was surprisingly neat and tidy, given that Galornyn considered Clarcom to be a country cousin of sorts. The gatekeeper recognized Taryn's plaid and sent a page immediately to the lord and lady while Taryn's band dismounted. Stablemen came for the horses as Lord Cunyr emerged from the great hall with his councilor at his side.

"Lord Taryn, we expected you no earlier than the morrow," Cunyr explained. He was a man of middling height with a goodly girth and cheeks veined with red. His breath attested that there was a fine flagon of mead within. Taryn's mouth immediately filled with saliva.

"Lord Cunyr," he replied. "We made good time in fine weather. My brother Egoran sends his regards." He removed the message tube from his saddle bag and offered it to the councilor.

"We heard of your father's death," Cunyr said. "Our condolences."

Taryn hadn't expected a mention of his father's death since it had been more than a month. He nodded and looked above Cunyr's head, hoping to hide his pain. A lass in the window of what was the women's hall caused him to completely forget about his grief. Cunyr saw his stunned look and took it wrong.

"Of course, you are still grieving. Would you care for a spot of mead before seeing your chambers?"

Taryn felt Gregyn's eyes upon him like a palpable force and it seemed as if the lass were also staring right at him. The thought of meeting her at table when he'd been drinking mead all afternoon filled him with dread for some reason. He swallowed and ran a hand through his filthy hair.

"I would much rather have a bath and change of clothes at this moment. Can we speak at the evening meal?"

"Certainly. I'll turn you over to the capable hands of Chamberlain Ogrynnyn." He indicated a man standing not far away before he and the councilor turned back to the great hall.

"One moment," Taryn told Ogrynnyn, who had to be old enough to be his great-grandfather. He turned to Gregyn. "You have this?"

"I do. Apparently, so do you. Keep it in mind. There's no shame in turning aside."

"I'll try."

The lass still stood in the window, now chatting with another lass, when he turned back to Ogrynnyn.

"We've a bath chamber. Let me show you and then I'll turn you over to a page. You're not traveling with an attendant?"

For some unaccountable reason, I neglected to arrange one for myself.

"Nay. I wanted a bit of rough living for this outing. On our return, Cullyn will serve."

"Of course. That's a smart way to get him back in the harness."

As they talked, Taryn followed him to a half-broch not far from the main broch, through a door and down a flight of stairs to a generous cellar with a row of tubs in stalls along the lesser curve. One of the tubs was already being filled with hot water from a stone trough that ran along the wall. Taryn observed it with a raised eyebrow.

"Lady Lydya's folk are from Denygal where bath chambers have existed for many years. She championed this.

"Where does the water come from?" Taryn asked, intrigued.

"A large tank above one of the kitchen fires. Baryk will assist you and see that you have clean clothes for the evening meal. Do you wish any refreshment in your bath?"

Taryn's stomach growled as his mouth thirsted for mead or ale.

Ogrynnyn withdrew, closing the door. Baryk was a young page, who tried not to look directly at Taryn as the older lad began to strip off his boots and clothes.

"There is still one set of clean clothes in this saddlebag," Taryn said, indicating. "Can I have some meat and cheese and a tankard of water flavored with ale."

Baryk's eyebrows wriggled.

"You drink your ale Denygal-style?"

He knew naught of the Denygal and did not think Gregyn would either, but it seemed as good an explanation as any.

"At this hour of the day, aye." He tested the water with his hand. Way too hot for his tastes.

"Let me show you," Baryk offered. He caught up a bucket from the floor, allowed it to fill from the trough, then closed the gate on the trough so no more steaming water spilled into the tub. He indicated a nearby stool. "You wash off with the bucket, sponge and soap. The dirty water goes down the drain in the floor and then you can get into the tub and soak, shave and the like."

Taryn felt his chin where his soft beard was getting rather shaggy.

"We could also bring the court barber if you prefer."

"I don't, but thanks. The food is all I require and that you hang my clean clothes so they lose their wrinkles and the smell of leather."

Baryk hung the clothes while Taryn washed, then left to go get food. Taryn tested the water again, pleased to see it was cooling. He slid into the chest deep water, leaned back, bracing his feet against the end. He was just starting to sweat when Baryk returned with a tray of food and a flagon of ale-flavored water. Taryn restrained himself from drinking the entire flagon immediately. He ate food first, drank half a tankard, ate some more food, before shaving and then drinking another half-tankard. By the time he got out of the water, his clothes were fresh and his stomach full and he managed to leave some ale in the flagon.

His chambers were on the fourth floor of another half broch, looking over the kitchen garden. Baryk had taken the rest of his clothes away to be laundered, so that Taryn had naught to unpack. He checked his shave in the mirror and checked the sky to see how many watches he had to wait to see that lass again.

He sat down in the window sill to watch the comings and goings of the dun. They seemed quite similar to the activities at Galornyn. He saw Gregyn stop at the garden gate to speak to Cullyn ap Riordan.

Now what's that about? Surely he knows that people will question why a common-born rider speaks with the spare heir of a great clan.

While he watched, Taryn became aware of a shimmering round the two that he'd seen before, when his grandmam didn't want anyone hearing her conversations. *Is he a mage?*

Nonsense! Why would a mage present as a mere soldier? I know, though, don't I? He can make use of the medallion in a way that I cannot.

But when the two separated, the glimmering moved with Cullyn not Gregyn.

Mayhap I am wrong?

The sun swung round the dun and dropped toward the west. Taryn could smell somewhat delicious roasting somewhere in the complex, so he headed to the great hall. There were servants scurrying here and there and two were setting out a fresh barrel of dark. Taryn dipped water and topped it with pale from a pitcher and told himself to stay very far away from the barrels.

She wore blue dresses and her long dark hair was caught back in a simple braid down her back. Ogrynnyn asked her a question, she gestured and laughed, then turned and saw him staring like a moon-calf in the market.

"You must be Lord Taryn," she said, extending a slim hand. "I'm Shyla nee Riordan."

Taryn shook hands with her and had no time to mourn his loss because somewhat seemed to explode in his brain. She was absolutely beautiful and gracious and whatever she said was brilliant, though he couldn't understand a word of it. Did he speak intelligible words in response to her greeting? Did it matter?

Other courtiers were coming into the great hall. She directed him to the honor table. He sat down upon a cloud of roses and quite forgot to drink any spirits. She sat across from him with her mother beside her. He tried to sort their words out from the nimbus of light that encircled both.

"We've heard there's plague at Galornyn," Lydya said.

Shyla's hands were long and delicate.

"It seems to be on the ebb. The chirgeon notes that infant palsy usually occurs in the summer and wanes in the fall. It's not fall yet, but the numbers are easing."

"I do worry about my son," she explained.

He stared at the nimbus surrounding her, pale golden and flame-shaped. He looked at Shyla, wondering if she saw it too, and saw a similar light.

What does it mean? Did Maddw know I'd see this? Is this what he meant by a mere taste of the power?

"We were sorry to hear about your father," Shyla said. "Was it the infant palsy?"

"Aye. He passed very quickly. Others have been ill much longer and lived."

"No one else in the family?" Lydya asked.

Chew your meat. It gives you time to ponder your answers.

"Nay," he lied and then pondered the look that came across her eyes. Does she know that I am lying? Am I that transparent?

Her aura shifted subtly.

"Of course, you are not allowed the share that information with us," she said. "With the succession so new, your family would want you to hold things close to your chest. I met your grandmam many years ago. How is she faring?"

"Wonderfully. I swear there are times when she seems to be younger than my mam."

"Some people age more slowly than others."

Taryn calculated swiftly and realized that Lady Lydya was one such. She had to be in her fourth decade and yet she had no baggy cheeks or wrinkles fanning out from her eyes.

"Aye, there are those who seem blessed that way."

Along the table, Cunyr had begun to slur from his wine as he spoke with a servitor Taryn had not yet met. Cullyn seemed to listen, but not to speak, while Lydya turned her head to listen to her husband.

"That is a fine vintage, Lord Taryn," Cunyr said. "Will you not join us?"

Taryn recognized his own weakness with wine as he watched his goblet being filled. Could he hold himself to a few swallows while there were far more to drink? He sipped the wine, but in his odd state, he didn't feel the usual wash of warmth through his limbs.

"It is fine indeed," he agreed, pretending to sip again before setting the goblet down.

"Lord Taryn, why did they send you on this mission rather than Shyla's betrothed?" asked a young Denygal lord who sat near at hand.

"Is it the custom hereabouts to do that?" Taryn asked. Shyla and Lydya both laughed. Kefyn had the same sort of aura as Lydya and Shyla, completely unlike the auras of anyone else at the table. A wash of green in the gold was curious. *Aye, my lord, we both love a woman who is totally inappropriate for us.*

"They have not met yet, have they? In Denygal, it is customary for the bride and groom to meet at least a couple of times before the wedding."

"I apologize," Lydya said, favoring Kefyn with a gaze Taryn didn't wish to interpret. "Denygal is a much smaller land than all of Celdrya, so meetings such as Kefyn describes are much easier to arrange. I did hope to meet Teddryn before the appointed date."

I can't lie here. She's already shown that she sees through me.

"Teddryn has duties in Galornyn."

"So he has not taken ill or aught?" Shyla asked. Somehow he did not think she was worried after his brother.

Lydya knows what I am thinking. I know it.

"He was ill for a bit, but was on the mend when we departed. There have been a lot of people ill this summer. My own sergeant spent an eightnight abed. He's hale now."

They accepted the change of subject. Taryn wondered if it would be possible to see Shyla alone, but he knew it would be inappropriate to attempt it. Thus, he was surprised when she drew up beside him at the door as he was leaving.

"It's stuffy in here. Have you seen the rose garden yet?"

The night scented heavily as they walked out a side entrance. His chambers at Galoryn overlooked a similar garden, but he'd never before been able to see flows of energy emanating from the bushes. He suspected Shyla knew what he was experiencing.

"My mam wants you to know that she understands why you can't tell us everything. Do you miss your father?"

"Greatly."

"It is sad when one so young dies. How is your mother keeping?"

"She has my sister to keep her busy and running the dun as Egoran is not yet married. I think she has little time for grieving."

And little inclination.

"How long will you be with us before you must take Cullyn away?"

"We can tarry an eightnight. I hear there will be a tourney."

"Aye. It's a tradition for the 14th summer."

"Lovely."

"Will you compete?"

"I haven't given it any thought." He considered telling her about why he was having so much trouble sorting out his thoughts right now, but a footfall on the path behind them closed his mouth. "Your cousin is following us, you know?"

"I do. Kefyn, who put you up to creeping round behind us?"

"I put myself up," the Dengyal explained. "If you can't go off with me privatelike anymore, you certainly can't go off with him."

"I will soon enough be her brother," Taryn reminded. As he said it, an image of Teddryn being fed by a spoon filled his mind. *Nay, this is only my fear speaking ... or my greed.* "Like as not I will be sent in the wedding party when Teddryn travels to receive you."

"I hope so. If I'm to repair with strangers, I would like at least one person along that I know."

"Surely you're selecting your retinue by now."

"Mayhap," she agreed. "I'll leave you two to talk. I promised Mam I'd join her after dinner."

She walked away toward a secondary broch while Taryn and Kefyn stared at one another in the indifferent torchlight.

"Do you know ought about Denygal?" Kefyn asked.

"Little. Why?"

"Because you will need to."

"What does that mean?"

"Just that I sense there's more to your future than you realize."

Kefyn turned on the garden path and walked a bit away before turning again to him.

"On the morrow, right after we break fast. Let's you and I go riding. We should get to know one another."

High Celdrya

The market faire was sad. It may once have been large enough to fill the plaza, but now there were many dilapidated booths along one side and the active booths lacked a robust offering of wares. Randodd bought a few items while he listened to the conversations of merchants and customers.

"My wool monger moved his herd toward Galconyn," the weaver told a customer who asked why his cloth seemed coarser than in the past. "I found another source, but his wife does not spin so fine a thread. I don't know but that mayhap I should follow. Custom's fallen off by half this year."

"All my chickens died of the smoke last summer during the siege. It takes time to rebuild the flock when there's few about to sell more pullets."

"The army killed all but one of my cows for meat last summer. Tren's men, the louts."

"My husband spent the winter down with the croup and my hand is not as good at leather as his."

When he'd seen what he needed to see, Randodd mounted the city walls at the north-east tower. It gave him a view of the work on the largest of the breeches. All of his knowledge of siege craft came from books, but he tried to make sense of what he was seeing. It seemed to him that what the Celdryan city folk rebuilt on their own was somewhat Howedd would not need to rebuild, but he had to admit that he didn't have the expertise to evaluate the work. During one of the meal breaks, a worker sat down near Randodd. An offer of high quality cheese bought some conversation.

"You're a traveler, aye."

"I am. My father's a merchant from Dun Llyr, hoping to move into the city. He'll be grateful to hear the walls are being repaired."

"Aye, hopefully the repairs will hold against Tren or Corbryn, whichever one comes this next time."

"You doubt they will?"

The worker gazed down at the repairing grounds as he chewed his cheese.

"The walls held for 90 years until Corbryn brought dwarven sappers a decade ago. You see how we must rebuild the wall from the deeper place? Some of our best material is being used for the foundation, which requires the use of other materials in the wall itself."

"I see that you have lighter stone mixed with darker. Is there an advantage?"

"There's naught of an advantage. The original stone was quarried from the Dome. That's the black stone. Very dense and strong. Even the smaller bits of it makes good rubble stone for the filling. The lighter stone comes from the southern palisades. It's granite, but softer."

"Why use the newer source?

"Because quarrying the Dome is beyond our abilities. The stone's too dense. Granite from the southern palisades is softer, so that we can work it, but it's also less able to withstand siege weapons."

"What happened to the original stone? Shouldn't it still be about near the breech?"

"We're using it for the foundation because it is so strong, but there's not enough. Our masons have lost the secret of working the hard stone."

"The secret?"

"There are some who say it were mages' work. Mayhap."

Randodd didn't much believe in mages, but it never paid to embarrass a source of information, so he nodded thoughtfully before asking his next question.

"Why will you block the way to the Mulyn men? Is not one of them the True King?"

"Hah, and how do we be knowing which one? That's a vexed situation at best. I'm thinking the True King will be proving himself to us, not just coming and saying he's the king. The city administration ain't be opening the dun to Tren or Cunyr, not in decades now. There's a key to entering and they don't know what it is."

"How will you know who the True King is when he comes?"

"I don't be knowing rightly. I'm more interested in keeping my family fed than in conveying some royal to the high place, you know?"

"So your loyalty could be bought with food?"

"Aye, lad! I think the old kings must have known that, to stay at the rule for so long as they did. Your da has your loyalty because he's your da, but if his business didn't provide for you, would you not sell your abilities to another who could afford to pay you? I've got to get back to work."

Randodd stood atop the wall, looking out across the vast landscape the other side of the Avercelt. Miles upon miles of farms had surrounded the city at one time, but now many of the fields lay fallow, with scrub trees starting to creep in.

"The city is starving," he told Howedd when he arrived in Llyr an eightnight later. "You can't take it by force of arms, but if you can appeal to their hearts by way of their stomachs, they'll be yours and will hold the city for you against Tren and Corbryn combined."

Howedd looked at the map Randodd had provided, weighing the points of the report.

Feed them and they're yours.

"This would be a massive undertaking," he noted. "I can't do it right now. There's naught time."

"Well, here's the beauty," Randodd told him. "So long as you get there before the Mulyn men do, you've won."

Howedd sat back, thinking, Randodd waited. His brother needed a bold move to secure his rule. Was this it or was Randodd playing at court craft?

A slow smile dawned on Howedd's face and then he clapped Randoldd's shoulder.

"You are brilliant, my brother. I need – five bards who are willing to relocate to Dun Celdrya for the winter. We can accomplish this."

Bards? What do bards have to do with this?

Randodd wagered he'd find out.

Clarcom

*T*he jade bracelet touched her goblet as she reached for her wine. He'd given it to her this afternoon, wrapped in silk and with a bouquet of flowers. She could hardly prevent herself from skipping up to him at the honor table and kissing him away to his chamber. Of course, she didn't. That would be most unpolitic. He'd not thank her for embarrassing Lydya, who held a seat on the rig council and might well seek her revenge.

The night they'd spent in the chapel flitted through her mind. Lydya was not all bad, but she must remember who put baubles on her wrist and gave her a place in the world that would not see her hands rough with hard labor.

The Galornyn ambassador was the youngest son of the noble family, a handsome fellow with brown hair and blue eyes. He tried unsuccessfully to keep his attention on Lord Kefyn of Denygal while Shyla sat across from him.

His brother's children are likely to be his if he remains in the same dun.

Her months among the nobles had taught her a deal
more than she had expected. She idly looked from face
to face on the dais. Bryan had arrived this afternoon, his
handsome face alive with laughter at somewhat Shyla
said. Though male and female, they were clearly brother
and sister, taking strongly after their mother. Truly, only
Cullyn favored his father, his hair neither blond nor dark,
his skin sallow rather than kissed by the sun. Even the
curve of his chin and the set of his blue-grey eyes were
more of Cunyr than Lydya. Six children. A blessed
woman. Cunyr leaned his head in to speak with Cullyn.
Shouldn't a lord have his heir at his elbow?

The meal at the ladies' table was a swirl of gossip
and laughter. It wasn't that Elora did not enjoy the
company of young ladies, but that she wondered if she
was going to a cold bed alone or if he might call for her
this evening.

The meal ended with dancing. When Cunyr joined,
she knew the answer. Amid the complicated swirls of the
dance, she eventually touched hands with her lord. He
was sweating from the dance and looking tired, but he
smiled at her and whispered "Wait for me" before the
dance broke them apart once more.

Lydya brushed skirts with her on the way out of the
great hall.

"Cautious, lass. It's always light before a storm."

*What did that mean? She drops hints that I'm in danger and
yet, I see only a jade bracelet on my wrist and a warm bed tonight.
Mayhap he will get me with child. I would enjoy that, I think.*

Elora stopped at her room to change into a dressing
robe before slipping away to Cunyr's chamber. The

servants had been about their work, setting flowers in a vase and laying out a board of cheeses, meats and fruit. The bed had been turned down on both sides. She climbed up and arranged the pillows to wait. Time passed. Far off she could hear laughter.

Cunyr must play at politics.

In time, he came, pausing in the door to smile at her. She smiled back, sliding off the high bed.

"Just where I want you," he said, pouring himself a goblet of wine. He offered her one. As she sipped the sweet vintage, he nuzzled her neck. She lifted her chin to make it easier for him to find her shoulder. He chuckled and held his arms wide to both sides. "Will you undress me, my lovely?"

He'd begun to go to paunch before she'd known him and had become increasingly stout since her arrival. She undid his belt and unhooked his sleeves. He untied her kirtle and slipped her robe from her shoulders. Soon they were on the bed, his grunting and puffing above her. This part was not so lovely, but the feel of the jade against her skin paid it back.

When it was done, he curled away from her, snoring heavily. She slipped out of bed and padded to her robe, placed some food on a plate and made her way back to her chamber off the ladies' hall. All the doors were closed, everyone asleep.

Is this the night I received the prize? she thought as she nibbled her meat and cheese.

How many of his mistresses thought that only to be set aside with a small pension and the promise of marriage to a landless noble?

Six children. It's not him then, but why are there no bastards?

Conspiracy

of

Compassion

The only women noble men treat worse than their wives are mayhap their mistresses. They'll be polite to a merchant, a dyer or weaver, who happens to be a common-born female, but after the rose loses its dewiness, they will treat their mistresses like wives that they can dispose of.

Macla of Llyr nee Moryn, Lady Umhall (FY 1002)

Past

Founding Year 931
High Celdrya

With the merchants balking over tax, Gerriant had asked Blethry to research the history of taxation. The only time there'd been a regency in Celdrya had been during the Time of Troubles. Blethry was deep into the annals when Travys interrupted him.

"The High Priest of Lugh is demanding audience with Gerriant," he announced in a low voice. He had been assigned to show Blethry round when he'd first arrived in High Celdrya. He seemed to think that made them friends, though Blethry had tried to dissuade him from the notion.

"For what reason should I be interested in that bit of gossip?" he asked.

"If the regent prefers Lugh over Bel, we may find ourselves very far from the halls of power."

"I still don't see the concern. Do you suppose me an ambitious man who would rather rule than learn?"

"I think you came rather soon to court at the king's calling."

"At the request of my father and Perryn, aye. The Lugh control the courts, the Bel are involved in learning. There's no rivalry."

"You claim so, but I've been a priest longer. The Lughan were the secondary sect until the Time of Troubles. They became powerful with the new dynasty. We were librarians for two centuries until King Vanyn promoted Naddyn."

"Thank you for the history lesson, but I still fail to see the concern."

"Is the Bel or the Lugh better suited to advise the king or the regent?"

"Mayhap it would be better if we each advised the king in the areas of our expertise. I'm advising the regent right now … or seeking to. But for your chattering, I'd be closer to that goal."

"Is Gerriant considering a purge?"

"Not to my knowledge. Please do leave me be."

Lady Wymffa, Councilor Dumyr's wife, approached at that moment.

"May I help you find a book, my lady?" Travys asked, playing the perfect librarian.

"Nay, but I wish to speak with Blethry."

Travys smiled but did not withdraw. Blethry marked his page and waited for her instructions.

"Young man, please do walk with me," she said, then to Travys. "I do not require your service just now."

Blethry left the codex he'd been examining to following Wymffa. She knew the library as well as any librarian and led him to a private corral along an outside wall.

"Do be seated," she invited, indicating one of the chairs. She cracked the shade on the window by a handbreadth, allowing them to see one another when she closed the door.

"I grieve for Queen Lillyana," she began.

"Everybody does," Blethry assured her. "They all loved her, though most did not know her."

"I enjoyed an afternoon's needlework with her," Wymffa explained. "We didn't become close friends in that time, but I think we would have. Do you believe Lord Deryk acted willfully to kill her?"

Blethry shook his head slowly.

"I do not," he admitted. "He seemed so stunned by his behavior. I believe he was ensorcelled."

"As do I. There was a servant that only Deryk appears to remember --."

"Talidd, aye. We haven't found him. There's a young lass – a groom's daughter – can't be more than eight – she remembers him as dark of hair and eye, swarthy, thin."

"Which is how Deryk remembers him as well."

"He's the only adult who does. How does he fare?"

"He was quite ill when Gerriant ordered him from the gaol to the donjon. He's better, but still weak. I think he has little hope of surviving, so he does not fight."

"Mayhap he does not want to survive. If he remembers what happened … imagine?"

They shuddered in unison.

"Why did you come to me?" Blethry asked.

"To learn what you know. Malona's not been found either, I suppose."

"Nay. It is quite astonishing how little we know of her. She's been the king's mistress for several years, but naught can remember where she comes from or if she ever spoke of her home."

"And no one found that curious making before now?"

"Nay, but this is a dun where servants can pop out of existence and none but small children and demented soldiers will remember they existed. I think we need to assume that there were mages involved."

"Mages and assassins?"

"Nay. I think the Assassins' Guild had naught to do with Vanyn's death. More and more I think it was mages alone, that mayhap the mages are the Assassins or that they use the Assassins to hide their activities." He saw that she agreed with him. "I've not worked out more than that. Mayhap those with more devious minds might have better luck."

"You know more than Dumyr suspects," Wymffa said. She shifted uncomfortably, looking at her hands. Like many ladies, her hands bore the marks of hours of seam sewing. "If mages killed Maryn, Vanyn and Perryn, will you still demand Deryk's death?"

"I'm not demanding his death now. I was angry at first, but when I calmed, I realized that we don't blame the net for catching the fish. Were that I could stay his execution, but there's no proof of what we suspect."

"The people demand revenge, Dumyr says."

"Is that what he thinks or just what he says?"

"He's torn. At their heart, servitors were raised to be soldiers and Dumyr wants to give whomever he serves a neat package in the end."

"Will he object to you depriving him of that goal?"

"Nay. Eventually, he'll come to my way of thinking. Why do you assume I will deprive him?"

There were risks in what he was about to do, but her aura was intriguing.

"Lady Wymffa, we keep secrets. You're from Denygal, a place where the Kindred are said to have magery power. My folk are Old Faith and there are mages still in Dunmaden. You and I see beneath the surface … of the folk round us and of each other."

"You're a druin?"

"The Old Faith call us druids and I have not been trained by the priests, so hold it to your chest, please."

"Of course. I would not want you telling others about my abilities. Dumyr knows, but none other. Aye, we've both seen Derek and know that magery is involved."

"Aye. While I hope he recovers, I rather doubt he will. It takes a stronger bit of ensorcelment than I would be capable of to force a man of his honor to do what he did. People rarely come back from it."

"If we can get him out of the donjon, I can get him away from the city."

Blethry stared at her in the dim light.

"You would risk hanging yourself to save him from hanging?"

"It would be right. I – somewhat knew of Malona."

"You think she ensorcelled him?"

"I think she ensorcelled Vanyn and Perryn as well. Looking back, I see her influence. Dumyr remarked that the king's mind had become changeable. And his health deteriorated. Is that a classic sign of long-term ensorcelment?"

"I'm druid taught. Our power comes from nature, not from men. I've heard that the Black take power from their victims or channel it through themselves, but I have no personal knowledge. To my knowledge, the Black do not take women. How do you know she was the source?"

"She always creeped my flesh. Dumyr's too. She had an uncanny way of gaining information that no one else seemed able to get."

"Like the Assassin's Guild in Glencarnyn? Gerriant suspects Burcan was ensorcelled for that."

"And yet he remains in possession of his mind."

"Mayhap more than one mage or sorceress is involved. Some are more gentle than others. I could influence a man to take flowers to his lass without stripping his will."

"Denygal assuage ensorcelment."

"It's frowned upon by druids, but useful like in the rare instance. Mayhap I could get more from Deryk and ease his torment."

"I cannot advise you on this," she said. "I think he needs to leave this place for somewhere he can rest."

Against his will or not, Deryk is a regicide. Slipping him free of here is not as easy as you suppose.

"Do you … have you any word of Donyl?"

"Nay, but my heart says he lives. Dumyr has sent messengers, but I predict they will not find him."

"Why?"

"The One moves in mysterious ways. I believe you are meant to find him."

"Me? I'm in Celdrya, he's probably in Denygal. How am I to find him?"

"You saw him before, the night of Perryn's death."

She's no mere dabbler.

"How do you …?"

"There's Kin blood in Denygal veins."

"You were party to the vision?"

"I saw Donyl follow you through the corridors and see his brother killed. I saw you warn him to run. I also saw that you were meant to go to Denygal."

Is that what it meant? Dream visions are always a mixture of sleep dream and vision. How does she know my destiny?

"It is one possible future. You still decide whether to travel to it."

Blethry shuddered and wiped sweat from his brow. She continued to stare at her hands.

"I don't know," he admitted. "I must think and consider how to do it, if I do. I am a mere priest. I don't have authority to send myself where I choose."

"My husband mayhap does."

"Mayhap, but I must meditate on it before we move forward. You understand?"

"I do. What you decide will mayhap affect all of our lives."

She rose from her seat and, without another word, let herself out of the carole, leaving him to explore his own thoughts alone.

Present

Founding Year 1028
Mirklin Wood

*T*he forest floor was a study in shades of green. Constantly shifting patterns of light and dark, but always green. Tamys had opted to remove the blind fold and had spent the day trying to make sense of what little he saw. He heard the brush of a bird's feathers as it winged from tree to tree, the scamper of squirrels as they ran up trunks. He could smell mushrooms growing in the dark recesses between roots and here the hollow sound of horse hooves on a paved road. Water dribbled into a pool somewhere to their right. One of the horses had relieved itself while they traveled. A long way off, he thought he heard an axe on a tree, but he was probably misinterpreting that. Padraig called a stop a fair bit before sundown, commenting that he might have trouble seeing in the shadiness of the forest. Tamys dismounted. Padraig set his hand upon a tree trunk before he led the bay away.

"Follow the tree round and feel for a fallen log. There's a depression that will be good for a fire and room enough to pitch a tarp over our beds rolls."

Tamys fumbled round until he found the log, where he sat listening to Padraig's activity.

"You seem less tired," Padraig noted.

"I think the cooler air in the forest and the sun not being so bright mayhap have helped."

"Good. You can lend a hand then." Padraig pressed a plate into his hands. Tamys could smell cheese and meat. "Mind the dagger by your right knee and be careful not to cut your fingers. I'll collect wood."

"I don't think I can …"

"It's that or collect wood."

Padraig left Tamys to work it out, fumbling for dagger, feeling round for the cheese. The dagger felt heavy and cold in his hand whilst the cheese smelled sharp. While it felt firm enough, there was enough moisture remaining that the scent came off on his fingers while he gingerly sliced bits. Easier than he had supposed, but a altogether disturbingly visceral experience. Padraig built a low fire just enough for making tea and then they sat beside it mostly listening to the forest sounds without talking. The green had faded to dark grey when Tamys dozed off. Sometime in the night, he began to dream of a riot of birds singing a melodious song. He tossed and turned, smelled cheese on his fingers, and fell out of the window time after time. The sound of Padraig packing their kit woke him.

"Must you make so much noise before it is even sun up?"

"It's past dawn, lad. Head hurting?"

"Aye. There was some song bird, warbling away throughout the night. I thought it would never sleep. Did you not hear it?"

"Nay, I dreamt of music though. Mayhap it's my elven blood responding to the song of the forest."

"Mayhap you're annoying me a great deal."

"Sit your saddle and hold your tongue, lad," Padraig suggested. While he tied the blind fold over his eyes in hopes that the headache would ease, he caught the fragrance of porridge when Padraig set a bowl at his knee.

They were in the deep forest now. After riding for a bit, Padraig announced he'd wandered from the trail. They paused so he could climb a tree and correct their path by some handful of yards. Tamys stood by his horse, blindfold in place, waiting.

His vision behind the blindfold was usually some form of grey, except when he "saw" the flowers he smelled. Now, in the grey, green began to leak through, to form pictures until he saw a well-kempt road through well-tended trees, and two graceful arches of multi-colored stones just at the beginning of a bridge over a babbling creek. As he watched, people with furled ears and odd dress began passing by, talking to one another, there one moment and gone the next. He still stared at it when Padraig grabbed his arm.

"What are you seeing, lad?"

"W-what? I – it makes no sense. I see the road as if it were brand new and there are people, I suppose elves, walking it."

"You suppose you see Kin? What do your Kin look like?"

"Odd tight clothes, men and women wearing the same. Their ears look twisted into shells."

Padraig stopped breathing for a heartbeat.

"And you say the road is new looking?"

"Aye."

"I see paving stones that are flat in the middle course, but some upturned on the edges outward, so that I don't know how we got off it. There's trees choking close and vines hanging over. The dwarves build to last, but even dwarven roads want maintenance and this road hasn't seen a dwarf in centuries, I'd wager."

The images had faded from his inner eyes, leaving an empty echoing hole. Padraig helped him back in the saddle, but the damage had been done. His head pounded, smells and sounds were magnified, and the horse's movements felt greatly exaggerated.

"The elves clearly stayed in this area for a long time after the Arrival," Padraig observed at one point. "I wonder why the dwarves stopped trading with them."

"I care not and my head hurts. I'd ignore you, but I don't seem able to. It's like every sound in the forest has somehow been made louder."

Padraig stopped the horses and soon Tamys felt something smooth and rounded touch his hand. A water bottle.

"Willow bark tea. Take a swallow."

Tilting his head back for the swallow caused his head to throb, but he managed to stay in the saddle and not drop the bottle. When they continued, the forward movement of the horses somewhat soothed him, but for some inexplicable reason, the touch of the bay's mane on his hands annoyed greatly. The pain eased from overwhelming to tolerable, but he felt exhaustion hanging on him like a wet cloak. When he dozed off in the saddle, Padraig called a halt.

"There's water here and you can rest. We'll stay the night, try to get your energy back."

"I'm sorry," Tamys said as Padraig helped him from the saddle to his blankets, hastily spread.

"Nay. Winter's a long way off and you are newly off the sick bed. Rest."

"You just want time to think about what I saw. What if it is only a hallucination brought on by not being able to see?"

"Mayhap. Sleep."

Tamys lay down, but the sounds of insects buzzing kept him awake for a good long time, until he heard the sound a hawk wing settling in a tree nearby. The world revolved slowly down into darkness and he slept.

Clarcom Court

*E*lora despaired of ever mastering stitch work beyond basic seams. She'd naught grown up doing embroidery. Her father was a dyer who had married a weaver. They would trade their product for finished clothing, already embroidered by people who knew a fair bit more than they about needlework. Common embroiderers did fine work, so why take time away from more lucrative endeavors to do it yourself? The noble women did all the sewing for the dun, even those of the common servants. They seemed all right with her only being able to construct clothes, but she knew she'd never be accepted in their world until she mastered embroidery.

Lydya was kind in her guidance and the other women were too, but Elora felt like such a clod as she made a mess of her practice piece.

"It takes time to learn a new skill," Lydya said. "Right, Ygerna?" Her younger daughter was struggling with her own practice piece. Elora fought frustration at comparing herself to an 11 year old.

She laid her practice piece on top of the trunk in her room and moved to select a gown for dinner. She'd just set the blue silk on the bed when the door sprang open to reveal her lover Cunyr, looking like a thunderhead.

"Where have you been?" he demanded, closing the door.

"I was in the Lady's Hall," she explained. *He knows this.*

"You're spending time with that cursed witch I'm married to? What's she offering you? Land in Denygal?"

"Naught, my lord." He'd been drinking, she could tell from his breath as he approached her. His hair was thinning, his gut going to paunch.

I should have seen him for what he was when first he complimented me. I was a child! And he's an old sot with an unnatural attraction to children.

"I'm learning to sew." What a stupid thing to say! She saw that immediately. He grabbed her arm. "That hurts."

He slapped her cheek.

"Are you going to cry now like I've hurt you?" He threw her on the bed. She tried to roll away, but her skirts wrapped round her legs, slowing her, until he caught her and forced her onto her back with his large bulk upon her.

Her hips hurt when he was done and she thought she felt blood. Her lips were swollen and her throat hurt where he'd choked her. He fell asleep beside her and left her to lay there, tears wetting her pillow, afraid to move for fear that he would do it again.

Light crept across the wall, pale dawn. She watched the light move inch by inch and when he stirred, she closed her eyes and pretended to sleep deeply, hoping he'd leave without incident. When the door latch dropped into place, she waited to count 100 and then opened her eyes. She was alone now and free to do whatever she wanted.

She wept.

Clarcom Court

*R*yanna fled the great hall. If she had to listen to another of Cunyr's stories of youthful bravado, she was likely to run the man through. She left Sarala to it and headed … away. She ended up on the rampart overlooking the countryside, watching Kefyn and Taryn ride in from the hills. She had watched last night with awe, trying to comprehend Taryn's aura. It had made sitting at the servitors' table listening to gossip almost worthwhile. She'd come to the conclusion that Padraig had missed a bit in his observation of the family at

Galornyn. It wasn't just Lady Berdda who possessed power, but her offspring.

Did she hide your gift for a reason or are you lazy with your shielding?

Taryn's aura appeared and disappeared at random intervals. What she'd been able to see indicated to her was uncertain and variable, somewhat as a child's might, but with an adult's intelligence. She'd seen an aura like that in an adult once before and he'd beaten his wife until she'd lost the child he'd claimed to want. The difference was that Taryn's soul was good at base and Gil's was not. Truth to tell, she'd been wrong about Gil at first glance too.

I wonder what Kefyn learned from you.

She closed her eyes and lifted her face to the wind off the lake, remembering pleasant times at Ama'na before things went badly.

Before Gil arrived ... before Maryanara came with child ... not, truly. She created a beautiful daughter.

The scuff of a boot on the walkway behind her caused her to turn. Kefyn paused.

"He's mage-born," he reported as if she had sent him off to find out.

"Taryn? Possibly. It runs in his clan."

"I think he's just learning of it himself."

They shook their heads, smiling ruefully.

"Celdryan nobles live in incomprehensible ways," Ryanna explained.

"He's smitten with Shyla."

"That's unfortunate for him since he's come to collect her dowry for his brother."

Kefyn leaned his back against the parapet and grimaced.

"What?" she asked.

"He says naught, but I think there's somewhat."

"About his brother?" Kefyn nodded. "There's been plague in Galornyn. That doesn't change your place, you know. She's betrothed to another and her father wants an alliance that matters to the kingdom, not a love match in Denygal."

"I know. She knows too. I suggested we run away to hand fast, but she claims Cunyr would have me killed just for spite."

"He would.

Kefyn sighed and turned toward her.

"I can't break through his shields. For all that he doesn't seem to know how to shield, I can't get past. I want to know if his brother will treat her with care."

"And you think I can help you?"

"I know you have the power."

"And you know that I won't violate Wisdom standards. I won't stop you from doing it, but I won't do it myself."

Kefyn sighed in acceptance, then straightened and nodded toward the ward below.

"What do you know of Taryn's captain?" he asked.

Ryanna followed his gaze to where Taryn spoke with a young man wearing Galoryn colors.

"I don't. I suppose I saw him at the riders' tables, but I didn't know who he was."

"See somewhat missing about Gregyn of Galornyn?"

Ryanna might have advised against such spying, if she had not been planning to travel with Taryn's band. She saw naught amiss with her eyes, but it was a moment's work to switch to another perspective and to see what concerned Kefyn.

"No aura." She shifted down several layers of weaves, feeling round the edges. "He knows what he's doing."

"Why would they send a mage with Taryn who pretends to be a rider?"

Ryanna had no answer.

"Mayhap it's a coincidence. There was an elven community in Dunmaden before the Lughan came to power in the Time of Troubles. Both young men could have a bit of elven blood, which would explain the ability to shield and the reported gifts of Berdda of Galornyn."

"That's your explanation? That what must be less elven blood than exists in any Denygalman has somehow produced such a vivid scope of psychic gifts? Surely you're jesting."

"The Old Faith encourages druins. Why do you care?"

"We could be friends."

"Loving the same woman appears to be a shaky foundation."

"We love the same woman that neither of us can have."

A shudder ran down Ryanna's back so that she shivered in the warm summer air.

"True," she said. "What is he like?"

"Young. Less worldly than many noblemen I've met. He's not unaware, but his hands are unsullied."

"Careful ... what you're thinking gets folk hung this part of the kingdom."

"Is that why you turned white?"

"Nay, but somewhat does feel out of sorts," she explained. "I can't explain it."

Kefyn stared at her for a long moment.

"If you won't violate Wisdom rules with Taryn, will you at least get close enough to learn somewhat of Gregyn?"

"His shields are such that I cannot gain access without his knowledge. There's other ways to get to know a man. I'll see what I can learn."

With that Ryanna left the parapet, careful to hook her thumbs in her sword belt like a proper soldier. She needed to see if Gregyn had joined the tourney and if so, if there was a contest that Ryan of Moryn might join with him.

Water

The elves left behind some manner of evil within the tangle of trees on the southern border. The trees do move about and the paths are twisted. You see movement in the shadows, but only at the edge of your vision. Men travel in, but do not return. Others return with their minds gone, raving of monsters and beautiful women.

**Radraig of Wwmgleadd, bard
(FY 1027)**

Past

Founding Year 931
Mulyn – Dun Joran

*G*etting Joran to attend him in his chambers had taken some effort. Talidd had despaired of ever reaching his mind, let alone influencing him. His own abilities were like a guttering flame and Joran was much distracted by the birth of his son. Last night, he'd channeled through a candle and finally managed to plant the idea that Joran should come to him. He'd slept long and hard, eaten a full breakfast and had the attendant light four candle lanterns as well as opening the window. He could sense the raven somewhere out in the forest, but it was a closed book, sealed from him for the time being.

What did Balyster's spell do to you, my friend?

Given the warm day, Joran wore his plaid breecs and embroidered siarc, but no cloak. He looked younger and happier than Talidd had ever seen him, though he had been to High Celdrya and back several times in recent months.

"How are you keeping?" Joran asked. "Is your leg healing well?" Ryla had advanced the tale of Talidd misstepping during the storm on the dark of the moon. It explained his working from his chamber.

"I'm on the mend, thank you. I've been going over the household accounts and meeting with the servitors. Collection of taxes is going well. Please do sit. The tea is warm."

The candles dimmed slightly as he put the thought in Joran's head that he should pour for both of them and move Talidd's mug to his right hand. Talidd swallowed a sip of tea to wash down the nausea. He had no doubt he could influence Joran now that he had the man in the room, but he had to meter his strength. A layered spell was less exhausting and more difficult to break.

"Have you spoken with your brother about Cadda yet?"

"Aye. She is the elder. It is only right that our son inherite. Still, Burcan is the elder of us and deserves the honor."

"Nay, he does not. He is plotting against you."

"Burcan? Nay. He would not."

"Aye, but he has. He forced his lady wife to give birth early, thinking that would win his place."

"Nay, he would not do that."

"Ask her ladies and you will know." Talidd held his shaking left arm down with his right, then tapped three times with his right foot to close the working. Joran stared out the window for a long moment, mouth agog, before turning to their conversation again.

"The capital is in turmoil," he reported. "Gerraint is refusing to execute Lord Deryk and the merchants are arguing over tax."

"Good," Talidd said. "That works in Cadda's favor."

"They know about the ensorcelment that caused Burcan to fire that village."

"Do they? I thought I covered my tracks rather well on that one. Who do they suspect?"

"Gerriant didn't say outright, but the Lady Malona."

"That moon witch? Aye. That will do. Do they know where she is yet?"

"I have no knowledge."

"Where is Burcan at the moment?"

"Dun Celdrya. Gerriant gave me leave, but not him."

"Hmm, so are you authorized to make decisions for the whole rigdon?"

"Aye. Loryna is much absorbed with her babe just now."

"Write to Lord Shalanar at the Pass of the Arrival. Tell him to contract with the dwarves for their weapons."

Joran rose from his chair and left the room. Talidd released the weaves, watched them dissipate like gossamer in the sunlight. He needed rest. The bed was farther away than he had supposed. He would have to rest here in the chair until his energy waxed. He shuddered with exhaustion.

Ryla entered the room. For a saeffic, she had proved surprisingly useful ... a skillful liar, a subtle nurse, a capable shadow hunter.

"Their honor keeps us at bay," she explained. "That you can overcome that is why you are useful. Cease to serve our purposes and learn how cold the moon can become."

Pity that I'll have to do somewhat about her when I've my strength back.

She came up behind him, placing her hands upon his shoulders. Under her breath, she spoke the language of Ariannhod. A tingling warm suffused down his left side. Exhaustion followed, so that he had no memory of repairing to the bed. When he woke up, he thought only of the need to use the chamber pot, so that he was sitting there before he realized that he had walked without help and used his left hand for the first time since Balyster's nasty spell. What had changed? He remembered ensorceling Joran and then … just the grey fog of exhaustion.

Present

Founding Year 1028
Clarcom Court

*G*regyn tried not to be insulted when the master of lists read his match to him. Most common-born riders couldn't read and he generally didn't draw attention to his ability. Ryan of Moryn was matched in archery.

The whole of Dun Clarcom had been given over to a tourney in honor of Cullyn's 14 summer. Lords had come from all over the rigdon to test their mettle in mock combat. Even the common born riders were allowed to participate in some of the events, though Gregyn knew from experience that they were not to win. Winning was the stuff of Braedyn of Llyr, a renowned swordsman who had been set upon the roads for daring to best a minor lord at tourney. With his abilities still impotent, Gregyn had no plans to atagonize the nobles by doing overwell in the lists.

"That's Shyla's cousin of sorts," Taryn told him. "Middle height, slim." He pointed to the lass wearing lad's clothing who stood at the side of the archery booths. "Apparently archery is quite an art in Denygal."

"How have you heard that?"

"Kefyn explained it. He's another cousin from Denygal. Why'd you sign up for archery rather than the melee? They let the common born fight against the nobles."

"They let us lose against the nobles," Gregyn corrected. "It mayhap boosts a fat old man's ego, but I'd rather have some real competition. Is she a noble?"

"She who?"

"Ryan?" Taryn frowned. Gregyn waited.

"I must have heard you wrong. He's a Denygal noble, which Kefyn explains means there's not much of a difference."

"Why is Kefyn telling you all this?" Gregyn asked the question to buy time.

How is it that everyone round us believes she is a lad?

"I don't know. He says I've got some future commerce with Denygal. I don't know how he knows and he doesn't seem to know specifics, but he felt obliged to educate me about the ridgon."

"I'm sure you'd much rather Shyla had done so."

"Don't tease," Taryn said, looking younger than his 16 years. "I know I shouldn't feel attracted to her, but I can't seem to help myself."

"I felt that way about the equerry's daughter last year," Gregyn told him. "Then I realized that I was nocking an arrow for too rare a bird and I decided to aim lower."

Taryn favored him with a pitying look. Although they'd never spoken of her, Gregyn felt certain he knew about Nalyna. When Gregyn looked away, Taryn continued with the subject at hand.

"Teddryn would rip me arm from leg and Egoran would see me hung for destroying an alliance with Clarcom. I know I can't pursue it, but I can't stop from sweating every time I see her."

"I thought nobles were betrothed practically from birth. You aren't, though."

"Too far from the rule. I was betrothed to some lass in Fyrgal until they declared a claim to High Celdrya. My father withdrew to protect his alliance with Mulyn. My father wanted the foster daughter of East Mulyn, but Corbryn was keeping her for his own son. Now that he's been dishonored and exiled, there mayhap be more talk that way." He straightened from the wall he was leaning on. "I wonder if anyone would notice if I went back to my quarters."

"What did you do, take a flagon of wine back to your quarters?"

"Aye, actually. It was only half, but I tossed and turned with odd dreams all night and morning dawned much earlier than I would wish."

"Mayhap you need to leave it alone entirely."

"Mayhap, though easier said than done. I suppose I should see what lists I'm on and act like I care. You'd better get to the line."

Gregyn pretended to sigh, but in reality, he wanted to talk to Ryan of Moryn, the lass hiding as a lad. She was tall for a woman and no doubt wore a jerkin of some sorts under her clothes, so that she looked narrow from shoulders to hips. Her dark hair, cropped short, shone like mahogany in the sun and her blue eyes were large and alluring. She didn't have an aura and that worried him a great deal.

Does everyone else think you're a lad because you've cast some glamour on yourself? Can you breach my shields?

He hadn't worried about that in a couple of years, knowing his depth of strength, but Naranddal's spell was a mystery to him. He didn't know how it manifested itself. *Am I hidden as Taryn is or am I merely unable?*

"Ryan of Moryn?" he asked.

"Aye." Her voice was dark enough to be male. "Gregyn of Galornyn?"

"Aye." They shook hands. Hers were as callused as his and her grip was strong, and yet he knew that she was a lass without any shadow of doubt.

"I believe we're at the line next," she offered.

His name was called first. They were using standard hunting bows. Gregyn sighted down an arrow to assure it was straight, nocked it and drew. He'd practiced some on the journey from Galornyn and gotten his strength back, but for a moment, he felt uncertain, finding it hard to hold the target in view.

Settle your breath. Plant your feet. Your body is a bow, strung, ready to push the arrow to the target. Breathe.

He felt the Source wash up his rear leg and into his back. The arrow settled and he released. It sank deeply into the bullseye. He lowered the bow and walked to the waiting area. Nausea washed over him and a throb of pain began behind his left eye and for a moment, black spots danced in his vision. Ryan stepped up, nocked and drew. She held the target for only a moment before releasing. A nimbus of light rimed her body as she walked toward him. He focused his gaze on her target. The judge's measured and declared them a tie.

"You're Taryn's man from Galoryn, aye?"

"Aye." *I touched the Source just now. Naranddal said that would not be possible. Is it her?*

"I admit I've only ever traveled here in the East, but I detect a Llyr accent."

"I was raised in Llyr as a small child," he admitted. *Careful. She may well be an elven mage.* "I suppose I form words in that way from time to time."

"What brought you to Galornyn?"

"I was a caravan guard. Teddryn came through seeking riders and I offered my sword. You've clearly some experience in archery."

"I've traveled a bit. Worked as a caravan guard some years ago. Archery is quite the sport in Denygal."

Vomiting at her feet is not a way to warm her to you. You want to know who she is. Control your stomach.

"You've traveled then – here in Dublyn?"

"Aye. Lived in Ama'na – the Southern Confluence – traveled into Blyan with a caravan and then took the mountain route back to Cenconyn."

Gregyn had studied maps of the kingdom and knew that the mountain route from Blyan to Cenconyn had been destroyed some years ago. *Wait – the Southern Confluence?*

"Was not the Southern Confluence destroyed a generation ago."

"I'm older than I look. Many Denygal are."

The implications of that made his head hurt more.

In the end, they were the top two archers. He was seeing double by the time he toed up to the line. Although reaching for the Source allowed him to hit the target at all, his arrow was a ring and a half off while hers hit the bullseye again.

"Are you all right?" she asked, catching his arm. "You've gone white as milk." He felt a tingling sensation where her hand touched him.

"The heat has given me a headache. I think I'll find somewhere cool to sit for a bit."

There was a shady and quiet location round the edge of the stable where he could sit and listen to the relatively distant sounds of the crowd. As he sat, that tingle in his arm washed across his body and cleared his head. He sat there in the shadows, considering the

Source in its raw and immense power and thinking he might dive into that ocean and live.

Mirklin Wood

*P*adraig sat upon a log, contemplating the forest. He'd heard the hawk somewhere far above mayhap a watch before. Tamys slept as if dead. There was naught to do but think. The remains of the dwarven road did not run straight, but occasionally jogged round hills and crossed streams over decorative bridges.

What keeps an old-growth forest clear?

For indeed, the floor of the forest was not nearly as choked as he'd expected. Aye, there were fallen trees and undergrowth, but he'd expected much more difficult travel. He recognized that the forest was thicker to either side of the old road, yet still not as overgrown as he'd heard virgin forest was. Padraig couldn't puzzle out a reason for this.

Tamys' horse nickered as if someone neared. Padraig stood to see to the beast. He never caught sight of what disturbed the horse, but felt a peculiar pricking between his shoulder blades. He whipped round to look behind him, but he saw naught to concern him. The sensation of being stared at lingered a moment longer, then faded.

Some unseen animal, no doubt. Mayhap the hawk.

He went about his business.

Tamys woke near sunset as Padraig was preparing a meal of dried meat and forest vegetables.

"How are you keeping, lad?"

"My head feels better," Tamys said, rubbing his eyes. "I hear a brook and I need to squat."

"We're camped in what might be an old caravanserai. There's a wall behind you. Go about 10 steps along it to your right when facing it and you'll be at the squatting pit."

When Tamys returned, having managed to lace up his breecs without asking for assistance. Padraig pressed the leather bucket into his hands.

"It's time you tried your wings a bit," Padraig decided. "What you hear is a spring. Get water."

"I can't."

"You can! Use the sound as a guide. A straight line will take you into a tree, but if you step a little to the left after about a dozen steps, you should be able to avoid that."

"I can't!" Tamys repeated, breath coming in gasps of terror.

"I think you have little choice," Padraig announced, pulling his hand free of the wall and causing him to stumble forward a bit so that Tamys stood swaying in the middle of the clearing.

"I can't!" he repeated a third time.

"Do you think I'm more stubborn or you? I think I am. After all, I can find my blankets without help and feed myself. So, it's time to branch out a bit, lad. Try."

"I can't see!"

"You can hear. You can walk. You can get water. You may bark your shins, but I'm pretty sure you can do this. Once you're there, I'll help you back."

"I can't!" Tamys insisted. Padraig refused to reply. They could stand there all night and discuss it or Tamys could comply. Padraig went to gather wood, though he stayed close.

Tamys stood in the clearing with the leather bucket in his hand for a good long while. Padraig was building the fire when Tamys heaved a sigh and oriented himself by the sound of the spring. He felt carefully with one foot at a time until a branch of the tree poked him in the forehead. That scared him into falling down.

"I said I can't do this."

"You're halfway there," Padraig commented. "It would be nice to have some water for tea and to soften some of this dried meat."

"I'm blind!" Tamys said unnecessarily. Padraig didn't reply. Tamys sat on the ground, frustrated, for some time. It grew dark while he sat there. Finally, he stood, waving a hand round until he found the tree branch and making his way carefully to the left. Then he listened for the spring again and began slow progress forward. When his foot caught on a fallen branch, he bent to remove it, but his fingers identified it as long and straight enough to be a frail walking stick. He then used it to feel what was in front of him. When he reached the spring it took him a bit of time to figure out how to stand so as not to get his breecs wet while he dipped water. When he turned from the spring with a nervous, but triumphant look upon his face, Padraig was there to offer an arm and help him to the campsite.

"I did it," Tamys whispered.

"I never doubted you could. Hang onto that stick. That seemed to help a bit."

They spent a pleasant, quiet evening by the fire, with tea and stewed meat and some vegetables that Padraig had brought from Wmgleadd. They fell asleep to the quiet song of the forest.

Clarcom Court

Shyla leaned her elbows on the parapet wall, watching as Bryan showed off his prowess with a practice sword. She was glad that he had chosen events that were far from the noble viewing stage where she would have to pretend to be the lovely lady of the tower. Lydya had given her leave to wander as if she were not fertile. It amazed her how often her mother chose to allow her children their freedom at the risk of incurring Cunyr's displeasure to herself.

A male body eased between her and the workman who had given her nobleness a respectful space. She stepped left, shooting a glance at the interloper and blushing in surprise when she saw it was Taryn.

"My apologies," he said. "You didn't hear me when I spoke. The shouting, you know. Ah, Bryan. Does he prevail in all events or is it an act?"

"The master at arms here says he's an excellent swordsman. Why aren't you down there?"

"I was, but I promptly lost my first event, and saw no one to call me to task if I didn't continue in the alternative tier, so …." He smiled at her. "I was actually hoping to catch Gregyn, my sergeant, in an event, but he must have found a lass after he lost in archery."

"He didn't lose. He was beaten by a Denygal. There's no shame."

"Kefyn explained that the Denygal use archery far more than they use the sword. This one knows he's fighting the heir apparent. You can see him parrying and not fully swinging."

"Bryan hates when they do that. Watch and see what he'll do."

In a moment, Bryan turned his sword on its flat and smacked his opponent's bottom. The opponent looked startled, Bryan shouted somewhat and then the opponent charged back into the event with renewed vigor.

"He's a reputation for embarrassing those who don't really fight. He used to have to make quite a show of it, but now they usually just need to be reminded."

Taryn grinned.

"I can respect that." The opponent was a good swordsman and now that he was actually competing, the event was more entertaining. Bryan would no doubt win … his reputation as a swordsman was earned … but the win was no longer assured.

"Do you hear from your family since you've been away?" she asked, eyes on the match as she was aware that his gaze was upon her.

"They would send a speeded courier only if someone died."

She turned to him, gaze meeting his boldly.

"You know what I'm talking of," she remarked. His gaze slid sideways and he looked confused. "Or mayhap you don't." She looked down to see Bryan sweep his competitor off his feet and tag him on the shoulder with the blunted practice sword.

"He won that fairly," Taryn assured her.

"You speak knowledgeably."

"I lost because I drank too much wine last night, not because I don't have any skills. My skills have not, however, been tested. Bryan has no doubt been to war."

"Smallish skirmishes against brigands, I think. It's awfully hot here."

He blushed.

"Will you walk with me?"

They made their way down the stairs to the ward. Shyla so hated the narrow underskirt she was expected to wear now that she was fertile. She had to hitch up her dresses to manage the stairs. Taryn proved a gentleman, not watching her as she descended and walking just ahead of her to shield her from view.

"The clothes they make lasses wear," she huffed.

"It does seem confining," he agreed, blushing again. "Is there any peace in this crush?"

"Come," she said and led the way to a closed gate in a high wall between two brochs. The rose garden was an oasis of forgotten tranquility.

"This is where we were the other night?" he noted. "I see it when I walk to the great hall from my quarters."

"My mother's touch of tranquility. There's even a water tap here." She indicated a niche in the wall where a tankard hung from a pipe that issued water that flowed in a stone channel that disappeared into the ground.

"It takes a while to fill the tankard."

"The water runs the fountain?"

She liked Taryn. There were things about him that concerned her … his over-indulgence in wine … but his intelligence was clear and his humor was spot-on. While she drank from the tankard, he dipped a hand in water flowing from the unicorn statue of the fountain that graced the center of the garden, rubbed it through his hair and then scooped a double handful to drink.

"Be honest with me. Teddryn … how ill is he?"

He stared at the space above her head.

"He has what appears to be the infant palsy, but he still had use of his body when I left. It doesn't kill or palsy everyone and my grandmam has methods to support him."

"Which is what we haven't talked about," she said. "You act as if her abilities are not known. You act as if your own abilities are not known to you."

He brought his gaze down to meet hers, his eyes widened in shock. His lips parted to say somewhat, but the words never came for a scream rent the air and a distant thud caused them both to turn and then run in the direction of the sound.

The rose garden had been created from a dead-end formed where two brochs were joined by a short corridor. Three stories up, the small rooftop walkway offered a great view of some of the events on the other side of the corridor. A small body lay crumpled on the cobblestones beneath the corridor. Shyla saw the brigga and screamed, running forward, dropping to her knees by her youngest brother.

"Nay, God, nay! Not Danyl. Nay!"

People gathered … Bryan, Ryanna who pretended to be Ryan, Kefyn, Taryn's sergeant, mayhap others she could not see through her tears. All she could see was her brother's spirit slowly rising to stand on his own chest, staring down on his body as if shocked to see it below him. A tiny winged creature settled on his shoulder.

For a moment time stood still, all light seemed to move toward Danyl, Shyla felt herself drained of energy and then Danyl's spirit floated back down into his body. His chest rose and fell slightly. Blood flowed from his temple and one ear. Ryanna's friend Saryl announced him alive and then she shouted for a stretcher and Taryn and Bryan helped Shyla to her feet to make room for Saryl to work. Saryl seemed the only one with her wits about her. Everyone else looked stunned, drained.

Shyla looked up at the roof and a hollow spot grew large in her gut. It was a miracle that anyone could fall that distance and live. She looked round the folk watching Saryl treat Danyl and thought

Who just played God?

Dun Llyr

*B*ranwyn had begun to wonder if Egoran were rejecting the marriage, since she'd hardly seen him in the time since her arrival. She did understand about formal periods of mourning and how they necessitated seating her away from him at the honor table. He must be appropriately grave and not be seen whispering to his betrothed. She had expected at least a chaperoned meeting not long into her sojourn at the dun, but when none came, she had begun to fret.

When the summons finally came, she scarce had time to bathe, do her hair and select an appropriate gown. She selected a set of blue dresses that brought out her eyes and made her blond hair shine. As large as a great dun was, there were few places that afforded any privacy. She paused at the door of the council chamber, awed for a moment at the formal table and many candles.

Egoran stood at the window, dressed in the usual plaid breecs and embroidered siarc of a nobleman. He still wore the black armband. He turned after a moment, gaze slowly measuring her.

"Come, Lady Branwyn. Do let's take our seats."

He met her on the way to the table and conveyed her into an upholstered chair before taking his own.

"You must try some of this wine," he started. "It's a very fine vintage from Dunmaden." He poured from the pitcher into a glass goblet.

"It's red," she noted.

"Are you unfamiliar?" he asked.

"Only the white grapes grow in the north," she explained. "We import red wine, but it is precious, not wasted on daughters generally."

"The reds are bolder than the whites, not as tart and dry. Breathe in the aroma before you take a sip."

The bouquet warned her that this would be a strong tasting wine. She'd expected it to be sweeter than she was used to, but instead she smelled peppery berry flavors. Her first sip filled her mouth with flavors. While she was used to the crisper white wines, she could easily get used to the more robust flavor of red. Her court training taught her to sip slowly and take her time consuming the goblet, lest she embarrass herself before her betrothed.

A serving lass brought a platter of fruit and bread. Fresh fruit was also rare in Mulyn, so that she enjoyed the taste immensely, especially served with a type of clotted cream that she had never had before.

After some casual questions about the comfort of her quarters and whether her entourage had been caught in the dark rain, he began to warm to her a bit. Though not a handsome man, his grey-blue eyes were shrewd and intelligent.

"I apologize for keeping you in the wings for so long, but my father's death caught us all unawares."

"I understand entirely."

"Good. May I ask … you're 19, aye?"

"My name day is an eightnight from now."

"Why did your father not arrange a marriage much sooner than this?"

The serving lass took away the platter while another brought the soup course. This gave Gwen time to think of the best way to answer the question.

"My father hoped very much to make this match with you, but your father insisted upon continuing forward with your first marriage. He then sought to marry me to Clarcom. Bryan ap Riordan is younger than I, but of high enough status to marry to the r-royal family."

She hated when she stumbled like that, but truth-to-tell, she didn't believe her father would ever sit the throne of High Celdrya.

"You mean, he hopes to gather enough support from your betrothal to actually take the city and the dun. Did you know that my mother was actually the one to propose the marriage, shortly after you were born?"

"I had heard whispers to that effect, aye."

"Ambitious woman, my mother, and I rather like the idea. Your brother Galryen hasn't married yet."

The fish soup required some getting used to. Branwyn took an obligatory second spoonful before setting the spoon down.

"Nay. Our father has tried to arrange a marriage with many of the high duns, but there's been a dearth of appropriately-aged girls. Gal won't take a child-bride. I'm supposed to try to talk you into ending the betrothal of Teddryn to Shyla of Clarcom. My father will offer his ward as replacement. Since she's not my blood sister, diversity will be maintained."

"And it would tie my dun much closer to Manahan. I'm sure you know why I might hesitate."

"I hear he's quite ill." Egoran stared at his bowl for a moment, clearly weighing his answer. She was not his wife yet. He could not trust her to not carry tales to her father.

"Does this ward come with a dowry that won't take three years to get to us?"

"She comes with some of the best farming land in Mulyn which will net your dun fat rents. Just two years of such is more than my dowry. Currently, the rents go to the Lughan temple by her father's will, but upon her marriage, the half the rents would go to Manahan and half to her spouse."

"Under different circumstances I would happily entertain that arrangement, but my father's death has revealed a dearth of coin. We needed your dowry three years ago and we need Shyla's now. In fact, my brother Taryn has gone to collect it."

Branwyn knew this to be a test of her loyalties to her husband. She had been well-schooled by her stepmother. It was tricky because her father considered himself their liege lord, but the vyngretroi had withheld that honor until after he took the dun.

"My father is a great man, but arrogant. He chose to delay the dowry in order to pay for his attempted conquest of the city. He had hoped your family would allow the marriage to go forward without it. I think he was surprised when you did not."

"I was still grieving for my first wife and did not really wish to marry again. Your father's delay was a blessing in my eyes, though now it means we must consummate the marriage and produce heirs rather sooner than I would like."

Gwen nodded as Egoran took a first spoonful of soup, because she really didn't know what else to say. She did rather wonder why Galornyn was short on coin. Several reasons sprang to mind, but ….

Egoran cleared his throat as perspiration beaded on his forehead. He wiped his mouth with his napkin, then rubbed his throat with shaking fingers.

"Are you unwell?" Gwen asked.

His eyes widened as he registered her voice and then his face flushed purple. Gwen sprang to his side, calling for help. The servants rushed in as his eyes rolled up into his head and then he began to have a seizure. More people came running into the room, so Gwen got out of the way. Standing back staring at the tableau, she could only pray to the gods that he would draw a breath. When he did not, all she could think was that she had barely gotten to know him.

Lair

Dwarven roads were a miracle of craftsmanship, but combined with elven magicks, they could do wondrous things. I remember when I was a child, traveling with my father from the coastal city all the way to the Dome in less than a quarter sector of the sun. Oh, it was marvelous! It's so hard to believe that it is all gone now.

Vandrysynpalador, elderman of the Blue Iris Holt (Kin Cycle 24567)

Past

Founding Year 931
High Celdrya

*B*lethry surrendered his dagger to the gaoler, recognizing his conflicted feelings. Would he seek Deryk's death if he were allowed? He banished the image of his sister's broken face. One did not blame the weapon for what its wielder did. *Yet* ....

"How is he this day?"

"He does not eat unless the Lady Wmyffa insists. Do you know the way?"

"Up, I suppose. Do I need a key?"

"He's too weak to escape. We've secured the door with a bolt, but there's no reason to lock it."

He didn't kill your sister.

He started up the circular stairs. Halfway up, a door was open into one of the cells. He wondered who had been held there and where they had gone. Unlike the gaol, the donjon had pleasant cells with beds and most of them had windows.

Scholar that he was, he occupied his mind during his climb with what he knew of the building. It was one of the oldest structures in the dun complex – a standalone broch that went three stories into the ground and many stories above. It had been built as a keep and had been used as such during the Time of Troubles. It had, he thought, saved the Trevellyn line when the walls of the dun had been breached.

His breathing was a bit ragged by the time he reached the highest floor. Here another door stood ajar. A shout came from inside, followed by a growl. Blethry rushed in to see a man standing over Deryk with a dagger poised to strike the man in the bed. Blethry instinctively wove Air, wrapped it round the assailant and slammed him into the nearest wall. The assailant rolled up off the ground and rushed into Blethry who tried to grab the dagger-wielding arm. The momentum carried him into the wall. The assailant twisted free of Blethry's grip on his siarc and ran for the door. The undergaoler hit him with his bandy stick and he tumbled to his knees. Blethry rolled to stand up as the assailant swept the guard's legs out from under him then rushed down the stairs. Blethry stumbled after him as the undergaoler scrabbled to get to his feet. The assailant cut right into the open cell as Blethry hit the stair behind him. He rushed into the cell to see the assailant turn the dagger on his own throat. Blood squirted across Blethry's face.

There was no saving him.

Guards were called and Blethry was compelled to give his testimony several times. Eventually, they gathered in Gerriant's council chamber for a last retelling of the events in the donjon.

"Who would want to end the investigation into Perryn's death?" Gerriant asked after Blethry finished telling his story.

"That is the question, isn't it?" Dumyr said. "There are no other prisoners in the donjon. This rider disappeared last night. How he got into that cell is any question. Clearly he slept there."

"What do we know about him?" Blethry asked.

"Ricyn came to us in a trade with Mulyn when Cadda and Loryna went north. He's been a good worker, steady enough that they noticed when he went missing and didn't just assume he'd gone to a tavern."

"I think we can assume that he is as much a weapon in the hands of a larger power as Deryk was," Blethry said. They both turned to stare at him. "He acted crazed … ensorcelled," he explained.

"There's a nest of sorcerers in this dun?" Gerriant asked.

"There doesn't need to be. There might just be one."

"Who?" Dumyr asked.

"I know naught. I suspect whoever was on the gate when Ricyn entered the donjon saw this sorcerer, which explains why nobody remembers Ricyn entering. Of course, they will not remember him or her any better than they remember Ricyn."

"The question remains … why try to kill a man who is likely to die in the Roman way at any point?" Gerriant asked. "Once he's dead, there is no real impetus to continue the investigation. I can say I've done what needed to be done, the matter is settled. Even if he died by an assassin's knife, there is little reason to pursue the matter."

The three men stared at each other without answers. A knock at the door caused Gerriant to call for entry. Wmyffa obeyed, closing the door behind her.

"How is he?" Dumyr asked.

"Shaken – almost sad that the assassin did not succeed. He's far from clear, but I believe he may know more than he realizes. When I was questioning him, he let on that he saw Talidd just after meeting with a Mulyn iron monger by the name of Llewys outside a tavern called the Golden Tankard."

"He would have been investigating the king's death for Perryn," Blethry added when she paused.

"He's struggled with remembering his affair with Malona, but I asked about and I would not be overly surprised if it started that night."

"This woman apparently was in half the beds in the dun," Gerriant complained. "There's some who claim she was sleeping with Perryn." Blethry flinched. "Sorry, lad, but royals are often less constrained than ordinary men."

"Knowing it and having it affect your sister's all too brief marriage are separate issues," Dumyr said. "We should send someone to Mulyn to speak to this Llewys."

"I'll speak with Burcan again, see if there's somewhat he knows of the man."

"Do you think that wise, sire?"

"I believe Burcan mayhap have been tricked as well. If there is ensorcelment going on, it means that Malona must not be the one."

"She might have been part of a larger conspiracy," Wmydda suggested. "There only needs to be one wielding this magic."

Blethry nodded, recognizing that he needed to make a decision soon. Deryk had almost died today because of his inaction. What if, locked within the young lord's mind, were the answers to the death that had swept the royal family? What if he knew where Donyl might be found? Was it right to allow him to die for somewhat not his fault? The disposition of his life lay with Blethry and he must needs make a decision sooner rather than later.

Present

Dragon Cycle 3045789
Dragon Lair

A harsh wind whistled round the back side of the Dragon's Head, swirling down the throat of a cave and waking Arqisalo, who yawned and stretched her full length against her mate, Gruniq. The stone beneath her belly scales exuded a subtle warmth that contrasted the wet wind. This had been a particularly comfortable lair for near 1000 cycles, but a rockslide in the spring had made the entrance tunnel much shorter. Gruniq promised a new lair by snowfall. He'd found a suitable one on a mountain a bit farther north, but as with all natural caves, it required some digging out. Arquisola laid her jaw upon one paw and tried to drift off to sleep once more. They really did need a larger lair and Gruniq promised the new one would suit. There were six of them now and mayhap a seventh on the way. She wound her tail against her lower belly where a strange new bulge had appeared this spring. She calculated the implantation had occurred mid-winter before last. If true, the egg would emerge winter next, which would leave her lair-bound for another two cycles until the pouchling cozied into her. She rather enjoyed the pouchling stage.

As if she had somehow spoken to him, Meliniq muttered in his sleep. It had been more than 100 cycles since he had climbed from her pouch into the world. For many targans, the youngling stage was preferred, but Arqisalo enjoyed the feeling of a pouchling. She did not love Meliniq or his siblings less because they were sub-adults, but to give them an infant sibling seemed the highest gift she might bestow.

Meliniq snorted as he awoke, shaking his head as if to free himself from his dream. He waddled past Arqisola's head on his way to the squatting hole. She waited a bit to let him relieve himself in private before following.

"Is all well with you?" she asked.

"No, targa, I had a bad dream," he admitted. She rubbed her snout against his short neck. He nuzzled under her body, slipping his head into the pouch to latch onto a nipple.

"Will you tell me of it?" she asked while he suckled. He had begun flying more than a 10-cycle ago and should not still be feeding on her, but it felt so good, so she allowed it still.

"I dreamt of a little cave with two-legged creatures." Although dragonkind could speak, they were a naturally telepathic species, so that they spoke silently, mind to mind.

"Humans?"

"Maybe partial humans. I forget what you call those."

"They call themselves Dengyal. Go on."

"There's a male waiting for me."

"You're to be a Companion. I've known this since you emerged from the pouch. Do you know where this dun is?"

"That's the word they use for their caves, yes?" She purred her affirmation. "No. It is not yet my time."

"Do you know when?" she asked, feeling the swelling in her belly.

"A few years at least. He's to ride me, tarka … like a horse."

"Are you sure you're not using your tartar's tales to fuel your imagination."

"No, this is not the first time I've dreamt this. It's just the first time that it is clear. My Companion will lead a vast army with me at its head."

Arqisola stopped purring as a shudder ran through her body, causing her scales to chuff several times before she settled.

"He is not of the way of peace?" she asked.

"I saw many carrying steel arms, surrounding a tall bald dome with a human city at its foot." He'd been displaced by her shudder and was now cleaning his talons.

She shook her crest vigorously to settle her scales. Meliniq yawned.

"Tartar says Companions are not slaves. That I must be wise in my counsel. Perhaps I am misunderstanding my dreams."

"What else did you dream?"

"I do not understand what I've dreamt. When I do, I will tell it to you."

He yawned again.

"I would sleep now. That deer had some good fat upon its haunches and it was my turn for it."

"Yes, of course, love. We'll discuss this later. A Companion bond is mutual."

Arqisola allowed him to return to sleep as she stared out the dumping hole to the semi-darkness of the summer sky, thinking of what she had just learned. As she thought, the image of the Denygal wielder came into her mind. She looked different from when Arqisola had last reached out to her. Her hair was very short now and she stood among many who looked similar to her rather than to the Kin. Something distracted her from the real world of word and thought, so that Arqisola could not reach her mind.

A chill wind howled down the dumping hole, so that Arqisola thought pleasantly of her nest next to Gruniq. There was time yet to speak with the enchantress and learn how she was connected to the one who would be her offspring's Companion.

Mirklin Wood

*I*n Padraig's dreams he danced in elven round dances with a tall, beautiful elven woman, but he awoke in the middle of the night to a yell.

In the dark of the camp, Tamys knelt upon his blankets, his dagger in his hand, blind eyes frantically trying to see.

"I can hear them, Padraig! I know they're there!"

A branch quivered at the clearing's edge. Padraig leapt from his blankets, long knife in hand, running into the forest edge. He thought he saw someone duck behind a tree. A lithe figure with lean face and high cheekbones, cat-slit eyes and peaked ears. Darting around the tree himself, Padraig saw naught, but began to shout in Elvish.

"I mean you no harm. My name is Padraig of Denygal. My mother is a half-elf. I travel south through the forest on a mission for the One True God – what you might call the Nameless One. Please don't be afraid. I come in peace."

There was no answer and total silence came over the forest. Padraig continued yelling the same thing until Tamys called him back, poised upon his blankets as though to defend himself. Padraig knew that he was perfectly capable of doing such.

"What was that language you were speaking in? Who were you calling?"

"Elves. I know they were elves."

"Elves! Padraig, we're a good long way from their range, most of the kingdom."

"When the Celtmen 'Arrived' here, the elves ranged along the great rivers. They ran in many directions. They had a great city in this area, north on the plain. It was truly an outpost of some sort, mayhap for trading with the dwarves, who don't like to get far from their beloved mountains. The city north of here probably lasted a good while after the Arrival, since humans only crossed into this area three hundred years ago. It only makes fair sense that the elves would have moved south into the forest with the encroachment of their enemies."

"If they're here, wouldn't we see somewhat of them? Towns, villages, somewhat?"

"Truly I have not seen any houses or fields since entering the forest, but I've seen an elf. That in itself is enough."

"Mayhap it was a dream. I thought I heard a two-legged being walking round our camp. I laid there a good while listening before I was sure I wasn't hallucinating. But, I woke you from a sound sleep and you might have still been part dreaming."

"Nay. It was elves."

"They might not even speak the same language after a thousand years," Tamys reminded him.

"That's but three generations for an elf, lad – well, closer to five since the Scourging."

"Scourging?"

"That's what the eastern elves call the Arrival. They view it as a punishment for somewhat in the society before the Celt arrived."

Tamys shivered and groped for his cloak, one hand still encumbered by the dagger.

"You can sheath the dagger," Padraig assured him. "This was a reconnaissance. I should check about the camp," he said. He rose and touched a torch to the coals of the fire. He walked round the camp, checking for footprints. Finally finding a bare footprint a bit longer than his own, he followed the trail toward the pile of gear until the prints suddenly smeared, probably when Tamys had yelled out. They ran quickly toward the forest edge where Padraig had seen the elven male disappear into the leaves. He followed the trail round the tree in question and then lost it in the underbrush. He returned to Tamys by the fire. The dagger was sheathed, but the lad's hand remained on the pommel.

"What did you find?"

"He came to spy us out, but I don't think he got far into the camp before you scared the living breath out of him. I'd say he'll naught be back tonight. Mayhap in the morning. Mayhap with others of his kind."

"No offense, Padraig, but you don't sound at all concerned and I think you're mistaken in that. These are not your mam's folks. Three generations or five is still a long time for bad blood to fester and, while you may speak their language, you look human. How do you know that they'll not come back with a phalanx of archers with those cursed long bows."

"Long bows are an invention these elves didn't see. The elves of Denygal took the hunting bows of the human Denygals and adapted them with their own ideas. Besides, we've done naught except scare them."

"And trespass on what they doubtless perceive as their land," Tamys reminded strongly.

"Elves are not like Celdryans," Padraig argued. "They don't hold land to their chest like a treasure. It belongs to all the elves. Didn't you see …?"

Padraig faltered to a stop, remembering that Tamys could not see the elven communities they'd passed through on their way here.

"Nay, I saw naught," Tamys snapped. "Do you have a plan?"

Padraig took a moment to decide not to apologize for his mistake.

"When strangers travel through the eastern lands, the elves expect certain behavior of them – not to use more than what they need, that sort of thing. I'm proposing we follow those rules. We'll eat what we have in our stores for tomorrow and build our fires small. Bury our offal when we have it. If they're like the elves I know, they'll respect that."

"Unless they've been watching us these last two days."

"I don't think so. Remember that dream you had last night?" Tamys nodded. "I dreamt of elven round dances. I'll wager we camped near a settlement last night and didn't even know it. The old dwarven trade road would make a handy trail for these folk to travel from one settlement to another. The lad who came into our camp might well have just stumbled upon us. Besides, I've been respectful of the forest, using only fallen wood, burying our leavings. Nay, we're all right so long as we are careful. Mayhap they can help us in our journey."

Tamys snorted lightly, but he didn't argue. He merely lay down upon his blankets and tried to sleep. His physical weakness finally forced him to do what good sense forbade. Padraig stayed awake a good long while, wondering of the elves of the west and thinking of the advantages there would be in speaking with them. He fell asleep thinking about what it would be like if he could actually get another elf to scry to Gly for him. He could perhaps find healing for Tamys or spiritual support for himself. Aye, it would be a wonderful thing. And perhaps this was why he was told to traverse the forest in the first place. These elves had not heard of Jesu, only the Nameless One whom eastern elves considered to be God the Father. Mayhap Padraig had found the reason for his mission. As sleep took him though, a portion of his brain reminded him that these elves had naught to do with the kingship of Celdrya. Did they?

Clarcom

*H*ow could a single day change life so much ... extinguish the sun ... age his sister into adulthood ... turn the world upon its head?

Bryan leaned back against the wall, eyes closed, listening to Shyla and Kefyn pray. He'd prayed earlier, but now he felt wrung out, but not at ease, as if between battles. He could almost feel an army looming outside the dun, though he knew the battle had naught to do with arms.

He heard the echo of Danyl's scream and his eyes snapped open. Taryn ap Galornyn had earnest blue eyes the color of a mountain lake. He had sat with them all evening, ignored their praying, and offered to bring food and beverages. He proved more use than Cullyn, who had not even shown up until they'd settled Danyl into bed. His brother had stood silent against the wall in the children's hall until he eventually had disappeared. Taryn had remained, gone and brought food and then tarried while they awaited news.

"I need some fresh air," Bryan announced. "Anyone want to come to the roof with me?"

"There might be news," Shyla objected. "You can go, but I should stay here."

She looked older than her years with her face drawn and pale.

"I'll stay with her," Kefyn said quickly. "We can go when you return."

Taryn stood.

"I'll go with you," he offered.

They climbed to the top of the broch. At this time of night, there was very little to see, just lights in windows above the darkness of the ward.

"I want to thank you for your help this evening."

"Of course," Taryn said, sitting down between two merlons and turning his gaze out across the town. "It's the least I can do."

"Why?"

"I'm a guest in your dun. My grandmam would approve."

"Your grandmam sounds like a well-bred lady."

"Aye."

"You don't mention your own mam much."

Taryn took a deep breath and let it out slowly.

"Ah, aye, the fresh fragrance of uncleaned dun ward," he quipped, coughing a bit. "My mother is … less than motherly, I suppose you could say. She has other priorities. My brother Egoran is the heir, so she's more interested in his life. Berdda tries to fill the void."

"And your da?"

Taryn looked briefly sad. It had been more than a moon, if Bryan calculated correctly. He supposed grief might last longer if your parent weren't a reptile.

"There were four boys before me and a gap between Teddryn and myself, so I didn't get the hunting trips with Da. They were all born before he ascended, you see. I had to compete with the rigdon. He did pay attention when I was learning to ride and he would come and watch my sword lessons and ask me questions from books. I might have been a better son if I'd been more appreciative of what attention he could give me."

"You're not the youngest?"

"Nay. My sister Rhodda is the youngest."

"What's she like?"

Taryn's eyes misted.

"About the same age as your brother." His deep breath sounded shaky. Now seemed as good as anytime to ask after his suspicions.

"You were among the first to reach him, aye."

"I think Shyla and I were first. How he survived that fall …." He stared into space, stricken

"Do you remember somewhat?"

"A feeling. I can't truly explain it."

"If it comes clear to you, mayhap you'll share. Let us go back now. Mayhap you can talk my sister into coming away with you for a bit."

"Me? Nay. Kefyn mayhap has that power, but I don't think she even notices me."

"You think? I know you notice her."

"I do, but I'm not … it isn't that way. I know my place."

"I believe you. I still think you should suggest it. Let's go back."

Bryan was fairly certain that Shyla did not know what she wanted. He'd seen some glances she'd given Taryn during the tourney and he suspected she returned Taryn's feelings … or could. While he didn't want her to cockold Teddryn with his brother, he hoped to break the entanglement with Kefyn. He believed his cousin was not encouraging her, but Kefyn wanted to maintain the friendship and that made it hard to end the flirtation. Bryan welcomed Taryn's interference.

In the children's hall, Lydya had finally come from Danyl's room to sit down on a bench, wiping tears from her cheeks. Saryl (or whatever the lass's name truly was) followed her.

"Has he …?" Bryan started to ask, stumbling.

"He still lives," Saryl assured him. "This sort of injury would be a crisis in the holts, so I can make no promises to his treatment here. I will do the best I can."

Chirgeon Traegyr had also come from the room.

"You are a foolish lad to give unsupported hope," he pronounced before stalking from the room.

"What did that mean?" Bryan demanded.

"Traegyr does not believe Danyl will recover," Lydya reported, fighting back tears. "I prefer to believe this young woman. It may be fantasy, but it is hope and I must have hope."

Shyla covered her eyes, weeping. Kefyn squeezed her shoulder. Taryn excused himself at this point. Bryan watched his retreat.

He's remembering somewhat, I think. It's too soon from his father's death.

"Prayer might help," he said. "Could we, now?"

So they did, all of them but Saryl, who returned to wait with Danyl. It didn't cure Danyl, but prayer gave them strength to wait for his recovery … if recovery was God's will.

Blue Iris Holt

*G*ly crushed cardamom, cinnamon and catsclaw powder together in a large bowl, watching the color blend to assure the proportions. The caravan had sold out of the herbal mixture this trip, so he intended to have more available for next year. He already had sent messages to the coastal holts to replenish his supplies.

A foot scraped the stone behind him and he left off his work to look. Tavoran stood in the doorway, tall and handsome as ever, eyes full of rage.

"Hello, son. What may I do for you?" Gly said, because there was nothing to be done about Tav. He'd learned the rules and lived as if they meant something, but Gly knew it was just an act.

"I've decided to return to Denygal this fall."

Gly shuddered. That never spoke well for some girl's future.

"Must you?"

"There's research to do. These marauders may be upon us any day, but we don't know how. We should, so we can prevent it."

What he said was true and he would spend his time in research. It didn't take long to destroy lives and then flit away before anyone knew you were there.

"Shanara believes Gil is involved," Gly reported, because that was important news and a bone for Tav to suck.

"Indeed? I'll see if that is information that is useful. Tell Madi that I've gone."

"I will."

And she will weep not for his absence, but for what he is doing in it.

"Do you suppose Ryanna traveled west to avoid our love?" he asked.

"Ryanna rides at the One's command," Gly corrected. There was a large knife near at hand. He could end this now before there was more heartache.

The feeling of a baby in his arms stayed his hand.

Tav closed the door on his way out. Gly sank onto a bench and wept for he knew his son was an evil man and he hated himself for not being able to stop him.

Honor Wood

There are many species of being in Daermad and not all sentients are human or even close. The elves (they prefer to be called Kin) live a very long time and their eyes and ears are naught like ours at all. They tell tales similar to the adventurers' tales — of griffin and flying horses and … dragons. Dragons are the most intriguing because they can take to the skies in ways we cannot imagine, but they also live forever. I wonder if they can die at all.

**Shyrtransdonyl, Moryn,
Founding Year 969)**

Past

Founding Year 931
Dengyal Wilderness

*J*anara held his staff in her hands, shifting it, sighting along it.

"This is honor wood," she remarked after a bit.

Donyl straightened up from poking holes in the ash at the edge of their fire. An unexpected thunder shower had forced them under the shelter of this rock overhang.

"I'm not familiar," he explained. "It looks like a rough stick of old willow to me. What is honorable about it?"

"They're given to some Wisdoms as a sign of honor. How did you come upon it?"

"It was given to me by a boy in the mountains on my journey here."

"A boy?"

"From Kylly Mines. He guided us to the paths to the citadel."

"Those who are of the way of peace?"

"Aye. How do you know about them?"

"They are related to the Denygal. We both worship the One and that citadel trains Wisdoms and guides for both of us. He would not have given this to you by happenstance."

"I'm no Wisdom."

She didn't respond, just looked at the wood.

"Do you whittle?"

"It's not favored in the royal circles, but aye, I've done some basic. Why?"

"You will understand this staff better if you reveal it. Its beauty is not found on the outside, but on the inside. As you reveal it, it will either accept or reject you."

Donyl frowned at her, but took the staff and ran his fingers along the furrows.

"What are these odd bits here?"

"You must reveal them."

Donyl sighed. They'd only spent half the day trekking and his body no longer demanded rest so frequently. It would give him somewhat to do while they waited out the storm. He scraped the end grain with his dagger, deciding that this wood only required a bit taken off the outside. It was relatively soft wood, so he slit the bark about two inches down from what he felt should be the top, girded the branch and then used his dagger like a draw knife to remove just the outer layer, revealing the yellow wood underneath.

Janara came back from walking in the rain, smelling as if she'd bathed. He watched as she squeezed water from her braid, then donned dry clothes. He was never going to get used to her walking round in her small clothes, although he supposed the trews she wore instead of a proper set of dresses were practical for the life she led.

"The storm is passing and we have many hours of daylight left. I suggest we move on," she announced.

Her suggestions were never really that. Donyl had accepted that she knew her way about here as he did not. He set the staff aside to begin to gather his meager belongings. He wondered what had happened to the treasure he'd given to the riders before they had fled Kylly Mines in myriad directions. Would he ever know?

They reached for the same item and their hands touched. Her skin was warm and damp. It made his stomach clench in a curious way. For a moment, they hung suspended between breaths, staring at each other's hands. And then the moment passed. She took the item to put it in her pack and they separated. She used a stick to pull the fire apart and kick dirt over anything still smoldering.

The woods dripped with golden liquid as they started along the path. The mountains remained high around them, the streams that crossed the trail remained bone-chilling cold. If her estimate of their progress was correct, they'd reach her family's dun in an eightnight. Unfortunately, the dark of the moon was only six days hence. Walking faster was a dream that left their goal dangling two days short of safety.

"Are there no horses anywhere?" he asked as he struggled to keep up with her distance-eating strides.

"To the east there's a trail that leads to the Dragon's Head and there's a steady stream of horses on it with dancers upon their backs, but before you reach it, there's the Milk and there's no bridges because it's too wide. It's another five days at our current pace before we reach the bridge into Fairhaven. There's horses on the other side."

"We won't live that long, Janara."

"You've lived so far, haven't you?"

"You didn't see – you can't know."

"We could run instead of walk fast … if you can keep the pace."

She scented the air like a hound as he bit his tongue from saying somewhat cruel and biting.

"You know, after I spent a year in bed, the chirgeon said I'd never walk again. I refused to accept that and spent another year learning to walk again. I've kept up with you as best I can."

The path was topping a wind-blown rise that offered a view to both sides of the ridge they were on. Far to the north a wisp of smoke curled up from an unbroken forest.

"A settlement of some sort?" he asked.

Janara stood stalk still, gaze pinpointing an image he could barely make out.

"Lightning is the enemy of the northern forest."

"What do you mean?"

"That's a fire. The wind from the south is normal this time of year, so it ought to blow away from us, but it's closer than I like and that I can smell it says there's some wind from the north. We should pick up the pace, just to be prepared."

She quickly settled into a ground-eating lope that he knew he couldn't match. He sighed and followed, because to stop was to be left behind.

Present

Founding Year 1028
Mirklin Wood

*O*n the morrow, Tamys couldn't wake up. Padraig tried several times to get him on his feet, but the lack of sleep from the preceding night had taken its toll. He remained groggy and weak, unable to eat breakfast or dress himself, so that it was well past dawn before he swung up into the saddle. They saw naught of the elves or any evidence that anyone was in the forest besides themselves. It occurred to Padraig that the evening before might have been an attempt to scare interlopers away. This forest might be known as the Mirklin Wood for a reason beyond the fears of superstitious folk afraid of densely growing trees. If the elves were aware of that fear, they might play it to their advantage. Certainly the elves to the east were not above practicing guile when the need arose. Humans had taught them well. Padraig wagered that the western elves were no less intelligent.

The day passed with few events. Padraig saw deer and birds, a fox once, plenty of squirrels, but no elves or humans and no trace of any had ever passed this way before. The only sign of sentient life was the remains of the dwarven trade road. But dwarves didn't build roads out of the mountains for no purpose. There must have been elves to trade with in the past.

The road led toward the mountains, maintaining a more or less straight path, except when it detoured round hills or to cross streams at fords. In one or two places, they encountered sturdy stone bridges, still standing over a millennium after they had been built. Moss covered the stones and trees encroached close, threatening to topple the structures. Padraig found the way the forest took back its own to be reassuring, as if the world wanted to return to the days of the elves, before humans had encroached. Tamys' edginess spoke volumes for how he felt about the forest.

"They're following – or watching anyway," he announced at midday when they stopped for cheese and water. "I can hear them."

"You're certain it's not forest sounds – deer, the like?"

"Aye. At first I wasn't certain, but I have listened all morn and they're just beyond what you can see, by the sound of it."

"I'm a quarter elf. What I can see is far more than an ordinary man."

"Then mayhap it's just beyond what they can see, but I know they're out there."

Padraig tried calling into the forest, speaking in Elvish, telling them again his name, that his mother was a half-elf, that there were others living in the east. He hoped they'd accept those credentials and come out of the trees, but it was not to be. Experience had taught them to trust no one.

Padraig saw a face in the tree tops toward evening, quickly gone. Tamys turned his nose in that direction.

"There's one overhead."

"Aye, I saw him briefly. Can we travel a bit farther? I'll never convince them I'm a quarter elf if they don't see me traveling in the near-dark."

"I thought so," Tamys said triumphantly. "All the time we've traveled together, you always had to be reminded that night was following. I wondered, but now I know. You see in the dark."

"Not truly dark, but I can see well enough to navigate by starlight."

"Can the horses?"

"Nay, which is why we'll stop by dusk, but I'd like to continue until the sun goes down."

"It's fine with me. I hardly need light to sit this saddle, so long as you can see."

Padraig glanced back at Tamys and saw the lad's face flicker with pain. He turned forward and continued the journey. Dusk found them at a small clearing that was less than ideal. Tamys accepted the mess bag happily enough and set out the cheese and bread. There was some jerked meat left, but Padraig feared they'd need it in the mountains, so they supped on the cheese and bread alone. They occasionally heard what might be a footfall at the edge of the clearing, but he couldn't see into the trees. Padraig had gathered a small stock of fallen wood, but he decided not to build a fire since the evening was warm and neither he nor Tamys needed the light.

With no sign of further encroachment, he eventually fell asleep, only to awaken and find a dozen elves sitting cross-legged on the ground in a circle round the camp, as if they'd been watching them sleep.

Clarcom Court

*G*regyn's head pounded, but there was no place to rest where he might find dark and quiet, so he assuaged it with a tankard of dark. The dun was in an uproar. Most of the tourney guests prepared to depart in the predawn gloom, but Gregyn had not slept, waiting for news from those allowed near the lad. All agreed the lad had a penchant for jumping from roof to roof, so nobody questioned his fall. Gregyn knew differently. He'd felt the presence. He'd deal with that later. Now he had to recover from what he'd done in the rose garden.

Interacting with Ryan had released Naraddal's spell mayhap a little earlier than the grey mage would have planned, but seeing Danyl lying there had unleashed somewhat in Gregyn that he had never experienced, that he'd never known he could do. As the child's spirit had been leaving his body, Gregyn had seen the incredible web of Talidd's spell, how it had spread across the land to find potentials, to uproot their lives and draw them to him. For whatever reason, it had swirled round Danyl and caused this. In a heartbeat, Gregyn had known Danyl laying on the cold stones was a mistake. In the second heartbeat, he'd realized that all of the people he knew as psychically gifted were there ... Taryn, Shyla, Bryan, Ryan, Kefyn, Lydya had just entered the rose garden. Gregyn had put his hand on the lad and drawn every bit of power he could using the people round him as familiars, then poured it into the lad until his spirit had slowly flowed back into his body, which began to breathe.

Gregyn's headache was easing, he wasn't nauseous and his hands weren't shaking. If he had harmed himself with working such large magicks without preparation, it didn't show. But had he done any good?

What are you thinking? You're a black mage apprentice. If Talidd finds out what you did, he'll burn you out himself!

Taryn joined him at the riders' table, sighing tiredly.

"How is he?" Gregyn asked, trying to ignore the crazy things he saw in Taryn's aura. No one with that much potential should be allowed to go about with his aura hanging out there like a cloak in the wind.

"It's bad. He ought to be dead, so bad is probably good. There's still hope." He rubbed his temple. "I don't know why I feel so tired."

Because I sucked life energy from you to give to him.

"After a skirmish, at first you feel energized, but later you feel drained. The excitement got you through the night, but now your body is feeling the hour."

Taryn nodded, then stared at the opposite bench as if waiting for it to divulge answers. Gregyn rubbed his burning eyes and waited.

"I think somebody pushed him."

Easy. If this is Talidd's spell, that makes sense. The True King might be asserting his primacy or showing his wisdom. Which is another reason no one should know of what you've done. Mayhap you should not have done it at all.

"Why do you think that?"

"I've been on that roof. It's the corridor that most directly takes you to the great hall from my quarters, so I took the roof walk."

That's consistent with how you live at Galornyn. Mayhap coincidence or mayhap ....

"The parapet is waist high on me. The lad is tall for his age ... he could see over without climbing up, but he couldn't fall over without help. I went up there just now and ... I can feel ... someone ... a malevolent someone."

With your gifts ....

"I believe you, but they won't."

"Won't they? If you haven't noticed, a fair number of them have gifts that are greater than Berdda's. One of them can stop a death from occurring."

Does he know about me? Would he shield me if he did?

Gregyn looked up to see Taryn's gaze on Ryan of Moryn who had just come down the circular stairs. She dipped herself a tankard of dark and came to sit down on the opposite bench.

"How is he?" Taryn asked.

"Saryl says he'll do what he can, but lad's brain is like a bruised arm incased in armor you can't cut off." Taryn's wince said he understood what that meant. "If he lives, there will likely be difficulties."

What have I done?

"A noble child ... he'll not go hungry, be forced to beg. There are worse lives than to be a disabled noble."

Gregyn remembered the first time he'd been aware of his gifts, when he'd used them to distract a beggar so he could steal his coins, confident that the man could not chase him since his feet were crippled. It had been a heady experience for a child of six or seven. If he'd saved Danyl for that sort of existence, at least his position in life would provide him with some dignity.

"It's a tragedy regardless of his status in life," Ryan said. Her blue eyes seemed to weigh and judge them. "Life is a gift and should never be lost lightly, but there's consequences to playing God. A death averted creates complications that should not occur." As she spoke, her gaze moved back and forth between them, finally settling on Gregyn.

My shields are back if they were ever gone. She cannot know about me.

Ryan drained her tankard and stood.

"I know we planned to leave day after tomorrow, but Cullyn shouldn't leave his family right this moment and some of us may be needed here for the next few days."

She strode away. Gregyn strictly controlled his reaction, swallowing another gulp of ale, while waiting for what Taryn might say.

"Berdda would use her gifts to strengthen him as she did with Teddryn." Gregyn forgot how to breathe. Taryn's nervous fingers brushed his breecs. "That's what it felt like – when she worked with Teddryn." *Are you saying you're linked? Nay, nay, nay.* "I wonder if they know how to do that here." He stood up abruptly. "I must get away from the smell of ale. You look done in. I'll let the men know we'll not be leaving for a few days longer."

He put a hand on Gregyn's shoulder.

"Get some rest, friend. You've earned it and I'll not have you ill on the return journey."

Taryn glanced longingly at the ale barrels and then fled the great hall, leaving Gregyn to nurse his headache and fight his fear.

Galornyn

*T*he summer heat meant a quick funeral, especially since so many were afraid of plague. His mother shrieked, bereft of her favorite. Rogyn withdrew into contemplation. Berdda pled exhaustion, having been up all night with Teddryn. After Egoran was laid to rest, Maddw walked with the family back from the litch field and then made his escape up to the roof.

Taryn's comfort with heights had its advantages. There were not so many people on the roof. Maddw found this not entirely true as Branwyn nee Manahan sat upon the parapet, face raised to the sun as it came around the eastern headland. Behind and below her lay the sweep of the Galornyn harbor with its bevy of ships going back and forth through the Narrows.

"I apologize for intruding," Maddw said. The sight of her threatened to bring the tears anew. He'd not truly been fond of Egoran, but he had loved him as a brother.

"There's no need to withdraw, sir. I needed some fresh air is all. I'll leave you if you prefer."

"Nay. I did climb here to be alone, but not from you."

"Thanks for saying it," she replied. He leaned against the next merlon. "Is the roof your away place?"

"Nay. It's my brother Taryn's escape. I usually take a horse out. You?"

"In Mulyn, I walk. Here – well, I suppose it doesn't matter. I'll be returning soon enough."

"Are you upset by that?" he asked. "Don't think me wrong here, but Egoran's disinterest in you was clear."

"Noble women go where they are sent," Gwen quoted. "In our short conversation, I thought mayhap we could find intellectual common ground. I'd have made a good wife for a vyngretrix."

He believed that. She was well trained, attractive and not given to panic. She had gotten Egoran help quickly, though it had already been too late.

"Did the chirgeon determine a cause?" she asked.

"Shellfish, they believe. Some people react to it and even someone who has eaten it often in the past might change to being unable to eat it. He must have ignored the first time it tickled. It's been the death of others in the past."

"That, I suppose, would explain why I ate the soup and drank the wine and didn't die."

"Hmm," Maddw agreed. He didn't think she believed it any more than he, but it was what they were left with, a comfortable non-answer. "You needn't worry that you are suspect."

"I assumed the chief taster examined both bowls and goblets and determined that there was no poison."

"You really were prepared for life as the spouse of a vyngretrix, weren't you?"

"My father meant to spend my maidenhead wisely. I'm sure he will do so now as well."

"Or spend it on his next war, aye?"

She sighed, but he could tell she'd already considered the possibility.

"Truth-to-tell, I don't really want to discuss this," Maddw told her. "I could use some light-hearted conversation. What really brought you to the roof?"

"The sea. I'd never seen it before I arrived here and I am utterly fascinated."

"I've always thought wide stretches of forest and sky-scraping mountains were fascinating."

"Have you ever seen?"

"Once after joining your father in sieging Celdrya, I was able to travel to southern Galconyn. Do you know if there are similarities?"

"Aye, we traveled that way on our way here. To eyes that have never known mountains, I think they are similar. Galconyn's mountains are steeper than the ones near Manahan, more like there are in the Pass of the Arrival."

"So my eyes are mountain novice eyes?"

"Somewhat like my eyes are with regards to the sea. I suppose in time, I would have come to miss the mountains, but I think I will miss the sea when I return. I'd have liked to learn the nuances, to know when a storm is coming and to recognize one ship from another."

Maddw looked out across the harbor and, for the briefest of moments, he thought he saw a fleet of small, low-slung ships throwing torches at the warehouses that lined the docks. History, he supposed, as it faded. A shudder ran down his back.

"Are you cold?" Branwyn asked.

"More like sad. You lost a brother last year."

"Aye. Trevyr died in battle. There's no easy way to lose a sibling, I suppose, but it mayhap made more sense."

"I got my report about your brother Tamys, by the way."

"Aye?"

"He traveled to Clarcom, but then headed to Celdrya. We believe he took a caravan job. We're still awaiting report from the west to verify that."

She sighed, then nodded, putting a pleasant face on it.

"Good to know. Gal asked that I plead with Egoran to allow Tamys to live should he arrive here."

"You have my word that I will do my best should he come here looking for you. My sources say he's under ban, but not under death sentence."

Now she smiled genuinely.

"It's odd, because he's younger and the son of a different mother, but he is my favorite brother. He's been far enough from the rule not to care about all the politics and that is much easier than what I've had to endure."

"I understand. I just became the spare heir, so I imagine my time will soon be taken up with all my brother needs me to know."

"Why were you war leader and not Rogyn?"

"I would wonder that myself if I hadn't lived through it. Rogyn always should have been heir, but for the fact that he was not born first. Some men are leaders of an epic sort and that will be my brother."

"And Egoran?"

"Well trained, but essentially soulless."

Gwen stared at him. She knew it, just from the short time she'd spent with him. Whoever had killed Egoran had known it too.

"Thank you for sitting with me," he said.

"When we met, that day in the corridor, I felt we could be friends. I am glad always to help a friend."

There were worse things, Maddw thought, then to marry a woman who could be your friend. That the thought had not occurred to her spoke well for her lack of personal ambition. That none had brought the mention of it to him made him wonder if he was just hoping his attraction would be satisfied.

Llyr

*T*he bedsheets were wrinkled under her back as she tossed restlessly in the summer heat. Outside rain clouds scudded across the black sky as the city lay under a blanket of humid air.

It had been winter that day, with rain pattering against the glass panes. She'd insisted only Nanyna should be with her for this. There was no need for a midwife, lest the child not be entirely normal.

An unseen hand tightened on her belly as she squatted to bring the child further down.

"Shouldn't you use the birth stool for that?" Nanyna had asked. She'd been very young that day, her brown hair shining where it showed under the head scarf.

When she could speak, Shyralan had allowed Nanyna to help her to the birthing stool, but she could not stay there. She rose to walk the room.

I should never have laid with him.

She'd been intrigued by another mixed-breed. It had been so long since she'd been with her own kind. He'd been handsome and glib of tongue and an attentive lover.

I should not have laid with him.

What would she do if the child showed features?

Children die all the time in birthing.

The contractions came more and more often, longer, more intense. No matter how many children you had, the last bit was overwhelming. Nanyna had arranged for a bath and Shyralan slid into the warm water, grateful for how it wrapped round her. Only three pushes there and the child pushed out. Most mothers counted fingers and toes while the child lay upon their chest, but Shyralan smiled at the rounded ears and the round pupils.

Aye, this child will live. I'll find somewhere for him in my world. I've needed a house master for some time.

She'd begun to lay aside money for him that day. He would need the best of educations. And soon he was a toddler and then a boy of six, tall and gangly.

She'd gone to sleep one night after tucking him into his bed. She'd dreamt that night as she dreamt this night that black daemons had slunk in his room and carried him away while she slept. She'd turned the Bottom upside down seeking him, but no one could find him.

She woke up crying out for her child, her hands grasping at empty air as a crack of thunder rattled the window panes. Beyond the growl of the heavens, she thought she heard him call out for her, but of course, no one was there.

Thin Edge of Life

The Summer Isles lay far to the south, beyond the Stormor. There are five islands in the archipelago, inhabited by a dark skinned people with curly hair, who apparently worship nature, which they personify with names. They are known to be very ebullient and casual in their attitudes toward marriage, but very fierce with regards to territory.

Dagvyn, priest of Bel, FY836

Past

Viking Year 742 (Four years ago)
Hansorfjord

*G*il considered his dagger all through dinner at the Kong's table. Erik was clearly besotted with Sygna. They spent all evening whispering one to another. Surely, she put on a good performance for her burden. Gil could show her far better goods if only he could get her alone.

It wouldn't do to kill Erik at his father's table. It would destroy the alliance with the Svard. While the Orental were prepared to enter the invasion, they wanted the Svard to soften the kingdom first. He needed both of them to accomplish the Goddess's goal, but he wanted Sygna. He could smell the *awen* on her and knew that such was the key to true power.

You thought that with Ryanna, the Goddess whispered. *Mayhap you are too hasty in your acquisition.*

War was dangerous and Erik was a war leader. Mayhap Gil would have to rid her of the young kong's offspring, but that was a small matter. He'd do it more subtly this time so she would not resent him as Ryanna had.

She's young and wants a handsome strong man with many riches. When this is done, I will be all that and more.

"The ships are coming well and Erik has the jals training crews," Kong Magnus reported. "What help will your employers give us?"

"You are to soften up the coast, disrupt their trade. The Orental will come in on the eastern part, into southern Dublyn and pressure to the west as you move up the river valleys."

"We can begin raiding as soon as Erik produces an heir, but the jals think we are stretching ourselves too far to take the elves in the mix. We are not mountain warriors."

Careful, the Goddess whispered. *I've a plan or two to that end. Patience.*

"My employer is dispatching me as an embassy to others who might like to join the fight. Of course, the spoils will be spread amongst the participants depending on investment."

"Of course," Magnus demurred. Erik had left off his incessant pestering of his bride to listen to the conversation."

"May we know of your plans, emissary?"

"Not at this time. Negotiations are delicate. I cannot promise the performance of parties who have not yet agreed."

Erik exchanged a subtle glance with his father.

Would that I could do this without these untrustworthy men?

"That is understood," Magnus said. "Our concern is that if we launch before our allies are ready, our efforts would be inadequate."

"Just continue building the ships and let me take care of the alliances."

And your daughter-in-law. Is there not some custom among you heathens about conjugal relations for visitors?

Apparently this was not the case because Gil was invited to return to the junque after the meal. He stepped up onto the deck where the Orental sailors would not even meet his eye. He had lived among them for months and yet they hid themselves from him.

His cabin was dark and chilled, but as soon as he struck flint to steel to light a lantern, she appeared, dressed in her breast skimming dress, her raven hair tumbling past her waist.

"My lady," he whispered.

"Farenlucgilyn, we should celebrate our victories and plan your next expedition."

"Yes, my lady."

Goblets of mead appeared as she dropped her dress and stepped free of it. He did not think to drink, but swept her up in his arms to carry her to the bunk. He didn't remember them discussing the next phase of their campaign. They drank mead and mated several times. He fell asleep eventually and awoke alone, as if she'd never been there, but he knew where he was bound to go now and he'd begun to realize that she would pave the way for him if he but trusted her.

Present

Founding Year 1028
Mirklin Wood

*T*he elves had indeed been watching them. They blind-folded Padraig and didn't bother with Tamys. As they rode to wherever the elves were taking them, Tamys tried to use his remaining senses to good advantage. The elves did not have horses of their own, but they allowed Tamys to ride.

~*They've put a bag over my head, Joy complained. Can your bird help us?*

Tamys had no idea what Joy was talking about. His occasional flashes of blind-sight told him that they were traveling a deeply shadowed path alongside a rock hill covered in green plants. He thought this might be a dwarven side road because the horses' hooves had the same hollow sound as the highway. He smelled what he thought were oak leaves and an occasional pine. After a while of riding silently through the grayness Tamys heard voices far ahead and smelled cooking fires. The elves helped him off the horse and gently guided him into a shelter of some sort. The air was cooler, the sun completely gone, the space lit by – not lanterns. There was light, but he couldn't smell flame. They guided him to a stool where a wall of living stone guarded his back. *A cave?* Someone guided his hand to close round his stick. The kindness did not reassure him.

Padraig had been silent this whole time. He smelled differently from the elves, which was how Tamys knew that he was still there. One of the elves spoke and Padraig answered, still with a bag over his head. Mayhap he'd asked for it to be removed because they did. Padraig spoke again. An exchange occurred between the elf and Padraig. It seemed respectful. Tamys didn't sense fear in Padraig's voice.

~*Have you looked through your bird's eyes yet?* Joy asked.

How did one answer a horse? Tamys didn't know, so he tried to focus on the cave.

~*Shielding? How'd you learn that?* Her voice was now much softer, so that he could listen to the cave.

He thought there were four elves and Padraig there. One of them stood at the entrance – the metal door behind him tasted different from the stone it was set in. The roof here was higher than the chamber was across. How did he know that? He knew naught.

"Tamys, stop trying to shield yourself from them. They need to believe us."

Padraig's sudden lapse into Celdryan surprised Tamys, but he still didn't know what shielding was.

One of the elves said somewhat. Padraig translated.

"They want to know your name. Answer honestly."

"Tamys ap Manahan of Mulyn."

The elf spoke again.

"Are you blind?"

"Aye."

"Why are you traveling through the forest?"

"Padraig, how do they even know what I'm saying?"

"They don't, but they can see your soul."

The elf said somewhat in what might have been an annoyed voice.

"Why are you traveling through the forest? Answer, lad."

"Padraig is bound for Morglen, the other side of the mountains and this is the shortest way."

The elf turned away, then spoke. There was a great deal of walking round the chamber and then Padraig took Tamys' arm.

"We've been accepted. They have a guest chamber for us to rest and refresh in."

"Are we free to go?"

"I wouldn't go that far, but it's our good fortune that they're not going to kill us as interlopers. Come, best cooperate for now. Trail your finger along the wall and count your steps. At some point knowing the way to and fro mayhap be useful-like."

Clarcom

Sarala placed her hands to either side of Danyl's head, trying to avoid the bruises, but knowing that was impossible. The lad didn't feel them at any rate. The nurse and Shyla moved him on her count, rolling him like a log onto his left side, settling his right limbs on pillows. Sarala released his head and stood back.

"There's blood in his brain," Shyla reported.

"I know," Sarala admitted. "His breathing is slowing. I can't explain why his bones are not broken, but it does not matter as his brain is swelling and I lack the ability to relieve the pressure."

"Elven healers can, though, right?"

"I'm merely an herbalist."

"You are at least trying, not like Traegyr declaiming him dead while he yet breathes."

"He may well die before the day is out," Sarala said. "Ryan is trying to find a way for a healer to connect with me, but my lack of gifts makes that problematic."

"Not impossible?"

"Nay. It's been done before. If the pressure doesn't become too much, he may live anyway. You do know, though, that injuries like this – he may never walk or talk – I may save an empty shell."

Shyla's eyes misted, but she was made of tougher stuff than her delicate appearance made one think and she did not actually weep.

"Mayhap prayer is the answer," she suggested in a hoarse voice.

"Prayer is always the answer," Sarala replied automatically. There would have been a prayer circle a lot sooner than this in the holts. I began to wonder if I was alone.

"Nay, I mean a prayer group, laying on of hands here."

"Recognizing that his care must come first, I've no objections, but …."

A tap on the door caused the nurse to move to the door to admit Taryn from Galornyn, who softly oozed power that he seemed mostly unaware of.

"How is he?" Taryn asked.

"He's …. " Shyla started.

"Dying," Sarala announced. *It was either you or your captain who prevented the boy's soul from leaving his body. Ryanna is rarely wrong obout these things.*

Taryn nodded.

"I mayhap can do somewhat to help," he said to Shyla. "My grandmam -- what I told you about how she helps Teddryn."

"You can weave in the same way?"

"I don't know," he admitted. "I have gifts, but I've not used them and I'm .. I don't know. Mayhap you can tell me."

He held out his hand to Shyla. She hesitated a moment before taking it, gaze askance.

"I feel the power and that it's been tapped by another before." She gasped and looked at him intently. "Why did she block you?"

"I suspect to protect me from my mother. It's a hard story to tell. Can you use it?"

"I'm not trained to know … but Ryan …." Shyla turned toward Sarala in question.

"He might act as a bridge," Sarala agreed. "Alinor, find Ryan of Moryn and ask him to join us."

"Also send summons to Lord Bryan, Lady Lydya and Kefyn of Donalshyr," Shyla added. Alinor nodded and left the chamber. "I hope you don't mind, but we need to pray for him as well and they are safe to be told. They won't tell others."

"I suspect Kefyn already knows," Taryn said.

A sound from the bed drew Sarala's attention. A shiver ran through Danyl's body. *A seizure. It's not the end, but it's not a good sign.* She put her hand on the back of his neck. He had grown warmer. He hadn't passed urine since what had wet his breecs on the ground. His pulse slowed further even while she was checking it.

The group that gathered included Glynn, Lydya's third son. Eight people filled the room to capacity. Ryanna grasped Taryn's hand with her left and placed her right hand on the back of Sarala's head. As Sarala placed her hands on Danyl's head, a seizure rippled through his body. Lydya continued whispering in prayer to the One as did the others. Sarala felt naught. She despaired that the boy would die under her hands.

God, help me to help him. I don't know what to do.

And, then ...

She felt a click like a latch being opened and she flowed into a dark red place filled with flashing fireflies. She had seen this described by elven healers, but it had been a place locked away from her by her natural inabilities. She thought about the bruise on his left temple and found herself in a dark red place with no fireflies. No, there was an occasional barely discernable flicker at the edges of her consciousness. She felt compressed, as if she were at the bottom of a deep pond. She thought about the pressure and felt her consciousness flow downward. The pressure grew until she feared she would stop breathing. Her heart beat frantically and she wanted to beg Ryanna to break this horrible connection. She pushed away from what felt like a barred door and then it opened and the pressure seemed less. She pushed on the barred door again and the pressure eased more.

She became aware of her body once more. She opened her eyes. Danyl did not look substantially different, but Lydya was smiling. The lad's body was not as hot, his breathing was stronger, his heart rate more steady. Saralya felt well-rested despite not sleeping for more than 24 hours and Shyla stared at Taryn like she had just seen him for the first time.

"Is he … healed?" Bryan asked.

Sarala put her hands back on his head and brought to mind that place once more.

"Nay," she reported. "We've helped him, but he's not cured. It will take time. You've taught me a new skill," she told Taryn. "Mayhap I will need a refresher, but if I can learn this healer technique from you, we may yet save his life."

"I don't know that I am teaching you anything, only that you can use what I have. I will remain if you wish it," he assured her.

At Sarala's insistence they all left the chamber except Ryanna, who sat down in the windowsill with her back against the closed shutter.

"How does it work with him?" Sarala asked in Elvish.

"I'm not sure," Ryanna answered in the same. "There's a fount of power there that I can tap and someone has used it for healing previously, so there was already a tap in place. He does not know what he's doing, but because you do, I can weave it to your purposes. It changed somewhat in you, didn't it?"

"It's talked about among the healers. For every Wisdom who wields the healing arts, there's a handful of healers like Padraig who come by their gifts through God's design, but there are some of us who can also learn skills that are not natural. Mayhap that is what Taryn's grandmother does."

"Why were you never trained?"

"They considered me too young. For all our mothers' people try to avoid prejudice, they still see things through catslit eyes."

Ryanna smiled.

"Aye, I remember. Twenty-one seems very young to them while we know we are mature enough. Celtmen are wives and mothers well before your age."

Sarala ran her hand down Danyl's vertebra from neck to mid-torso.

"How is he?"

"People keep asking that," Sarala said. "The answer is the same in Elvish. He should not have lived. Help me roll him onto his back."

Ryanna never moved. Pillows shifted and Danyl was rearranged without his spine being moved out of alignment. Sarala gave her a rueful grin before indicating the left side of Danyl's head.

"If I read what I saw correctly, this part of his brain is very bruised and bleeding. There's other parts damaged too, but that's the worst. There's a place, deep inside, where there's … hmmm, a blockage created by the swelling. When I open it, blood and … other fluid … drains away. That will help for a while. I'll need to do it again."

"When?"

"I'm not sure, but I know the signs now. Taryn and you must remain close in case I can't do it alone."

"We will. She fancies him, you know? And he her."

"Shyla and Taryn? I suspect she fancies him more now that he holds the key to saving her brother, but aye. Kefyn's heart is breaking."

"Kefyn knew he shouldn't love her. The heart is a changeable beast."

Sarala nodded, though she had never fully allowed herself to be carried by hers. Cai had been too old for her. He'd been a kind friend, no more.

"I need rest," she admitted in Celdryan. "Mayhap you will remain with him and wake me if there are changes?" Ryanna looked at Danyl with a slight askance view.

"I can do that," Ryanna replied, also in Celdryan. "It's interesting how the aura shrinks tight round an ill person. Mayhap we can use Taryn to teach you the skill of aura reading as well."

"Mayhap. 'Tis a useful one, no doubt. Ryanna, who do you think …?"

"Go rest, Sarala. There are mysteries you do not need to resolve."

I do have more important things on my mind.

"I'll wake you if there's change. Should I turn him or …?"

"Every watch, to his right side, then his back, then his left."

"Done. Go now. I'll be here."

"Thank you. How is it, do you suppose, that I am here for this?"

"The One knew this would happen. Take your ease and question naught."

Sarala took a deep breath and did as told, too tired to question further, but knowing that somewhat had changed in her plans going forward and that the One had known all along that they would.

Galornyn

*B*reathing took so much effort. Teddryn awoke struggling to expand his lungs, each breath an agony. His head hurt as his body burned with fever. Berdda's cool hand brought some relief, but he feared he would die before the day was out.

Breathe! Lift your chest. Let your lungs expand. Now, breathe out. Easier, but then you must breathe in.

He would doze off sometimes and wake up light headed, his desire for air paramount. Breathe in, breathe out. Death was round every nap.

Maddw's face wavered above him, speaking nonsense words. The roaring pain in his body eased, his breath came easier and he dozed until he forgot how to breathe again and then the struggle began anew.

His muscles were aflame and it felt like his head would burst like an overripe melon. He heard Nudd stalking the halls, calling his name.

I thought I'd die in battle, among the honored dead, not in my own piss, crying for the pain to stop.

Breathing eased at Berdda's next visit and he slept for a time before he woke struggling once more. Now it was Rogyn standing over him.

They're using their gifts to keep me alive. I'm so tired. Mayhap it would be best if they allowed me to go.

"Water," he whispered, but when they put the cup to his lips, he couldn't swallow. Pain seared through his head, down his neck, setting his back and limbs afire. His lips were moistened. He concentrated on the next breath and the one after that.

Any moment Nudd would find his room and provide him with relief. Just one more breath – in and out – wait until the gods take a hand – breathe and breathe and breathe ….

Sleep overwhelmed him and this time he didn't awaken. He felt himself float free of the bed and then found himself upon the field of battle with the clang of swords all round him.

Mirklin Wood – Elven Village

They didn't allow me to see on the way here.

Joy's complaint proved to Padraig that these elves knew about Companions and did not want Padraig to have the information he needed to make an escape. On the other hand, they knew naught of horses and allowed Padraig to care for them, which got him outside.

This was a tree village. Except for the stone hill that served as some sort of village center and guest hall where Padraig and Tamys were housed, most of the village was built up into the trees and joined by swinging bridges. On the ground, there were a few fields of food crops, but mostly the woods were free of signs of habitation. The western elves had been hiding for a long time and they left little trace of their passage. Their clothes were doe-skin that faded into the trees. They spoke in subdued voices and did not meet his eyes.

The clearing of the understory should have been a clue. They need wood for heating in the winter.

But what did they want with Tamys? Padraig was certain he himself was not the main quarry. There was somewhat about Tamys that brought their interest. They treated Padraig as a translator and aid to an honored guest, while exuding reverence toward Tamys.

"Are you well?" Mylan asked. She was the head of this village, far as Padraig could tell, the primary person to speak with them. While it was impossible to know age with a full elf, he suspected she remembered a time before the elves had come to the forest to live. She'd seen horses before, though she didn't seem to like them much. That was consistent with the tales of the older Kin talking about their parents' fears for them capturing horses and learning to ride.

"We are. Thank you for allowing us to rest here."

Her eyes were enormous, pale green, in sharp contrast to her black hair.

"There are those who thought we should allow you to pass. They don't remember when half-breed lived with us. I see the face of a daemon wrapping the heart of a person."

Padraig didn't much like that term "person", but he reserved his judgement for now. These elves had never known Jesu and did not know that the One saw all the same.

"Our healer is seeing to your friend," Mylan said, brushing a long-fingered hand along her leather trews.

"Do you think your healer has medicinals for his blindness?"

"Maybe. We cannot know this yet. Are there many like you out beyond the forest?"

"Half-elves?" She inclined her head. "Not this side of the kingdom, far as I know. We all live far to the east, in a place called Denygal. Mostly, what lays near here is Celdryan lands now."

"The daemons did not stop until we came here. They feared the trees. We made sure they feared them more."

"They call it Mirklin Wood – Dark Wood, Ghost Wood."

"Good, then we have done what we needed to do. Why did you choose to travel this way?"

"I'm not afraid of forests and I needed to get south of the mountains before winter."

"Hmm." She composed her face in an expression that he could not read, but a shiver ran down his back.

I suspect the mountains will be no closer if we stay here.

"Explain these – things," she instructed, pointing to the packs piled against the wall where the horses were tied.

They know naught of horses.

"Horses need weight upon their backs," he fabricated. "I must come here every day to put these saddles and packs upon them so they will remain healthy."

To prove his point, he hoisted a pack upon Earnest's back.

"Very interesting. Mayhap that is why the horses that used to roam the prairie died?"

"Very likely," he agreed, buckling the straps. He suspected they'd been rounded up by the Celts, but he didn't intend to share that theory with her.

"We are very pleased that you have brought Tamys here to us," Mylan said. "It is our wish to make him whole and healthy once more."

"Thank you."

She inclined her head and withdrew from him. Padraig allowed a previously-suppressed shudder to shake down his body.

There's somewhat wrong here. I must figure it out and decide my next move. I doubt it will be to remain here for the winter, so my God, please guide me.

Shadow of Guilt

The Fey have no king. They claim they never needed one. Each village had a council selected by a vote of the people. The village council would select representatives to regional councils, but there was no central authority. We are glad to have brought them to civilization, though they have not yet realized that their lives will be better when they have come to live under wise guidance.

Aiden ap Shalar, Priest of Bel, FY 139

Past

Founding Year 931
High Celdrya

When Gerriant received word that an ambassador from Galornyn had arrived, he had been dictating the death warrant for Deryk ap Trevellyn.

Whatever might they want this day?

"I have properly prescribed the manner and time of his death, aye?"

"You have," the Lughan scribe agreed.

"Is it dry enough to sign and seal?"

"Nay, regent. It will require some time to cure."

"I will speak to the ambassador in the greeting chamber then. Excuse me."

The scribe bowed slightly and Gerriant made his escape. He rather didn't like the Lughans now that he'd gotten to know the Bel a bit. He hated that he could not continue the investigation into Vanyn and Perryn's deaths, but the Lughan were insisting that there were statutes of limitations. He risked losing Deryk completely if he did not act.

The ambassador from Galornyn proved to be a man he was acquainted with – Staryg, a minor noble who had served page in Dun Fyrgal some dozen years ago.

"Thank you for seeing me on such short notice," the short, barrel-chested man said. "I did not want to make too much of my visit, but it is of some urgency."

It appeared so, for he had not paused to bathe or change clothes. He still had road dust upon his breecs.

"What is it?"

"When you sent out requests about the Assassins Guild, I began to ask round since there are known enclaves in Galornyn and Dunmaden. I felt they'd hold things to their chests, but there are always some who will speak if you cross their palms with silver."

"You've found somewhat?"

"Aye. You aren't going to like it, I'm afraid." A serving man entered with a tray of meat, cheese and bread, a flagon of water and a pitcher of summer wine. Staryg poured for himself, mixing water in after an exploratory taste. "Apparently, there have been several contracts let with the Guild having to do with the royal family. I certainly hope you have a taster employed."

"I do. Tell me."

"The Guild was hired to kill all three."

Gerriant knew his mouth hung open like a fly-trap, but some heartbeats passed before he could think beyond being stunned.

"All three?"

"Aye. Maryn's death was beyond suspicious, don't you agree?"

"Aye, and Vanyn's death spoke strongly of the Guild. I'm confused as to how the Guild induced Deryk ap Trevellyn to do its craft."

"As far as I can tell, Lord Deryk had naught to do with it. The Guild employs mages who can twist a man's mind to do almost anything."

"He was caught with the dagger in his hand."

"He is as responsible for Perryn's death as the dagger, but of course, it is your decision."

"If you're saying Deryk is innocent of the charges, you must know who hired the Guild."

"Aye. The Guild is more than willing to allow us to punish the man responsible since he turned on them and killed several rather than pay their ending fee."

"Who?"

"Burcan ap Mulyn."

"You're certain."

"I'm certain the Guild was paid in Mulyn marked coin. The Guild is certain that Burcan was the one who offered it. Physical description matches. The Guild may be assassins, but they have their own honor about these things. They're not given to lying outright. Besides, who else would gain so much – being as his wife is in the line of rule."

"Actually, her sister is the first in line, but mayhap is not about himself ruling as his family ascending. Hold this to your chest for now. I must ruminate on what you've told me."

"Aye, regent. I'll tarry for a few days before returning to Galornyn. Do call on me if you have further questions."

Gerriant promised that he would. As soon as the man withdrew, Gerriant poured himself a full tankard of wine and drank it down straight. His hands were still shaking after he'd swallowed the last drop.

Present

Founding Year 1028
Clarcom

Gregyn found Cullyn shortly after deciding he couldn't sleep. He had forged a note from Taryn asking Cullyn to meet him on the roof and found the young lord hanging over the parapet with a self-satisfied smile on his lips.

"You pushed your brother off this roof, did you not?"

Cullyn laughed.

"Of course I did. Annoying little rooter is out of my way now."

Gregyn balled up his fist and slammed it hard into Cullyn's gut.

Never leave visible bruises and don't break bones, Sawyl had taught. Cullyn gasped and choked, sagging against the wall.

"What in the hells makes you think I shouldn't kill you right now?" Gregyn demanded, his voice echoing off the hiding spell. Cullyn coughed, panting, unable to speak. "If I didn't think it would cause a stir, I'd toss you to the same fate." He saw a flicker of fear in Cullyn's eyes. "Good, you know who your master is. I suppose you thought I mightn't still have the ability to sniff that out for a while there, but I still do. What was the point of killing your brother?"

"Traegyr suggested a sacrifice."

Gregyn promised himself that Traegyr would not enjoy their conversation when it came.

"He surely did not mean a human sacrifice by a lad who has learned only basic rituals."

"We sacrificed a rabbit. It's not enough power."

"For what?"

"For me."

Gregyn felt a shudder run down his back as he recognized a spirit somewhat akin to the one he had often sensed in Sawyl. Such a mage would do whatever it took to amass more power for himself, even push a child to his death.

Gregyn slammed him against the wall with the force of another punch. He grabbed Cullyn's hair and twisted his face up to him. The lad still had no shields from Gregyn. There were naught signs that Traegyr had been able to enter beyond Gregyn's controls. He watched as the boy's pupils dilated with fear.

"I can't call back what you've done to Danyl, but you will never do that again – ever without my direct permission. Cully ap Riordan of Clarcom, you will do no blood sacrifice at all, not even as a participant until I grant direct permission."

"Aye," Cullyn said in a dreamy voice. Gregyn held the ensorcelment a moment longer before releasing him.

"Why did you try to kill Danyl?" he demanded. Cullyn had no choice but to answer truthfully.

"I hate him. None of my siblings is worth half as much as I am, but he's a bastard and part-elven in the mix."

Gregyn felt ice run down his back. *Not Cunyr's son, part elven and somehow mixed with the True King? What am I missing?*

"What are you saying?"

"I'm saying my mam put horns on my father's head and the product of that needs to die."

"Your father keeps a mistress close at hand. Far as I can tell, your mam's not trying to kill the whelp she's carrying. He's a child, Cully ap Riordan of Clarcom. You will remember this conversation with terror and never speak of it with anyone except me in private. You will dream every night of what you have done until I tell you to stop. You will regret it every moment. And you will not work magic outside of my presence until I say." Gregyn tapped his hand three times on the parapet. Then he strode off the roof to leave Cullyn to regret his actions alone.

Mirklin Wood

*T*he guest quarters of the western elves were pleasant enough and food was brought at regular intervals. Still, watching Tamys sleep grew old quickly, so that Padraid had been glad when the healer had asked him to join her in her workspace.

Ba'ra'na'la offered Padraig a sip of the tea she had just made. Padraig took the wooden cup and sipped. A fungal tea, it tasted strongly of birch.

"Are you familiar with this?"

"No," he explained. "What does it do?"

"It stimulates the blood and encourages healing. Your friend has a bruise in his brain." The elven woman pointed to the back of her own head. "It's healing. There's no risk of causing more bleeding. But by increasing the blood flow, it will help the bruise to dissolve."

Padraig could accept the lore. It was similar to using hot and cold soaks to reduce a sprain. He wanted to test the tea on himself first to assure it wouldn't make Tamys sick, but he rather thought Ba'ra'na'la would not poison Tamys. Everyone who interacted with them seemed to consider Tamys somewhat important, but Ba'ra'na'la was the only western elf who seemed to present a wholly honest face.

"Your heart rate will increase a bit and you may feel warm and wide awake."

Padraig felt naught at this point, but he was willing to wait. The healer reminded him of a friend from Blue Iris Holt, Farana, who was tall and ridiculously thin. Her braid was so tight that it seemed to pull her face back from her nose. While that part was very distinctive, her hair was a non-descript color and her eyes were a silver-gray. Ba'ra'na'la would not be considered beautiful among the Kin, but her intelligence was clear, so she would be valued.

"May I ask … what is it about my friend that seems to interest the People?"

He didn't much like that term. The Kin had set it aside not long after embracing Jesu, but the western elves did not know the One in this way. They still thought of themselves as the center of the cosmos.

Ba'ra'na'la poured some of the elixir into another cup and cut it with water just as she had done for Padraig's. She sipped it.

"Do you know of the *troth aldor*."

Padraig felt his sinuses clear.

"I'm a half-elf and raised outside the circle of Kin. I think I've heard the term, but I don't remember its meaning."

"*Troth aldor?* This is a sacred story. Before the Rending, there was a belief that the *troth aldor* would come to set the world aright."

"*Troth* – guide. *Aldor* – voice."

"Yes. The guiding voice. He will herald the One's *Ama'lumin* and will speak on his behalf."

"*Ama* – peace. *Lumin* – beacon?

"Yes. You know of this?"

Harbinger of the one who will bring peace? Nay, the Kin believe that will be Jesu. Oh, my Savior, Navaransen would not believe that. He'd use old terminology. What if I've been looking for a king all this time and instead was meant to find his harbinger?

He'd been wrong before.

"How is my friend involved?"

"Are you ready to take the tea to him?"

I do feel remarkably awake and recharged, not
overstimulated. Why are you not answering me? Or do you think I
will find the answer when I am with him?

"Yes."

Tamys had been sleeping almost continuously since
they arrived. When Padraig stepped into the bed
chamber where Tamys lay wound with blankets,
Ba'ra'na'la's blue-light ball lit the walls. Earlier in the day,
the interior wall had been draped with a cloth painted
with depictions of just what they had been talking about.
The scenes had not interested Padraig until now.
Ba'ra'na'la placed a hand on one of the images – a man
with his eyes covered with a cloth, a staff in one hand
and a sword at his waist.

"*Troth aldor*," she identified. She then indicated
another figure on the wall. "*Ama'lumin*." While Padraig
did not recognize the *ama'lumin*, he stared at the figures
in the background – a sorrel horse, a black dog, a hawk, a
wolf, and several objects of art and jewelry.

The elves had no horses.

Tamys opened his eyes and turned his nose toward
Padraig.

"What's she saying?"

If he noticed Padraig's moment of disturbed
distraction, he didn't ask. Padraig shook himself.

"We've brought a healing tea. How are you feeling?"

Tamys needed to use the bucket before drinking the
tea. He ate some fruit and a round of a bread-like loaf.

"That's curious," he remarked.

"Somewhat?"

"My mind feels clear for the first time since the fall. No headache and that vague sense that the ground is moving slightly has stopped."

"Is your eyesight any clearer?"

Tamys wriggled his fingers in front of his eyes.

"Nay. I think it's about the same, but I feel that I could sit a horse all day and not be exhausted at night."

Padraig related the description to Ba'ra'na'la, who nodded sagely. She held a light up to Tamys' eyes and tapped his joints with a practiced finger.

"It's helping, but the elixir's benefits will be temporary for now. It will get better with time. Will you return to my workshop with me, Padraig?"

Padraig would much rather have stayed to contemplate the painting, but he didn't want to seem too interested, so he went with Ba'ra'na'la, telling Tamys that he would return shortly.

"Good, mayhap you can take me for a walk. I have boundless energy."

"He may well sleep before you return," Ba'ra'na'la predicted. "He is not as well as he supposes just yet."

In her workshop, she handed Padraig a bag.

"When you go, he will need this."

"When we go?"

"The *troth aldor* should not be among us. Soon enough, you will know this and you will go. I would not have Tamys untreated in that event." She smiled.

"Why are you doing this?"

"A dream that I had so long ago that I had forgotten it. I painted the tapestry when I was but an adolescent. It was from a true vision. Tell no one that you have that. I do not fear for myself, but that Mylan will know that you intend to flee if she becomes aware."

Padraig nodded and slipped the bag into his siarc.

"I will not betray you. Thank you. May I ask … we call ones like yourself 'wisdoms' in the east. I haven't heard mention here."

"And you won't. Wisdoms disappeared in the Threshing. Those of us born with these abilities learn not to mention them. There is a belief here that ones like us caused the Threshing."

"How is that?"

"The old ones pled for those before me to do something to stop it, but they could not, so there are no more of us … openly."

Padraig stared at her.

"How many?"

"Hundreds. They know about me because of the painting, but my parents were important, so I was not driven out and I have pretended all these years that it was a fluke. Your friend … he must be free to find the *Ama'lumin* and you will help him do this. He must come to know the One as you know Him."

"You know that I worship the One in a different way?"

"I have seen it and I know that this One is the True One who resides in the heart and not in the mountains. But you must go when the opportunity presents itself."

Tamys dozed off by the time Padraig returned to the chamber. After eating a bit of the tray of food that had been left, Padraig sat down on the floor with his back to

Tamys' bed to stare at the painting and contemplate how it impacted his immediate future decisions.

Clarcom

*B*ryan smiled at his father's joke, despite not understanding it. Jokes in general made no sense at the moment. He supposed Danyl meant no more to Cunyr than any beggar child in the streets of Clarcom, so what did it matter if he joked?

Danyl matters to me.

"You must break out of this glum mood," Cunyr warned, taking another long swallow of mead. "The common cannot see the nobility beset by the same common concerns that they wallow in."

"My brother lies near death, father. What mood should I adopt?"

"He continues to breathe. You should laugh, for he has cheated Nudd."

I think not. The Lord has buoyed him, mayhap. Nudd is but a myth to frighten children.

"I'll try, father," Bryan said instead of the truth. He'd been to visit Danyl this morning. The healer Sarala explained that the twisting of Danyl's right arm and leg were to be expected. Seeing it had left a chunk of ice in Bryan's belly. "Ah, Duncyn, joining us?"

The Dengyal lord, brother to the current squire, approached, but he did not look celebratory.

Careful, man, my father will proclaim you inappropriately funerary.

"A messenger has just ridden in from the Crossing," Duncyn explained. He held a message tube out to Bryan. His normally cheerful face was drawn.

Bryan broke the seal and twisted the tube open. The message inside was a single page, written out by a scribe for Lord Darryl.

> *It is with deep regret that I must inform you that my daughter, Gwendolyn, passed quickly from a sudden fever this morning.*

It was dated yesterday. Bryan's hand began to shake. He'd never met his betrothed and yet she had been a part of his future for most of his life. He could not cry for a stranger, but his future stretched forth like a black tunnel of unknown darkness.

He dumped the tube and message in the chair between Cunyr and himself.

"I have a funeral to attend," he told Duncyn. "Tell the messenger we leave in a watch, soon as I've packed."

Cunyr fumbled with the parchment and then frowned after his heir. He smirked and swallowed another long draught of mead, but nobody saw it.

When Bryan returned to the Great Hall, Lydya was there speaking sharply with Cunyr.

"I'm so sorry, my son," Lydya said, enveloping him in a much-needed hug.

"Widowed before he even had a chance to bed her," Cunyr noted. "Well and good, for truly I have a better match in Mulyn for you. Unfortunately, the Lady Branwyn has been married to Galornyn, but Malyna, Corbryn's ward, ought to still be available. You go to the funeral, play the dutifully bereft betrothed and then, we'll plan a spring wedding."

Bryan straightened from hugging Lydya. There were words that came to mind that he could direct at Cunyr, but he didn't. Instead he looked into his mother's exhausted face.

"I'll be back as soon as the funeral is over. Danyl will be in my prayers the whole time."

"Of course. There's no time to arrange an honor escort for you. Duncyn's agreed to accompany you."

"I thank him for that. Surely you did not have to arrange it."

"I didn't. He offered. It will pry Kefyn away as well. They'll need to return to accompany the Galornyn band, but that will give Cullyn a few more days to settle his grief."

Cullyn does seem to be sulking about somewhat since Danyl's injury. Mayhap only that his tourney was ruined.

"Aye," was what he said instead. "I won't be long. Since I didn't know her, no one will think it strange that I return from whence I came as soon as the grave's been closed. As for Malyna of Mulyn, I will remind that I am of age and have a say in this union. You can send messengers of inquiry, but there is to be no bargain struck until I have had opportunity to review it."

Cunyr looked choked while Lydya hid her smile behind practiced facial expressions.

"Now I must be off," Bryan said as Duncyn paused in the doorway in travel clothes. He shouldered his saddlebags and took his leave.

They were halfway through Clarcom's streets when it occurred to him that the death of his bride after his majority meant he was no longer a complete slave in betrothal. He had a say and that felt a good deal like freedom he had never known.

Ice Holt

*T*he fields overgrown with chicken weed clenched Cai's stomach with anxiety as he and Eamon rode their horses through the holt's gates.

Finding the iron gates standing open hadn't really worried either of them. Blue Iris had never closed its gates until Ama'na. Why should a holt so far north, that had never known an incursion, close its gates on a fine summer's day?

Because somewhat black rose on the horizon.

The chicken coops smelled of death and the cistern they passed was covered in green slime. Eamon dismounted and drew his sword as the wind sighed round a granary.

"I think we're too late," he whispered. His catslit pupils were so wide as to almost seem round. Cai dismounted, drawing his own sword.

"The doors of the residences are closed," he remarked, hopefully. Their footsteps echoed as they approached the first door.

They tried several of the iron doors before one gave at their tugging. Opening it assaulted them with the odor of putrification so bad they both turned aside to vomit. When Cai managed to light a torch with shaking hands, the light revealed what they had suspected – piles of bodies swollen with rot and eaten by flies. They tied handkerchiefs coated in mud and packed with chicken weed over their faces to block the smell so they could investigate.

As they pushed into the residences, Eamon noted this had been the Hall of the Wise.

"The assault must have happened in the night," Cai remarked. Many were still in their beds.

At the back of the hall, they found the stairs to the baths, which were deserted. There were no bodies here. They tried the stairs to each of the other residences, but they found no one alive. In the single males hall they found themselves staring at an open tunnel that seemed to lead straight to the Celdryan hells.

Eamon bent to pick up a heavy haft.

"Dwarves?" he asked. Cai held it under the torch light.

"No, trolls. They must have tunneled in."

Cai leaned into the tunnel, tossing his torch as far as his arm would allow. It landed on a bend of the tunnel, allowing him to see that it continued on for a very long way.

"We should go," Eamon said, plucking at his shirt. "Diseases come with this many dead bodies and … you don't know what might come out this way."

"This was a moon ago, at least," Cai reported. "But you're right. We need to burn these bodies and head down the trail to warn the other holts."

Burning the bodies took much of the day. They chose not to move them, to fire them in place within the residences once they'd opened the doors to the outside. Eamon noted that there were far fewer men in the singles residence than normally would be seen.

"Do you think they got away?"

"No," Cai said with a shudder. "I think they were taken as slaves. We need to be gone, now."

They decided to head south and continue through the night. There would be enough light for them to see and neither wanted to remain so close to so much death.

Cai wondered, as they rode, would they find the other holts in such a condition.

"We cannot know until we get there," Eamon told him. "But if the trolls can burrow into Ice Holt, what is to say they can't attack any of us, at anytime."

Cai flung himself off his horse to vomit again. Things were much worse than they had supposed.

Mirklin Wood

*T*amys sailed over the forest on strong wings. Movement far below gained his attention and he circled lower and lower until he lit upon a tree branch beside a clearing before the mouth of a cave. Many elves gathered here while an elven female with silken black hair stood upon a massive stump of a tree and spoke to the gathered.

"We must do the will of the One who knows that that daemons mean only harm to us. This male who claims to be both elf and daemon would take the *Troth Aldor* from us. We must seek to send him on his way so that our harbinger may then be set before the One as is required in the ancient tales."

"Yes, the *Troth Aldor*. Lift up the *Troth Aldor*. Present him to the One."

"We must assure that this great spirit the daemons want will not come to use to tie us in ropes and keep us from living. We must prevent the *Troth Aldor* from going forward."

"Yes, the *Troth Aldor*. Lift up the *Troth Aldor*. Present him to the One."

The chanting grew louder and more rapid with every statement the black hair woman said. Tamys thought it must be a dream since he did not speak elvish, but this did not feel like a dream. The wind ruffled his feathers and he could feel the rough bark beneath his talons.

"*Troth aldor. Troth aldor. Troth aldor.*"

"The blood of this sightless one will be *Pada'wa'la'anero'ama.*"

"Pada'wa'la'anero'ama. Pada'wa'la'anero'ama. Pada'wa'la'anero'ama."

The elves now danced frenetically, in beat to some drums. The sky purpled with clouds and thunder rumbled. He saw no lightning, but as the black face of the heavens glowered down upon them, he felt the sizzle in the air.

Crack! Lightning struck above the entrance to the cave, but the dancing and chanting did not stop. The black haired elf stood with arms stretched wide, seeming to suck in the energy and grow strong and stronger.

Tamys gathered himself to launch into the air … and woke up panting in his bed in the elven village.

Pivotal Moments

Samyel spoke the One's words to the people of Ysrael who demanded a king. "Kings do certain things that enforce their rule over you. He will conscript your sons into his army so that they may run before him into battle. He will appoint leaders over you who will do his bidding ... plowing his land and reaping his harvest to fund his wars. He will take your daughters to make perfume, and to cook and bake on his behalf. He will take your best fields and vineyards and give them to his own servants. He will demand a tenth of your seed and of the produce of your vineyards so that he ay give it to his administrators and servants. He will take your servants and the best of your cattle and horses and assign them to his own use. He will demand a tenth of your flocks and you yourselves will be his servants. In that day, you will cry out because your king whom you have chosen for yourselves, but the Lord won't answer you in that day.

But the people refused to heed Samyel's warning. Instead, they said "No! There will be a king over us. We will be like all the other nations. Our king will judge us and lead us and fight our battles."

**From the Scriptos of the One,
Writings of Samyel
Recorded by Blethry, Priest of Bel,
Moryn FY 942**

Past

Founding Year 931
High Celdrya

*D*eryk jerked his head up from his knees, trying to dismiss the memory of the girl's brains splattering across his face.

Don't doze off! he told himself.

Sleeping upright with his back against the wall made it easier to wake, but it didn't stop the memories. He put his feet on the cold stone floor and lurched up to follow the wall to the window. His legs still had no strength and his hands shook uncontrollably. He sank down on the windowsill to stare out the glass to the ward. He saw Perryn's face in the glass, obscuring the activity below.

Behind him, he heard the door open and Lady Wymffa entered. He turned to give her his attention.

"How are you keeping?" she asked, placing her basket on the table and sitting down on the stool. If what was in the basket was meant to tempt his appetite, it failed.

"Sleeping or awake, I see them," he said. "I know you think I'm innocent, but it does not matter. I feel my guilt, just as a sword bears the dings of turning on mail."

"Do you trust me, Deryk?"

Deryk stared at her. She had always been one of his favorite court denizens, practical and well informed. She laughed easily, but not lightly. She had a way of lifting him up from the blackness and getting him through the day. He nodded.

"I can face my death knowing the One God does not hate me, though I do not understand why He forgives."

"I believe that if you are executed, the investigation into Perryn's death will not continue and it is vitally important that it does. I know you feel it's your due, but I must ask you to let us help you so that we can find the real killer. Then, if you still want to die, we'll find a way for that to happen."

For a span of a breath, Deryk felt a sword in his hand and heard the clash of battle.

"I trust you," he said.

"Good then. First, you must eat to get your strength back."

Deryk watched as she brought out some bread and cheese. His hand shook as he took it from her and it took a swallow of water to get the first bite down.

"What's second?" he asked.

"Be ready when the time comes and don't argue, just go with Blethry."

"Blethry? I k-killed his sister. Why would he save me?"

"Because he's already saved you once and he knows you are naught but a dagger wielded by a foe. Please, lad, trust me because your choice to live might change the world."

Deryk took a second bite and chewed stolidly.

I will still die for my crimes, just not before the whole truth is known ... I hope.

It was better to die for a righteous cause than to die because you'd been used like a playing piece in a game of hounds and hares. Truth seemed righteous enough.

Present

Founding Year 1028
Mirklin Wood

*P*adraig thought to hide his worry from Tamys so the lad might rest and heal. His headaches subsided and he began to explore the chamber with his stick and more courage than Padraig had expected. Days passed before Travorlyndotrynmylan invited Padraig to come out of the chamber. As near as Padraig had been able to tease out, the western elves were ruled by a council somewhat like the Wise in the eastern mountains. Each of them seemed to have a different task assigned to him or her. Mylan's hair was black as midnight and her catslit eyes were silver.

The guard assigned to Padraig led him out of the caves and up a bridge that led to the top of the hill. There, Mylan waited in a hut with large windows and an unused wood heater. The side of the bridge were planted with trees, the hill was topped with them. Padraig didn't wonder why he'd had no hint they were so close to an elven community.

"Please to have seat," Mylan said, indicating a cushioned bench. Padraig sat down. She was beautiful with high cheek bones, and looked to be his own age. He wagered coin she was much much older. He didn't trust her in the least.

"Have you comfort in the resting house?"

"I do and my friend is healing."

"This is what we give. Your friend is newly sightless?"

"Aye. In a fall, two moons past."

"This sound is the word of monsters. You speak our language oddly, but you look monstrous."

"I explained this to the council before. My father is a Celdryan and my mother is an elf."

"We have such born when the monsters take our females."

"My father was not a pleasant man, but I don't think he raped her."

Mylan poured a liquid into a wood cup and offered it to Padraig. It would be impolite to refuse, but he struggled to trust her.

"The friend of yours … he is both monster real-people also."

"Is he Kin? How do you know?"

"We read his aura. Was his mother not raped too?"

"I don't know." Mylan brought her cup to her lips, but she didn't drink. She was waiting for him. Having no choice, he took a sip. The liquor burned down his throat and made him cough. Mylan smiled and sipped without drama. "W-what did your healer find in her examination?" Ba'ra'na'la had cautioned against seeming too familiar with her.

"It is a brain bruise." Mylan indicated the back of her head.

"Will his sight return?"

"Treatment is vexed. He heals … or not."

Padraig had expected that prognosis. *There is no healing but through the Lord*. He also thought Ba'ra'na'la mayhap had not been telling her superiors the full truth.

"May I ask … how long have you been here? In the east, we thought we were the only true-people left."

Padraig did not like that term "true people". The Kin had stopped using it after the Scourging. He used it to placate his host.

"Traelagaleana fell when I was a child. Without trade roads, cities collapse. We move to villages. Then monster come again. Many die. We came here. Monsters fear forest. We help them fear it. And now you come. Why?"

"My people know about the highways. When my friend was injured, the delay made it so I couldn't travel to Morglen – the southern land beyond the mountains – by winter if I took the usual route."

"The highway wants repair. You may traverse it, but your friend will remain here."

"If he wants."

"There is not choice. It is so."

"Why?"

"It's been decided."

"Will you explain your decision?"

"No! You leave at first light, day following next day."

"Why?"

"Because the One God speaks to us from sundown to sundown and we are not able to lead you until it is done."

"The One God? You worship the One God. Tell me what you know of Him."

"It is known. The One God threshed us like gain, tossed us to the wind. Some of us came down and others flew very far. We remember the days."

"So it's like a feast day?"

"Yes, much like."

"On feast days where I am from, we don't care for our animals except what is absolutely necessary. May I tend my horses now so that they will be well-cared for through the day?"

Mylan stared at him with her catslit eyes.

"You may. You and your friend will remain in cave all during feast."

Mylan gestured to a guard who escorted him to what passed for a stable here among people who knew naught of horses. There was a trough of grass and a bucket of water in a small open cave that contained three large ewers of what Padraig's nose told him was wine. Joy shook her mane in greeting.

~They plan to drink this vile vinegar for a ceremony to their false god.

Yes, that's exactly the thing.

The saddles, panniers and saddle bags were exactly where Padraig had left them when he unloaded the animals.

What can I use here to my advantage?

The elven guard had no idea what Padraig might need to care for the horses, so didn't question his activities and even wandered over to speak with a fellow guard. As Padraig examined the contents of the panniers, his hand came to rest on a sack of powdered valerian. The yellow-brown dust would mix well in the wine, if he could find a way to get it into the ewers before the ceremony.

Just then, two of the elves started arguing over a female and every elf in the vicinity ran to watch the fight. Seeing the hand of the One in the distraction, Padraig poured equal measures into each ewer, finished caring for the three horses and was wandering back toward the resident cave when his guard remembered his duties.

~Now if we can figure out how to escape and not be followed.

~If three horses go in three different directions, would their trackers be able to follow us? Joy suggested.

~Tamys cannot ride unaccompanied and he's the one they want.

Padraig waited through an unexpected silence from his Companion.

~He could ride me … just this once. I can send Earnest on a circuitous path and you can ride that dull lump to a safe rendezvous. The bird is scouting.

~The bird? Padraig asked. *The hawk? You can talk to it?*

~Not quite talk, but communicate, yes. It knows things, Padraig.

Padraig paused at the door of the quarters he shared with Tamys. The lad lifted his sightless gaze to the door when Padraig entered.

"I was starting to think they'd done somewhat with you," he admitted.

"My apologies. I was speaking with our hosts. How would you feel about remaining here?"

Tamys fumbled for and caught Padraig's sleeve and drew him onto the bed. He barely spoke above a whisper.

"The bird keeps intruding on my thoughts, somewhat to do with Joy and forest pathways and these pillars at the start of a bridge."

"I don't know about the pillars, but the rest of it …. They want you to stay here while sending me on my way."

"Nay, I would not choose that, but we're being watched, so how …?"

"I've a plan. Well, Joy, the hawk and I have a plan. You might need to be braver than you want."

"Better that than an exhibit in a grotesquery."

"Is that how you feel here?"

"They want somewhat from me. They keep saying a word. I can't say it, but Joy knows it."

~Pada'wa'la'anero'ama

Padraig took several heartbeats to remember how to breathe.

"What does it mean?" Tamys asked.

"They don't speak exactly the language the Kin speak. *Pada* is the word for Nameless. *Ama* means peace.

It translates sort of as 'the chosen whom will bring peace with the Nameless.'"

"I don't understand."

"Nor do I. The Nameless god of the elves had lots of mythology surrounding, but the Kin don't refer to it much, so I don't know if this might not be a mythological convergence."

"You mean how the Rawmaynes saw our god Aeron has their god Ares because they did the same things and had similar names?"

"Aye, just so. Mayhap there is mythology …."

~*Why are you discussing this?* Joy demanded. *He needs to know our plan.*

~*You're right, of course.*

~*I can hear this, you know?.* Tamys entering the conversation surprised Padraig.

"You can? I mean, you can."

"Can they?" Padraig had not considered that.

~*Hush, Joy. Be a horse until I tell you otherwise.*

"This is the plan," he whispered aloud to Tamys. "Listen carefully. You will need to trust Joy and the hawk."

Clarcom

*L*ydia looked as though she had not slept in days. Ryanna watched from the servitors' table as Taryn and Shyla talked together and Cunyr played the ass. Ryanna had tried to set aside her feelings about Ama'na, but his first act as vyngretrix had apparently been from the heart.

"When are we going to let the child go?" he demanded of Lydya where everyone might hear. "He's dead already. Just forgot to stop breathing. Traegyr can take care of that."

Lydya stared at her husband with an expression Ryanna had often felt.

She'd run him through with a sword if she could. *Taryn looks like he's trying to talk himself out of drawing steel in his host's court.*

Shyla fled the table in tears, leaving Taryn without an object for his affection.

"It would be a kindness," Cunyr's mistress remarked. To keep herself from hurling a dagger at the young woman, Ryanna wondered again about the bruises on the lass's throat.

Abuse didn't excuse her comment, though Ryanna understood the source better.

The look Lydya gave the lass sent a shovel of snow down Ryanna's back. You could steal a man from a woman's bed, but don't threaten her children.

"Mayhap we can discuss this in the morning," Taryn suggested. "When we're more rested and less drunk."

"I am not drunk," Cunyr protested sloppily. "I am merely stating a fact."

Lydya stood with perfect poise and dignity.

"I am tired. I think I will withdraw for the evening. Ryan, would you escort me please? I know you are leaving soon and I hope to speak with you before you depart, cousin."

Ryanna rose to follow her up to her bed chamber, which was a large slice of the family hall. Ryanna closed the door softly behind her, casting a hiding spell before Lydya could tire herself.

"Thanks to you," Lydya remarked, kicking off her slippers and sitting down on an upholstered divan. "Will you leave Sarala with us?"

Ryanna swallowed before nodding. She did not wish to leave Sarala with this burden, but the One True God had awakened her last night to remind her of her calling. Sabre was complaining of eating voles on the prairie round the city. Sooner or later, she would have to move beyond this comfortable city with familiar faces to travel with two unknowns who were hiding secrets of their own. Well, one unknown. Taryn had been open enough about what little he knew. Gregyn, however ….. He could be forgiven for playing God. He was not a Believer, after all. He couldn't be held to the same scruples. Though why he had saved Danyl in the first place had her scratching her head. As far as she knew, he'd never met the child. Saving him might have been instinctive, but she did not find Gregyn as innocent and forthcoming as Taryn. The rider knew how to hold his secrets close to his chest.

And then there was the matter of Cullyn. His aura had not concerned her in the least until Bryan had mentioned a change in it.

"My brother has always had an aura shot with darkness … well, since I've been able to read it anyway. It's sort of large, extended from his body by grandiosity. Now it is constricted tight round him, like he's ill."

Or guilty.

Gregyn and Taryn had both been at Danyl's side almost as soon as she had been. They were not the presence Shyla had felt upon the roof. She hadn't seen Cullyn until much later. Ryanna watched him laughing with his father at the honor table and she wondered if she might perhaps need to find out more about this lad before she traveled with him.

Or not. I'm a gifted psychic and a skilled warrior. If he were to come against me … do I think Taryn and Gregyn are on my side or his?

"If she is willing, I have no objections."

"I spoke with her this afternoon. She says his condition is stable. She knows some technique for relieving pressure from the brain swelling. It has to be done several times a day, but he's not getting worse."

"She needs to stay here, but if she wishes to travel on with me, I won't stop her. I will speak with her tonight, to make clear her intentions." She hooked her thumbs in her belt, quite liking that sensation now that she was getting used to it. "You may need to put guards on his chamber." Lydya looked started. "Your husband and Traegyr wish Danyl harm. It's not personal, but they see him like damaged livestock."

"I'm aware. Surely Sarala's presence will keep them at bay."

"Since you have begun to call her Sarala, I assume the whole dun knows she's a woman. While she does have some skills as do all Kin females, she cannot grapple hand to hand with a male assassin. I suggest guards for her sake as well as Danyl's."

"I'll see to it. May I ask … how do you feel about traveling with Taryn's group now that you've come to know them?"

"It's not a concern. Taryn has shown his character in his care for Danyl."

"Aye. I suppose it's looking at things from a Celdryan perspective. You are a woman."

"I am not without skills and I don't think Taryn would permit his men to harm me. Lydya, you do know there are fell magicks about this dun? Someone tried to kill your son, but someone else used the Source to keep him from dying."

"Shyla and Kefyn have told me their suspicions. Bryan claims to have felt it too." She breathed out heavily and closed her eyes a moment. "I don't know what to do about it. Bryan was scanning auras before he left. You?"

Do I tell you that I suspect Cullyn? Nay, that would be cruel at this juncture.

"I have. There are a fair number in your court who can shield. That is instinctive for some, so I can't say that it is suspicious. The ones I can read are not evil, but that does not settle my fears on this matter."

"It could have been a guest, now long gone."

"Aye, it might have been. I would stay if I thought I could do more, but I am being called."

"I understand. God go with you and may you always remember Who you serve."

They embraced. Ryanna left Lydya to contemplate her life on her own. Sarala left Shyla with her brother to come out and talk with Ryanna.

"I've decided to stay. I'm fairly certainly I was meant to come this far just for this."

"The One knows all."

"He does. I wish He'd show me how to heal the lad, though I am learning a great deal about brain injuries. When you reach your destination, scry to Lydya to let me know what's going on. I will like as not travel with you back to the holt. I can't imagine that I will be held here longer than the winter."

"I'll do that. And if I do not turn back this way?"

"Kefyn will escort me back. He's to winter here in the south. I will have a stop to make regardless."

"Stop?"

"Marya – the lass we met …."

"I know. She told you?"

"Aye. I wasn't prepared to discuss it with you and then we met Kefyn and there was no privacy. You know who my father is, don't you?"

"I suspect."

"You said he was dead, but he isn't."

"He mayhap be and he will be if I ever see him again. I thought myself paranoid when I would wonder, but Marya confirmed it for me."

"He's your husband …."

"No, he's not," Ryanna said, brushing her fingers through her short hair. "I begin to wonder if I was not seduced rather than wooed. In either case, I must be about the One's business and so must you. Be careful. The Celt can be tricky."

"I've discovered. Thank you for introducing me to this world and showing me my name."

"Aye? What would that be?"

"Amanasarala."

"It suits you. I'm off to tell Taryn that I'll be ready to leave on the morrow."

Taryn had left the great hall. Ryanna dipped half a tankard of dark and sat down on an empty bench to enjoy it. Gregyn settled onto the bench beside her.

"Can we talk?" he asked and she felt the hiding spell.

"What will we be discussing that you don't want anyone else to hear?"

"That. I know you are aware of Dunmaden. You know about Taryn. I suspected you know about me. It would make the journey uncomfortable for us not to be honest with one another. Both Taryn and I know you're a female. I understand why you're hiding behind a glamour, although I do hope you let your weave go for Saryl before you leave as she is an incredibly lovely lass who should know the fun of suitors. Cullyn is an issue, of course. He doesn't know. Can't see through the glamour or read auras."

"He's the only one in his family that's reached puberty who can't."

"Except his father, of course. You're right. He has a smallish gift from his mam, but he'd want a great deal of training to breach your shields."

"And you?"

"You've felt as much round mine as I've felt round yours. Let's not pretend otherwise. I mean you no harm, lass, and I trust that you will not come against me so long as I do not come against you. I wish I had time to learn what you know and I pray you will teach Taryn."

"Such as?"

"Shielding. His family sought to protect him from his mother, who dabbles in the black arts. Meeting Shyla unlocked their hiding. I can't mend it, but I would not want to have his mother know. I suspect you can teach him."

"Why can't you?"

"Because I'm a common born rider and if the other men caught me out, I'd be a common dead rider." That was partial truth, she thought.

"Does Taryn know about you?"

"He suspects. He's a talented one for no training. When he gets to Galornyn, his grandmam and brother can teach him all he needs to know, but I would not want to have him riding up to the dun with his mam watching. It would ruin all they strove for."

"I can try, but Kin are not Celt, so …. We'll see. I don't suppose you'll tell me how you came to be trained."

His grey eyes sparkled for a moment and then he shook his head.

"I can't and I shan't."

He moved to stand up.

"Were you the one who saved Danyl?"

He froze, telling her all that she needed to know.

"I didn't mean to do it," he explained. "Compassion run amok. I've thought about whether I could heal him the same way, and … I think naught." He swallowed. She realized that he was younger than she thought. It was the quiet surety he had that made him seem older. "I'm not sure I entirely regret it. Mayhap he'll recover. The children do with the infant palsy. Mayhap they do with this."

"Mayhap," she said. And then the buzzing dissipated and Gregyn was gone. *Are you on my side or just seeking to put me off suspicion? And exactly what is the extent of your power?*

Galornyn

*T*eddryn's breath paused and Berdda's ceased. Maddw looked up from the book he was reading, *Teddryn breathed.* Berdda did as well. Maddw returned to staring at the same page he'd been reading for a watch, fooling Berdda not at all. Time passed at its snail's pace and then Teddryn's breath stopped again and this time it did not resume. His eye flickered behind the lids.

Maddw reached him first. Placing a hand on his forehead, he drew power up from the stone beneath his feet and poured it into his brother. Teddryn's chest rose and fell, rose and fell.

"He's no longer breathing automatically," Berdda acknowledged. She felt heavy with exhaustion and feeling every year of her age. Maddw's efforts were greatly appreciated, though they seemed as small as her own. She wiped a tear from her cheek.

"Others have survived this."

He's weakening. I am missing somewhat in treating this. I have delayed the plague and prolonged his succumbing. His agony as well.

"Truth-to-tell, I need Taryn to effect a cure. Unbarred from his gifts, I believe I could use him as a conduit for healing. I should not have allowed Egoran to send him away."

"Grandmam, Eg judged rightly that Taryn needs to be away, leading men, so that he might at last mature into a man."

Maddw is so pure of heart. He does not realize that Egoran believed Teddryn might not recover. He moved to forestall giving back the Clarcom dowry should that occur.

Maddw washed his face in a basin of water.

"It mightn't be a bad idea," he mumbled into a towel. "What do you suppose Rogyn will do about Branwyn?"

Mayhap not as pure as I thought. Did the idea already occur to you, lad?

"Taryn should be returning soon. Somewhat has him distracted. Mayhap his gifts have him in confusion, but it's possible love has him dizzy. Still, he doesn't seem as close as I wish him to be. I fear Teddryn will die before he gets here."

"That's in the hands of the gods, is it not? You're doing all you can. Take not responsibility where it is not yours."

Tears spilled down Berdda's face at her grandson's use of warrior wisdom.

"Mayhap it is just my grief over Egoran, but I am so weary and hopeless."

"Mayhap you are just that, exhausted. You should rest while I stay with him. I'll send a servant if I need you."

Sleep. Aye. It has been days since I've had a full night and I grieve for Egoran as much as I fear for Teddryn

"Aye, I will do that. I love you dearly, Maddw. I know my concern for Taryn has a times overshadowed that you are my favorite, but it is true. You have such a strength of character."

Maddw peered into dark places for a moment.

"You ever wonder if the strength of our gifts can change the world round us?"

This is much too philosophical on no sleep.

"I believe there are those who can use forces to deliberately bend the world to their will. I don't believe you have done that. What you're feeling is just the guilty grief of those left behind, especially when one dies so young. What if we had done this or not done that … it's not for us to know. Now I'm off for that nap."

Berdda kissed him on his cheek and slipped out of the room. She could only pray to Bel for his support of Teddryn while she slept.

Escape

The Companion link is ordinarily found only among those with high amounts of elven blood. There are relationships that seem similar among the magery, but these are not actually the same. Either the man twists the animal to his will or the animal twists the man to its. This is entirely unlike the Companion relationship which is mutual and loving.

Saroynan, scribe of the collegiate.
FY 111

Past

Founding Year 931
High Celdrya

*D*umyr rolled to the side and pulled Wmyffa into the hollow of his shoulder. She sighed contentedly as she settled the blankets more smoothly over them. Sometimes they would just doze off now and wake in the morning tangled together, but tonight, his period of sleepiness lasted only a short while and she sensed when he became more fully awake.

"What are you thinking?" she asked.

"You know me so well, love," he said, pulling his head back a little to see her more clearly. "I'm wondering what you're thinking."

"That's some sort of circular reasoning," she teased affectionately. "Do we need to pleasure each other again?"

He sighed. There'd been a time … but he was older now … and there were more pressing matters to discuss.

"You aren't going to do anything drastic to save Deryk's life, are you?"

"I'm tempted," she admitted. "I doubt much that I could spirit him away with no one the wiser. I'm not 20 anymore."

"My parents were so stubborn! I thought for certain my father was going to skin me alive when we came back from the hand-fasting. That was the finest day of my life, truth to tell. But seriously – we need to discuss what we're going to do. Gerriant won't wait forever to decide his fate and while he favors the ensorcelment theory, he is not king to make arbitrary decisions. The council will demand Deryk's life unless we can produce the sorcerer and maybe even then."

"So we must get him away. It's a simple matter to take him through the bolt hole, but not so easy to get him out of the donjon and where do we take him that he will not be pursued?"

"And how do we not destroy our own lives in the process?" Dumyr reminded her.

"There is that. If it were just you and me … but our children's lives would be in the bargain too." She sighed. "I think Blethry may yet do it. He's young and protected by his family's connections and the Bel temple. He could take Deryk to his mam's people. They're so far deep in their mountain fastness that it's unlikely he'd be found. A simple life is likely all he can handle now."

"He does seem very fragile. I keep wondering when his father will send an emissary. We sent messages to Dun Trevellyn the day after the murder."

"The two branches of the family are close. I find it odd as well."

She paused, a contemplative expression upon her face.

"What is it?"

"The Trevellyns. Why did the council not choose a regent from the Dublyn branch?" Dumyr chuckled. "What are you humored by?"

"If you had been born a man, you'd have my position. I've been asking the same question and I'm not satisfied with the answers. They're of Bel and that mayhap have some influence. The vyngretroi are not at all comfortable with Bel-guided leadership. They prefer the Lughan."

"Gerriant is Bel also."

"He's … balanced. They can accept that. And I'm uncertain that is the reason. It may be a reason among many which I am having difficulty grasping."

"That's because women control the breeding lines. Mayhap this is not just about Maryn and Perryn, but an attempt to bring down the entire dynasty."

"Explain."

"Ordinarily, if the mainline were wiped out, wouldn't they go to the Dublyn branch?"

"Aye. I think I kin your meaning. It's not easy to do that when a member of the Dublyn branch killed the king."

"He was there for all three deaths. It's a simple matter to blame Dun Trevellyn, thereby relegating them to an inferior status."

"For what purpose?"

"A regime change. Isn't that how the caesars did it?"

Dumyr tried to remember the Rawmayn books he'd read as a younger man, but they'd all sort of washed together over the years.

"I suppose. Regime change to whom?"

He could see she hadn't thought it through, but she had a deliciously devious mind when she let her imagination engage.

"The lasses are in Mulyn and it appears the signs point there. Burcan fired that village. Cadda is next in line. The iron monger was from Mulyn."

"It does make sense and yet …."

"What can we do to stop it?"

They stared at the ceiling for a bit.

"There is one possibility," Dumyr finally said. "It appears Maryn got Lady Gilyan of Llyr with child."

"Did he? Aye, quite fertile young people. How do we know this?"

"She wrote a letter to Vanyn asking for land and small stipend. It arrived the day he died. Perryn mean to adopt the child. He wrote to her, but she never replied. My eyes and ears tell me that her father disowned her, which suggests political pressure."

"From whom?"

"Now there's the question. They aren't allied with Mulyn. They're allied with Fyrgal. I can't imagine if Fyrgal were manipulating this that Gerriant would be so honorable in how he is investigating it."

"Do we know where the lass is?"

"I can guess. How do we prove the child would be the heir? And is that even true?"

"Aye. Perryn died without issue and Maryn had already produced a child, so a druin can vouch that the child is his. Assuming Donyl isn't found, of course. Have you noticed we're talking as if he's gone?"

"He can't be king, Wmyffa. He's lame and untried in battle. A 16-year-old regent with no offspring would need the protection of someone stronger and older – Gerriant most like. But if an heir were found, the scales are subtly shifted."

"If Donyl adopted the child, it would clear up all sorts of issues of succession. Certainly more power shifted to Mulyn is not a good thing."

"Llyr has enough power as well."

"If her father disowned her, there will likely be a period of rift. What's her brother's stance on it all?"

"I suspect he's the one that let my eyes and ears know of the disownment."

Wmyffa yawned suddenly.

"We need to return to this topic in the morning, but it seems clear that we need to find the lass, protect Deryk and figure out the role of Mulyn in all this."

"And while you're at it – we should make sure the Avercelt runs northward in the spring."

"Don't tease me. You know I'm right."

"I do, but I also see it as a big task that we cannot do alone." He kissed her on top of her head. "We'll sleep on it and see what we think in the morn."

Present

Founding Year 1028
Blyan

*T*aryn's band reached Dun Blyan at the Crossing the morning of the funeral. They'd brought along five riders as an escort for Bryan. Duglas and Kefyn had been more than pleased to be upon the road and Bryan had sent them cheerfully on their way. The first camp after the Blyan Crossing was a pleasant stream valley still within Blyan. Duglas noted with pleasure that the honor band did the majority of the work.

"I'm not much used to that," Duglas said as they sat by a fire in front of the honor tent.

"The common do not serve the nobles in Denygal?" Taryn asked. Gregyn, face half-hidden in shadow as he sat at guard, smirked. Duglas had been watching him since Clarcom, uncertain of what to think of him.

"There's barely a distinction between common and noble in Denygal," Kefyn explained.

"Who rules then?"

"Elected councils for the most part. The Squire of Moryn is appointed by Lydya, but as a representative between the councils and the Celdryans."

"What an odd system! Where ever did it come from?" Taryn asked.

"The elves," Ryanna said when the two Dengyalmen paused in discomfort. "We elect our guides for a period of time – to do certain jobs with the guidance of the holts. That is the way we did it in the camps that formed after the Scourging. Some think it mayhap have been the order of society before the Scourging. Denygal came about when Celt and Kin intermingled."

Kefyn leaned back against a log, watching Taryn.

"And it works?" the young lord asked. Duglas nodded. Ryanna laughed. Duglas was surprised that the lad smiled back. "My tutors would not have thought that possible. They'd quote the Philosophies and say selection of rulers by the commons will only lead to common rule." Duglas bit his tongue, waiting for more direct criticism. "When Kefyn told me that Denygal was quite different, I didn't take him seriously until I saw you help to pitch camp. Do these elected leaders live common lives during their – uh – what do you call it?

"Time of service," Ryanna offered, turning game bird on spits. "And, aye, by most measures there is little difference between those who are elected as representatives and those who work as drovers, weavers, bakers, and so forth. They must still work to support themselves and contribute to the community."

"Contribute to the community? You didn't mention this," Taryn chided Kefyn.

When were they talking … and about what? That lad has no sense.

"I'm Denygal, not Kin," Kefyn reminded. "The only community contribution I know of is the two tithes. One-tenth of the churches and one-tenth to the store houses. The first 10th is a true tenth and the second tenth is on what's left."

"Wait. What does the, uh, squire live on?" Taryn demanded.

"The rents from the lands attached to Dun Moran," Duglas explained. "We don't collect taxes in Denygal. The Celt nobles tried to divvy the land up as they do here in the south, but we resisted. In the end, to keep up the nobility imposed upon us, Donyl of Shyr created an estate round Moran for the support of the dun, which the squire manages. There are rent holders who work it for him in exchange for a third-tenth."

"And that's enough?"

"If you aren't supporting an army or a great many retainers, it is," Kefyn said, feeding sticks into the fire.

"How do you protect the rigdon then?" Taryn wanted to know.

"Voluntary levies and individual landholders."

The fire crackled and popped in the thoughtful silence that followed.

"Sounds like a paradise," Taryn remarked. "What do you think, Cullyn, of a world where noble and common are the same?"

The young page scowled and threw a stick in the fire.

That one doesn't like Taryn much. I wonder what's about with that.

"It won't work. The wisdom of the ages says that rule by an educated elite is far better than the chaos of the rabble."

Gregyn shifted his weight to look at the young lord.

"What do you think, captain?" Duglas asked. The rider did not answer immediately.

"I think it's a world where men like me have to work honest jobs toiling in the dirt rather than serving at the pleasure of a lord."

"Doesn't much appeal?" Ryanna asked.

What was it about that statement that makes our youngest member smile while pretending not to?

"I've never been a farmer, but it looks like hard work."

"There are more trades than farming," Duglas pointed out. "I'm a messenger."

"And, Kefyn, what's your livelihood?" Cullyn asked.

"If my father gives me leave, scholar and pastor."

"Pastor ... what's that?" Taryn asked.

Duglas stared at his brother while Cullyn's eye brows shot up.

Fool boy! Do not speak of things Denygal outside of Denygal!

"It's like a priest of Bel," Ryanna offered in a matter-of-fact tone. She turned the game birds again. "What's ahead on the road?" she asked.

The corners of Taryn's eyes crinkled. He recognized a change of topic when he heard it. He glanced toward Gregyn, who gave his report.

"Farms mostly – a dun ever so often. I've never been on the section between the Crossing and the border with Dunmaden, but I don't think there's much to concern us."

"Brigands?" Kefyn asked.

"Doubtful. I can't speak for Blyan, but we cleaned out a nest of brigands from Dunmaden this spring. I think we'll not encounter much interesting besides druids on the roads."

"Druins? I thought they stayed to their temples," Duglas said. He'd never traveled west of the Crossing and had jumped at this opportunity to find Padraig for Lydya.

Curiosity killed the cat and it died by drowning, but I do so want to see the rest of the kingdom.

"Druids aren't the same," Taryn explained. "They're Old Faith. They mostly haven't got temples. They live here and there, usually among common folk. This time of year, they begin to gather in northern Dunmaden because there's a conclave in the Black Forest. I've never been, but my grandfather talks about it some times."

"Your mother's folk are from Dunmaden, aye?" Duglas asked, hoping to keep the conversation a long way from Denygal.

"My grandfather was lord of a dun there. I paged for a while at Dun Tomyr. My uncle's lord there now. It's been – hmm, five years since I was there."

"Were they always so stand-offish?" Gregyn asked.

"I heard about that," Taryn said. "Teddryn was most annoyed. Of course, a rural dun in spring is short on supplies. Coming with 30 men is a strain on resources."

"The village seemed prosperous enough." Gregyn said. Duglas wondered why the rider seemed so comfortable with the young lord. They were of an age, but friendship between nobles and commons were not common south of the Dragon Wall.

"I was only 10, Gregyn. I don't think I knew what was what about rural duns then, but I do remember the discussion about resources being one reason they sent me back to Galornyn that spring. Are the cocks ready? They smell ready."

Why did he just change the subject?

They were cooked to perfection. Cullyn and Ryanna went to the tuck wagon for vegetables and bread. The sky had grown completely dark, clothed in unproductive clouds, but with the cocks off the spit, Kefyn threw some wood upon the flames and soon their circle was well lit. Duglas noted that Gregyn set aside his trencher of food while they ate.

"Are you expecting somewhat?" he asked.

The rider quirked one corner of his mouth.

"That's what I am tasked with, isn't it? I don't expect trouble this moment, but I must always expect trouble."

Duglas wanted to argue. He knew for certain that Ryanna and Kefyn would have Sensed trouble if it were headed their way, but he held a belief that both Taryn and Gregyn were psycically gifted as well. Even his own gut feeling found naught to be concerned of. These were settled lands, beyond the range of the pirates.

What do you fear, rider? Somewhat the rest of us cannot sense. And what, do I suppose, might be that causes you to keep a close eye on our young Lord Cullyn?

Naught came, but when Cullyn gathered their tankards and trenchers to act as scullery, Gregyn finally ate, Duglas noted that the rider never took his eyes off the young lord … almost as if he expected trouble to come from him.

Mirklin Wood

*T*_{amys!}

He had been on the edge of dozing off, but now he was awake.

~Who is that?

Joy's presence bumped at his brain.

~Padraig's medicinal has worked. They are sleeping … or near enough that it doesn't matter.

Padraig had taken what few belongings they had to the stable earlier in the day, telling their captors that he was packing for his departure. Tamys had made a show with Mylan of being upset with Padraig. She didn't understand Celdryan, but she understood body language and whining. Tamys had not thought of himself as a minstrel, but Padraig reported that she had praised Padraig for right thinking. Apparently Padraig had taken credit for deciding that Tamys should remain. Tamys had begun to sort out some words of the elvish language, enough to guess that Mylan was not going to let Padraig live to ride away.

Tamys gathered his staff and donned his boots and cloak and felt his way to the door.

Outside he could hear lusty singing in Elvish. He waited a moment, listening. Three elven men were talking drunkenly among themselves. There was no way he could pass among them as one of their own, so he felt the wall on the left, trailing a finger along the rough stone. Nobody called for him to halt as he continued toward the large communal room. His foot encountered a pitcher on the floor. He winced at the scraping noise, but nobody raised an objection, so he continued. Padraig had taken him this way before, so he somewhat knew the path. When he reached the door of the communal room, he paused, nervous of the larger room which seemed to echo vastly.

He listened. Four elves breathed heavily with sleep. One male had his face down on his arms on a table. Tamys could hear his restricted breathing in front of the crackle of a low fire in a dwarven built hearth. That he knew from Padraig's description. The door was opposite the hearth. Using his staff, he felt his way across the room, encountered a stone wall, felt to the right and found the door.

Smelling the greenwood round the elven camp triggered blind sight. He knew it was night, but the image he saw was a strange wash of green with ghostly images striding across the space.

~*Joy?*

The horse did not answer, but in a moment he saw the camp from above. A bonfire, which he could feel some heat from, lit the center. The hawk's vision was as odd in its own way as blind sight, but he could make out the warm bodies of elves asleep against walls and upon benches. He also saw that Joy was coming to him.

"I told them horses need the exercise of being saddled for part of every day," Padraig had told him. "They know naught of horses."

The hawk vision faded as Joy nuzzled his shoulder with her velvet nose. He found the halter, followed her strong neck until he found her withers and the saddle peak. To his left, he heard an elf mumble in his sleep. He located the stirrup. Padraig and he were of similar heights, so he ought not need to adjust them. In fact, he realized this was his saddle. He swung up into the saddle. For a moment, he thought he might have misjudged and he might fall, but his leg settled over the saddle.

~*Cling to the saddle peak and let the sighted judge the path.*

Every instinct said not to trust the horse, but she had a point. The grey was dark this night and he had naught a clue of what was beyond the camp. He settled the staff into the sling where war darts normally rested and squeezed with his calves to signal he was ready.

Joy's gait differed from the bay's … smoother, more settled. The smell of the bonfire and wine dropped behind them. Padraig had said for him to lie over the saddle peak, to keep his head down to allow Joy to follow her own path. Tamys remembered this and dropped his face into her mane.

"Thanks to you," he whispered.

~*We're not away yet. I'll do my best.*

At first, they trotted along the narrow pathway. He could hear the hollow sound her hooves made as she trod on paving stones. When she paused, he moved to sit up.

~*Stay down. We're leaving the road.*

He lay back down across her neck and he felt branches brush his sides as she entered into the forest. They headed uphill, his seat sliding backward until he remembered to brace the stirrups. Then they turned down a game trail. He could smell deer scat and hear birds breathing in the trees. A branch rubbed here and some small animal hid itself there. Joy maintained a pace that was both graceful and quick. Occasionally, branches would rake along their side. Once he felt a thorn bush grab at his breecs.

The night grew from cool to cold, so that he asked Joy to stop long enough for him to wrap his cloak round his body. He dozed off then, fingers entangled in her mane, to awake to a drip of dew and the songs of birds. Joy had stopped and he could hear her drinking water.

"Is it a stream?" he asked.

~*I'm a horse, you realize. Why do you assume I understand your speech?*

Tamys gathered a double handful of her mane to swing down from the saddle. When she felt his foot leave the off stirrup, she began to move again. He nearly lost his seat and had to scrabble to settle in once more.

~*It might have made you sick and we can't afford for you to go stumbling about,* Joy said.

~*I need water and food and to squat. And I can't go on much longer without sleep,* Tamys protested.

~*When humans sleep they drool and my mane is wet. But I'll find you a stream to drink from and squatting. There's some edible in the saddle bag. It does not smell good to me, but I've seen you and Padraig eat it before.*

When they stopped, it was already starting to warm. Tamys drank several mouthfuls of cold clean water from a trickle over a stone ledge and then sat down to gnaw on the journey bread he found in the saddle bag. He felt surprisingly refreshed and his head didn't hurt. The sound of the miniature waterfall proved restful.

~*Where's Padraig? Where's the elven camp?*

Joy sent an image of them circling the elven camp, first going north and then off to the west. They were southwest now, on a game trail. Padraig had headed northeast away from the road while Earnest had traveled south by way of the road. The hawk waited at the elven village. Padraig had found a game trail to follow that was headed generally south.

~And the elves?

~The hawk claims they're just now waking. Some of them may never wake. I think Padraig perhaps overdid his medicinal.

~Why should I care about that?

~No, why should you – anymore than your hawk cares about the fate of a rabbit. You need to be upon my back so we can continue forward.

Tamys realized that while his head was completely clear for the first time since he'd fallen from the window, his physical energy flagged so that it was difficult to regain the saddle. Once he lay across her neck, Joy's warmth, combined with that of the sun, sent him into a light doze for most of the morning. When he lifted his head in preparation of asking to stop to make water, his blind sight blossomed into a forest tunnel of glimmering green and gold, with a carpet of what he thought were blue flowers until they burst into fluttering flight.

Butterflies.

The image faded like sparks thrown up from a night fire and he settled into the long afternoon's journey. His head pounded and his back ached by the time the horse stopped.

~I can't see in the dark. This is well hidden. There's some fallen branches here that might make a bed for you.

Tamys allowed the horse to lead him as he clung to the saddle. She was right about the fallen bows. He would have liked to sleep, but he knew she wanted care as well. He fumbled with the girth and lifted the saddle down. She turned her head to nuzzle at his shoulder in thanks. Exhaustion was dragging him downward. He lay, teeth chattering from the cold while Joy rolled in the path. He was startled when she rolled her back against him. Cloak wrapped about him, he tried to put as much of his body in contact with hers as he could. Heat slowly seeped into his limbs and, finally, he slept.

Tomyr, Dunmaden

*T*here were flowers planted outside the tavern in Tomyr as if they thought they were an inn in the city that might need to compete with other establishments. The other riders remarked on it, but Taryn didn't have that sort of knowledge and the Denygal seemed to think it was perfectly normal for a tavern to plant flowers at its entrance.

I'm losing my mind. Did I ever notice flowers before?

Gregyn supposed it was a side effect from the healing of his gift. For weeks he'd felt like the world and the aethyr were just outside the reach of his fingers, on the other side of a wet woolen blanket. Now his senses were heightened. The sun shone brighter, the air smelled purer and he noticed flowers growing in front of village taverns.

Maddw and Kefyn had seen Taryn to the dun, leaving Gregyn and the common born to fend for themselves with some coin from Taryn's purse. Gregyn remembered the tavern from the spring. The tavernman liked silver in exchange for good bread and better ale. He admitted he didn't have room for their horses or the men themselves.

"There's a field a bit back toward the dun where you can pitch your tents and turn your horses out. It's dun land, so your lord's folks ought to not object."

After they'd eaten, Ryan offered to take some of the men back to the field to set up camp, which allowed Gregyn to enjoy another tankard and keep an eye on the men who might not be so respectful to the tavernman's daughters. Although he still saw a lass with short hair dressed in men's clothing, the men were completely fooled by the glamour Ryanna cast on herself. Even Cullyn seemed not to see through it.

Cullyn annoyed him greatly. The lad had seemed to have promise last winter, but now rebellion was writ all over him, muffled by Gregyn's ensorcelment. Gregyn began to see now why apprentices sometimes had to be broken. In the hurly-burly of the camp, it was difficult to take him fully in hand, but there would be lots of opportunity in Galornyn.

He had sent the second group of men toward the field and stood on the tavern yard still marveling at the flowers when he felt a chill breeze run down his back and turned to see Meryk riding his way. The journeyman subtly indicated he should follow him out of town. Gregyn pretended to adjust a stirrup, then mounted to follow him. Meryk stood in a copse of trees a stone's throw from the road. The lowering sun cast deep shadow for them to hide within.

"I thought you dead," Meryk said as Gregyn walked his horse up to him. "Everyone else is."

"I nearly was," Gregyn admitted. "I couldn't use my powers until an eightnight ago and I'm still struggling with control." That was close enough to the truth that he would remember what he said if anyone tried to verify it. "So, did everyone else in the circle die?"

"As far as I've heard, aye. Talidd too."

Gregyn controlled his breathing, but couldn't help a swallow.

"How close to journeyman are you?" Meryk asked.

"I just started second. What does it mean for the apprentices when the master dies?"

"You should find a journeyman to finish with. Not me. You scare the hells out of me, surviving a spell that killed Talidd."

"It might mean I'm stronger than he was," Gregyn scoffed.

"It might and I might be a fool to rebuff you, but I've no mind to end up strangled in my bed right after you take the oaths."

Is that my reputation?

The thought had never occurred to kill Meryk … Sawyl. He wanted Sawyl's blood on his hands.

"Who is left of the journeymen?"

"Sawyl is in Llyr. You know about Werglidd. There's a journeyman in Clarcom. Werglidd can probably give you referrals. Jaryn has ascended."

"Jaryn?! He can't even talk. How do you know?"

"I scried the compound and saw him. You haven't?"

"I survived the spell just barely. Scrying the compound seemed a shaky idea. What does it mean that Jaryn's ascended?"

"For now, so long as Jaryn doesn't hold our names, we can go where we want and rise on our own. Sawyl is in Llyr."

"Our names?"

"You didn't know?"

"Know what?"

"Well, technically, an second level apprentice doesn't know, but you've always been smart. I thought you knew."

Gregyn pinned Meryk with his hardest gaze. His neck pouch started to warm as Meryk started to squirm. Gregyn shouldn't be able to force Meryk to explain, but he knew instinctively that he could.

"It's called name magic. The master controls each of us by our true name. But Talidd didn't name Jaryn successor, so I don't think he passed our names to him."

And nobody knows my true name, not even me. What does that mean?

"That explains some curious matters. Thank you for telling me," Gregyn said. For a moment, he was seized of a thought to slip a dagger into Meryk's belly, but then he'd have to explain returning with an extra horse. "We'd best stay clear of one another," he warned.

"It's best, aye."

Meryk stepped back away from Gregyn, smelling of fear. Gregyn held a placid expression. Meryk was already afraid. There was no need to terrify him. This time.

After Meryk mounted and rode toward the dun, Gregyn pulled the medallion out of his pouch.

"You're no mere bauble, are you? You're some sort of focus."

The lapis stone held striations that seemed to move as his gaze flitted over the surface. Heavy, warm.

Is this how I healed the boy? How? Why? Is this what healed me?

He'd have to find out … later. For now, with a journeyman so close, he thought it best to keep the medallion close and let it do what it could do.

Laughter Match

Would that I were allowed to kill a black mage for his excesses. The boy is ruined. I am impotent to repair it.

Naranddal, Grey Level 32, FY 965

Past

Founding Year 931
Dun Celdrya

*B*urcan awoke of a morning determined to take a river boat for home. He'd been too long away from his wife and child. He was saddling his horse when Gerrient appeared in the stables.

"Off somewhere, Lord Burcan?"

"I've been here too long, Regent. I need to see my son again before he is sitting. Is there somewhat you require?"

"Answers."

This is a man who loves to be oblique.

"What are the questions?"

"Why did you hire the Assassins' Guild?"

Burcan stopped adjusting a stirrup, blinking.

"What are you talking about?"

Is he mad?

"I wondered why you fired that village rather than bringing the assassins to questioning, but I didn't believe you would kill your own father-in-law."

"I didn't. I was on the other side of the table. I had no opportunity to drop poison into his goblet."

"There was a servant, a man scarce anyone remembers, who served that day and then disappeared. Deryk remembered him. A child remembers him better."

"What are you talking about? A servant?"

"I suspect this Talidd is an assassin, but it doesn't matter truly because I have on good report that you paid the assassins in Mulyn coin."

"I didn't. Talidd? I know that name."

The exits were blocked with guards. Burcan estimated his chances of escape somewhere between poor and none at all.

"Of course you do. You hired him to kill Vanyn."

"I didn't. But, Talidd …."

Nay, nay, nay … it cannot be. Mulyn coin and now the man is in his court.

"How do you know it's me who did the hiring?"

"You were described."

"I'm not the only one who looks like me, you realize?"

"Aye, but you're the one most likely to gain by the death of Vanyn and his heirs."

"Why do you say that? Cadda is the elder and she's married to Joran, not me."

Gerrient hesitated for the briefest of moments.

"You didn't realize that, did you?" Burcan challenged. "I know Talidd because he is my brother's councilor."

"He's at Dun Joran?"

"Aye, last time I was there. I don't believe my brother is a regicide either, but mayhap the Assassins Guild is using him."

Gerrient let out a slow breath.

"We will investigate it. Guards, take him to the donjon. He is to be held in the same condition as Lord Deryk. Briscyus, I need someone to travel to Mulyn to verify his statement and take this Talidd into custody if he is there."

Loryna … Joran … forgive me … I cannot help you if my head rolls on an executioner's block.

Burcan slammed his fist into the face of the first guard to get close to him. He followed through, taking the man to the ground with his shoulder. Gerriant couldn't catch him because of his twisted leg. Burcan popped a foot into a stirrup and smacked the horse's rump. It bolted forward, scattering the riders who had come to arrest him.

An ill-planned daring attempt, it surprised him that it worked. He swung up into the saddle at the stable doors and kicked his horse into a gallop. Folk scattered as he rushed toward the gate, winning clear as the portcullis was dropping. He veered to the right, carrying him across a grassy meadow. Although it was impossible to get into Dun Celdrya, he knew there was a place where he could get upon the wall and if he did it right, he might win free. Back at the gate, he could hear guards being called to arms. He jumped the horse across a narrow bridge and clattered up onto the wall. On the river side, he flung himself free of the saddle, slapped the horse on the haunches and jumped free of the wall, falling straight for the water.

Hitting the water took his breath away. Dressed in full clothing, weighted with sword belt and coin purses, he struggled to the surface and swam toward the dyers' yard on the far shore.

I am away, but I am far from safe. How will I reach Dun Mulyn without discovery?

Present

Founding Year 1028
Mirklin Wood

*T*he bay had not been trained for rough country, so that Padraig had to pick his way through the woods on a mount that wanted a road, or at least a trail. No matter. Truth to tell, the elves were meant to think he was Tamys, so a roundabout route suited a blind man well. He and Joy had agreed not to talk mind to mind for fear they might be overheard, but he had general impressions of her and Tamys' journey through the western forest. Earnest had taken the riskier trail, the dwarven road. So far, he seemed unmolested. Padraig wondered how Joy had imparted the plan to her little friend and why she would risk him, but he had accepted that Companions did not share all thoughts with one another.

It took most of the first day to work his way south of the elven camp. Toward evening, Joy reported in images that the elves were searching along the road. He'd tied branches to Earnest's pack saddle to sweep the road behind him, but he'd not been certain it would work until Joy showed that the hawk had baited them north and the lack of trail to the south had convinced them not to go that way. Sooner or later, they'd figure out the ruse.

He slept a bit in the dark of the night before setting out southward before dawn. When the sun rose, the world turned pearlescent with mist. As Earnest appeared, Joy emerged from the forest and the three horses were united. Padraig and Tamys dismounted to allow Earnest to roll for the first time in a day and a half and the men to squat, as the mist to the north swirled, reaching out seeking tendrils like somewhat living.

~Joy, where are they?

"We need to move on immediately," Padraig informed Tamys. "Can you keep this pace?"

"I've no choice. I will not let them kill you. Help me mount."

~The hawk says they're coming, but this is some form of dark magic.

As they rode, Padraig looked behind them to see the mist darkening, coalescing, and roiling toward them. Tamys picked up the pace, the bay blowing and sidestepping. Joy converted to a trot. Earnest could not hold that pace for long, but they all felt the need to move quickly. The road turned upward as the growling of myriad voices echoed out of the mist.

The One wants you, Padraig. Come to us and be free. Come to us and destroy those who hate you. Cure Tamys. Find the One's True King.

Far above their heads, the hawk screeched as a cat-like beast launched itself at the bay's haunches. Tamys unexpectedly guided the horse sideways to avoid the cat as Earnest tumbled it in the dirt beneath his sturdy legs.

Tamys pulled his staff free of where he kept it and caught another one across the muzzle.

"How are you seeing that, lad?"

"I'm not. I can hear them. I'll likely miss more often than I swing."

Padraig stabbed at anothr cat with his sword. It hissed.

"Do you see it?" Tamys asked.

"See what?"

"Ahead. It's a gateway of sorts, in the mountain."

Padraig saw where the roadway entered a canyon. The horses all surged forward, eager to only need worry about their fore and aft. A cat clawed at Joy and she skittered sideways. Padraig sensed sheer terror in her rather than the usual rational mind of his Companion.

The canyon closed round them, high walls compassing them in security. The cats yowled at the entrance, apparently unable to enter. A sense of singing hooves came from Joy.

"It's warded ground," Padraig decided. "They cannot follow."

Just then the hawk lit on Tamys' saddle peak, chuffing its wings several times before settling.

"There's a caravanserai mayhap a watch ahead," Tamys reported. "There's also a party of elves coming our way on the road. Do you think the canyon is warded against them?"

"I don't know. How far back are they?"

Tamys petted the hawk and then shrugged.

"It doesn't know time. Its descriptions are in wingbeats. I can't yet interpret that."

~I'm stumbling, Joy complained..

"We've no choice but to stop," Padraig decided. "The horses are exhausted and you are as well."

"Nay. I'm tired, but my head doesn't hurt nearly as much as it might. If we had to go on, I could."

~Joy, had he been borrowing energy from you?

~I suppose that would explain it somewhat, but it may just be that I didn't sleep much. He's tireder than he realizes, I think.

Padraig saw that when he guided Tamys to his blankets and the lad almost immediately fell asleep with his boots still on. Padraig sat guard for half the night, alert to every noise of the forest, but sometimes past midnight, he dozed off sitting with his back against the canyon wall.

Galornyn

*M*addw choked on his mead when Rogyn announced that he would see Branwyn married before her father heard of Egoran's death.

"Do you think that wise?"

"The Lughan say it is perfectly legal. He's compensated us for her hand. We shouldn't risk the alliance."

"Won't we risk the alliance with a poorly considered match?"

"Of course not. I wouldn't match the lass to someone not worthy of her. She is clearly a prize to be treasured."

"I agree wholeheartedly, but I'm still confused. Who do you plan to marry her to?"

Rogyn frowned and then guffawed.

"Mayhap you are slower from grief and worry than I thought. I mean to see that you marry the lass. I thought you mayhap would enjoy that."

Maddw smoothed his breecs with large hands.

"I would. I am fond of her. It's just … she was our brother's betrothed. Is it not considered incest?"

"If they had consummated the marriage, aye, but we're within the legalities of it. Does it bother you?"

"Nay. They spoke only twice. I may have more knowledge of her than Eg did. When?"

"Immediately. I can arrange a priest and witnesses by morrow evening."

"Has anyone told Branwyn?"

"Nay, but you do have the right of it. Grandmam is with Teddryn, so I suppose I'll have Derdydda explain the matter to her. I know it's rather a short turn, but her father's demanding the dowry's return would be a disaster for us."

As if that is a good reason to make a marriage.

"May I tell her?" Maddw asked.

Rogyn and he had similar looks, though Maddw was taller and broader. His brother smiled and Maddw thought it might look very similar to a mirror.

"If you wish, that would be fine. Before you go … how is Teddryn?"

"Struggling. The chirgeon says it's a matter of time, but Grandmam holds out hope that Taryn will return soon."

"She means to use him for some sort of sorcery then?"

"Naught that should hurt him. You know that's not her way. But, aye, the lad might help to save Ted."

"I opposed Eg sending him away. I knew – could sense what Grandmam was doing with him. Dangerous game that, with Mam hovering about. I think that's why Egoran sent him away, as much to get him out of Mam's circle of interest as to gather the dowry and hope he'll impress the Riordans."

"You don't think he'll accomplish that."

"He's well mannered enough, if he had someone to keep him from the ale barrel."

"I've scried him out and I haven't seen him drink anything at Clarcom. Even saw him wave away wine. It might have helped if someone had told him he was expected to audition for marriage, but he seems to be doing well on his own."

"Mayhap being free of scrutiny has had good effect. The question I must decide … if Teddryn survives and is palsied, what of this marriage?"

"That's somewhat you want to discuss with Gram, I think. I'm off to locate Branwyn. Pray she takes it well."

"I offered sacrifice this morn. Sorry to have to put you out to stud, brother, but truly, the fortunes are such that I must not waste any opportunity."

"I never expected to have much of a choice, but I admit I enjoy her company."

With that Maddw went seeking Branwyn, finally finding her in the dun library.

"There you are," he started. "I began to think you had left for the north without telling anyone."

"And without an entourage. How daring of me!" She was wearing a dark dress and a black kirtle, in keeping with mourning, but her head remained uncovered as befitted an unwed woman. "What was it you needed?"

"To show you somewhat. Come."

The dun sat above a strand of beach on the eastern headland of the bay. It was a bit of a walk down a long series of stairs broken by balconies that commanded breathtaking views of the harbor. When he told her what he was about, she declared herself to be part-mountaingoat and agreed to go the whole way down with him. Once there, she kicked off her slippers, stripped off her stockings and wriggled her toes in the sand like a child.

"This is so amazing. It's warm. And the smell – salty, but fresh." She tilted her chin up to let the sun caress her creamy cheeks.

Maddw smiled to watch her and was glad for the opportunity at this romantic gesture. He wished he had flowers for her, but there would be other times.

"Branwyn, I'm glad you like it here, because … well, Rogyn has consented for me to marry you."

She opened her eyes and stared at him, then the corners crinkled slightly.

"He doesn't want to let go of the dowry. Can't blame him. How do you feel about this match?"

"I've enjoyed our conversations."

"As I have yours," she agreed. She dropped her skirts into the sand and held a strong boned hand out to him. "Rogyn had best act quickly before my father realizes the dowry's in play."

"By evening on the morrow, you and I will be sealed. We best start the climb back up as the sun is turning toward the horizon and it's twice as long up as it was down."

"But I'm part mountaingoat and may well surprise you."

"You see, this is what I am not knowing, the child of sea that I am. What is a mountaingoat?"

She laughed, snatched up her slippers and stockings, and flitted up the stairs ahead of him.

Aye, this is a lass who'll keep me laughing for a lifetime.

Llyr

Shyralan tried to reckon how long it had been since she'd poured water into a basin and spent an afternoon swirling it for the reflections. It had been years. She didn't know how many years. When you lived centuries, it didn't much matter.

She didn't rightly know why she was scrying for home now. Why was she even thinking of home? Mayhap it had somewhat to do with that Hanolan captain sniffing her out. Woods witch, indeed!

The scrying image proved illusive. Lack of practice no doubt. A watch passed before the reflections finally cleared to a narrow window where Mylan looked as young as she ever had. She also seemed distracted. The emotions vibrated through the scrying link … rage, grief and somewhat that tasted curiously of … hope.

~*What's going on there?* Shyralan asked.

~*When do you care?*

It was hard to think in Elvish when she hadn't spoken it in decades.

~*When it suits me, true, but I do care. What's happened?*

Mylan turned so Shyralan could look through her eyes at the two funeral pyres.

~*Plague?*

~*No.* Mylan paused. Shyralan could feel her grief though the scrying link. *Do you remember the legends?*

~*The pretty fairy stories? Yes, some of the more entertaining ones. Why?*

~*Troth aldor.*

This was old Elvish, not spoken at anytime in her generation. Shyralan had to translate the meaning.

~*The Herald. Why would so many people die from a legend about a herald?*

~*The legend rode into the forest.*

Shyralan almost scoffed, but then thought better of the instinct. Mylan appeared to be completely serious.

~*The Herald?*

~*A half-elf rode with him. He's blind as the legend says he will be. But we lost him. He fled and somehow … death followed him.*

~*What does he herald?* Shyralan asked, curious despite herself.

~*The One's Ama'lumin.*

~The beacon of the gods? Madi, it makes no sense, Shyralan insisted. *Why would he show up now a thousand cycles after the Rending.*

~Light shines best in darkness. Will you come home now?

~I am home! How many centuries does it take for you to understand that I left?

~And what of Reniran?

It had been years since Shyralan had heard the Elven name of the boy she had runaway with. Both half-elves, he had felt the need to flee even more than she had. Here in the city, he'd become jealous. Sometimes he'd come back round, but it had been nearly two decades.

~He lives his own life now. I will tell him you asked if he comes my way again. The troth aldor … you said he was with a half-elf, but if he came from outside the forest … he isn't elven?"

~He's part, but that surprised us very much, that he would look like a daemon.

Shyralan felt ice settle round her heart once more.

~You mean, he looks like me. I must go, Madi. I have no time for legends. I'm sorry for your loss.

~More die than are born. We need breeding women to replace ….

Shyralan tipped the water into the slop bucket. There was no use explaining to her mother that she had more important things to do than save a race of people who refused to admit that their time was past and she didn't mean to waste the mental energy trying.

Dunmaden

*D*un Tomyr proved cold and parsimonious. Ryanna could see no reason for it. The land about seemed prosperous enough, but the dun's inhabitants counted every turnip. There were signs that this had not always been the case. Taryn had a private chamber in a side broch and there was real glass in the casement. Threadbare tapestries warmed the walls and faded bedhangings wrapped the well-crafted bed. Taryn closed the door and dropped the latch into place. When Ryanna created the hiding, he smiled.

"You're new to these gifts, but you recognize them," she noted.

"My grandmam's been using hers round us my whole life. Kefyn says you can help me learn to control mine."

"Mayhap. I'm Kin and you're not, so we may not use our gifts in the same way. You are badly in need of learning to shield."

"Shield? That would be where I can't see the glowing color round the outside of your body, but I can see it round other folks."

"That's an aura and, aye. Yours is here one moment and gone the next, which is expected for someone new to their gifts."

"How do I control that if I am unaware of it? I don't see my own aura."

"I can't see mine either. Most wise can't see their own."

"Wise?"

"It's a Kin term for those who can see beyond the veil."

"Mages?"

"We don't use rituals to twist the powers to our will."

Taryn looked thoughtful.

"I don't think my grandmam does either, but you're right, of course. Some do."

"You can see that?"

"Not your way, but aye … it's the intrigue of the Galornyn court. What is needed for this training?"

"We can do it right now. You avoided alcohol at the meal, so this should be easy."

"Do spirits affect the control?"

"Aye to varying degrees."

Ryanna relaxed her shields and Taryn gasped.

"You can see my aura without having to shift your Sight?"

"The whole time at Clarcom, I felt like a mooncalf. I couldn't control what I saw. Will shielding help with this?"

"Mayhap. Look at mine. Now watch. I'm going to envision wrapping that aura up as though it were a cloak and putting inside my siarc."

"It disappeared," Taryn whispered.

Ryanna relaxed again. After demonstrating it three times, she encouraged him to try. Almost immediately, his aura disappeared from her view. He could only hold it for a short period, but he'd learned shielding far quicker than she had ever known.

"Continue practicing. I'm told you might want to hide your aura from your mother and others in Galornyn, so you will want to have gained mastery by the time you reach there."

"Thank you. It's interesting. It feels as if I pull some portion of myself into myself."

"Aye. When you've practiced sufficiently, you should be able to actually disappear in a crowd, to walk unnoticed unless someone looks directly at you."

"Intriguing."

"I should be headed back to the camp."

"Before you go, do you know what transpires back in Clarcom?"

"Danyl still lives. You can't scry?"

"I don't know how."

"You can teach Sarala medical care, but you can't scry. This is the difference in our two ways of working with the Source."

"I suppose learning can wait until I see my grandmam. I'll walk you out."

"Tell me. What is it about this dun?"

"I don't know, but I feel it too. I'm coming back to the camp on the morrow and whether we travel on immediately or not, I'm remaining. There is somewhat … concerning here."

Crossing the ward, Ryanna looked up at the roof of the dun and gasped. Taryn's gaze followed hers. His throat apple bobbed.

"Do you see it?"

"Like a toad only enormous? I may not sleep tonight. What does it mean?"

Ryanna shook her head. Taryn waited while she prepared her horse.

"Naught's changed with it," he noted.

"Nay. It's an old force, here for some period of time. How long have your grandparents been gone from this dun?"

"Eg was young when my mam stopped fulfilling her duties as lady – mayhap 25 years."

"Don't investigate it, Taryn. Trust me. If you are even tempted, ride for the camp."

Taryn turned to stare up at the toad apparation.

"I'll go get my saddlebags," he announced. "This place is ill-omened."

"I'll wait," she offered. He stalked quickly back toward his chambers while Ryanna stared at the apparation. A groom came out of the stable.

"Somewhat?" he asked.

"Nay. Just waiting for Lord Taryn."

"Right enough. My master does not much like when his relatives come poking about. He'd be more comfortable in his camp, I think. I'll saddle his horse."

The toad's head turned and its gaze seemed to follow Taryn as he stalked back toward the stable. The groom came out almost immediately.

"Good fortune to you, sir."

"And you," Taryn returned. Ryanna turned toward the gate as Taryn mounted and then they were away.

"Good riddance," Taryn muttered as they both shuddered violently.

As they rode toward the camp, Ryanna looked up at the tor that gave the village its name and knew that its summit would be in her very near future.

Clarcom

*T*he pressure relieved from his brain, Danyl relaxed from the seizure contorting his limbs. Shyla's face looked sucked of life as she stared at her brother. Sarala straightened his limbs. His right arm tucked up against his belly and the foot on the same side turned inward, toes pointing down. Sarala put a hand on Danyl's lower belly and, using the same technique Taryn had taught her to relieve pressure on the brain, she caused Danyl to void his bladder into the toweling between his legs, which she immediately changed. She scooped up a small ball of mush from a bowl and massaged Danyl's jaws so they would open and she could place the food in his cheek and then massage his throat until he swallowed reflexively. She did this three times and then let him rest. She did the work, but she knew somehow that it tired the boy. The left side of his face was a mass of swollen bruises, the eye sealed shut, but the swelling was going down, so she thought they were moving in the right direction.

"You should go get some rest," Sarala told the lass. "I will want you to be here while I sleep later."

"Aye," Shyla grunted after a moment's rebellious thought. "I'll return at dawn."

"Thanks to you."

Sarala ate the bread and cheese she had neglected earlier in the evening then bathed the lad. She could still straighten his palsied arm and fingers, but the spasticity was growing stronger. If she tapped his left cheek, he turned that way and protuded his tongue like a babe on the tit, but not on the right side. She did not look forward to the day when he opened his eyes and his family saw what had been left in the wake of his injuries.

Sarala covered Danyl's still form with a blanket and sat down in the window sill. With the shutters closed, she could lean there and sleep for short periods. She'd managed two watches last night.

She dreamt of round dances in Blue Iris Holt and then of Cai traversing dark passages alone and fearful. Her forehead rested on her knees and her bare toes curled against the stone on the other side of the window opening. She dreamt she stood at the foot of Danyl's bed, able to see the sworls of energy that were his life force. His heart was strong, his kidneys good. His stomach hungered and his head … heat poured off it in waves of red gas that spoke to her of pain and injury.

The door opened, all but covering her resting place in the window sill. A dark figure stalked forward in the dark. Danyl's breathing muffled as somewhat was put over his face.

Sarala came fully awake. She slipped off the sill on nearly silent bare feet. The man turned in the dark and smacked her across the face. She careened into the table where her gear rested. Her hand closed on the hilt of her long knife. Shaking stars from her eyes, she swept the long knife side to side as she charged forward. The tall dark shadow grunted and then collapsed forward onto Danyl.

Sarala grabbed his belt with both hands and hauled him backward to spill upon the floor. She pulled the pillow from Danyl's face. The lad breathed in deeply and then blew out. Sarala opened the candle lantern shade. Before she could inspect the bleeding man on the floor, he scrambled up against the wall, drew his dagger, and cut his own throat, just as Bryan ap Rhiordan burst in the chamber with his sword drawn.

"Someone heard you scream."

"Did I?" she asked. She rather doubted that, though her cheek throbbed with pain and her left eye was swelling shut. "He tried to kill Danyl."

"You killed him?"

"I stabbed him, but he killed himself."

Bryan took her long knife from her and wiped the gore on the dead man's breecs. Then he rolled the man onto his back to inspect him.

"He's a servant. I saw him carrying water earlier." From his position on his haunches, he indicated the pillow on the floor. "Is that what he tried to kill Danyl with?"

"Yes." As far as Sarala could tell, Danyl had not been injured by the attack. He surely would have been if the pillow had remained on his face for longer than it had, but she had intervened before any permanent damage could be done … more than had already been done.

"Perhaps he is the one who threw Danyl off the roof," she suggested.

"Mayhap, but I think …." Bryan picked up the pillow to examine it. "This is of fine material and if I'm not mistaken, so is the embroidery. I think this mayhap have come from an honor chamber – family or … high-level servitor or …." He put his face into the pillow and breathed deeply, turned it over in his hands, viewing it in that way he had.

Not long after, Lydya had been called as men came to take away the body. She turned the pillow over in her hands as well and then handed it back to Bryan, her face white as milk.

"Do you know how stitched that pillow case?" Bryan asked.

"Aye, but I fear any justice from the knowledge."

"What do you mean?"

"Unless I am mistaken, Elora stitched it."

They all three stared at the pillow in shock, recognizing the implications.

Companion

Burcan has escaped. Quite the bit of daring-do and once he was on an ore barge for the north, his own people protected him. This is a delicate matter. Gerriant is not king to make sweeping decisions, but Burcan's treachery cannot be allowed to stand.

**Dumyr, High Councillor,
Dun Celdrya FY 931**

Past

Founding Year 931
High Celdrya

*G*errient has not chosen to stay your execution," Wmyffa had reported that afternoon. "Dumyr says he believes you might have been ensorcelled, but he can find no grounds to not execute you for the crime nonetheless."

"I understand. I have accepted my death as just consequence for my action."

"Nay, this is not what will occur. Dumyr says Gerrient all but winked and nodded. I think he knows our scheme."

"Does that translate into gaolers turning their backs as I walk out the front door?"

"Nay. Dumyr doesn't believe that is the case, but – this is the oldest part of the dun and old brochs hold secrets. Be ready when Blethry comes."

Deryk had donned the clothes she brought in her basket and tried to rest as much as he could, but anticipation made him restless. It was the deepest part of the night when he heard a grinding noise in the inner mason's wall and the clothing cupboard swung inward to reveal the young priest dressed in traveling clothes standing at the top of a dark staircase.

"How did you …?"

"Vanyn and Gerrient were children in this dun."

"The regent is part of this."

"He said to tell you that he knows you didn't kill Perryn willingly, but he can't claim you were ensorcelled and let you walk free. It's not a legal excuse."

"Where does this lead?" Deryk asked, peering down the stairs while Blethry swung the cupboard back into place.

"Lower than the gaol levels. We need to make haste."

Deryk took the torch the priest offered and followed the man down the stairs. The light provided a view of only a few steps.

"This broch was a keep at one time. This stairway existed for getting the royal family out in the event the rest of the dun was overrun. Although it runs through the inner wall, most of the access was sealed when it became the donjon."

They reached a landing where they had to reverse direction to continue downward. After several of these switch backs, they began to hear voices.

"The guards and then the gaol. We need to be quiet as we go through."

The steps were damp here and moss grew on them. Deryk put his foot down and nearly fell, bracing himself against the stone, the sound of his boot scraping echoing off the walls of the tiny space. He was much more careful of his footing after that. The steps became slicker and the air danker the further they traveled. Soon, Deryk could hear water running. They splashed through a foul stream and he could hear rats squeaking in the darkness. Then they climbed up a short staircase, Blethry opened a door and they entered the cellars of Dun Celdrya.

Deryk had grown up playing down here in the winters, but somehow he and Maryn had never found the secret door that gave Blethry and him entrance. Mayhap that was because they hadn't wanted to investigate the sewers.

Dumyr and Wmyffa awaited them at the bolt hole.

"Another sewer?" Deryk asked.

"Nay, though it does go under the river. There's a farm to the other side where horses await you."

"This is the fabled bolt hole. I thought only the king and his heir were allowed to know of its location."

"There's not much the king knows that the councilor does not," Dumyr explained while Wmyffa handed them haversacks. "There's food and water. Blethry will take you through Galconyn."

"To where? I can't go to my family. That's the first place they'll look."

"Nay. Your family never responded to our inquiries, so we can assume Dun Trevellyn is not safe for you at the moment," Blethry explained. "There's a mountain holdfast Dumyr knows about."

"Wmyffa and I came from an area in the mountains" he explained. "No one will think to look there, but your disappearance will allow us to continue the investigation. It will excuse Gerriant being dogged."

"I cannot yet thank you for my life, but I thank you that you want to find out who really killed Maryn and Perryn. Vanyn too, of course."

"Of course. You should be going now. The guards won't know you're missing until the morn, but you need to be out of the dun by then."

Deryk turned to Wmyffa.

"Thank you for believing me," he said. "For convincing me to at least believe in myself enough to let you prove – well, not my innocence – my manipulation."

"It's the least we could do. Go on now. Wait until we call for you."

Deryk followed Blethry into the bolt hole. Dumyr swung the door shut behind them. It was a long stone corridor that stretched downward into the darkness.

"Why are you doing this?" Deryk asked as they walked. "I killed your sister."

"In Dunmaden, we don't hold folk responsible for being ensorcelled. I can't change the laws of the realm, but I can refuse to obey them when they're wrong."

"Aren't you angry?"

"Some, but that's just my grief warring against my head. I promise you, Deryk, we will find the answers to this."

"And then I can die for my crimes?"

Blethry stopped walking and turned round to stare at him. He sighed and shrugged.

"If, when that time comes, that is still what you desire to do, then aye, you may at that."

"Good, because I do not want to live with her blood on my hands."

Blethry sighed again, turned round once more and headed down the tunnel, walking fast, as if to avoid further conversation.

Present

Founding Year 1028
Mirklin Wood

With the hawk flying reconnaissance, they slept the night at the caravanserai. The morrow dawned cold. They left the canyon and rode unmolested through the forest. When Padraig saw faces in the trees, he held his knowledge until Tamys reported hearing footfalls. The elves were watching.

"The elves from the village have not breached the canyon," Tamys reported from the hawk.

"These must be a different band then or we would be captured and held."

After a bit, Padraig risked talking in Elvish to the trees and one of them revealed himself, face drawn in curiosity. By midday, they encountered a band of five elven males and two females standing in the road. They nodded their heads peacefully and parted to allow them passage.

"What does that mean?" Tamys asked.

"Ba'ra'na'la said there were folk pushed out by her village It's possible these bands are at odds with one another, which would explain the warding that doesn't allow elven magic through. I frankly have no idea, but they're not trying to kill us or enslave us, so I say we don't demand explanations."

Midafternoon they rode another hewn canyon between stone walls and came out into a small pleasant valley with a stream running through it. A bear looked up from its meal of fish and fixed its weak-eyed gaze upon them. Padraig pulled Joy to a stop, halting the procession. The wind shifted and Tamys' bay snorted, rolling its eyes. Consummate horseman, Tamys wound his fingers into the rein and pulled back on the bit, bringing the horse under control.

"Somewhat –?" Padraig hushed him.

~If that beast sees us, I say we abandon the human and outrun it, Joy thought. Padraig ignored her.

"Don't move," Padraig whispered. "Sit like stone."

Tamys looked like he might be straining his eyes to see what the danger was, but he waited. Padraig pulled his long bow free of the case under his leg, wrapped his leg around it and strung it. Then he drew an arrow and nocked it. Padraig prayed to the One True God for deliverance. He knew that the elves he knew would not countenance the wanton destruction of an animal and he had no means for transporting the meat through the forest. However, he remained unwilling to become dinner for the beast, so he prayed for an alternative. When the bear suddenly looked away, scented the air and ambled off over the hill to the east, Padraig breathed a relieved sigh.

"It's gone," he assured Tamys.

"It?"

"A bear." Padraig stowed the arrow, but hung the strung bow over his saddle peak, leery of what besides elves might be beyond the trees. "It's moved on, but I'll admit to a spot of terror for a moment." He explained the dilemma of a defensive kill.

They continued on to the stream and the sturdy stone bridge that crossed it, fetching up to a spring round evening. Here a firepit had been constructed of stones and a small stock of wood had been laid by. Padraig dismounted to investigate and knew that he was meant to camp here. None but elves might have provided this newly minted caravanserai.

When they woke, instead of finding a party of captors, a basket of eggs and dried plums awaited them with a bundle of elven ribband tied to it.

"What does it mean?" Tamys asked when Padraig described it to him.

"Elven ribband messages are complex, but they're not usually given to enemies. I suspect this new tribe is separate from those in the village. If this were the east, I'd say it's an invitation to return, but after what happened to us, I'm loath to assume anything. We should move on, try to reach the high mountains today."

When they set out, Tamys seemed to gaze out upon the brilliantly colored mountains.

"Fall?" he asked. "Have I lost track of the days?"

"This high up, it comes early. We must make haste for the pass."

"The hawk says the elves cannot breach the canyon. I suppose we're safe now."

"Nay, not safe, but not pursued. It could snow any day in the mountains and we'd be trapped at altitude."

"Then we should make haste. Padraig, before we do, I want to thank you for not leaving me with them. You could have gotten clean away without me."

"That was never a choice I would make."

"How did you convince Joy to carry me?"

"I didn't. It was her suggestion. Was she rough to you on the journey?"

~*I was the soul of compassion,* Joy huffed.

"She was actually kind," Tamys reported. Just then his hawk landed on his saddle peak, a still warm rabbit in its talon. It rubbed its beak against Tamys' shoulder and launched back into the sky, leaving its prey. Tamys held the rabbit out to Padraig.

"I don't know if he realizes that I'm blind, but I think he may return with a second rabbit."

"The relationship between us and Companions often starts with basic instincts of the animal. Joy communicated carrots and alfalfa to me for a good many days."

~*While you talked to me about dark friends,* Joy teased.

"It's ordinary to sense an alien mind, then?"

"It is. That's a wild raptor. What I don't understand is why your hawk can communicate better with my horse than it can with you."

"I think it's to do with my head. And mayhap with my not having been raised with it. I kept pushing it away at first. Will you explain to me …? Do Celts often have companions?"

"I doubt it. Your grandmam is from Denygal. That mayhap afford enough blood to form a link."

"What are you suggesting? My mam was get by an elf?"

"That never occurred to me. I know of no elves near Mulyn. I was thinking mayhap your grandmam was pregnant before she traveled from Denygal to marry your grandda."

"Hmm, that mayhap not be utterly impossible. There's a bard's bawdy about nine months to the day. It's meant to praise my grandda for his virility, but that's some close figuring. Still, it takes months to travel from Dengyal to Mulyn. Wouldn't she have whelped sooner?"

"Not necessarily. If your mam's sire was an elf, they live many centuries and their pregnancies are near two years long. A half-elven child might grow inside for a year or more. You don't seem much upset by this thought."

Tamys rode quietly for a bit. Padraig allowed him to contemplate. The hawk returned with another rabbit.

"A hawk has chosen me for Companion and secret elven societies believe I am somehow important enough to abduct." He handed the rabbit to Padraig. "I suppose that my grandmam might have had a secret lover before her marriage to my grandda seems as good an explanation as anything else." He raised his sightless gaze to the sky.

"What is it?"

"How am I supposed to explain to a hawk that horses don't eat rabbit?"

Galornyn

*T*eddryn swam up out of the fog and into the light. For the first time in what seemed like months, his head didn't feel ready to explode like an overripe melon in the sun. The act of opening his eyes tired him, but he could breathe without thinking about each inhalation and exhalation. He wanted water, but he had forgotten how to speak. Berdda placed a hand on his forehead.

"Your fever's broken," she reported. "Taryn is near Tomyr. I can feel the link growing in strength."

She used her sorcery to heal me? Taryn? Aye, I've always known without knowing. He's like Maddw. Water! I need water.

It took a supreme effort to peel his lips apart and then to form them into the shape needed to say what he needed. Berdda began bathing him. He could smell the salt in the water.

"W-wwaaater," he whispered.

She filled a cup immediately and brought it to his lips, lifting his head for him. He took a sip, and another. She pulled it back.

"Slowly. You don't want to make yourself sick."

"Thanks," he whispered. He could feel Berdda's hand and the rag on his arm. He didn't like it. He wanted to be left to himself. He tried to pull his arm away, but naught happened. Pain spiraled up through his arm, but he couldn't move it. He tried the other arm and it was the same.

"Am – I – palsied?" he asked. Speaking took energy and he had so little.

"Aye, for now. Some have made full recoveries. That you're still breathing is a good sign."

The room started to swim before his eyes. He did not know if it was just exhaustion or if she had drugged him. Sleep meant he did not have to think about what palsy meant for his life. As he slipped into unconsciousness, he thought he heard the ring of swords and shields and a tear ran down one cheek.

Dunmaden

*A*re we pulling stakes?" Kefyn asked Ryanna as he returned from a nearby lake where he'd bathed.

"Taryn is ill."

"Ill?"

"He came to the camp ready to travel on, but then he started to feel sick during breakfast and Duglas ordered him to bed."

She leaned against a tree, eyes on the horizon.

"You see them too?" she asked.

Tomyr rested at the foot of a tall grey tor that towered over the surrounding forest. Kefyn had been trying to ignore the images that flitted at the corner of his eye, but Ryanna was clearly a realist.

"Aye," he admitted. "I've never seen so many elementals in one place. You?"

"I see them all the time, everywhere. They're always plucking at this emotion or causing that catastrophe. But they usually gather round people, not places."

Kefyn slid into etheric sight and saw the many varied beings coming and going from the summit of the tor.

"Tormyr – that means dark hill in Denygal."

Ryanna nodded. There was somewhat about her expression that made Kefyn think of soldiers on the eve of battle. He supposed she had ridden to war a few times. She certainly carried herself like the soldier she pretended to be.

"What are you thinking?" he asked.

Ryanna slowly turned her eyes toward him.

"You are a nice young man," she said in Elvish. "Which is why I will not be telling you my thoughts anytime soon."

With that, she walked away toward the cooking fire where a stew was underway. Gregyn was detailing men to move the horses for better pasturage.

"Is Taryn's illness concerning?"

"Nay," the escort captain reported. "His grandmother was using him to strengthen his brother through an illness. I think somewhat happened. If he's still sick in the morning, we'll get the dun chirgeon out here, but I suspect he just needs rest."

"Will we be traveling tomorrow?"

"We won't. Ryan thinks he needs sleep, so I'm not waking him. The men could use the rest and tis a pleasant caravanserai. You, Duglas and Ryan are allowed to travel as you will, of course."

"Are you from round here?"

"I lived south of here for a while before I landed in Galornyn, but nay, I'm from Llyr originally. Can't you tell by my accent?"

"Nay, you all sound like you're speaking with rocks in your mouth," Kefyn admitted. Gregyn laughed. "Do you know any of the tales of Dunmaden?"

"It's rich farm land. The druids protect the forest. What more is there to know?"

Kefyn considered the young rider who seemed incredibly comfortable with Denygal gifts for a man who did not possess them himself.

"If you were raised in Llyr … are you not Old Faith then?"

Gregyn's eyes narrowed.

"I'm comfortable enough with it," he said. "I wasn't raised observant, so it doesn't matter much to me."

Why does that feel like a lie to me? Why do I think you can see the daemons on the tor as well as I can? How do I find out the truth you keep so closely hidden?

Across the camp Cullyn erupted into harsh words for a rider. Gregyn excused himself and walked that way. Kefyn looked about for Duglas and saw Ryanna instead, still staring up at the tor as if it was calling her.

Path of Fire

The raptors fight over the aviary, but only one can rule and no bird of a feather will mount the throne. The dragon stirs and the One's Beacon will arise.

**Navaransen, Sentinel,
Kin Cycle 17602 Old Calendar**

Past

Founding Year 931
Dengyal Wilderness

*T*he trees to one side of the trail blazed, flames licking higher and higher as hot smoke burned Donyl's eyes and seared his throat. They ran, hunched low, wet blankets covering their packs. Somewhere ahead, Janara had promised, was a dwarven highway that would take them out of this inferno. Donyl kept running because he knew she would stop if he did, but he had no belief in their survival. Having traveled so far by sheer miracles, he felt consumed and finished.

Janara turned aside to the stream that babbled to their left. She soaked her blanket, so Donyl did the same. Here the fire was mayhap thirty feet away, consuming a fringe of trees that was all that separated it from the trail. Donyl dropped to his knees to gulp mouthfuls of water, but surged back to his feet when Janara tugged at his shirt.

They didn't talk. They couldn't spare the breath. They ran ... ran for their lives ... ran to a place she said would be safe.

It seemed that he'd been running forever, his whole life … since Maryn's death.

How did I come to be here with this exotic alien lass running through a daemon-wrought forest fire?

Tears poured down his cheeks so that he could barely keep track of Janara as she ran before him. Flames surged above her as a tor rose before them. She stumbled to a stop.

"There! Mayhap a mile."

"We're not going to make it."

"If we keep running, we might. Move!"

She stayed beside him now, encouraging him with her presence. It was so hard to breathe with the air so hot. A spark brushed his forehead. Was her blanket steaming? The path was smoother in the middle, but safer near the stream. They stumbled into the water for a moment, up onto dry stone the next.

They might have made it, had Janara not stumbled over an errant rock and fallen headlong onto the stone of the path. Donyl slewed back to help her up and she cried out, grabbing for her knee where blood gushed from her torn trews. The flames arched above them, the air filled with hot fire and Donyl prepared to breathe his last.

Water poured through the flames and smoke, flooding the path, soaking their clothes, clearing the air. Janara lurched to her feet.

"We're saved. Move!"

They clung to each other, stumbling toward the opening in the rock face. Heavy smoke drifted across their path and sent Donyl coughing once more. A cooling wash of water came from the sky as they staggered up to the entrance. Janara paused to form a glowing orb of light and Donyl looked up through the smoke to see the glittering belly of a dragon as it turned to avoid the tor.

"The dragon …," he whispered.

"Saved you again." Janara coughed. "We're safe now. On the far side of this is Farhaven and my mother and father. Come. We'll be there in a watch and it will be safe."

Tendrils of smoke curled in the air of the tunnel, but as they trudged farther in, the air was fresh and cool. Donyl stumbled and lowered himself to the floor.

"I need a moment," he told her. "And we should look at your knee."

She limped back to him and lowered herself beside him. Together they rolled up her trews so that he could examine the deep cut across the bone below her knecap. He tore cloth from his siarc to bind it. Their hands met, they lifted their gazes to one another. Her pink lips parted. His heart beat fast as his stomach clenched. Their lips touched. She tasted of smoke and roses. After several heartbeats, they parted, staring into each other's eyes.

"W-w-we should keep moving," she whispered.

He kissed her again instead. She giggled. His cheeks grew warm. She kissed him on the nose, then slewed round at the crunch of a boot on gravel. Donyl pulled his sword free of the scabbard and then gawked as a dead man walked out of the shadows.

Present

Founding Year 1028
Mirklin Wood

*T*he long slow climb into the high mountains gave Padraig plenty of time to observe the road. He reported it in much better repair than it had been in the forest.

"Either the dwarves built it better for the mountains or mayhap they remained in these mountains longer," he observed.

Tamys didn't much care. The higher they climbed, the more tired he became. He slid out of the saddle at night exhausted and Padraig had to drag him to consciousness come morning. The bay labored and even the hawk took to riding atop Earnest's pack saddle for much of the day. Joy and Earnest, being mountain-bred, had an easier time of it, but the slower pace held dangers. A frosting of snow one morning reminded them all that they were in the high country.

On the morn of the third eightnight traveling through the forest, they encountered a cliff ledge path running alongside a deeply running river.

Tamys heard a vast echoing hole to his left. Wind tugged at his hair and clothes.

"What is that?" he asked, pointing

"A river canyon."

Tamys reined his horse in and sat listening. He could hear the chasm to their left and the cliff to their right. He felt like he was sitting on the very precipice of death.

"I'm not doing this," he insisted.

"There's no other way round, Tam. I wouldn't ask you to be go anywhere near a height of this sort if there were alternatives."

"You can't ask me to do this."

"Tam, I am called to the other side of these mountains, which means I have to continue forward."

"Are you threatening to leave me?"

"Nay, of course not, but if we stay here, we will freeze to death soon enough. You know how cold the mornings have become."

As if by command, a cold wetting rain rushed down the canyon, dampening Tamys' clothes.

I promised to follow him as best as I am able or die in the way. Padraig did not leave me to my fate among the elves. What more can I do?

"I'm terrified."

"I will keep you away from the edge to the best of my abilities."

The echoing edge remained close at hand with a sheer cliff to the right. They followed the road along the shelf until they reached a stone bridge that spanned a deep, but narrow canyon. Padraig dismounted to give the structure a good looking over. Tamys dismounted and stood by his horse, head cocked to one side, listening. His blind sight had been absent for days now, so he had to use his ears.

"We're to cross the river now?" he asked. Anxiety tightened his chest.

"Aye. There's a bridge, but I'm not sure I trust it."

"Is it in poor repair?" That's what the wind sounds like when it catches a bridge?

"Nay. Truly, it looks well enough. I'm just thinking it's not seen its makers in a good long while."

Tamys put out a hand to feel what was about and encountered a pillar of stone beside the bridge. Surprised, he snatched his hand back.

"What is it?" he asked.

"I suppose it's a marker stone – or mayhap an anchor stone. It's more than thrice your height and there's a second one opposite it."

Assured that it wouldn't topple onto him, Tamys touched the stone again and his blind sight bloomed. Made of a smooth stone that glowed pale golden in the sunlight, the pillar rose above him, graved in a looping pattern of vines, branches, song birds and deer in rich hues of blue, green, purple, red and colors Tamys had no names for.

Tamys turned to ask Padraig if he could see what he did, but his friend had walked out onto the bridge to further his inspection. Tamys saw the other pillar as misty and indistinct. Keeping his hand on the one, he reached across to the other.

Purple storm clouds darkened an otherwise sunny sky, crouching low like a beast over the bridge of perfectly fitted stones. Wind blasted hot into Tamys' face, so that he had to avert his eyes. In the edge of his vision, he saw elves of old walking cross the bridge. They seemed unaware of the storm above them or the dragon that flew out of the storm. The bridge warped and twisted and the wind tore at Tamys like a beast's claws. A thunderous roar beat down the canyon followed by a shriek like hinges of a long closed door. At the far end of the bridge, a lass strode into view, her short dark hair tousled by the wind, her men's clothes pressed flat in some areas and flapping in the wind in others. She stared at Tamys in shock, her full lips parting in speech he could not hear. Behind her, Tamys could barely make out a man with his arms spread wide as Tamys' were. The lass held out her hand to Tamys just as Padraig grabbed a double handful of his clothing to pull him free of the pillars.

Tamys dropped to his knees, retching, shuddering, and completely blind once more. Padraig had left him at the sound of panicked horses. In fear of being trampled, Tamys reached for the bridge rail, but his hand encountered rough stone. He crawled to press himself against a wall he didn't remember seeing before and waited while Padraig calmed the horses.

"Come, lad, let's get you up off your knees," Padraig said after a bit. Tamys allowed him to help him stand.

"How far forward is the bridge and the canyon?" he asked, afraid to move from the wall.

An awkward silence ensued.

"They're not a concern," Padraig reported.

"I don't understand. What happened?"

"You triggered somewhat when you touched both pillars. I can't explain it, but we're nowhere near the bridge. I'd wager this is the far side of the mountains, actually. Can't you feel the dampness?"

Tamys did not know what he felt. He lowered himself to the ground, shaking, the world spinning about him like a vortex that revolved down into darkness and silence.

Dunmaden

*G*regyn awoke earlier than the entire camp, just at the cusp of dawn, and walked out to sit on a log and enjoy the fresh air while trying to figure out the medallion. Although his powers had returned, he hadn't managed much more with the medallion than to give himself a headache. It wanted to be unlocked, but it was a finesse spell and mayhap beyond the capabilities of an apprentice.

Is an apprentice still that when his master dies?

Gregyn did not know. For most of his time with the black mages, he'd assumed there were no choices, but the information about name magic raised questions. Had he ever been compelled by Talidd to do anything? If not, he was responsible for his actions. Mayhap he was also capable of working magic outside of their guidance. He knew that to be true. No one had taught him blood magic. He'd guessed from rituals and then caught a small croc to test the theory. He had stumbled onto the use of a female companion. Mayhap he could learn on his own, which would make him free of the black. He'd still need access to the knowledge of the ages. Mayhap the Grey … might entangle him in rules of their own.

His head started to hurt. He leaned back to rest a moment and watch the Wild Folk come to and fro from the tor. He had almost hiked to the summit yestermorrow to assuage his curiosity, but he was loath to let his gaze wander far from Cullyn ap Rhiordan. He'd worked name-magic on him, but he didn't know the correct spells and he couldn't be certain that he was actually in control of the murderous young lord. Naranddal would know the answer ….

And likely chide me for being so careless.

The morning fog was burning off, but it allowed enough of a screen that Ryan didn't see him sitting quietly against the tree as she crossed the road to the trail that led up the tor. He dropped the medallion back in his neck pouch and hurried after her.

She intrigued him and not just because she was a beautiful woman hiding in the guise of a man. Her power was undeniable. He'd been intrigued by Berdda's power as well, but Berdda was so far above his station that he could not hope to learn her secrets. Ryan was here and now and he felt as though he could learn from her … if she would allow it.

The trail up to the tor proved well trod, with steps cut into the stones. Ryan showed her mountain-raising by being surefooted and swift in her climb, no doubt using the staff she carried to good effect. Gregyn had all he could do to keep his breath on the upward slope. At first, it was merely a hike in the woods to learn more of an exotic companion, but as they climbed higher, Gregyn watched the Wildfolk gathering in the trees, some racing ahead to the bald fist of rock above them. He wondered if Ryan saw the Wildfolk too.

The trail emerged from the wood to a shelf strewn with rock fall through which a path had been meticulously gleaned. Ryan waited for him at the cave mouth. He jerked to a stop as she laughed.

"Low landers! You think I could not hear your breathing as you huffed your way up the mountain? Your sword rubbed against trees at least thrice and mayhap you should learn to lift your feet while you walk. Your boots will last longer."

The Wildfolk twittered silently. Ryan turned her head to where his gaze wandered.

"Daemons inhabit this place, but they shouldn't," Ryan noted. "This was once an important place to the elves."

"Daemons?! Is that what you think they are?"

"What do you call them?"

"Wildfolk. Elemental spirits."

"Same same," she retorted.

"What is your plan here?" he asked.

"Exploring at this point. I suppose you can come with, so long as you don't interfere."

The dog and her exchanged glances and the dog turned to stalk down the path the way they had come before she turned to the entrance of the cave. Gregyn meant to suggest a torch when a ball of golden light blossomed above her left hand. He ducked under the lintel and stepped over the offerings in the antechamber.

"Do you know about this worship?" she asked, leaning over a basket of rotting fruit.

"I'm from Llyr. I don't think it is Old Faith. We could ask Taryn when we return to camp … he who will be cross with us for wandering off on a fine day for travel."

"Peasant worship," she said. "There's naught of great monetary value here."

A sprite trailed a long yellow finger along the edge of a basket.

"Mayhap to appease the Wildfolk."

"Appease them?"

"They like to play tricks on folk. This is ancestral land of Taryn's maternal folk. Mayhap many here have the Sight and do not wish to anger the Wildfolk."

Ryan straightened.

"The question is – why are they all gathered here?"

Gregyn agreed. He'd never seen such a gathering of them. Hundreds, mayhap thousands, clinging to the walls and ceiling. Ryan's ball of light was insufficient to make out those walls. Gregyn called forth an orb of his own, a blazing blue. It was his first since his healing and the brightness of it astounded him. Ryan glanced at it and then away. She already knew about him and didn't question his abilities.

The better light provided a view of the walls, graved with looping vines and clear drawings of folks with furled ears and catslit eyes.

"Are those elves?" he asked.

"They are." Ryan scanned the walls. The Wildfolk moved away from her gaze.

"Can you see them?" he asked.

"The elementals? If I wish." She walked toward the rear of the chamber, where two giant metal doors lay on the ground, pitted with rush. In this second chamber, there was more wall art and a type of dais bracketed by two pillars of an unusual stone. Here even more offerings were piled up on the dais and in front of it. Ryan stepped over them to climb onto the stone altar. Gregyn's chest tightened as he stepped up behind her.

"What are these?" he asked, touching one of the stones. A warm tingle ran up his arm and his ears hummed with vibration.

Ryan bumped her orb higher to view the startlingly well-preserved painting behind the pillars.

"This was used for some sort of transportation," she whispered.

"Transportation? It's in a cave," he reminded her. "It looks more like some sort of temple to me," he suggested, reaching across to the other pillar to trace a pattern that looked like a deer.

Some force rose up from the floor, entwined his legs and flowed out through his hands. He vibrated with an elemental fury like none he had ever encountered. Wind slapped his clothes against him and wrapped his hair cross his face as he stood helpless in the flow of power. Ryan turned, shouted and grabbed for him and then he slammed onto his back at the foot of the dais, breath driven from him.

For several terrifying heartbeats, he fought to move any air. When it flowed back in a gasp, he had to lie quiet for a moment to stop his head spinning. He sat up into utter darkness and silence. Calling forth power, he formed another orb to light the space so that he could stare at the dais. Ryan and the baskets of sacrifice were gone as if they had never been there.

The Void

*T*he back of the cave disappeared. The archway opened into a sunny sky bruised by purple storm clouds that crouched low over a bridge of perfectly fitted stones. Wind blasted hot into her face, so that she wanted to avert her eyes. In the edge of her vision, she saw full elves in archaic clothing walking cross the bridge. They seemed unaware of the storm above them or the dragon that flew out of the maelstrom.

This is the conveyor the elders talk about. How did it work?

Ryanna felt an ice cold wash down her back followed by an incredible upwelling of power behind her. She turned to see Gregyn caught between the pillars, seizing, a nimbus of energy glowing about him.

The bridge warped and twisted and the wind tore at Ryanna like a beast's claws. A thunderous roar beat down the canyon followed by a shriek like hinges of a long closed door. At the far end of the bridge, Padraig strode into view, clothes pressed against his body by a massive wind. Ryanna stared at him in shock, then tried to shout at him, to get his attention. Behind Padraig, she could barely make out a man with his arms spread wide as Gregyn's were.

Gregyn was going to die if he didn't release contact. With a shout, she struck him mid-chest with power directed out of a straight arm. The rider disappeared, the vortex slammed shut and she tumbled backward heels over head. It seemed eternity before she came upright, gasping and dizzy.

Caught up in purple thunderclouds, she didn't know which way to go. A shriek like rusted door hinges deafened her momentarily. Enormous catslit eyes stared at her from the storm.

Kin? Dragon? Lion? Am I food for a giant feline? She saw a light in the thunderheads and moved in that direction. A young man stood at the far end of the maelstrom, arms held out like Gregyn's had been.

How am I so far away?

How could he still be there?

She dragged herself along the bridge against the wind until she saw Padraig, who turned to gawk at her. He spoke, his words shredding on the howling wind. Then he turned to grab the young stranger who held the gateway open. The bridge dissolved and breath-takingly cold water washed her thighs. She saw an arm emerge from the surging water. *Padraig!* She flung herself forward to catch his wrist. The current grabbed her and the weight of him dragged them both under the flow.

To Be Continued ...

Time Flow, Geography & Culture in Daermad Cycle

This book occurs in a number of time periods. The first quote in The Willow Branch - Fate explains why – the present is built on the past and when we forget the past we imperil the future. This is also why the larger series is entitled Daermad Cycle – daermad meaning "forgetful" in Gaelic. Pay attention to the subheadings because they tell you whether you're in Founding Year 931 or 1028. There are two main stories. The past with the doomed princes Maryn, Perryn and Donyl follows the destruction of the kingdom. The present with Padraig, Tamys, Gregyn and Ryanna follows the restoration. Unless the present actors can figure out what went wrong in the past, they are doomed to repeat it. Yes, Talidd shows up in both time lines as does the Morrigan and Shyralan.

In writing the tale of Daermad, I found that I had two separate stories that could run in different books or different sections of the same book, but really were not stand-alone stories. They need to be told together to arrive where I want to arrive, so please bear with me because the past really is the foundation of the present in reality as well as in Daermad.

I tried to make it easy for you by obeying my own rules. Each chapters starts with a quote from the literary history of the peoples of Daermad, followed by a scene from Founding Year 931 (the past). The rest of the chapter focuses on FY 1028 (the present), though there are a few subchapters that follow Gilyn, who would be the destroyer of worlds. If you pay attention to the headings, you should have no problem staying oriented.

The people of Celdrya are the descendants of a Treverri tribe of Celts that somehow stumbled through a "portal" back in the 4th century AD, which was the early Christian era for parts of Northern Europe. They have been in Daermad for about a millennia and so they are not exactly European Celts anymore, but they share some common history. You will also find other familiar Earth cultures living in Daermad. Where did they come from? You'll have to buy more books to find out. Where did the Kin and dwarves come from? Daermad!

The Kin speak Elvish, which is rendered largely in American English. The Celdryans speak some form of Gaulish, which accounts for the lilting narrative voice in those sections. In a nod to my immense admiration for Katharine Kerr, writer of the Deverry series, I've tried to follow her language conventions as to spellings. I make no claims to perfection.

Those extremely long names for the Kin are their full names. Just as I would be Lela Amanda Davis Markham, Morynsionryanna is Ryanna, daughter of Sion from Moryn. Similar to Asian naming conventions, the clan name is given first. Because Ryanna's father is Denygal, his place of birth is listed rather than his clan, following the Celdryan fashion of common names.

A Word About Language

This is a fan's nod to Katharine Kerr, writer of the phenomenal Deverry series. I tried as much as possible to render the writing of names in keeping with her linguistic guidelines from that series. Any errors are my own.

Celdryan is a Celtic language, which is closely related to languages that exist in our own world, principally Welsh. However, it is not identical. The Celdryans left Gaul a millennia ago. Of course, their language has drifted. The following guide might be helpful in pronunciation.

DD is voiced "th" as in thin or breathe. There is also a hard form of TH, as in The or breath.

Y is never a consonant. When long it is voiced as the "i" in machine or the "ee" in teeth, when short it is voiced as the "e" in butter.

DW, GW, and TW are single sounds as in Gwendolyn or twit.

Wmgleadd would be pronounced "um – glath", for example.

Ll is a breathy l sound, somewhat like combining l with an h.

Some terms to know —

Daermad – derived from Gaelic for "forgetting" or "mistake" It is what the Celdryans call the world they live in. It's the equivalent of Earth or planet.

Kin – Daermad native race of elven type. They tend to be tall, slender and long of limb, with large cat slit eyes and furled ears. When they mate with humans however, these resulting "elflings" can have a mixture of features. They are naturally psychic, though some are more gifted than others.

Celdryan – the descendants of Celts who arrived in Daermad a millennia ago.

Denygal – a mixed race of nominal Celdryans who share ancestry with both Celdrya and Kin.

Basketlands – the former home territory of the Kin, it has been under Celdryan rule for centuries. It is the fertile lands of the valleys between the great mountain ranges and the Stormmor.

Aver – Celdryan for "river"

Temple of the Moon – women's religion dedicated to the worship of goddesses, principally the Morrigan. Psychically gifted priestesses are called domas.

Cult of Lugh ¬– a sect of the Celdryan religion that has done away with personal sacrifices and relies on political power to control society. They oppose all magic and reject diversity of religious beliefs. They are currently the dominate religious sect in Celdryan society

Cult of Bel – a sect of the Celdryan religion that emphasizes academics and charity. Their druins are ecclesiastical-approved mages. They are secondary to the Lughans, but not necessarily happy about it.

Old Faith ¬– a sect of the Celdryan religion that performs personal sacrifices and emphasizes honor and community. Their priests are known as druids and have the gifts of mages. Their granias are herb women who also work in psychic gifts. Although limited in territory mostly in Dunmaden, their nobles have a prodigious childbirth rate so are represented in many duns throughout the kingdom.

Mages – there are various sects from various traditions. Sometimes they work together and sometimes they work against each other. The Black mages want to control society by gaining control of the True King.

Goi'tan – a voluntary period of servitude in Kindred society for the purposes of repentance. It involves a public acknowledgment by wearing grey robes, shaving one's head and keeping silence. After a period of goi-tan, a Kin's transgressions are never to be mentioned again.

Cotan – a soft fabric similar to our cotton that is cultivated by the Kin and highly valued by the nobility of Dublyn.

Breecs – baggy woolen pants worn by Celdryan men. Nobles wear plaid breecs that distinguish their clan.

Trews – form fitting pants worn by Kin and others

Siarc – a linen shirt worn in Celdrya. The yokes are often embroidered. The nobility adorns theirs with their clan symbols.

Dun – a fortress including the main keep and outbuildings surrounded by a wall. The city that supports a dun is often called Dun also.

Broch – a dun tower, a round building preferably built of stone.

Companion – another Kin term indicating a sentient non-human animal that has a psychic connection with a human, usually a Kin or Denygal, but sometimes a Celdryan mage.

Lumina – a type of translucent building stone used by Kin in former times to build cities. The art of working it has been lost.

Excerpt from
Fount of Dreams

Viking Year 742 (Four years ago)
Hansorfjord

Sygna had not slept in anticipation of the departure. Erik had shown his ardor earlier in the night and then slept like the dead. Sygna had slept briefly and then awoke from an enlightened dream, unable to return to sleep. She'd finally risen to sit on the tiny private balcony in the solstice twilight, mulling over the dream.

Flights of dragons gliding out of purpose storm clouds ... a man-sized chrysalli and a beautiful woman dressed in manly clothes and wieldly a sword to protect the pupa within ... a hawk grappling with a raven ... a

Viking ship burning odd round buildings and Erik leaping free of the ship with his clothes on fire. She had no interpretation, except for fear for Erik.

The morning dawned bright and sunny and the great hall, filled with viks eating their last meal before a campaign laughing and jesting. She'd served beer and porridge and avoided Gilyn Kinsen to the greatest degree possible.

The emissary creeped her flesh. He thought himself subtle with his ardor, but the lust elementals poured off his skin whenever he looked at her. There were other elementals as well – greed, violence, hatred. Thought of him brought the cloying scent of overripe lemons to her nose, the feeling of a hand squeezing her throat.

Whose memories were these? Not hers. She kept a hand upon her dagger whenever he walked near even as she tried to stay with others. Should she have told Erik? Orma counseled against. Women must be strong to protect their men so the men could be strong to protect them. She wanted to understand Orma's wisdom. The kong's wife had duties beyond that of an ordinary woman and must needs be braver.

As the junque coursed its way down the fjord, followed by the first rank of long ships, Sygna felt buried by the stuffiness of the great hall. While the other women and the few men left returned the great hall to an ordinary condition, she sought the open terrace overlooking a graceful waterfall that started in the sky and plunged past the keep into a deep chasm that roared with tumult. The sun kissed her skin and a breeze lifted the damp hair free of her neck. Cool spray from the waterfall dappled her cheeks. She closed her eyes and breathed deeply of the flower-scented air.

The slight taste of copper tickled her tongue. She opened her eyes to stare at the waterfall as a scrying focus. Through the veil an unnaturally large raven kited, a black dog in his talons. The black bird bent a wing to turn toward the yawning mouth of a cave that wasn't there in reality. A skua emerged from the cave, carrying a salmon in its beak. It flew straight for the raven, who continued its course unfraid. They passed each other, skimming feathers. The skau dropped the salmon and turned to savage the raven. Then a green dragon soared up from the waterfall's chasm. The raven screeched and flapped desperately away from the dragon while the skua circled it. With a single pump of its wings, the dragon closed the gap. The dog fell free, tumbling in the mists and the dragon dove downward after. When Sygna glanced toward the raven, it had disappeared. The skua flew through the veil of the waterfall and when she looked downward the dragon and dog were gone.

The penny taste faded and she saw with natural eyes once more. She turned toward the great hall, paused to stare at the bronze goblet laying by the railing. Wine red as blood trailed across the stone and over the precepace. What did the salmon in the skua's mouth represent? Heart caught in her throat, Sygna stretched to see over the railing. Far far below, a man lay spread upon a narrow ledge … unmoving.

Stay Tuned … the Story Continues …

About Lela Markham

Hi. I was raised in a house made of books in Alaska and told tales from the time I could talk. A teacher eventually made me write one of them down. I hated the exercise, but it was the spark that ignited a fire that has never gone out. Come explore my imaginary worlds.

My daring husband, two fearless offspring and I live the adventure of a lifetime here on the Last Frontier where the midnight sun encourages wandering the wilderness and the long dark winters favor reading, writing and staring at the northern lights … hence the moniker Aurorawatcher. We share our adventure with a sentient husky who inspired Joy and Sabre's characters in The Willow Branch and a very dominated, but extremely happy yellow Lab.

Check out my Smashwords interview for more details or visit me at my website. Feel free to drop a comment or ask me questions. Lela

Aurorwatcherak.wordpress.com

Or you can reach me old-school at lelamarkham@gmail.com .

Check out my publisher

Breakwater Harbor Books

www.breakwaterharborbooks.com